The TENDER REBEL

VIRGINIA GAFFNEY

F GAF

HARVEST HOUSE PUBLISHERS
Eugene, Oregon 97402

Cover by Left Coast Design, Portland, Oregon

THE TENDER REBEL

Copyright ©1997 by Virginia Williams
Published by Harvest House Publishers
Eugene, Oregon 97402

Library of Congress Cataloging-in-Publication Data

Gaffney, Virginia, 1957–
    The Tender Rebel / Virginia Gaffney.
        p. cm. — (Richmond chronicles; #3)
    Sequel to: Carry me home.
    ISBN 1-56507-669-9
    1. United States—History—Civil War, 1861–1865—Fiction. 2. Richmond (va.)—History—Civil
    War, 1861–1865—Fiction. I. Title. II. Series: Gaffney, Virginia, 1957– Richmond chronicles;
    bk. 3.
PS3557.A314T46 1997
813'.54—dc21   97-12381
                                                                                                         CIP

Printed in the United States of America.

97   98   99   00   01   02   03   / BC /   10   9   8   7   6   5   4   3   2   1

For
"Mop"
Bobbie Pell

*My special friend whose open-hearted
love and acceptance have been there for
me during almost 22 years of friendship.
Thank you! I love you!*

One
May 1862

The stillness was making Carrie nervous. She had stepped outside to get some fresh air but the heavy sultriness surrounding her, clutching at her, offered little relief. The yellowish tint of the sky, combined with the buildup of cumulus clouds on the horizon, spoke of an approaching storm, but there was more. . . . Carrie's heart told her the ominous day was prophetic of what was soon to be released upon her beloved city. Richmond waited with bated breath for the inevitable. The tens of thousands of Union soldiers camped at her gates would eventually no longer be content to just prepare for battle. When would the fury of the Federal forces be unleashed against the capital of the Confederacy?

Trying to control the nervousness clutching her throat, Carrie took several deep breaths as she looked down on the swirling rapids of the James River cascading its way over rocks and boulders on its way to the Atlantic. It never ceased to amaze her that she was gazing on the same river that flowed so placidly by her family's plantation farther south.

The view from Chimborazo Hill was breathtaking, the plateau of nearly forty acres commanding a grand view of the city. She loved to come and stand outside and turn slowly as the different panoramas spread before her eyes. Now as she stared down at the river, she looked farther south to see the many ships in harbor, with the bridges spanning the river in between. Turning east she gazed out at the long stretch of country—cultivated fields, forests, and hills that spread as far as the eye could see. Once again the fields of Cromwell Plantation flooded her memory. Impatiently she pushed aside the pictures of the place she had been forced to flee. Now was not the time.

To the west she could see the splendor of the city—the church spires needling their way toward heaven, the Capitol building reflecting the rays of the sun, the factories and the wonderful homes that gave Richmond its charm. From here she could pretend the horrible overcrowding in the wartime city had not clouded the beautiful city with litter, filth, and crime. As she completed her revolution, she stared long and hard at Hollywood Cemetery. Richmond natives called it the "city of our dead." Many fresh graves dotted the hillsides. How many more would lie with those gone before?

Carrie shook her head impatiently and pushed at the strands of black wavy hair that escaped the bun she captured them with each morning. Daydreaming and imagining what was coming was doing her patients no good. Taking another deep breath, she turned and reentered the hospital.

"See any Yankee gunboats out on the river, Miss Cromwell?"

Carrie smiled at the young soldier lying closest to the door. "Don't be ridiculous," she scoffed. "You know after the beating the Union received at Drewry's Bluff a couple of weeks ago, they aren't going to try that avenue again!"

"We whupped 'em good, didn't we!" another soldier called out.

"We got 'em that time," a dark-haired lad retorted, "but they ain't gonna give up easy. There's going to be the devil to pay around here soon enough!" The ward fell uncomfortably silent, the bedraggled soldiers nodding in acknowledgement.

Carrie looked around at the saddened faces and forced a cheerful note into her voice. "There will be no more of this kind of talk, gentlemen. Your only job right now is to get well. I think that should consume quite enough of your energies. Let the fighting be done by those who have to fight. Your turn will probably come soon enough, anyway." Carrie paused. Many of the soldiers would never be able to fight again. However, most would be called back to join their units— pushed back into the boiling cauldron they had just barely escaped. She pushed on with determined cheer. "Who is ready to write home?"

"Right here, Miss Cromwell!" one young boy, barely sixteen, called out. "My momma is worried sick about me. I've got to let her know I'm getting along just fine."

Carrie's heart went out in a rush of sympathy. She smiled at the boy and walked over to his bed. Pulling out paper and pencil, she settled down in a chair beside him. "All right, Samuel. What would you like me to say?" She wrote as the young soldier talked, but privately wished she could just whisk him away to the love and care of his momma.

Carrie had lost track of what battlefield Samuel had come from, but the constant reminders of that day would be with him forever. The bandaged stump of his amputated right arm and the sling encasing his left one spoke of the horror he had been through. Yet she had never once heard him complain. The words he was sending home to his momma were ones of strength and confidence. How many mothers, miles from their loved ones, were helpless to save their boys from the pain and suffering they endured here?

It was the same with the rest of the men. There were hardly any murmurs or complaints. They seemed to have accepted this war as their lot in life, and if they were left less than whole, well, they weren't alone. Once this war was over there would be lots of one-legged, one-armed men running around. They were fighting for a cause, and everyone knew great causes demanded great sacrifice. That was just the way it was. When the South had soundly whipped the North and sent them running back with their tails between their legs—and it was bound to be soon—then all of it would be worth it. They would all be heroes, and they would rebuild their new country the way they wanted it to be.

Carrie was not going to be the one to challenge or destroy their hope. She had hated this war from the very beginning—when it was still a murmur in the streets. Her feelings had only intensified as she witnessed the suffering and senselessness surrounding her. The only thing that helped her make any sense of it was her work at Chimborazo Hospital.

She had only been here for a week, but already she loved her work. Every morning she would walk from her father's house on Church Hill to the sprawling complex of buildings and tents. The hospital had begun receiving patients earlier that year and was constantly being expanded for the anticipated increase in casualties. Dr. McCaw, the founder of the hospital, did not share the naive beliefs of many that the war would be over soon. He was preparing for the long haul. He was also preparing for the worst.

"Hey, Miss Cromwell!"

Carrie looked up from the letter she was just finishing. "Yes, Walker?"

A rough-looking boy from the mountains of Tennessee smiled brightly at her. "Tell us the story of how you got to Richmond."

Carrie groaned as a chorus of men voiced their agreement.

One of the hospital wards, a kindly man in his mid-forties, laughed as he entered the room. "Looks like it's going to be a while before they get tired of *that* story! Kind of nice to have a hero around here," he said. Dropping a pile of fresh bandages onto the table next to the door, he winked at her, chuckled under his breath, and left.

"Come on, Miss Cromwell. Tell it to us!" Walker urged again.

Carrie had told the story so many times that even in her dreams she narrated the events. Yet, the soldiers seemed to love it, and she could see the hope it sparked in their eyes. If a lady could outwit the Union army, then there was not so much to be afraid of, after all. A quick look around satisfied her that there were no immediate needs in the ward. Laying aside her writing supplies, she forced her thoughts back. "Just a few weeks ago I was busy growing crops on my father's plantation."

"Cromwell Plantation," Walker interrupted.

Carrie nodded, then continued, "Anyway, we were going to feed the hungry people in Richmond with our harvest. Instead of planting our usual tobacco, we were planting food crops. We had corn, beans, peppers, okra—oh, all kinds of things." Carrie paused, looking from face to face. "I didn't realize how close the Union army was until I heard the sounds of the battle in Williamsburg."

"That's the one where I lost my arm!" Samuel said proudly.

Carrie heard the tinge of pain in his voice and smiled at him compassionately. "The day after the battle, my father's slaves had finally convinced me to leave the plantation and come to Richmond, but before I could leave, the Union soldiers came searching for food. They broke into my house."

"If they was looking for food, why'd they break into your house?" a new patient asked. "I heard they were clearing fields and smoke-houses. I thought most everyone had already high tailed it for Richmond, anyway."

Carrie frowned, anger sharpening her usually pleasant voice. "There was a man who betrayed me. He told them I was still on the plantation." Her eyes took on a remote look as the memory of that day flashed before her. She clamped her jaw shut, a muscle twitching in her cheek. Her father's old overseer, Ike Adams, had sent the soldiers to rape her.

"How'd you get away?" one of the men near her asked anxiously.

Carrie knew Howard, a Georgia farm boy, had just come in that morning. This was his first time hearing the story. "I managed to hide from them until they quit searching the house. Then I snuck out to the barn and waited for it to get dark." Once again, she wasn't telling the whole story, but the secret of the tunnel under Cromwell Plantation was going to stay just that—a secret.

"How in the world did you hide from them?" Howard asked. "I've heard about how Yankees search a house!"

"Let's just say I have my ways. . . . " Walker sang out in a high falsetto.

Carrie laughed with the rest of the men at Walker's imitation of her standard response. Then she continued, "Anyway, I waited till about midnight and then managed to jump on my horse and race past the guards outside the barn."

"And get this," Walker broke in again. "She was riding that horse bareback. A great big thoroughbred! This pretty, little thing rode that horse just like a man!" Then he sobered. "I'm sorry, Miss Cromwell. I need to let you tell your own story."

Carrie told the rest quickly. People had tried to turn her into a hero for jumping Granite over a tall fence after being shot in the shoulder during her escape. She still had occasional dreams about that ride through the dark woods before she had finally connected with Warren Hobbs, the soldier Robert had sent to help her. She had made it. That was what counted.

Her story worked its usual magic on the listening patients. If turning her into a hero helped their own morale she would just keep on telling it. And it took her focus off Robert. Daily she battled the fear of what this war could do to the man she loved.

"Them Yankees ain't no big deal!"

"Yeah, even a woman can outwit them!"

"It may have been a Yankee that put me in this hospital, but I bet there's three or four I put in one of theirs!" another boasted.

The men continued their banter as Carrie moved from bed to bed checking on the condition of her patients. Not that she could do anything if she found a need—other than call a doctor, or nurse, or one of the ward aides. It had been made clear to her from the beginning that her sole job was to dispense comfort to the soldiers by reading to them, listening to them, or writing letters for them. Anything medical was to be done by one of the male employees. Her eyes flashed with anger as she recalled the words of a doctor when she had tried to point out to him that one of the soldiers was developing an infection in a wound.

"My dear Miss Cromwell," he had drawled in a patronizing tone. *"I hardly think I need your assistance in this matter. Such a thing is not really suitable for a lady. I would think you would be rather embarrassed to have an interest in such things as medicine. Such a thing would be nothing but injurious to the delicacy and refinement of a lady."* He had looked at her with a smirk on his condescending lips, as if he had doubts about her being a lady. Then he had continued, *"I realize you are probably just trying to be helpful in this, most trying time, but it will not help our cause to have our ladies' natures become deteriorated, or to have their sensibilities blunted. You just give our soldiers a little comfort and care. Leave the medical care in our hands."*

Patting her on the hand, he had walked from the ward, leaving her to fume and pound pillows into shapeless submission on the beds she was straightening. All her anger had done was cause her shoulder to ache. Since that day her defiance had steeled into determination. She had wanted to be a doctor since she was a little girl, but she had a long, uphill battle ahead of her. There had already been plenty of warnings that she would be greeted with prejudice and ignorance at every turn. She would just have to get used to it. Someday it would be different.

"Your green eyes are flashing up a storm, Miss Cromwell. Did one of the soldiers in here do something to make you angry?" Samuel asked. "You just give me the word. I'll take care of it!"

Samuel's concerned voice broke into Carrie's thoughts. Instantly she replaced her frown with a smile. If she was going to bring cheer into this ward, she would have to do a better job of hiding her feelings. "Of course not, Samuel!" she said brightly. "You boys are the light of my life." She settled down in the chair beside him again. "Didn't you tell me you have a grandmother who is very special to you? Don't you think she would like a letter from you, too? One just for her?"

"Granny? Why, sure. I bet she'd think that was really something—getting a letter from a real war hero!" He grinned, obviously proud of his self-proclaimed title.

He had started dictating his letter even before Carrie picked up her paper and pen. Writing swiftly, she filled several pages. She had just added his signature to it when she heard her name called. Carrie looked up, smiling broadly. "Hello, Janie."

"Are you planning on staying here all day? You promised your father you would have dinner with him tonight."

Carrie glanced quickly at her watch. "I completely lost track of time!" Gathering her things, she called a good-bye to her patients and followed her friend out the door. A quick look up confirmed her earlier suspicions. The sky, now a deeper yellow, was outlined with boiling black clouds, and the heavy air was stagnant—no doubt a strong wind would be assaulting the city soon.

"I think we have time to get home, but it looks like it's going to be a bad one." Janie spoke quickly as she strode down the hill.

Carrie matched her stride. She missed the plantation and all her father's slaves who had become dear friends, but she was glad to be in Richmond with Janie. They had exchanged letters daily since that fateful day when Carrie had saved Janie from a drunken soldier. Next to Rose, her best friend since childhood, Janie was her closest friend. "How did your day go?"

Janie shrugged. "It was fine." She hesitated. "If watching mere boys learn how to live their life without arms and legs can ever be fine." Her voice sharpened. "We lost three today in our ward. Their bodies just couldn't fight anymore. . . . " Her words trailed off and her eyes filled with tears. "I don't know if I'll ever get used to it."

"I pray to God you don't!" Carrie exclaimed, her eyes welling with moisture. "I hope we never become immune to the death and suffering around us. When that happens part of us would die. I'd rather deal with the pain than become hardened."

Janie nodded, then changed the subject, obviously wanting to tread on lighter ground. "Matron Pember got a letter from her sister today."

Carrie looked up at the sound of amusement in Janie's voice. "The one in New Orleans?"

"Yes. It seems the ladies of that fair city are not taking kindly to Union occupation."

"What do you mean?"

Janie made no effort to hide the laughter in her voice. "Matron Pember's sister evidently has the same strong personality she does. Her letter said she was arrested on the charge of laughing as the body of a Federal officer was being carried past her residence. She claims she was having a party at the time and the laughter was the result of something a child had done. General Butler . . . "

"Who is certainly not a popular figure around there!"

"Exactly. General Butler didn't believe her and demanded she apologize."

"Which of course she didn't."

"Of course not. When she refused to apologize, General Butler called her a 'vulgar woman of the town' and banished her to Ship Island."

"That barren island of sand in the Gulf of Mexico?" Carrie exclaimed.

Janie nodded. "She wrote Matron Pember with her response to the General's banishment, telling him, 'It has one advantage over the city, sir; you will not be there!' "

Carrie laughed along with her friend. "You're right. She's definitely the matron's sister." Then she sobered. "I feel so badly for her, though. What a terrible thing to be stuck out on that island."

Her sympathy was compounded by the genuine affection she had developed for the no-nonsense, outspoken Matron Pember. The matron had overheard the doctor's comments that had so infuriated Carrie. She had waited for Carrie in the hallway and told her not to be bothered by the doctor, that soon the South would be begging for women with medical ability. Her exact words still rang in Carrie's mind. "The South is sending off all its men. The time will come soon enough when it will be the women who will save the day. Things will never be the same after that!"

"Matron Pember says the Union will probably send her back home. She is sure her sister will give them no rest," Janie said, interrupting Carrie's thoughts.

Carrie laughed. "From what I can tell there are a lot of women in New Orleans like her."

"The matron's letter told about how the women there spit on the soldiers and regale them with derogatory remarks and gestures. Why, one lady even dumped the contents of her chamberpot on General Butler's head as he was passing under her balcony." Janie's laugh rang out.

Carrie spun and regarded her with flashing eyes. "Janie Winthrop! You can't possibly think that is respectable behavior. Those soldiers are just doing their job!"

Janie shrugged. "Maybe. But I think I would feel the same way if those Union soldiers out there take over Richmond. How would you like having to bow to their every whim?" She turned to glare at Carrie.

Carrie thought about it for a minute. "Pouring a chamberpot on his head. Ugh!" The sound of Carrie's disgusted voice sent Janie off into peals of laughter again. Soon both of them were doubled over with mirth. In the midst of war it was difficult to find a reason to laugh. You took what you could get.

An ominous rumble of thunder and a distant flash of lightning got them moving back down the hill. There was quiet between them for several minutes.

"Are you scared of the future, Carrie?" There was no amusement in Janie's voice now. Her normally bright, blue eyes were dark with worry, her attractive face pinched with fear. "Oh, I suppose I'm being silly," she suddenly exclaimed without waiting for Carrie's answer. "I guess this storm is just getting to me."

Carrie looked at her quickly. The glib response on her tongue died at the expression on Janie's face. "Yes," she said slowly, "I suppose I am scared." They had not talked much about the thousands of Union soldiers outside the gates of Richmond. The Union cry of *"Forward to Richmond"* had become a frightening reality. Carrie hated the war and wanted it to end, but the idea of being in a captured city was not appealing. While the people in the outlying areas had fled to Richmond for safety, many residents had fled to escape possible Union occupation.

It seemed everyone in Richmond had been in a state of panic when she had reached the safety of the city's borders after fleeing the plantation, but the panic had now settled into a calm defiance. She had heard some people describe it as apathy but as far as she could tell there was no apathy on the part of Richmonders—they simply realized they could not stop what would happen. They could only deal with it and fight as hard as they could. Until then, they would wait. They would not give up their city without a mighty resistance.

"What if our boys lose, Carrie? Will the Union destroy our city? I've heard that many Northerners are calling for it."

Carrie listened in dismay. Should she tell Janie what her father had told her just last night? It would only frighten her more. On the other hand, Carrie had decided it was better to know the truth. "I talked to my father about that last night," she finally admitted.

"What did he say? Surely he knows what they plan to do since he works with the government."

Carrie spoke slowly, remembering the pain she had seen on her father's face as he had talked. "The military authorities have decided to make sure the Union doesn't get its hands on the valuable supplies here in the city." She hesitated. "If the Union enters the city, all of the tobacco and cotton will be burned."

"But the warehouses are right in the heart of the city! What if it spreads? It could destroy all of Richmond!"

Carrie knew Janie was fighting to keep panic from overwhelming her. "They know that. And the very idea of it scares them to death. But they feel it is the only thing to do. But all of that is only *if* the Union captures Richmond. That is still a long way off. Our army is strong and about to get stronger," she finished with forced optimism.

"General Jackson is coming back from the Shenandoah Valley?"

"My father says he is on his way. He did the job he was sent to do wonderfully. President Lincoln was so certain Jackson was heading to attack Washington, that he called off the reinforcements he was sending to McClellan. General McDowell was called back to guard their own capital. Father says it makes the odds a little more even."

Janie shuddered. "There is going to be so much suffering when the fighting finally starts here. We already have so many patients from the Battle of Williamsburg. What's it going to be like?"

Carrie said nothing. She had a good idea what it would be like. It was too horrible to contemplate.

After a long minute Janie looked at her again. "Do you want Richmond to fall? Neither one of us believes this crazy war should be happening."

Carrie almost smiled. Janie was so much like Rose. She always managed to cut through to the crux of the matter. Suddenly she wanted to cry. Where was Rose? How was she? Carrie knew her friend had reached the safety of Philadelphia after she had helped Rose and her husband, Moses, escape slavery, but were they still all right? Fear clutched her heart. Lately she found that her emotions could swing from one to another in seconds. She supposed it was just this crazy war—but it was exhausting. Suddenly she remembered Janie's question. A quick glance at her friend told her she was patiently waiting for a reply.

"Do I want Richmond to fall?" She shook her head helplessly. "I want this crazy war to end, but I hate the idea it might take the destruction of the city to make it happen. I've lost one home. I don't want to lose another. And I know it would kill my father. Working for the Virginia government saved him after my mother died. He has thrown all he is into building a new country. I can't wish more pain for him! And what about Robert? The man I love, out there fighting. If the city falls it will mean even more Southern deaths. But maybe it would stop the escalation of the war. If it's not too late for that." She shook her head again. "Yet, I can't wish for the South to win. It would only mean the continuation of slavery. I can't abide the idea that more helpless people will have to suffer and be denied their freedom." Her words tumbled to a halt as her eyes filled with tears. "I just know I hate this whole stupid war!" she cried.

Janie reached out and held her hand for a long moment. Nothing more was said on the way down the hill.

Carrie had just changed into a fresh dress when she heard a knock at the front door. She wasn't expecting anyone, so she continued to smooth her hair into place. There were so many people living in the house now it could be for anyone. For a moment she gazed into the mirror, wishing she was back on the plantation and could leave her hair loose without having to confine it to a bun. Wild and free, she would race across the rolling fields on Granite and let the wind whip it. Closing her eyes, she could almost imagine the feeling.

"Miss Cromwell."

The sound of her name startled Carrie back to the present. Quickly she finished her hair and moved to the door of the room she now shared with Janie. "What is it, Micah?" She smiled at her father's butler.

"Lieutenant Borden be at the door for you, Miss."

"Robert is here?" Carrie exclaimed. Swiftly she ran down the stairs to the front foyer. "Robert," Carrie exclaimed, "when did you arrive? I wasn't expecting you." She took his arm to lead him into the parlor.

Robert shook his head. "I don't want to be inside. Can we go out on the porch?"

Carrie frowned at the serious tone in his voice. A closer look revealed tension on his handsome face. "Of course," she agreed quickly.

Once outside, Robert moved slightly away from her to stand against a column on the porch. Carrie gazed at him for a moment. The wind had already begun to stir the city and was tossing Robert's wavy dark hair. Outlined against the threatening pallor of the sky, he looked like a mighty warrior in his Confederate gray uniform. "You're leaving," she said simply.

Robert continued to look at her, as if he was trying to burn a vision of her into his heart. He had told her how much the memories of her had helped during the long campaign of the winter. She fought the urge to run into his arms.

Finally Robert nodded. "General Lee is sure something is going to happen soon. He has promised to send General Johnson every available man."

"When do you leave?"

"In a few minutes."

Carrie fought to control the raging fear in her heart. As hard as she tried, though, she couldn't hide the tremor in her voice. "I see." She didn't know what else to say. Thankfully, Robert saved her by opening his arms wide. Without a word she walked into his embrace.

Several long minutes passed as they stood in silence. The streets around them bustled with activity as people rushed to escape the encroaching storm. Doors banged open as women dashed out to save their laundry hanging on the lines. The trees, just a few minutes ago swaying in the breeze, were now bending low under the powerful gusts the storm was sending their direction. The roll of thunder grew louder as the flashes of lightning lit up the sky with increasing intensity.

Carrie longed for the moment to never end. If only wishing hard enough could make all the horrid realities of the war melt away, could transport them back to her secret place by the river. It had only been two weeks since she and Robert had moved beyond all the turmoil of their relationship. The issue of slavery was still a bone of contention between them, but Carrie was no longer pretending her whole heart did not belong to him. What if these two short weeks were all they were to have?

Robert was the first to step back. "I have to go, Carrie." His voice cracked, as if straining to keep the pain of their separation at bay.

Carrie gazed up at him, trying to etch his face into her memory. She fought to stop the tears welling in her eyes and managed a tremulous smile. "I love you, Robert. Take care of yourself."

Robert looked at her hungrily a moment more, then moaning slightly, he bent his head and covered her mouth in a warm kiss. Carrie responded to his touch, unleashing all the longing hidden in her heart. They both knew they might never see each other again. A loud crack of thunder startled them and they drew apart. Robert raised his hand, letting it rest on her face, then stepped back.

"God bless you," Carrie said tenderly.

Robert nodded, turned, strode down the stairs, and vaulted onto the tall thoroughbred waiting for him.

Carrie ran down the steps after him and laid her head against the horse's face. "Take good care of him, Granite. You better come back to me, too," she whispered. She had given Granite to Robert just days after arriving in Richmond. He needed a good mount, and there was not enough food in Richmond to take care of any non-working horses. She was glad for Robert to have him but it ripped her heart to think something might happen to her beloved horse as well as the man she loved. Stepping back, she smiled brightly at both of them. "Go save my city, Lieutenant Borden!"

Robert smiled, tipped his hat at her, and urged Granite into a fast canter down the road. Carrie watched until they had rounded the curve and were out of sight. Even when she could no longer see them, she stood there, oblivious to the whipping dirt stinging her face and arms. It was the sharp crack of a limb that brought her back to the present. Looking up she watched as limbs and leaves did a frantic dance in rebellion against the gale battering them.

"Carrie! Get in this house."

Carrie turned and managed a smile at Janie. "I rather like it," she shouted above the din. "When I see a storm like this it helps to remind me it takes a very powerful God to create such a thing. It gives me hope that maybe he really is in control of all this."

Janie strode down the stairs and took her arm. "And it would give me hope that you still have some sense in your head if you wouldn't keep standing out here waiting for a limb to knock you silly!" she retorted.

Carrie allowed Janie to pull her onto the porch, then turned to stare back out at the building fury.

"Was that Robert I saw leaving?"

Carrie nodded. "He has been called to the front."

"I'm sorry," Janie said simply. She took her friend's hand and stood silently.

Carrie was grateful she said no more. There was nothing to be said anyway. This same scene was being played daily in every town in the country. There were no words to ease the pain or take away the questioning and worry in each heart as loved ones left for the battlefield. It was simply to be endured.

Finally Carrie spoke, "There seem to be nothing but questions about the welfare of the people that I love." For just a moment it seemed as if it would overwhelm her. The pictures swirled through her mind, fighting for first position. Moses, who had helped save her from the Union soldiers on the plantation, was himself a Union spy.

Where was he? And what would happen to him if he was caught by the Confederates? And what about Rose? The last Carrie knew she was safe in Philadelphia, but what if slave hunters were still pursuing her? What if Ike Adams went after her again?

Pictures of Aunt Abby swirled into the collage. Her special friend, who was so much like a second mother to her, lived in the now foreign land of the Union. There had been no communication, save one smuggled letter through the Underground Railroad, for over a year. And Matthew—Robert's close friend from the North who had recently been released from a prison in Richmond. Would his job as a war correspondent once again put him in danger?

Overlaying the collage of swirling pictures was the image of a tall, handsome lieutenant mounted on a towering, gray thoroughbred.

A deafening bolt of lightning ripped through the darkening sky. The sound of an explosion and a flash of light told Carrie a tree had attracted more than its share of the storm's fury. As she stared out, the first huge raindrops fell. Within seconds, the drops had turned into a roaring deluge that made all talk impossible. Stepping farther back into the shelter of the porch, Carrie allowed the anger of the storm to carry some of her feelings of helplessness and powerlessness away with it. She had always found strength in storms. This one was no different.

Tomorrow would come. There was nothing she could do to stop it. All she could do was wait and see what the new day would bring.

Carrie tried to look like she was listening as she forced herself to eat the supper May had fixed for the household. But she was distracted with thoughts of Robert and the approaching doom. Overcrowding in the city had filled every house to capacity. Until a month ago, her father had lived in this house by himself along with his two house servants. Now the household totaled twelve. She and Janie shared a room upstairs. The other seven were men employed by the government. All of them were pleasant enough, but Carrie had been busy at the hospital and had had little time to become acquainted with them.

Thomas Cromwell cleared his throat as he reached for his glass of water. "I have proof today that all of our city is indeed trying to do their part for the war effort." He allowed his voice to trail off, inviting questions.

Carrie forced herself to pay attention. Her father had been casting anxious looks at her since reaching the table. She had seen Janie talking to him just before they were called to dinner, so she was sure he knew Robert had been called away. She forced a light note into her voice. Giving into despair would do no one any good. "And just what evidence did you acquire today?"

Thomas turned to her eagerly, obviously relieved by her show of interest. "Even the proprietors of our gambling halls have embraced the patriotism of our time."

"And just how, pray tell, have they done that?" Janie asked in an openly skeptical voice. "Are they opening their doors to Union soldiers so that they might make more money?"

Thomas laughed, but shook his head. "They have *closed* their doors for a while."

"What?" That was enough to get even Carrie's attention. She had only been in town for short periods during the last year but she was well aware of the gambling halls' reputations.

Thomas nodded. "They've decided to suspend operations for a while because too many of our officers were being lured from their duties. But that's not all," he said, pausing dramatically. "They have also voted to give twenty thousand dollars to our cause."

"Be still my beating heart!" Janie cried dramatically as laughter rang through the room.

"They have decreed it be used to purchase articles needed to treat the wounded in whatever may be coming."

Carrie felt the now-familiar fear clutching at her throat.

Her face must have betrayed her emotions, for her father looked at her regretfully and said, "I'm sorry, Carrie. That was thoughtless and insensitive of me."

Carrie pushed aside visions of Robert lying wounded on the battlefield, and reached forward to take his hand. "Nonsense. I am very glad the owners of the gambling halls are finally going to do something constructive with their money. It will be much needed. Our soldiers deserve the finest care." She searched her mind for a way to change the subject and let her father off the hook but it took all her mental energy to keep from bursting into tears.

"Well, they took care of another Union spy yesterday." The statement was offered by Warren Pucket, a clerk in the War Department. The slightly built man, in his early forties, had been turned down for entrance into the army because of medical reasons but that had not stopped him from making the trip from Alabama to offer what services he could.

Thomas turned toward him with obvious relief. "I've heard a little about it, but I don't really know the story. Do tell us."

Warren complied. "Evidently Timothy Webster was a master spy. Since last October he has been dispatching letters to the North detailing the Confederacy's military secrets. From what I have been told, he managed to work himself into Baltimore's Confederate Underground. They actually sneaked him over the lines because they thought they were helping their own cause."

"Rather ingenious," Thomas muttered angrily.

"It gets worse," Warren replied. "Webster posed as an Englishman here in town and made friends with officials on every level. He hung around the newspapers and the War Department. Why, both General Winder and Benjamin used him as a dispatcher."

"He was used by the Secretary of the War Department? Judas Benjamin was taken in by him?" Thomas exclaimed.

Warren shrugged. "He was evidently very good at what he did."

"How did they catch him?" Janie asked.

"The story I heard said Webster fell ill with extremely painful rheumatism. He went so long without reporting to Washington that they got worried about him and sent two men down to check on him. Someone recognized the two men as northern detectives. They hadn't been here long before they found themselves in jail."

"But what about Webster?" Carrie asked. She found the story fascinating, even though she was appalled to think these were all American citizens spying on each other.

Warren smirked. "The two men in jail didn't take too kindly to the idea they were going to hang for being spies. With a little persuasion and promises of mercy, they broke, telling all about Webster and his mission. He was really the big fish in the whole operation. Until yesterday he has occupied one of our prisons."

"What happened yesterday?" Carrie asked.

"They hung him," Warren stated flatly.

Carrie turned white and stared at him. "They hung him?" she repeated.

Warren's face hardened with anger. "You don't get away with spying in the Capitol. There is no telling how many of our men died needlessly because of the information he was passing out."

Carrie saw her father open his mouth to break into the conversation, but Warren hurried on, reveling in the story.

"There weren't many people out there to watch the hanging. A whole crowd of folks showed up for the hanging of his two buddies but were disappointed when it didn't actually happen. I guess they decided this one wouldn't really happen either. They missed a great show!"

"You were there?" Thomas asked.

"Yes. I was asked to record it for the War Department. Anyway, the first time the trap was sprung the rope was too long. He fell straight to the ground. It busted him up a little but it certainly didn't kill him."

Carrie shuddered as the picture sprang into her mind. She listened in horrified silence.

Warren, oblivious to the fact that not everyone was enjoying his story, hurried on. "They picked him up, helped him up the stairs, fixed the ropes, and sprung it again." He paused. "He hung for thirty minutes before he was cut down. Then the detectives sliced up the rope for souvenirs."

Carrie could control herself no longer. "How can you find anything good in such a horrible thing! These are Americans killing Americans!"

Warren's voice was flat and emotionless when he turned to her. "I'm sorry if the reality of the war is disturbing to you, Miss Cromwell. It is disturbing to all of us. I freely admit I find satisfaction in knowing another threat to our way of life has been destroyed. Timothy Webster knew the risk when he decided to come down and betray the people who put trust in him. We are at war, Miss

Cromwell. A war we intend to win. We will do whatever it takes to win it."

Carrie stared at him as his chilling words sank into her heart. Suddenly she was tired. Very, very tired. "Excuse me. I think I will retire now." She slipped from her place at the table and climbed slowly up the stairs to her room. Halfway up, she heard her father's chair scrape back and his footsteps following her. Turning and smiling at him, she managed, "I'll be all right, Father. I just need some time alone."

In her room, she curled up in the windowseat and stared out at the rain still pounding the city. She heard the echo of words spoken by a Richmonder earlier in the week, *I have begun to feel like the prisoners of the Inquisition in Edgar Allen Poe's story—cast into a dungeon of slowly contracting walls.*

The walls were closing in.

hen Carrie woke the next morning, she lay still and watched as a slight breeze ruffled the curtains. A quick glance revealed that Janie had already departed for the hospital. Carrie stretched and allowed the bed's softness to envelop her body for a few more moments. This was her first day off in a week. She hadn't realized how tired she was. The light outside told her it was mid-morning.

Several long minutes passed while she listened to the sounds of birds outside her window. To be sure, they were competing with the sounds of a noisy city, but if she pretended real hard she could almost imagine she was still on the plantation. Funny, she had been in such a hurry to leave the plantation, to follow her dream of becoming a doctor. Her decision to stay and grow crops had been her own, and it had been easy to throw her whole heart into it, but she had yearned for the day she could begin to follow her dream in earnest.

Well, here she was. Only her dream hadn't included thousands of young men needlessly killed and wounded from battles pitting Americans against Americans. It hadn't included countless amputations and infection that sapped the life of vibrant young men. It hadn't included infectious diseases that spread like wildfire, claiming countless lives, as they swept through the camps that bred them.

Carrie had dreamed of going North—to the school established by one of the first women physicians in America, Dr. Harriet Hunt. She would have lived with Aunt Abby in Philadelphia, while having the support of other women who had braved the cold waters of change before her. Now Philadelphia was in a foreign country. She was indeed in a medical hospital, but every step she took was going to be a battle. For just a moment, fatigue caused her dream to waver in front of her. The picture dimmed and grew hazy as she envisioned the obstacles she would face.

But only for a moment. With a snort of contempt at her own self-pity, Carrie forced a defiant laugh and threw back the covers on her bed. "Get out of bed right now, Carrie Cromwell!" she muttered. "Lying around feeling sorry for yourself is a stupid thing to do. You are right where God wants you. You have a chance to make a difference. So what if you have to fight a little? Isn't that what you do best?" she demanded of herself in an exasperated tone.

Throwing her long, flowing curls over her shoulder, she stepped to the window. A deep breath told her the storm last night had cleared the air only temporarily. Thick gray clouds still captured the sky. Already a sultriness was invading the morning freshness. Just like the day before, the air hung heavy, seemingly burdened under the threatening events it was being called upon to convey. Carrie felt the heaviness reaching for her heart, but tossed her head and retreated back into her room. "I have a whole day to myself," she declared brightly to her empty room. "Now, what am I going to do with it?"

A soft knock at her door caused her to spin. She had been sure she was alone in the house. Whoever was still around would think she was a trifle daft for carrying on a conversation with herself. "Yes?" she called, slightly irritated.

"Do you think your old father might share in all this talk with you for a while?"

Carrie laughed and flung open the door. Her father was used to her habit of talking to herself. She had done it from the time she was a child. "Father! What are you still doing home? Nothing is wrong, is it?"

Thomas shook his head. "I've already been to the Capitol. I had to retrieve some papers. My next meeting is not scheduled to start for a couple of hours. When I heard you, I thought I might talk you into having breakfast with me."

"The two of us alone? I can't think of anything I would like to do more," Carrie exclaimed. "Give me just a few minutes to get ready. I'll be right down." She smiled as she slipped into her dress, then tamed her hair into a braid and bun. She had not been alone with her father since the few minutes they had talked when she had come to after the surgery to remove the bullet in her shoulder. There were always other people around. Whistling softly, she closed the door to her room and ran lightly down the steps.

Thomas was already seated at the table. "May will be in in a few minutes with our breakfast." Laying aside one of the papers he had been perusing, he fixed a loving smile on her. "Now, daughter, tell me how you're doing."

Carrie slipped into the chair next to him. "Feeling quite refreshed. I didn't realize how tired I was until I got to sleep so long."

"You have barely slowed down since you arrived. You should have given yourself more than five days to recover from your injury before jumping into work at the hospital." He grinned when Carrie merely shrugged. "Not that I would have expected you to do anything less."

"You are hardly the one to talk, anyway," Carrie responded with an impish grin. "You are at the Capitol both day and night."

"You're right," Thomas sighed. "There seems to be no end to the things that need to be done. Helping to govern a state at anytime is a continual challenge. When war is added into the mix it becomes..." His voice trailed off.

Carrie leaned forward and laid her hand on his. "How long since you've had any rest yourself?" she asked tenderly.

Thomas shook his head and straightened. "Rest will come when there are no longer thousands of soldiers camped at our door," he said firmly.

Carrie was concerned at the deep lines of fatigue she saw etched on his face, but said nothing more. She knew it would do no good. Her father had found salvation in his work with the Virginia state government after his wife died. She would not interfere with the very thing that had saved him. Giving his all to the state he loved had been the only reason he had found for living. "What is going to happen?" she asked quietly.

"Only time will tell," Thomas said heavily. "I'm afraid there is discontent behind the battle lines as well."

"What do you mean?"

Thomas shrugged. "I'm afraid our own President is unable to find out what is going on. He and General Johnson don't have the best working relationship. My understanding is that the General is a very capable commander. He just doesn't feel any great need to communicate what is going on on *his* battlefields."

"Not even with the President?"

"It seems President Davis didn't know how far Johnson was retreating from McClellan until he rode outside the city limits and found our own army camped just a few miles away," he commented drily. "Word has it that Johnson initially wanted to take his stand against McClellan right where he is, but Davis and General Lee persuaded him to take the battle to McClellan down on the Peninsula. Johnson went but he's been retreating ever since. Now he's right where he wanted to be all along."

"It can't remain a standoff forever, though."

"You're absolutely right," Thomas said grimly. "There seemed to be some movement of the troops yesterday but no one really knows what is going on. Except for Johnson, and he's not talking."

Carrie heard the ripe frustration in her father's voice. "Have all the stragglers gone back to the army?" She vividly remembered the day last week when she had gone down into the city. There had been weary, ragged men everywhere—sprawled on the sidewalks, cellar doors, porch overhangs. Tired, hungry, and discouraged, they had poured into the city seeking a respite from their suffering. General Johnson had sent troops in to bring them back to their duties.

"Most of them are gone," he said angrily. "Others snuck out of the city toward the west, I'm sure."

Carrie looked at her father thoughtfully. She could find no anger in her heart toward the confused men who had come to fight this war—either voluntarily or conscripted. No one had been prepared for the slaughter and suffering that had met them. It was little wonder many of them longed for home and made the decision to let other men fight the battles for them.

A long silence stretched between them as visions of what the immediate future might hold paraded before them through the room.

Thomas broke the quiet first. "There is a possibility the city will fall, Carrie."

Carrie knew how it must be tearing her father up inside to admit even the possibility. "What will you do?"

"There are a lot of things being said. You already know they plan to torch the tobacco and cotton warehouses. Other men are threatening to set fire to their own homes—and to the Capitol. They are even planning on destroying the magnificent statue of Washington if the Yankees succeed."

Carrie whitened at the thought of the destruction that would flood their city. "Surely the North would do no more harm than what we plan on doing to ourselves," she protested.

"I agree," her father replied wearily. "But emotion can play a much bigger role than reason at a time like this." He paused for a long minute, and then his face tightened with anger. "By God, we've not fallen yet!" he exclaimed as his fist pounded against the table. "We will not go down without a fight."

"Or without thousands of soldiers being killed and wounded in the process." Carrie made no attempt to hide the bitterness in her voice.

Thomas sobered instantly, but his face was still hard. "We didn't ask for this war. But we're going to see it through—and we're going to win." Another long pause. "We have to win." His words were spoken more to himself than to Carrie.

The first boom of cannons and pop of gunfire erupted just after one o'clock that afternoon. The wait was finally over—or was it just beginning? Only time would tell the outcome of the battle. Would Richmond still be the capital of the Confederacy when the noise died away?

Within minutes the streets were thronged with people hurrying to the higher elevations to view the fighting. Carrie hurried to join them. In spite of her revulsion of the war, it was impossible to not want to know what was happening. There was no way she could stay in her father's house and simply listen. She had to be with the people. She had to be a part of what was going on in her world.

The book she had been attempting to read earlier had been tossed aside unceremoniously. Right now, she couldn't even remember the title. It was one she had idly chosen from her father's extensive collection when she was trying to decide how to spend the day. Not that it had held her attention. For the first time in her life no book could interest her. The events surrounding her made the fiction she had been trying to read look comparatively flat. Nothing but the drama that was unfolding in Richmond today would be able to arrest her attention.

The crowd surging up the hill was, save the quiet mutterings of a few people, silent. Their tense, strained faces spoke of their anxiety. Carrie noticed a few of her neighbors who seemed content to listen from the safety of their porches, but most of the town seemed to be migrating to the highest points around them. From there they would be able to look out and possibly see the battle play out before their eyes. She was sure everyone wanted to know if the Federal troops broke through the Confederate defenses. Not that the knowledge would do much good. There was nowhere to run.

The thunder of cannon rivaled the fury of the storm the night before. Buildings shook and windows rattled as it rolled into the city. Carrie gazed around her, frightened as the mutterings of the people took on a panicked note. The steady popcorn staccato of gunfire drifted on the breeze between the loud explosions. Allowing the flow of people to pull her onward, she took comfort in the very numbers. Finally they all reached the top of the hill. When Carrie turned to look, there was nothing to see except the already thickening cloud of smoke that blended with the slate-colored sky.

"What's happening?" one lady cried.

"Those Yankees are fixing to get a taste of Rebel fury is what's happening!" a stout gentleman shouted, waving his cane defiantly.

"Who started the fight?" another asked anxiously.

"There's no way of knowing," another responded. "All we can do is wait and find out what happens."

Carrie stood quietly, staring out at the scene, thinking only of Robert. Where was he? Was he already wounded? Would she see him again?

"My son is out there in that cloud of smoke," one nearby lady said softly.

"Both my boys and my husband are out there," another responded.

Carrie watched as the two women clasped hands and stared off into the distance. Suddenly she turned and strode rapidly back in the direction she had come. Standing on the hill and staring was going to do no one any good. What was going to happen was going to happen.

There was nothing she could do to change it. Experience had already taught her what the result would be, however. The place she could do some good was the hospital. She knew the flow of wounded would start flooding in before the day was over.

Janie looked up in relief as Carrie stuck her head in the door. "I knew I could count on you to come," she said simply. "We need help preparing beds for the wounded."

Carrie nodded sharply and turned toward her assigned ward. She completely lost track of time as she moved from bed to bed, covering them with fresh sheets, laying out bandages, filling pitchers with water. As she worked she tried to keep up the spirits of the wounded soldiers, chaffing in their helplessness.

"The firing done stopped!" Samuel called. "I reckon that means our boys let them have it!"

"We don't know what it means," Walker replied. "It could mean we're about to have Yankee nurses."

Carrie opened her mouth to reply but the sounds of the shelling intruded into the brief silence.

"They're after them again!" Samuel cried. "Give it to 'em, fellas!"

Carrie couldn't help but notice the looks of relief on some of the faces surrounding her. These boys had seen the horrors of battle first-hand. They were not eager to be pulled back into the carnage. For now, the hospital was a haven of safety for them.

Once Carrie had finished in her own ward, she hurried into the buildings that until now had been empty. There was no doubt in anyone's mind that by the end of the fight for their city, all the wards would be full. Her arms and shoulders ached as she made bed after bed. Resolutely, she ignored the pain—it was nothing when she thought of what the soldiers were experiencing. It was infuriating that men determined to have their own way were willing to send other men to suffer and die in such a horrible manner. Fatigue soon deadened her anger. She moved mechanically from bed to bed wondering what face would soon be lying on the pillow she fluffed.

Carrie wasn't sure when she noticed that the firing had stopped. Silence replaced the constant rumble of cannon and guns. But it was not a silence that offered peace. It was heavy, like the calm before a great storm. The soldiers had done their job for the day. Now it was up to the citizens of Richmond to do theirs. She still had no idea who had won the battle. Were Union troops moving into the city even now? She would find out soon enough. Right now she had a job to do.

Carrie had finished in one ward and was moving with several other women to another when the sound of wagons drawing up the hill arrested their attention. The women exchanged knowing looks. "It's our turn," Carrie said simply. Ahead of her, she saw the rush of medical personnel hurrying to meet the first of the ambulance wagons pulling into the hospital yard. Resisting the urge to examine faces for any sign of the man she loved, Carrie walked quickly back to her assigned ward.

Changes had been made there during her absence. All of the remaining soldiers in her ward were Virginians. Those from other states had been moved to other buildings. There were bound to be a lot of casualties in a battle such as this. This way, with the men divided into wards with others from their home states, it would be easier for family members who were searching for their loved ones to find them. Carrie had been told of the changes but it still was hard to lose the patients she had grown so fond of.

Sighing heavily, she moved to prepare the newly emptied beds. Then she straightened and hunched her shoulders, trying to work out the soreness. Her work for the day was just beginning. In a matter of minutes, a broken mass of humanity would begin pouring through the doors. She could greet them with fatigue and self-pity, or she could cast aside her own cares to be able to give to them whole-heartedly.

"God, make me your instrument to the ones you bring to this ward."

Carrie had barely uttered the words before the first of the stretchers was carried in. She knew from the briefing they had received earlier that many of the soldiers would have to wait for medical attention. Their job was just to make them as comfortable as possible until one of the doctors could get to them. Carrie watched as the first man was carried in. Suppressing her groan, she tightened her lips and hurried forward.

She could tell he was fairly young, but his entire body was caked with mud and black powder from the guns. His shirt, crusted with blood, stuck to his body in some places, and gaped away with holes at others. Someone had wrapped a coarse bandage around his head, but it, too, was a reddish brown from dried blood and was matted to his forehead. The broken bone of one arm protruded through the gaping skin, causing it to twist on the stretcher at an awkward angle. In spite of it all he was conscious.

As soon as the stretcher carriers deposited him on the bed, Carrie moved to lean over him. "Hello, soldier."

"Howdy, ma'am," he said weakly.

"You're going to be just fine. We're going to take good care of you."

"I appreciate it," he managed as he grimaced with pain.

Carrie dipped a cloth in water and began to gently bathe his face. Now that the crisis was finally here she was oddly calm, a steely determination and compassion flowing through her body. "What is your name, soldier?"

"Johnny . . . Johnny Whitestone."

"Well, Johnny Whitestone, I'm just going to try and clean you up a bit. It may be a little while before the doctors can get to you, but they will see you just as soon as they can."

"Yes, ma'am. There ain't no big hurry. There's other fellows hurt lots worse than me," he said with a heavy accent.

"Are you from the mountains, Johnny?" Carrie knew talking would keep his mind off his injuries. Once the adrenalin of the battlefield ebbed away there would be nothing but searing pain to take its place.

"Yes, ma'am. From up around Charlottesville."

"This your first battle?"

"No, ma'am. I been fighting ever since Manassas. I guess I'm luckier than most. This is the first time I've got hurt." He paused for a moment, then his face brightened. "We stopped 'em, ma'am. We pushed those Yankees back. I reckon our capital will be safe a while longer."

Carrie continued to wash away the grime from his face. She could tell the effort of talking was beginning to get to tire him. "Just lie back, Johnny. The doctor will get to you soon." She longed to take the bandage off his head and tend to the wound underneath before infection had more of a chance to set in, but she knew she didn't dare.

"I be right thirsty," Johnny muttered.

Carrie touched his forehead—his eyes were already taking on that familiar fever-glazed look. Steadying his shoulders, she helped prop him up, then lifted a glass to his lips. His broken arm shifted, causing him to cry out in pain. She watched his face harden with determination as he gulped some water and then settled back against the pillow.

"Thank you."

"Miss Cromwell!" a voice near the door called.

Carrie looked up sharply and sprung up as another stretcher entered the ward. There were three other women working with her so every fourth patient would be hers to care for.

"Hello, soldier—" Her words died on her lips. The man they were carrying in was seemingly lifeless. The bandaged stumps of his right arm and leg were bright with blood. Thankfully he was unconscious. The reality of his situation would be a brutal presence soon enough. Carrie tightened her lips and went to work. At least he would have a clean face when he woke up. As she gently wiped his filthy face with a warm, soapy cloth she prayed. Prayed he would not give up hope when he awoke and realized what had happened. Prayed infection would not set in and sap the fragile life that even now hung by a thread.

The hours blurred as the ward quickly filled with men in all conditions. Carrie had no idea what time it was when she was able to make her way back to Johnny Whitestone. She had seen him taken from the ward and later carried back in, attended by one of the male nurses. He was just coming out of the anesthesia when she leaned over his bed.

"Hello, Johnny," she said cheerfully.

"They took my arm, Miss Cromwell," he said dully, his pain-glazed eyes searching hers for some understanding of what had just happened to him.

Carrie laid her hand on his shoulder. She would never understand the cruelty of a world in which a young man in the prime of life could wake up without an arm. "So they did, Johnny. Now you're going to have to use all your energy to get well." She fought to make her voice sound encouraging.

Johnny stared at her. "I'm a blacksmith, ma'am." His voice wavered as confusion filled his eyes. "Least I used to be. Don't reckon I'll be one now."

Sudden tears slipped from Carrie's eyes. She smoothed the hair back from his forehead. "You've got to take one day at a time, Johnny. First we've got to get you well. God saw you through that battle. He's not going to stop taking care of you."

Johnny seemed to drink in her words. After a long moment he said, "My momma told me she would be praying for me every day. I sure hope she's praying."

"I'm sure she is, Johnny," Carrie said tenderly. "What you need now is sleep. Close your eyes and try to get some rest."

Exhausted blue eyes stared at her a moment more with a look that said he was afraid to go to sleep, afraid he might never wake up. Finally his body won the battle. The blue eyes flickered shut. Moments later the haggard face was lax with sleep. Carrie watched him and prayed he would sleep a long time. He had only pain waiting for him when he woke up.

As Carrie watched him, she became aware for the first time of how achingly tired she was. Her shoulder, not entirely healed, was throbbing. Shaking her head, she tried to push the pain aside.

"Miss Cromwell?"

Carrie lifted her head toward the voice. She managed a weary smile when she saw that it was Matron Pember.

"It's two o'clock in the morning, Miss Cromwell. All the other women have gone home. You must get some rest."

Carrie stared at her. Had she had been in the hospital for twelve hours? "The patients," she murmured.

"The patients are resting. They will need you again when they wake up in the morning. You'll be no good to them without some rest."

Carrie smiled. "I'm not sure you're the one to be talking about rest."

"I'm on my way to get some right this minute. Will you walk with me to my quarters? I'll have one of the men see you down the hill to your father's house."

"Where is Janie?"

"She left a couple of hours ago. She looked in here for you but didn't see you. She assumed you had gone home."

Carrie nodded and fell in beside the matron. "How bad is it?" she asked as they walked across the yard.

"Bad," Matron Pember responded bluntly. "Every hospital is filled to capacity. Wounded soldiers are filling warehouses, homes, hotels. I have been told even the sidewalks are full of men waiting for a bed and a doctor."

Carrie shuddered.

"The estimates are up around five thousand," she continued grimly.

"Five thousand men!" Carrie gasped.

"Dead and wounded. It's hard to get an exact number of Confederate casualties. It will take some time. We've taken in quite a few Northern soldiers as well."

"I'm glad," Carrie said fervently.

Matron Pember nodded. "Humanity is humanity. Our job is simply to ease the suffering as best we can."

Carrie walked in silence for a few minutes, then asked the question that had been burning in her heart all day. "I have a friend. His name is Robert Borden. Did you by any chance . . . ?"

The matron put her hand on Carrie's arm sympathetically. "I haven't heard the name, Miss Cromwell."

Carrie nodded. "Of course you haven't. It was silly of me to ask."

"Silly to ask? Silly to care that someone you love might be dead or wounded? I think not. You have a deep capacity to care, young lady. Never lose that. You will lose yourself if you do."

Thomas was waiting for Carrie when she walked in the door. Neither one said a word. Carrie took one look at her father's fatigued, worn face and melted into the arms he held out to her.

After a long moment her father pushed her back gently. "We can talk in the morning. It will be here soon enough. We both need some rest."

Carrie kissed him on the cheek gently, then turned to trudge up the stairs. She entered the room quietly so as not to disturb Janie.

"Carrie?"

"Yes." She should have known her friend would be awake.

"Are you okay?"

Carrie was silent as she tried to decide how to answer. A breeze ruffled the curtains, carrying with it the lingering scent of smoke from the battlefield. The faces of all the young men she had comforted that day flooded into her mind. The pain on their faces, the confusion and fear in their eyes. She bit her lip against the memories. And then there was Robert's face as she had last seen him the night before. His strong voice, his tender eyes, the feel of his lips on hers. . . .

"Carrie?" Janie's voice once more broke the darkness. Moments later she was standing beside her friend. "You're exhausted. Let me help you get ready for bed." Wrapping her arm around Carrie's waist she led her toward the closet.

Janie's touch undid the control Carrie had fought all day to maintain. With a low moan, she turned into her friend's arms and allowed the tears to come. Tears for all the pain surrounding her. Tears for Robert. Tears for the present. Tears for the future. Janie stood quietly, her arms encircling her friend while Carrie cried.

Finally Carrie stepped back. "Thank you," she gulped.

Janie still said nothing.

Within a few minutes Carrie was undressed and in her nightclothes. Willingly she allowed Janie to lead her to her bed. When Janie pulled back the covers, she slipped into the clean sheets, her eyes already drooping in sleep.

"Tomorrow is a new day, Carrie. Sleep tight."

Three

The noise of voices downstairs woke Carrie the next morning. Stretching her aching muscles, she looked around. Janie was already gone, her bed neatly made. Why was Janie gone so early? Why did she feel so tired? Why were her eyes swollen? Suddenly it all came rushing back. The battle the day before. The never-ending flow of wounded soldiers. Pushing back the covers, she rose and moved quickly to stare out the window. It was still dark—the stench of gunpowder and smoke still heavy in the air. To the east she glimpsed the faint lightning of the sky as the sun prepared to arrive on the scene. The morning air was quiet. Even the birds were silent, as if in mourning. If there was to be another battle today, it had not yet begun.

Thomas was finishing his breakfast when she entered the dining room. "Good morning, dear."

"Good morning." Carrie's heart was still heavy but her cry the night before had released some of the pent-up emotion. She sat down in her place and looked at her father expectantly.

Thomas drank a sip from the cup he was holding, then made a disgusted face. "I don't know that I'll ever get used to this stuff they call coffee."

"I understand one can develop a taste for ground sweet potato peels," Carrie said with a small smile. She had tried one cup of the concocted brew and decided she could do without coffee till after the war.

Thomas took another sip, then put the cup down on the polished wood. "You had a rough day yesterday," he stated. "I saw enough on the sidewalks to make me ill. I can only imagine what it's like in the hospitals."

Carrie took a deep breath as the images from the day before swarmed into her mind like a mob of angry bees. It was all she could do to control her tears as the pain she had witnessed once more rose to taunt her. "It was terrible," she responded flatly. "The South's best young men are being slaughtered and mutilated. When this war is over, their lives will never be the same."

Thomas sat silently for a long moment. His voice was heavy with both sorrow and defiance when he finally spoke. "I realize the cost of this war is high. But it is a cost that must be paid."

Carrie remained silent. She wished she could be so sure it was all worth such a high price.

"The great objective of the Confederate states is to bring the war to a successful close. Every other consideration must yield to that— surely you see that!" Thomas said sharply. His voice softened as he continued. "Without victory we can hope to enjoy nothing we possess, and nothing we do possess will be worth anything without it."

Carrie had never wanted the war to start in the first place. Now that it was here she was doing her best to make a difference and alleviate a small part of the suffering. Yes, she wanted the war to end because it would mean the end of the suffering, but ... "People once thought the war would never come to pass. They were sure the North wouldn't come down here to fight. Then they were sure one taste of the Confederacy's might would send them running home with their tails tucked between their legs. What are those people saying now?" she asked softly. "What do they say when they see the thousands of wounded men filling our cities?"

Thomas hesitated but his voice was tinged with defiance as he answered her. "The South has been forced by the North into all-out war. We didn't want it, but now that it's here we will fight it. Victory is all that matters. No price can be too high, no matter what changes we are forced to accept."

Carrie gazed at him. "They brought in a woman last night," she said finally. "She was wounded while trying to help tend the men on the battlefield—shot in the back. They don't know if she'll make it." She paused for a long moment. "What if that had been me, Father? Would that price have been too high?"

Thomas shifted under her steady look, but his face did not soften. "I hope to God I never have to pay such a price. I'm glad you're safe in the hospital."

"Is that why you're willing to pay the price? Because no one you love, no part of your family, can be hurt by the war? Does that make the price easier?" Carrie demanded, aware of the bitterness in her voice. She *knew* what price she might have to pay. She was all too aware that Robert might even now be dead, or lying wounded in another Richmond hospital.

"You know that's not true!" Thomas responded sharply. Then he grimaced and reached over for her hand. "I'm sorry, Carrie. I know you're worried about Robert. I am, too." He paused. "War is simply a horrible thing. But can't you see this is a war that simply must be won? Can't you see that right is on the side of the South?" he pleaded. "We are fighting for a just cause," he finished firmly.

Carrie was silent for several minutes. The silence in the room seemed to grow, her father's questions flowing around her, taunting her to find an answer. Finally she looked up. "Maybe," she said slowly, "but tied up in the *just cause* is slavery. Thousands of our country's best are suffering and dying to maintain the slavery of millions of others. Where is the justice in that?" she finished quietly.

"Would you rather the South lost?" Thomas demanded. "That our way of life be destroyed? That all these deaths be in vain?"

"I already think these deaths are all in vain!" Carrie snapped. "There is no reason for a sixteen-year-old boy to have to live the rest of his life without an arm and a leg." Other hot words surged to her lips but she bit them back. Her country was already divided. She knew families were being split apart by differing loyalties. Carrie turned and touched her father's arm. "Father, I don't want to fight. I love you." She gazed at his angry face as she implored. "Our country is at war. I know there are things we disagree about, but we can't let the war destroy us as well."

Thomas' face softened. "You're right, Carrie. Somehow we will deal with the differences between us."

"It's your fault, you know. You made me this way," Carrie teased, trying to inject a lighter note.

Thomas managed a slight smile. "Because I let you grow into a stubborn, strong-willed young lady? Would that I could do it all again!"

Carrie leaned forward. "Would you do it differently this time?"

"Not a bit," Thomas responded immediately. "I raised my daughter to think for herself—to be her own person. Granted, I never thought we would come down on different sides of such a volatile issue. . . . " his voice trailed off. Then he shook his head. "I love you the way you are, Carrie. Just do me a favor," he said in an attempt at humor. "Don't go fight for the Union. We would never win this war."

Carrie stood and moved to where he sat, then leaned down to wrap her arms around his shoulders in a fierce hug. He seemed so tense, so tired from these wearying days. "I love you," she said tenderly. "Now, tell me what is happening in our city." She hoped that talking would release some of the tension he was holding. It was at times like these that she imagined how much her father must miss her mother. They had talked about so many things. She had always had a way of making him laugh—of making the worry lines disappear from around his eyes. Carrie had watched the life ebb from her father's eyes when he lost his beloved Abigail. How she wished her mother was here now. She would know how to help him through these times.

Thomas sighed. "From what I can tell, which is not much at this point, we were able to push back McClellan's troops. It is too soon to have the whole story, but it was a miracle that even that happened."

"What do you mean?"

"General Johnston issued orders that were never received or were hopelessly misunderstood. Whole regiments never even saw the battlefield because they didn't know where they were supposed to be. McClellan's troops far outnumber our own. We have no idea why he didn't just sweep down and take the city."

"Robert told me General Lee said McClellan is overly cautious."

"It may be all that saved us," her father said grimly.

"What does President Davis think about what's going on?"

Thomas shrugged. "The last I heard our President didn't even know there was going to be a battle until he heard the gunfire. Evidently neither he nor Lee had been advised of a plan to attack the enemy. Then someone told me General Lee had to order Davis back from the front before he got shot."

"President Davis used to be an army officer himself, didn't he?"

"Yes. And old habits die hard."

"Did he go back?"

"Yes, but not before helping rally the troops."

"One of the soldiers who came in last night told me they pushed the Union troops back."

Thomas nodded. "They did. But we paid a high price for it."

"Matron Pember said somewhere around five thousand were killed or injured."

"Including General Johnston," Thomas said grimly.

"General Johnston!" Carrie exclaimed. "What happened?"

"I don't really know. All I do know is that he was severely wounded and will be out of service indefinitely."

"Who is leading our troops?"

"General Smith."

Carrie studied her father. "You don't sound pleased."

Thomas shrugged. "I don't know much about the man. I've simply heard that President Davis is not overly impressed with him. It could just be talk. One thing for sure," he said heavily. "He'll have his chance to prove himself. There is sure to be more fighting today."

Carrie grimaced as she drank the last bit of her tea. "The sky is getting light. I need to get back to the hospital."

"So early? You've only had a few hours of sleep."

"I suppose you've had more," she said wryly, then managed a small laugh at her father's offended expression. "I thought as much. There are thousands of wounded men in our city. Sleep seems to lose its importance." She was reaching for the last morsel of her biscuit when a loud boom penetrated the morning air. "Father!" She ignored the teacup that went clattering to the floor as she jumped up from the table and sprang to the window.

"It's begun again," Thomas said solemnly as he stood close beside her and stared outside. "I have to leave now. They will be needing me at the Capitol." His face was hard as he moved to gather his papers. Then he turned back. "Take care of yourself, Carrie."

Carrie stared at him, certain there was more he wasn't saying. Their conversation from a week ago played through her mind. She knew that if the city fell, the government would flee before the Union occupied it. They would move to another location and continue the fight. Her father had begged her to go with him if he was forced to evacuate. She had refused. Her place was here in Richmond. She would face whatever came. Both of them had cried when she told him her decision. Carrie simply knew she must stay—she belonged here—and she must be where Robert could find her.

Carrie wrapped her father in a big hug. "I love you. And I'm very proud of you." She forced a smile, not willing to believe Richmond would fall.

Thomas laid his hand on her face for a long moment, then kissed her cheek gently. "I love you, too."

The sound of cannon and gunfire followed as Carrie hurried up the hill toward the hospital. Somehow, in spite of the already crowded condition of the city, they would need to find a way to accommodate the fresh flow of wounded from the newest battle raging. Richmond was indeed discovering the price it would pay for offering itself as the capital of the Confederacy. The shadows of glory and honor were quickly ebbing into the deep darkness of reality and responsibility. Laughter and bravado were disappearing beneath the moans and cries of the wounded. Grim determination had already replaced lightheartedness. The whole city was at war.

There were still wagons with men waiting in them as Carrie reached the top of the hill. As she walked quickly down the wide street surrounding the buildings, she gazed out over the sight. People were everywhere, hurrying in and out of buildings. Stretchers were being carried; food was being delivered. She could smell the smoke from the bakeries as they worked to produce bread for the masses. Soon the aroma of fresh bread would spread through the air, along with the scent of soup steaming in the tobacco-factory boilers down the hill. And of course, the brewery was turning out beer as fast as it could.

Rounding the corner, Carrie stopped suddenly and held her hand against her mouth, trying to control the sudden gagging reflex in her throat. She wanted to scream her horror at the sight of severed hands, legs, and arms piled outside one of the surgical buildings. Already the mound was attracting swarms of flies as it cast off its deathly odor. Closing her eyes tightly, Carrie forced her legs to carry her past the awful scene. These buildings were full of young men who desperately needed medical help. Somehow she must block out her own feelings of helpless horror and give them hope.

Almost running when she finally reached her ward, Carrie took one deep breath and ducked into the building. Immediately she was thankful Dr. McCaw had insisted on plenty of ventilation for all the buildings. Even so, the air was thick and heavy.

"Howdy, Miss Cromwell."

"Good morning, Johnny," Carrie said brightly. "And how are we doing this morning?" She took special care not to stare at Johnny's bandaged stump. Instead she concentrated on his eyes. They were still dulled with fever, but he was at least alert.

"Oh, I'm all right, I reckon. My arm hurts right much."

"I'm sure it does." Carrie spoke soothingly as she reached for a water pitcher and filled his glass. Holding it to his lips, she urged, "Drink plenty of water. It will help wash that fever right out of your body."

"Tastes right good, Miss Cromwell. I'm real thankful for what everyone is doing."

"It's the least we can do, Johnny. We just want you to get well."

Johnny smiled weakly, then managed a grin. "You heard how we pushed them Yankees back?"

"I certainly did," Carrie assured him.

Johnny seemed eager to tell his story. "The fighting was mighty fierce, Miss Cromwell. Why, most of the time me and my unit were fighting down there in that swamp. When we first got to fighting, that water was up to our knees. I even saw a snake or two slither by. I reckon they were trying to get away from all that noise."

Carrie shuddered as she listened.

"When I done got shot I thought I was just going to slip down into that water and drown. Then one of the boys came by and propped me up against one of them stumps. I guess my momma's prayers were answered sure enough, 'cause I didn't catch no more bullets. I must've passed out at some point, 'cause the next thing I knew I was in one of the ambulance wagons heading this way."

Carrie tried to force the picture of Robert fighting in conditions like that out of her mind. The only way she knew how to deal with not knowing was to give all she could to the men surrounding her. Gently she washed Johnny's face and hands. "Drink some more water, Johnny."

"What you trying to do, Miss Cromwell? Drown me?"

Carrie laughed, a genuine laugh, as Johnny looked at her suspiciously. "The water is good for you. You don't want that fever to take you, do you? Drink as much as you can. I promise it will help."

Johnny drained the glass she offered him, then he laid back against his pillow.

"I sure would appreciate some of that water, ma'am."

Carrie turned quickly and met the eyes of a young man two beds down. "Why, of course!" She filled a glass with water and hurried to him. "What's your name?"

"Alexander Bedford, ma'am."

Carrie looked at him closely. She was almost certain she had seen him before, but the dirt and strain on his face made him hard to place.

"I'm from Bedford Plantation, about fifty miles down the river," he said, as if in answer to her thoughts.

"Of course. My father, Thomas Cromwell, knows yours."

"And I know who you are, Miss Cromwell. I was there two years ago when that gray thoroughbred of yours beat Nathan Blackwell."

"I think the man riding my horse would like to take some of the credit for that," Carrie said with a laugh. The tournament at the Blackwell Plantation, when Robert had ridden Granite to victory, seemed an eternity ago. It had been a time of lighthearted fun, when her largest concern was whether or not Robert would capture enough of the rings to be declared winner in the competition. She forced herself back to the present. "How badly wounded are you?"

"Well, I suppose I'm luckier than most. I caught a couple of balls in my left leg, but they decided to leave my leg attached after I objected most strenuously to their suggestion of taking it off," Alexander said indignantly. Then his voice dropped. "I realize they may still have to take it, but as long as there is a chance . . . "

Carrie laid her hand on his arm. "I know everyone will work as hard as they can to save it."

Alexander nodded. "Yes. Of course they will." Then his eyes filled with pain. "I have so little to complain about. My best friend . . . Mark. He—he didn't make it. I watched him die. A bullet hit him in the head." He gulped as his face twisted in pain. "At least he died quickly. I don't think he even felt it." His eyes darkened as he traveled back to the horrors of the day before. "Men were falling all around me. I barely managed to drag myself behind some trees when I got shot. There were about five hundred of us who took part in that charge. Less than half of us made it out."

Carrie listened as Alexander told his story. It was a wonder he was alive. How long would he have to deal with the horrors of his memories? "I'm so sorry," she whispered.

Alexander shook his head and looked at her as if he were surprised to see her still there. "Please forgive me, Miss Cromwell. I shouldn't be burdening you with stories like that. You're a lady."

"A Southern lady, Mr. Bedford. Which means we're all in this together," Carrie responded crisply. "You drink that water, then I'll pour you another glass."

Alexander laughed, then nodded his head toward Johnny. "I think you're right. She's trying to drown us."

Carrie laughed with him, then moved down the line of soldiers, talking with each one, dispensing water, fluffing pillows, straightening linens, and doing anything else she could to try and make the men more comfortable. Sickness and pain seldom made sense, no matter what the cause. Somehow, since she had come to the hospital that morning she had realized she could waste energy with anger and frustration, or simply accept what was and do the best she could to make a difference. If she wanted to be a doctor she was going to spend her whole life surrounded by senseless pain and suffering. She would have to deal with it.

Sometime during that long morning, the sounds of battle ceased. Carrie had heard story after story of valor tempered by suffering. Their voices held both pride and agony; their eyes courage and fear. In each face she saw both determination and lonely homesickness. And in her own heart she was finding the way to deal with her fear and questioning about Robert. As long as she could give wholeheartedly to the men filling the ward she had no time to consider her own situation. She would always see Robert's face on every gurney, hear Robert's voice with every request for water. Although her fear that it might actually be him one day was terrifying, the comfort of helping those like him was the one redeeming factor. Instinctively, she knew the hospital would be her saving grace through the long months, and possibly years, ahead.

"There are more wagons coming up the hill!" a ward nurse yelled as he dashed out the door.

Carrie tightened her lips and followed. The newly wounded were already being transported in. Moving to the side, she stood and watched as the long line of ambulance wagons wound their way slowly up the hill. Tents were being hastily erected to handle the overflow of soldiers who would not fit into the buildings.

"Does anyone know what happened?" a nurse asked as he stood with the rest of them waiting for the wagons. "Our boys must have held them or we would be seeing Yankee soldiers streaming into the city before we saw the wounded."

"Maybe the battle didn't last too long this time," one attendant said hopefully. "The Yankees have decided to go fight their battles somewhere else."

"Fat chance!" another snorted. "They didn't fight their way all the way up that Peninsula to give up that easy."

Carrie watched and listened as the voices rose around her. She was sure the last man was right. The fight for Richmond was surely not over yet. She watched the first wagon cross the bridge over Bloody Run Creek, and then hurried back to her ward. There were only a few empty beds. She was sure they would be filled soon.

"Did we whip 'em again, Miss Cromwell?" Johnny Whiteside called as soon as she entered the building.

"I don't know, Johnny. But I didn't see any Union troops escorting the wagons making their way up the hill."

"Ah! You mean more of our fellow soldiers are coming to join in the wonderful hospitality and care we are being blessed with."

Carrie smiled down at Alexander. "Do I detect sarcasm in your voice, Mr. Bedford? Are we not treating you well enough?" she teased.

"On the contrary, Miss Cromwell. It's just that I can think of other places I would rather be right now."

"You got that right, Bedford," a man a few beds down cried out. "About now my fields are exploding with new growth. I reckon my momma and sisters are having a rough time trying to do all the work on our farm. My daddy and two brothers are fighting here with me. Momma was real brave when we all left but there just ain't no way her and my little sisters can take care of all that work. We have to end this war soon so they can have some help."

"Your momma would feel a lot better about her men fighting this war if she knew all of them was really fighting!" a defiant voice cried out.

Carrie turned around to stare at the man. Why did he sound so angry?

"Why don't you just shut up, Wiggins," the young man who had been talking called out.

"Shut up yourself, Green. I'm tired of hearing you talk about your momma and sisters. You still got a daddy and brothers who are out there fighting. They're out there fighting your battle 'cause you couldn't stay away from the ladies." Wiggins was a heavyset man with thick jowls. He scowled with disgust and then looked up to see Carrie watching him. He hesitated, then evidently decided to explain. "Green here never actually got to the battlefield. He couldn't seem to make his way past the ladies offering their services in fair Richmond. He done caught a disease from one of them. He's been lying in this hospital for two days because he has venereal disease!" He snorted his disgust again. "His countrymen are dying while he . . . " he let his words trail off.

Carrie nodded briskly, then busied herself pouring and dispensing more water. She knew, of course, about the prostitutes who had flocked to the city, especially now with so many soldiers here. And she had heard of the awful number of men who were being stricken with venereal disease. This war seemed to have no end to the ways it could strike down young men. A quick glance revealed Green staring down at his blanket with a forlorn, beaten look on his face.

Quickly she filled a glass with fresh water and carried it to him. "Have some water," she said kindly. Green stared up at her, searching her eyes. Carrie held the water out to him. "We all make mistakes, soldier. You're paying for yours already."

Green stared deeply at her and swallowed hard. "Thank you, ma'am."

Carrie smiled down at him, then moved away as a new stretcher was carried in the door. The newest patient was laid on the only bed still available. Experience was giving her the ability to look beyond the grime, blood, and black gunpowder. A quick perusal identified another young man barely out of his teens. "Hello, soldier."

"Howdy, ma'am."

Carrie looked at him more closely. There was no mistaking the familiar pain resting on his features, yet his voice was clear and strong, and his eyes still shone with life. "My name is Miss Cromwell."

"And I'm Bobby Macintosh," he responded with a smile. "I tried to tell my colonel I didn't need to come here, but he insisted. Seemed to think a few bullets in the leg were something to be concerned about."

"I think your colonel might be right!" Carrie retorted with a laugh. She already liked this young man.

Bobby shrugged. "I told my colonel I'd come and let them take the bullets out, but only after he made the medics promise no one would take my leg. I still have a lot of fighting to do, ma'am. Kinda hard to do on one leg." Not waiting for a response, he continued on, "I've got to tell you, Miss Cromwell. This city has a lot of people who don't think so straight living here."

"What do you mean?"

"This morning when my squad was bringing me in to one of the ambulance wagons, there were regular streams of people heading from Richmond out to the battlefield."

"More soldiers?"

"No, ma'am. That would have been what you'd expect. Nope. There were just hundreds of regular folks. Some of the guys with me told me they recognized the governor, some ministers, clerks, people in the war department. And lots of regular folks. I reckon they thought they were going to help somehow. Or maybe they just wanted to share some of the glory since we pushed them Yankees back. Course, I saw a good bit of them picking through stuff on the field. Guess they were looking for souvenirs or maybe something to sell."

Carrie listened, fascinated. "What happened when the battle started again?"

Bobby laughed loudly. "Funniest sight I ever saw. As soon as the first shell hit the ground, that whole group turned and started running as fast as you could imagine. Wagons and carriages were trying to outrace the other. Yep, I reckon they wanted to share in our glory, but they didn't have no intention of sharing in the fight!"

Carrie joined in the laughter as the whole ward chuckled at such foolishness. These men knew the dangers of the battlefield. That others would consider it nothing more than a playacting stage seemed absurd. They were all learning swiftly that they must find whatever they could to laugh at—then somehow manage to endure the rest.

Carrie was exhausted as she made her way down the hill toward home. She and Janie were silent as they watched the sun sink low on the horizon. They had smiled wearily at each other, but neither had spoken since they left the hospital.

"Carrie, look!" Janie suddenly exclaimed.

Carrie raised her head to look in the direction her friend was pointing. In her tired state, she had not even been aware that they had turned onto their own street. As she stared at the house, her heart leaped with joy. Tied to the post outside, Granite was staring at her with his ears pricked forward. "Granite!"

His nicker of delight rang through the air as Carrie lifted her skirts and began to run, never taking her eyes off the house. Just as she reached the walkway, Robert stepped out onto the porch, then leaped to the bottom of the steps. She ran into the arms he held wide.

Carrie was laughing when she finally stepped back. She looked up at him with shining eyes and opened her mouth to speak, but Robert held a finger to her lips.

"Don't say anything yet. I just want to look at you. This is always how I remember you best. Staring up at me with your shining green eyes, your beautiful face more alive than anything I have ever seen. You give me courage to keep living."

Carrie stopped laughing and looked deep into his eyes. "It was bad." Robert didn't answer. He didn't have to. The shadows in his eyes and the tense lines of his face said it all. Without speaking, Carrie raised her hand and laid in against his cheek.

Robert reached up and grabbed it, holding it there, while he continued to drink her in with his eyes. Carrie stood quietly, the tenderness rising and swelling until it seemed to choke her. She could not bear the sorrow she saw in Robert's face. Slowly, the tension seemed to ease and his eyes began to clear. Only then did she speak. "I love you, Robert Borden. I'm glad you're home."

"I love you, too, Carrie Cromwell." Smiling slightly, he once more opened his arms.

Carrie melted into them and stood for several long minutes, letting him absorb the strength of her presence, while she did the same. Could this be what love was? Each giving to the other the strength they found in being together?

It was Janie's voice that finally broke into their world. "I think you have one very jealous horse here," she called teasingly.

Carrie pulled back from Robert's embrace. Seconds later all of them were laughing at the sight of Granite staring intently at Carrie and Robert. He was allowing Janie to pet him, but he was paying no more attention to her than he was to the sounds of traffic on the road behind him. It was clear he thought he was due some consideration for bringing Robert home.

Carrie went to him immediately and held his big face between her hands as she gazed into his eyes. "Thank you, Granite. I knew I could count on you to bring him back." She untied the reins quickly, then turned to walk to the back of the house. "I'll be in in just a minute. I'm going to find him a very special treat."

"He deserves it," Robert said gruffly.

Carrie nodded, but didn't ask any questions. She had heard enough horror stories to last a lifetime. They were safe. That was all she needed to know for now. She would listen if Robert needed to talk, but for now she was content.

Thomas was the first to ask a question while dinner was being served. "Is it true the North regained their lost ground?"

Robert nodded. "About the best you can say of the last two days is that it was a draw. We pushed them back yesterday. They pushed us back today. Everything is exactly where it started two days ago."

Not exactly, Carrie thought. *There are now thousands of men, both Southerners and Northerners, who are dead or wounded.* She and Janie exchanged long looks, guessing what the other was thinking.

"How did General Smith handle himself today?" Thomas asked.

Robert shrugged. "He was in a rough position," was all he said. "President Davis commissioned General Lee this afternoon. He is now in charge of the army."

"You seem pleased."

"Yes, sir. I am very pleased. General Johnston was a fine man, but Lee holds my complete confidence. I believe President Davis will find this may be the best decision he ever makes."

Thomas nodded. "Lee has my confidence as well." He hesitated, then pushed on to the matter pressing them all the most. "What will happen to the city?"

Robert paused. "It's too soon to know. One thing I know for sure. It's not over yet. Not by a long shot."

Four

Robert was whistling cheerfully as he slung his saddle onto Granite's back and cinched the girth tight. Double-checking his rations, he repositioned his hat and swung into the saddle. He didn't know for sure what this mission was that General Lee was sending him on, but from the casual shine in his commander's eyes, he held out hope it was going to be different from what he had experienced so far. Looking back toward Richmond, he gazed at the steeples poking their heads above the distant tree line. It was all that could be seen in the bright moonlight, but it was enough to pull his thoughts to Carrie. They had said their good-byes earlier that night. Both knew each good-bye might be their last—it was one of the cruel realities of war. Right now he had a job to do.

It was close to midnight when he rode up to the tent of Brigadier General J.E.B Stuart. Robert had never met the twenty-nine-year-old Virginian commanding Lee's cavalry brigade, but he knew the stories that had already made him something of a legend—just from the way he dressed for battle. With his gold-braided jacket, yellow sash and cavalry cape, his gauntlets, jackboots, and ostrich-plumed hat, he cut an impressive figure among the other cavaliers. General Lee had told Robert about the genius Stuart had for reconnaissance and intelligence gathering. According to Lee, no other intelligence source could surpass his eye for recognizing and evaluating a military landscape or an enemy's strengths and dispositions. From what he gathered about Stuart, Robert could only surmise their mission was connected with reconnaissance work.

"Who goes there?" a soldier barked into the night.

Robert pulled Granite to a halt. "Lieutenant Robert Borden, sir."

A figure materialized from the shadows. "General Stuart is expecting you, sir. You may go in."

Robert nodded and ducked into the tent covering.

Stuart sat at his table, poring over maps and charts. He pushed them away and leaned back in his chair. "Hello, Lieutenant."

Stuart's compact, muscular body spoke of great strength. His face was florid, with a broad forehead and prominent nose. A thick, reddish-brown mustache curled over his lips and spreading beard. But it was his eyes that pulled Robert in—they were a brilliant and penetrating blue that burned with the intensity of his concentration. He was a man to be trusted. "Hello, General."

Stuart wasted no time on pleasantries. Once he had waved Robert to a seat, he turned back to his papers. "My men have no idea what is about to take place," he said.

"I don't find that difficult to believe, sir. Neither do I," Robert commented dryly.

"Good!" Stuart laughed. "Lee has requested secrecy. I believe it has been accomplished."

Robert said nothing. It was obvious Stuart was comfortable with him being there. He was content to wait and watch what would develop. Which, as it turned out, was exactly what he did. Not another word was spoken for almost two hours.

Finally, at two A.M., Stuart rose from his chair and moved to the door of his tent. He spoke briefly to an aide outside the tent, then turned to Robert with a smile. "I believe it's that time, Lieutenant. Your horse is ready?"

"Yes, sir!" Robert replied crisply, springing up from the chair where he was fighting sleep. All thoughts of rest had flown. Whatever Stuart was planning, he was sure it was going to be eventful.

By daybreak, a long column of cavalrymen stretched along the turnpike leading out of Richmond. Twelve hundred men strong, it had gotten underway with no bugle call or fanfare. Secrecy was a primary concern, so the men moved on unaware of their destination.

Robert listened as the men around him, talking in low voices, tried to guess where they were going.

"We must be going to join up with Stonewall Jackson in the valley," one rough-looking soldier from Mississippi said. "I heard he won a dazzling victory up there. Maybe they're sending us up there as reinforcements."

The man riding next to him shook his head. "I reckon we're heading for McClellan's flank," he said in an excited voice. "I think we're about to see some more action."

Other voices joined the argument, throwing in their suspicions and guesses. Robert was content to ride along quietly. They would find out when Stuart was ready for them to find out. It was good to be in the saddle again. Granite was stepping out proudly, tossing his head in the cool morning air. The sky was exploding with orange and purple as the sun edged its way into a new day.

The first day passed rather uneventfully. By the time they made camp about three miles outside of Ashland, Robert figured they had ridden twenty miles or so. The most exciting thing all day had been the local people, rushing out to greet them, excited to see Confederate gray.

Back in the saddle early the next morning, the line of cavalry moved off again. All guessing and wagers ended when the long line turned east. There was no more speculation of joining with Stonewall Jackson. It was now clear McClellan's flank was their objective.

"By jove! We're finally going to get a crack at those Yankees!" the man nearest Robert exclaimed.

"I knew that's where we were headed," another said firmly. "It's high time we got to meet them head on."

"Son-in-law against father-in-law," another said laughing. "This should be some show."

That caught Robert's attention. "What are you talking about?"

"You don't know?" the soldier said, still laughing. "General Cooke is the commander of the Union cavalry. Our General Stuart is his son-in-law."

Robert smiled, but didn't join in the laughter, once more realizing the ironic brutalities of a war that pitted family against family.

"Lieutenant Borden! General Stuart wants you at the front."

Robert joined the other members of Stuart's staff as they circled around him in the field.

"By now you realize what our objective is. Or at least you have a good guess. General Lee needs information on the strength of McClellan's right flank. Our job is to get it for him."

Robert listened intently as Stuart went on to explain that they were to push as far as they could. They were to put down any resistance they found, take prisoners if need be, and destroy what they could of enemy supplies. Excitement pulsed through his body as he contemplated what was to come. He was mounted on the finest horse he knew, with a commander he could trust. A quick look around confirmed the other men felt the same way.

"I've been waiting for this!" Colonel Rooney Lee, General Lee's son, exclaimed.

"Those boys are going to be mighty surprised to find us on their side of the lines," his cousin, Colonel Fitz Lee, agreed with a grin.

The line of cavalry moved forward quickly, easing through woods and past open fields where young corn was pushing toward the sky. They were greeted warmly by citizens who had not seen Confederate gray for over a month.

"Billy! Billy, it's you!"

Robert watched as a young soldier broke from the ranks, sprang from his horse and wrapped a laughing woman in his arms. The reunion lasted just for a moment, though. After kissing her cheek, he turned, vaulted back into the saddle, and galloped to retake his place in line.

"I love you, Billy. Take care of yourself, son!" the weeping woman called after him.

The rest of the morning passed rather uneventfully. The few Federal outposts they discovered were easily overrun. The Yankees seemed to have no desire to take on an outfit so much more powerful than their own. They either scattered or were taken as prisoners.

Robert was in front with a unit when they were nearing Haw's Shop. Out of the corner of his eye he caught a flash of blue. At the very same moment, a surge of Federals came forward with a roar.

"Form fours! Draw saber! Charge!" Stuart commanded.

Granite sprang forward at Robert's command as the Confederates swept forward. Robert watched, bemused, as the Union soldiers dashed almost to the front of the column, fired a shot or two, and then veered off.

The only result was a few captured Yankees who had been dismounted when the attack took place. The rest of the soldiers had made good their escape. Robert ground his teeth in frustration, even though he knew the mission was going extraordinarily well. He was longing for a confrontation that would result in a glorious victory, not these aborted skirmishes by the Union. A ruckus over to the side drew his attention. "What's going on?" he asked a man watching the proceedings with a grin.

"Colonel Lee done caught some of his old friends over there!"

"What?"

The man nodded. "Sure enough. Some of those men we just captured used to serve under the Colonel when he was in the U.S. Cavalry. They sure look glad to see him and he seems mighty pleased to see them as well."

Robert watched in amazement as Colonel Lee sprang from his horse and exchanged handshakes. Laughter rang through the air as they talked. All he could do was shake his head. No one would ever believe the captured, laughing troopers and the smiling young Colonel represented opposing armies mustered to slaughter each other.

Their first serious opposition came when they reached Old Church. They knew that this, if anywhere, was where the Federals would offer serious resistance because wagon trains carrying supplies to the Union troops north of the Chickahominy would have to pass this point. Robert was watching when one of the scouts raced up to General Stuart. Seconds later the order came.

"Charge!"

As Granite leapt forward, Robert could only surmise Stuart had just received word of a force waiting for them and was doing what came naturally to him—advancing on the offensive. Unsheathing his saber, Robert leaned low over Granite's neck. The blood raced through his veins as he caught his first sight of the enemy ahead. He was perhaps ten columns back when the units met.

Bedlam reigned as swords and pistols met in a loud clash. Dust swirled through the air as yells and shouts exploded all around. Robert saw an opening in the lines and surged through, his saber drawn and ready. Just as he broke free he saw the Federals spin and take off. Reluctantly he pulled Granite in and sheathed his weapon. He stared after the retreating bluecoats for a long minute, then turned back. There were several dead on the ground, all of them Federals. He noticed a knot of men standing to the side. Frowning, he rode over quickly.

General Stuart was just catching up with the regiment, and he called out sharply, "Who is it?"

"Captain Latane, sir," one trooper quickly replied. "He was shot, sir. But not before he badly wounded his assailant with his saber." He paused and shook his head, "He's dead."

Stuart nodded shortly and turned to ride off, a look of sorrow on his face. Robert knew the general had wanted to pull off his mission with no deaths. It was only one, but he knew how much Stuart cared for the men under him. Even one fatality would be hard for him to bear.

Just then Colonel Lee rode up. "Let me go after them, sir. They're my old regiment. I'd like to be the one to rout them."

Stuart agreed immediately. "Go ahead. But do it quickly. We need to push on."

As Colonel Lee's regiment was galloping off, Stuart called Robert over to join in a meeting.

Robert waited expectantly with the other officers to ascertain their next move. Surely they had accomplished their objective. The right flank of McClellan's army was woefully weak. If this is where General Lee wanted to mount his offensive—it was a good decision. Robert's guess was that they would turn back now.

"We are going to continue on," Stuart said firmly. "The enemy expects us to return the way we came. They might even now be burning the bridge across the Totopotomoy River. If they're quick they will have a force waiting for us back at Hanover Court House."

Robert stared at him. There were twelve hundred cavalry troopers well behind Union lines. What did Stuart presume to do with them?

The General's answer came swiftly. "We're going to go all the way around them," he said with a quick grin. His smile grew wider as he took in the looks of astonishment from the men surrounding him. Not waiting for comment he quickly outlined his plan. "We'll continue on and go through Tunstall's Station. From there we'll move on to the Chickahominy River and cross over. Then we'll follow the James back up to Richmond."

The men were quiet as they absorbed the startling news. Finally one man stepped forward. "We're going to Tunstall's Station, General? Don't you think it will be heavily guarded? The York River Railroad is McClellan's main line of supply. Their main depot is only a few miles away." His voice indicated he doubted the wisdom of his commander's decision.

Stuart nodded. "It will be risky but I think we can do it," he said confidently, his gaze sweeping the knot of men, challenging them to share his confidence. "We might even be able to tear up some of that railway. Think of it! If only for a day—if only for an hour—we might be able to separate the Federal army from its base of supply!" He laughed, then grew serious. "I know it's risky, men. But we have speed and surprise on our side. From Tunstall's Station it's only eleven miles to the Chickahominy. Once we cross there I don't think there will be a threat."

Again there was silence as the men contemplated what he said. The same man who had questioned him earlier spoke again, "If you see fit to go on, General, then I'm going with you." A murmur of agreement rose.

"Thank you, men." Just then Colonel Lee rode up with a flush of victory on his face. Stuart turned to him. "I take it your expedition was a success."

Colonel Lee nodded. "The camp was deserted when we found it. We put fire to everything we found there and picked up a few more prisoners but nothing beyond that. It appears those boys were not eager to be in the same vicinity as us."

Robert laughed along with the rest of the men. Tension gripped him at the thought of staying behind Union lines, but it was the kind of bold move Robert admired.

Another of the men spoke up. "I think the quicker we move now the better." His wry tone made them laugh harder. Then they sobered quickly.

What they were doing was dangerous and risky. Any of a hundred things could go wrong. Their best defense was to move before McClellan could pinpoint their position and send a strong force after them.

Within a short period of time the column was once again on the move. It was late in the afternoon when they drew near to Tunstall Station. Stuart gave his command. "Charge!"

Robert was alert, but surprisingly relaxed as the cavalry thundered down the road. It was becoming obvious that no one in the Union army had ever anticipated an attack from within, and behind, their own lines. The small units defending each outpost were scattering in the face of such a superior show of force. As long as they kept moving fast, they might actually pull off this bold, crazy maneuver.

As expected, the Federal units guarding the train station at Tunstall fled. Some were captured. Others disappeared into the woods.

"Do your work, troopers!" Stuart commanded with the wide grin Robert was becoming accustomed to.

With a loud yell, the troopers scattered to their designated duties. Robert vaulted out of his saddle and sprang to join the men tearing up the railroad. If they succeeded they would separate McClellan's army from its base. His heart pounded with excitement as they reached the tracks. He saw one of the men disappear into the woods. Robert knew he was on his way to set fire to the bridge across Black Creek. The scouts moved forward with axes to chop down the two telegraph poles nearest the station. The remaining troopers, still mounted, cheered and whooped as they kept guard against approaching troops.

Suddenly a shrill train whistle split the air. Immediately all action ceased. From the boldness of the whistle blast, the engineer could not possibly know the station was in the hands of the Confederacy. Robert turned with the rest of the men toward Stuart.

"Lieutenant Borden. Throw that switch. We'll derail the train!" Stuart yelled excitedly.

Robert sprang forward as Stuart continued to shout orders. Within seconds, nearby men were hurling obstructions onto the tracks. Tree limbs, rocks, anything they found were heaved in a desperate attempt to block the track before the train approached.

Robert raced for the switch, but groaned with dismay when he saw the heavy padlock holding it. Looking around quickly, he grabbed a large bar of iron and began bashing the lock. The rest of the troopers were hurrying into ambush position alongside the tracks. They would open fire if the train stopped or left the tracks. Sweat poured down his face as he pounded at the lock, but it did not budge.

"Forget it, Lieutenant," Stuart called. "The train is almost here. Remount and prepare for battle."

Robert threw aside the bar and sprang for Granite. He was barely in the saddle and moving toward cover when the train—a locomotive and a string of flatcars loaded with soldiers—roared around the curve. Granite dove for the woods. Had the engineer spotted them? Robert held his breath as the engine continued to slow. A smile spread across his face as it drew almost to a halt and several Union soldiers stepped off.

Bang!

Robert groaned as a pistol shot exploded in the stillness. There had been no order given to fire yet. Someone had gotten too excited. Now, there was no choice but to press the attack.

"Fire!" Stuart's voice boomed a second later.

"Rebels!" one of the startled Federals yelled. At the exact same moment, the engineer put on full steam and the engine began to pull away from the station.

Just then a barrage of gunfire exploded from the hidden troops. Robert watched in grim satisfaction as Union soldiers dropped or threw themselves face first on the boxcars to avoid the onslaught. A single horseman broke from cover and raced alongside the train. At a full gallop, the horse drew even with the engine. Robert heard a gunshot and saw the engineer slump in his seat, but the speed of the train continued to increase. Within moments it was out of sight. Wild cheering followed it.

When the celebrating ended, Stuart reluctantly gave the order to press on. Robert understood his reluctance. Their mission so far had met with nothing but success. It was tempting, knowing they were only four miles from White House, the main supply depot, to make that their next objective. If it was destroyed the Federals would be forced to retreat. Robert smiled as he thought of what a coup it would be for twelve hundred cavalry troopers to force a hundred-thousand-man army to retreat. His smile quickly disappeared, however. General Stuart was making the wisest decision. White House would surely be better defended than anything they had approached so far.

If they were to end up in a prolonged battle, McClellan would have time to send in reinforcements that would close off their line of retreat. They had accomplished their objectives. Now it was time to get out of there.

Robert was sure the long night would never end. The cavalry had the advantage of a bright moon to light the road, but exhaustion dogged them every step of the way. There could be no stopping or rest. There was no way to know how close behind them pursuing troops might be. Horses stumbled wearily as men nodded into sleep, almost falling off their mounts. In order to keep up the needed pace, prisoners rode double on the mules Stuart's troopers had captured. There was little talk as the line crept determinedly on.

Robert fought sleep by thinking about Carrie. Her face rose before him, her beautiful eyes shining with love, giving him confidence. He could hardly wait to tell her all about this mission. He knew she would rest her chin in her hand and absorb everything he said. He still could hardly believe Carrie loved him. He had vacillated between rage and grief when she had turned down his proposal of marriage because of their differing beliefs about slavery. An entire miserable year had passed while he tried, to no avail, to erase her from his mind and heart. That he was hopelessly in love with her he could not deny. Robert had vowed not to talk of marriage until the war was over, but there was not a day that passed without him dreaming of living his life with Carrie by his side.

Suddenly he frowned. He realized there were still many obstacles confronting them. If there was anything left of his plantation after the war, he would go back and rebuild. But Carrie was determined to be a doctor. How would they achieve both those things? His plantation was in the South. The only place Carrie could find a medical school that would accept women was in the North. Questions rose up to taunt him as fatigue blurred his eyes and mind.

How would they resolve their differing opinions about slavery? He had learned to respect what Carrie believed, even if he could not believe it himself. He knew there was no way he could run the plantation without a large number of slaves. How could he give up all he had ever wanted and dreamed of because Carrie believed slavery was wrong? She had made it clear she would never own a slave. Robert ground his teeth in frustration. There seemed to be no way to solve the dilemmas facing them. Yet there was no other choice. He loved her completely and could not imagine living his life without her. Somehow they would have to find a way.

The bright moonlight created a milky corridor as the horses wound their way through thick woods and across open fields. Moonlight caught on leaves tossing gently in the breeze, casting off creamy sparkles. A sea of stars twinkled their indifference at the world below. Robert gazed around, astounded that there could yet be so much beauty in a world so crazed and hate-filled. The beauty seemed to call to him, seemed to pull him in as he crept along. Slowly the confusion of his questions melted away to be replaced by a confidence. He was too tired to question it. Gratefully he let the confidence seep in, filling him with a new strength he could not identify.

Suddenly Robert recognized the strength. It was the same strength he had experienced when he had somehow managed to pull himself from a ditch just before a wagon crashed down on top of him. It was the same strength he had felt on the bitterly cold battlefield when he had been full of despair and hopelessness. Somehow he knew the strength he was feeling was the presence of God. Somewhere in the last year of war he had stopped denying that God was with him, but he still was incapable of understanding it. His heart told him God loved him, but he couldn't fathom why. Silently he stared up into the heavens. All he could do was trust God to hear his heart. He had no idea how to put his feelings into words.

The clatter of rapid hoofbeats roused Robert from his thoughts. Startled, he straightened and automatically reached for his saber. Had the pursuing Union troops caught up with them? Gradually he realized the hoofbeats he was hearing belonged to just one horse. Relaxing a little, he watched as a lone horseman dashed toward them from the direction they were headed. It could only be a scout sent ahead to report back to Stuart.

It was not long before Stuart called his group of leaders together for a conference. "One of my scouts lives nearby. Forge Bridge has been burned out."

Robert's heart sank. Crossing the Chickahominy was their one chance to get away from whoever might be pursuing them. Had they come this far only to be trapped?

Stuart smiled, but exhaustion lined his face. "My scout knows of a shallow place where we can cross the river. It will save us many hours of work if we don't have to rebuild the bridge. Once we reach the river we can all gain a little rest."

The sun was just dimming the glow of the moon when the front guard of the cavalry reached the place where they were to cross the river. Wordlessly the men stopped and stared at the raging water. Was this the easy crossing that had been described to them?

Robert frowned as he looked at the wide, swift, evil-looking water that had exploded far from its banks. He knew what had happened. Spring rains in the mountains had turned the normally placid Chickahominy into a raging torrent. There was only one way to find out if the ford was nothing more than a death trap.

Robert vaulted from Granite's back and stripped his uniform. Handing Granite's reins to a nearby trooper, he walked resolutely toward the water. No one tried to stop him. Someone would have to determine if the ford was crossable. The lives of twelve hundred men depended on it. Stopping just long enough to take several deep breaths and stretch his cramped muscles, Robert forged into the cold waters. He was prepared for a battle, but the actual force of the river shocked him. He was a strong swimmer, but the river seemed determined to conquer him.

Pushing forward with powerful strokes he swam slightly upstream as he made for the other side. Still the river pulled him along. His muscles ached and screamed their protest as he threw all of his strength into the effort. The river tugged at him, pulling him under and then thrusting him back to the surface. Finally, defeated, he turned back. It would do him no good to reach the other side. He would only be able to sit, separated from the cavalry until Stuart figured something out. There was no way they could ford the river here.

Stuart was waiting for him when he pulled himself out of the water. Robert managed a weary smile. "I think we're caught, sir."

Stuart frowned but didn't say anything. Robert knew he was deep in thought. Silence fell on the column as others tried to swim across. A few men who were excellent swimmers were able to make it to the other side, but it quickly became obvious that another way was going to have to be found.

As the morning wore on, the sun rose high in the sky, bringing with it fresh fears of a Federal attack. Several plans were conceived but quickly aborted. Finally Stuart gave the order. "We will rebuild Forge Bridge."

Robert pushed aside his fatigue and threw his energy into the job at hand. A large, abandoned warehouse became the means of their salvation. Supervising the exhausted men in his unit, Robert directed them to use battering rams to knock down the frame of the hulking structure. Once it was down they lifted the main timbers and carried them to the river. The watching troopers held their breath as they were pushed across on a skiff, then with great effort lifted up to the abutments that were still left from the burned-out bridge.

"It made it!" an excited trooper yelled as the timbers settled down securely on the abutments with just a few inches to spare on either side. A shout of celebration rose into the air as renewed hope sprang into every face.

Once more the men moved into action. More wood was hauled from the collapsed building to cover the floor of the bridge. Within minutes of its completion the column began to flow over the new bridge. Even the guns made it safely across. Robert watched as the last men rode across, then grinned as five men rushed back with torches to burn the bridge. There would be no way for the Yankees to pursue them. A deep sense of satisfaction filled him as he stood quietly watching what they had so quickly built send flames shooting into the sky.

Robert was turning Granite to join the rear guard of the cavalry just disappearing into the woods when a shot rang out. He spun Granite around and laughed aloud at the sight of Federal uniforms on the opposing bank. "Too late, boys!" he yelled in defiance as the men with him whooped in laughter and urged their horses into a swift gallop.

Carrie made no effort to hide her excitement as she moved with the flow of people to the heart of Richmond. She had received word that Robert was with the cavalry returning as heroes to the city. Stories of their escapades were flying around like missiles as crowds of excited Richmonders pressed forward to view the returning troopers.

At first Carrie had been frightened when her father had burst through the door the night before. He had barely been able to contain his excitement as he told her of General Stuart's daring exploits. Stuart, once he was convinced his troops were safe, had ridden ahead to report to General Lee.

"The city needs some good news, Carrie," Thomas had said hopefully. "With the exception of Stonewall Jackson's victory in the Valley, there has been nothing but bad news for too long. Young Stuart's bold mission will be like a tonic to the people."

Her father had been right. Excited voices rang through the air as each person tried to outdo the other with what they had heard about the mission.

"That young Stuart rode all the way around McClellan's army," an old man boasted, waving his cane in the air for emphasis. "I reckon we can handle those Yankees all right. I bet there are some mighty red-faced men outside the city right now."

"I reckon they'll just turn around and head back North!" another cried. "Why, if they can't handle twelve hundred cavalry troopers, how are they going to handle General Lee's army?"

"I heard the Union army was crossing onto that bridge when they set fire to it. I wish I'd been there to see those Yankees dropping into that river."

Carrie looked at Janie and laughed. "I'm glad I know what really happened. What they did was incredible, but if I listened to too many of these stories I would begin to think our soldiers were gods."

Janie laughed with her. "It's good to hear the people so excited. Who cares if they embellish the stories a little? It makes them happy. Goodness knows there is little enough to be happy about right now."

Carrie knew Janie was right. Many of the wounded soldiers had recovered and been sent back to the front, but the hospitals were still crowded with men too sick and weak to go back into battle. The dead had finally all been buried or sent off to their own states for burial.

The stench of death was beginning to lift from the city but everyone was aware it could be renewed at any moment. McClellan had not budged from his position outside of Richmond, and even though General Lee had dug in securely, no one was relaxing.

"It's been ages since I've been downtown," Janie said, breaking into her thoughts. "I feel like my whole world is the hospital. It seems strange to know there is another world out there."

Carrie nodded her agreement and gazed around. She had heard from her father that shortages were beginning to be felt, but she couldn't tell it from looking. She knew many of the people crowding into Richmond had brought money with them. People were buying, but the supply was having a hard time keeping up with the demand. "There are so many new shops," she commented. "And so many of the old ones almost look like they're new."

Janie shrugged. "If things don't change soon, everything will start to look a lot different."

"Why do you say that?"

"From what I hear the blockade is getting harder to run. It's still possible to get most things in other cities, but between the blockade and McClellan's army perched out there, goods just aren't getting through. Not to mention the speculators," she added darkly.

"Speculators?" Carrie was beginning to feel she really was spending too much time in the hospital. The world she was staring at seemed a foreign one. It helped to remember Janie had been here since the beginning, while she was had been on the plantation until recently, but that didn't change her desire to understand her surroundings.

Janie nodded and frowned. "Inflation is becoming rampant. There is no end to the amount of people in town who are willing to buy supplies and then stick them away until their prices go up. When they sell them they make quite a handsome profit. I've heard that something bought one day will return a hundred percent profit if they hold on to it for just a week."

"But people can't pay those kind of prices!" Carrie protested. "Most of the men are off fighting. How do they expect the women to feed and care for their families?"

"I'm afraid the portion of our population interested in speculation are not very distressed at the idea of families starving. Their priorities are how much money they can make before that happens."

Carrie sighed as one more cruel reality of the war was made clear to her. But from what she could tell there was not yet a shortage of supplies. Stopping in front of one shop's window, she examined its contents. Colorful bonnets rested on the legs of cavalry boots. Bright ribbons adorned crossed rifles and dingy umbrellas. There were loaves of bread, packages of food, gloves, packs of cards, prayer books, and canteens.

Janie seemed to read her thoughts. "Check out some of the prices."

Carrie leaned forward to read the price on a can of coffee sitting temptingly toward the front. "Four dollars!" she exclaimed. "For coffee? No wonder my father has given it up."

"That's just the beginning. Good tea costs between eighteen to twenty dollars a pound, butter almost two dollars. Corn is fifteen dollars a barrel, and wheat is four-fifty per bushel." Her voice hardened. "It's a crime. These people have so many hardships already. They have already given so much. If this war doesn't end soon there will be a lot of people starving."

Carrie stared at her. Janie looked chagrined and reached out her hand to grab Carrie's arm. "I'm so sorry. There is enough trouble in the world without talking about more. I didn't mean to spoil your day. Let's move on. Robert and the rest of the men will be here soon."

Carrie allowed her friend to take her arm and move her up the street, but her thoughts were troubled. Now she understood the things she had overheard her father's boarders talking about a few nights ago. She had only caught snatches of it but she'd heard enough to realize even people in the government thought the fortunes of the Confederacy were declining. The conditions in Richmond were worsening daily. Murders, looting, arson, and assault were reported by the press almost daily. Such lawlessness, especially for native Richmonders who had never experienced it before, was very disturbing. When it was compounded with news of defeats and losses, uncontrollable inflation, and scarce food, it was little wonder people were beginning to question what a just cause had to do with *this*.

"Here they come, Carrie!" Janie exclaimed, pulling her along faster.

In spite of herself, Carrie felt her excitement returning. Cheers were beginning to swell from the crowd, and music was blaring forth from the band. She leaned forward to catch her first glimpse of the horses moving up the street. Where was Robert?

"Those poor men look exhausted," Janie murmured. "But aren't they proud!" she added in delight.

Carrie smiled. Janie was right. Even the horses seemed to pick their heads up a little as the cheers swelled and soared over them. She watched as men straightened their backs and held their heads high. Suddenly she caught a glimpse of Robert on Granite. His face was lined with fatigue, and she could tell Granite was tired, but their eyes were bright. Her heart tightened with pride and love. Suddenly she found herself cheering wildly with the rest. She might not agree with this crazy war, but these men had done a noble, brave deed. They deserved the recognition and applause.

As if he were able to pick her voice from the crowd, Robert turned and looked straight into Carrie's eyes. Tears blurred her vision as his face lit with a huge grin. Suddenly his back was even straighter, his head a little higher. Carrie's heart swelled with tenderness. For all his bravery and courage, Robert still needed her love and approval. Her mother had often told her that there was a side to her father that would always be a little boy. Carrie hadn't understood it then. Now she did.

Five

oses leaned back against a big oak tree and gnawed on the hardtack he had just pulled from his haversack. It was easy to understand why the rock-hard mixture of flour and water had been given the nickname of sheet-iron crackers. Still, it was food. He had never thought that soldiering would be an easy job.

"Hey! Moses!"

Moses looked up as Joe, one of the men in his unit, sauntered up. "Yes, sir?"

Joe squatted down next to him. "Captain Jones is asking for you."

Without asking any questions, Moses stuffed his hardtack back into his haversack and rose easily.

"Moses . . ."

Moses looked down at Joe and waited.

"I just wanted to say thanks for helping us find fresh water. A lot of the men are real sick. Hanging out in this crazy swamp is going to kill more of them than all the Rebel guns together," Joe said bitterly.

Moses nodded. "Bad water can do a man in." He had watched as scores had dropped from typhoid and malaria. Sickness was rampant in the camps.

"How'd you know where to find it?"

"My daddy taught me when I was just a little kid. Told me it might come in handy some day." He didn't add that he had told him he needed to know how to find good water in case he had a chance to escape someday. His daddy had dreamed of freedom for as long as Moses could remember.

"Is your father still alive? Still on one of the plantations?"

All any of the soldiers knew was that Moses had lived on one of the plantations near Richmond. They knew he had been accepted as a spy for the Union because he knew the area so well. Moses had figured that was all they needed to know. Joe was asking a lot of questions. He decided to take a chance and answer honestly. "My daddy is dead. Hung by the men who caught him when he was trying to escape." There was no bitterness in his voice. He had made peace with his past long ago.

"I'm sorry," Joe said simply. "Slavery is a terrible thing."

"Not all the Union soldiers feel that way," Moses said evenly. "From what I can tell a lot of them think I should run on back to the plantation and be a good slave so this war can end."

Joe shrugged. "Different people feel different ways. I know there are some Southerners who think slavery is an evil thing. From what I can tell it doesn't matter what part of the country you're from. It's what's in your heart that counts. There are some people who just want to have power over others. I guess it makes them feel better about themselves if they have someone to look down on."

Moses looked at him thoughtfully. He had been right to trust Joe. This was a man who cared about others. He extended his hand. "Thank you."

Joe smiled and shook his hand firmly. "The captain is waiting."

Moses nodded and strode away. The deep loneliness in his heart had been assuaged just a little. He knew he had made a friend. As he wove his way through camp he allowed his thoughts to return to Rose. Where was she? What was she doing? Was she safe? Part of him longed for the days he and his beautiful wife had lived with Aunt Abby in Philadelphia. They had been happy there. Their freedom had been worth all it took to accomplish it. The miserable months of escape had faded into a dim memory.

Then he looked around the camp and knew he was right where he was supposed to be. He had worked hard to be accepted as one of the first colored spies in the Union army. He fully believed that one day negroes would be helping to fight the war, but that day hadn't arrived yet. He was doing his best to show that ex-slaves could be valuable to the war effort. Everyone must make sacrifices if any real changes were going to be made. He could deal with loneliness as long as he knew he was making a difference.

He drew up short when he reached Captain Jones' tent. His commander's head was bent over a piece of paper. He didn't want to interrupt the man's concentration.

Captain Jones looked up when Moses' shadow fell over him. "Moses, thank you for coming. Come in."

Moses ducked his head and eased his massive frame into the tent. "Yes, sir." He waited for the captain to speak.

Captain Jones looked down at a sheet of paper for a few more minutes, then lifted his head, stretched his long legs out in front of him, and settled back in his chair. Reaching for his pipe, he took several long pulls while he stared out over the bustling activity of the camp. "General McClellan needs more information."

Moses leaned a little closer. It had been almost two weeks since the Union had clashed with Confederate troops outside of Richmond. Was General McClellan going to make his next move soon? McClellan had claimed a glorious victory but nothing had changed as far as Moses could tell. Both armies were still stationed where they had been before the two days of fighting. The only difference was that thousands of Union soldiers were horribly wounded, with many of them being transported by boat back to Washington's hospitals. If that was a glorious victory, then he surely didn't want to see the results of a defeat.

"McClellan wants more information from behind the Confederate lines."

Moses waited silently. He would not respond until he knew what the captain had in mind. He had learned a long time ago to listen and then wait until he was asked for his opinion.

"I have heard of other spies infiltrating the Confederate camps, finding out as much as they can, and then returning to our side. I told McClellan that if anyone could do it you could, Moses."

"What do you have in mind?" Moses fought to control his pounding heart. Roaming the Southern countryside with a unit of Union soldiers was one thing. But going back alone, into the world that had once held him captive, was another.

Captain Jones stared at him thoughtfully. "I want you to sneak into a Rebel camp. Live there for a week. Find out as much as you can. Numbers of soldiers, what their guns are like, what their plans are. You've told me Southerners tend to talk freely around their coloreds."

"Yessir, they figur' us darkies ain't got no mind of our own." Moses consciously slid back into the slave dialect he had fought so hard to discard. Not many people in the South had any use for an educated negro man. If he was going undercover as a slave he would have to work very hard to make sure he talked like one.

Captain Jones grinned appreciatively. "You'll do it, then?"

Moses nodded. "I told you I would do whatever I could to help the Union win. If that means going back into slavery for a week, then so be it."

"Can you do it, Moses? You used to live around here. There aren't many men your size. Your height and massive build are going to make you stand out. What if someone recognizes you? Rebels don't take too kindly to slaves escaping and working for the enemy."

"You're not telling me anything I don't know, sir. I guess I'll just have to take my chances. When do I leave?"

"Tomorrow."

Moses thought for a moment. "I'll leave tonight. It will be easier to sneak into the camps when it's dark." He paused again. "Can you do something for me, Captain?"

"Such as?"

"If I don't come back—will you get word to my wife, Rose? I want her to know what happened." His heart caught at the idea of never seeing her again. Had they gone through all they had to reach freedom, only to have him end up back in slavery—probably in a prison or hanging from a noose?

"You have my word, Moses," Captain Jones said in a rough voice. Then clearing his throat, he muttered, "This is nonsense. You'll be back. I figure you have about a week, but if the action starts sooner, figure out a way to get across the lines and back to our side." His voice became brisk as he cleared away some of the things on his desk. "Now, what will you need?"

Moses forced a grin. "Don't reckon as how I'll be needin' much, Massa Jones. I sho be needin' to get rid of these here clothes, though. Ain't no slaves dress like this. I be needin' me somethin' a bit more plain." He looked down ruefully at his blue pants and shirt. It wasn't a regular uniform but it definitely identified him as a Union man.

"You'll need to carry some kind of identification so you can cross back over to our side," the captain protested.

Moses shook his head firmly. "I won't carry any identification, Captain. Not behind Southern lines, anyway. The papers I have right now will do just fine. I'll get rid of them when I need to. Rebels don't hesitate to search a negro if they have even a glimmer of suspicion about them. I'll be hanging from a tree for sure if they find anything hooking me to the North. No, sir," he said, shaking his head again. "I'll figure out a way to get back here. Right now I reckon I'll just go rustle me up some clothes that be more fittin' for a slave," he drawled.

Captain Jones' laughter followed him as he moved easily away. There was no answering smile on Moses' face—the thought of giving himself into the hands of Rebels was too sobering.

Moses started out as soon as it was dark enough to obscure his movements. His plan was simple. He would go several miles north in an attempt to reach the end of the lines. Then he would circle back down on the Southern side and into the Rebel camps. It was risky but it sounded a lot better than trying to sneak through lines where hundreds of guns were waiting in either direction. Walking rapidly down a back road, he stayed deep in the shadows and fingered the identification he would carry until he left Union lines. Thankfully the sky was heavy with clouds. The full moon hiding behind their murky depths would not be able to betray him tonight.

Two hours later, Moses figured he had gone far enough north. Cutting west he continued to walk rapidly until he reached a road he guessed would take him toward Richmond. He could only hope he was well behind Confederate lines. It was nothing but guesswork at this point. Stopping beside a stream, he pulled his identification papers from his pocket and tore them into tiny pieces, then leaned down to pick up a large rock. He held the papers tightly, dipping them in the water until they were soaked through. Water dripped from his fingers as he laid the papers in the shallow water on the edge of the stream and placed the rock over them securely. Even if someone found them before they had a chance to disintegrate, it would be impossible to read them.

Satisfied, Moses stood, looked around carefully, then continued his journey. He wanted to be within Confederate lines before the sky began to lighten. He didn't want to be seen skulking. That would only make him look more suspicious. As he walked he allowed his mind to wander. The idea of walking back into the slavery he had fought so hard to be free from sent a flood of memories rampaging through his mind.

He would forever carry the image of his daddy hanging from a tree after he was caught during an escape attempt. Just as he would always carry the image of his momma and sisters being separated from him and sold on the auction block in Richmond. The same auction block that had landed him on Cromwell Plantation almost two years ago. He had made a vow that day that he would find his momma and sisters some day and set them free. His efforts now were part of that vow. If his actions helped the Union win the war, one day all slaves would be free.

Moses scowled. As far as he could tell there weren't too many Yankees who were fighting to free the slaves. Sure, there were some like Joe who understood and hated slavery, but too many of them couldn't care less what happened to the slaves. They just wanted to save the Union so they could go home and continue living their lives. If people in the South wanted to own slaves that was their own business. Yet Moses still hung onto the hope that one of the eventual results of the war would be the freedom of his people. It was the only reason he was willfully walking back into the life he had longed to escape.

His thoughts returned to Carrie Cromwell. He wished he had some way of knowing if she had indeed made it to the safety of Richmond after he had helped her escape the Union troops that had descended on her plantation in search of food. Thank goodness his captain had never figured out that he had played a key role in her escape. He had heard the stories of how Carrie had flown from the barn on Granite and then jumped a high fence to make good her escape. Beyond that he had no idea whether she had made it to Richmond. He had done everything within his power to help the friend who had made his escape from slavery possible. He just wished there weren't still so many questions.

Then, as it always did, his mind turned to Rose. The image of her beautiful face and slender body rose up to both soothe him and taunt him. There was not a moment he did not miss her. He carried the memory of her gentle voice and loving smile close to his heart. She had given him the courage to follow his dreams. She had taught him to read and given him a thirst for knowledge. Her confidence in him was what kept him going. Surely it would be all that would carry him through the week ahead.

"Halt! Who goes there!" a stern voice shouted.

Moses jerked to a standstill and raised his hands above his head in submission. "It just be ole Samuel," he called out. "I be lookin' for my massa. You be knowin' my massa?"

He moved not an inch when three soldiers stepped from the woods. The beating of his heart slowed when he recognized Confederate gray. At least he was on the right side. Now he would have to trust his wits.

"What are you doing here, boy?" one soldier demanded in a hostile voice. "Don't you know I could put a bullet through you right now? You must really be as stupid as you look!"

"He sure is a big one!" another of the soldiers whistled. "Keep your guns on him, boys."

"Y'all keep your guns on him," another one, whom Moses quickly identified as the leader, snapped. "I'm going to check our darkie here out. Let's see what he's carrying on him."

Moses thought with relief of the soaked papers buried under the rock a few miles back. He managed to stand still as the soldier searched him thoroughly, then stepped back to scowl at him.

"You don't have papers of any kind, boy."

"No, sir. I know I don't be havin' no papers. I ain't no free man. I be a slave. I had to come find my massa. I know he be here fightin'. He be needin' me, sir."

The soldier who had searched him laughed derisively. "What does a soldier need from you, boy?"

Moses was watching him carefully, even while he kept the pleading look on his face and the whining tone in his voice. He had to keep the man off guard. "Why, my massa been needin' me all his life!" he exclaimed indignantly. "I been takin' care of him since he was a little thing. There's plenty I'se can be doin'. He be needin' someone to bring him his meals. He be needin' someone to keep an eye on thin's while he tries to sleep. I been hearin' the horrible thin's happenin' on these here battlefields." Watching the men closely, he pulled himself up to his full height. "I reckon this ain't just be a war to be fought by the white man. These Yankees be down here trying to take my home, too. I reckon I need to be doin' whatever I can to help!"

The three men stared at him for several long moments before the leader allowed himself to relax. "What'd you say your name is, boy?"

"Samuel."

"Where are you from?"

Moses' mind raced. He was taking a big chance. What if these three soldiers knew the area well? He would have to trust that their strong accents meant they were from much farther south in cotton country. "A plantation 'bout forty miles from here. A place called Crumpton."

"How in the world did you get here?"

"I walked," Moses said proudly. "I done walked all this way to find my massa."

"Well, Samuel, my name is Mitchell Palmer. And I'm afraid you aren't going to find your master."

"Why not?" Moses asked in alarm.

"Do you know how many men are out here?" Palmer laughed. "Over eighty thousand the last I heard. How are you planning to find him in this many men?"

Moses remained silent, allowing a look of confusion to play over his features before he hung his head to stare at the ground.

Palmer continued in a slightly kinder voice. "Look, if you're really wanting to help, then I guess we can find a place for you in our unit."

"What!" one of the men exclaimed. "You're going to bring that slave into our unit? Are you crazy? He ain't goin' to be nothing but trouble."

Palmer silenced the man with a glare. "He sounds like a boy who knows what side his bread is buttered on. There is a lot of those wealthy plantation brats who have their slaves with them. I've seen how easy these black boys make it for them. I don't see any reason I shouldn't have some of those same benefits. I always wanted to own a slave. This may be my only chance." He paused and stared thoughtfully at Moses.

Moses knew Palmer was relishing the idea of having power over him. His little game was working just the way he wanted it to, so far.

"I say he comes," Palmer stated with finality.

The other two men muttered and shook their heads, but said no more.

Palmer turned back to Moses, his voice hardened. "You give me any trouble, boy, and I'll shoot you square between the eyes. I've killed a lot of Yankees and I sure won't have any trouble killing you. You've put yourself on a battlefield with the crazy idea of looking for your master. As far as I'm concerned you're nothing but a runaway slave. And that means someone might come looking for you. Give me any trouble and I'll make sure they only have a corpse to carry away."

"Yessir!" Moses said eagerly. "I ain't gonna cause no trouble. You'll see. You'll be mighty glad you let me come along!"

"Yeah. I better be," Palmer said as he swung around. "Let's go. Our watch is up."

"Samuel! Bring me some fresh coffee," Palmer snapped.

"Yessir!" Moses responded as he jumped to his feet and moved toward the fire. *Only one more night,* he reminded himself. Forcing down the anger surging through him at the degradation and humiliation he had suffered during the previous six days, he fixed a submissive look on his face as he carried the coffeepot to where Palmer lounged against the tree.

Palmer, in spite of the fact he had never owned slaves, had moved easily into his role of master. Moses had watched him carefully all week long. He seemed like a basically decent man. He showed consideration and respect for the men around him, and they looked up to him. But he treated Moses like a piece of meat. Moses had watched slave owners long enough to understand what was going on. Ownership of another human being required a certain deadening of the soul. It hardened a man, and gave him a sense of power, but it left the slave dehumanized.

"Here you is, sir. Can I be gettin' you anythin' else?" Moses asked quietly.

"Yeah. I left my hardtack in the sack on my horse. Get it for me."

"Yes, sir." Moses was glad to escape into the darkness of the night. It allowed him to relax his vigilance. Only under cover of darkness could he allow the studied submissiveness to leave his face. This past week had left him wondering how he had ever endured all the years of slavery before he and Rose had escaped. It took every bit of effort he had to not release the anger he felt when they treated him as if he were just a stupid animal.

Nonetheless, he had gained valuable information to bring back to Captain Jones. He had listened carefully as the soldiers discussed what they knew of the defense of Richmond. Moses walked toward the horses as he allowed the information he had gleaned to flow through his mind. He knew General Lee was working hard to dig in around Richmond—to build fortifications and breastworks to withstand the attack the Confederates were sure would come soon. He had managed to hide his amusement when the soldiers returned from a hard day of digging, complaining bitterly about the "King of Spades," as they called their new commander. He had gained some idea of the strength of the Confederate forces, and he was convinced McClellan had the power to take on the South. Tomorrow morning he would carry his report back to the Captain. His job would be done. Assuming he could get back through the lines.

"Easy, fellows." Moses talked soothingly to the horses as he stepped up to Palmer's big bay gelding and pulled out the hardtack and salt pork he found there. Holding it, he turned to stare into the woods. Would he be able to cross over the next day? He had tried to avoid the question all week, knowing he would lose his ability to listen and concentrate if he was focused on crossing back to the Union side. Now it could no longer be avoided. His only hope was to wait until late that night and pray everyone was asleep as he stole out of camp. He would try to go around the lines and return in the same way he had entered onto the Confederate side, but if his attempt failed he would be forced to push through the lines and pray he wasn't shot. He thought longingly of the shredded paper beneath the rocks, but pushed the thoughts aside. It had been necessary to destroy his identification. He would just have to trust God to get him back safely.

Moses took a deep breath and turned back to camp. Now was not the time to arouse suspicion. He had almost reached the circle of light when he heard a voice that stopped him dead in his tracks.

"I got a message for you boys," a voice rang out. "The colonel said to prepare three days' rations."

Moses knew what that meant. A battle was imminent. Now he really did have to get over the lines—or risk being caught in the battle. None of that seemed important right now, though. It was the voice itself that made his blood run cold—and boil with fury.

"What's going on, Adams?" Palmer asked.

"All I know is what I just told you. Prepare three days' rations."

"Why'd they send you to tell us? Where is the colonel's aide?"

"Busy, I guess. How would I know? How would I know anything? I shouldn't even be here fighting this stupid war. This whole conscription thing is a violation of my Southern rights," Adams said bitterly. "I ain't even supposed to be fighting. I'm an overseer."

"From all I've heard, you lost your job on the plantation. Been hunting runaway slaves for a while," Palmer said sarcastically. "Besides, I don't know that you're any better than the rest of us. There's a war going on, in case you didn't know. It takes real men to fight a war."

Moses could imagine the fury tightening Ike Adams' face as Palmer taunted him. In spite of his fear, he allowed himself a small smile. It vanished quickly. Palmer was going to notice he hadn't returned in just a few minutes. But there was no way he could step out into the firelight. Adams would recognize him in a heartbeat, and then it would all be over. Not only his mission—but his life. There was not a Rebel around who would not be eager to hang a black man serving as a spy for the Union. Especially after Adams told the story of how Moses had disposed of him on the side of the road.

Moses stifled a groan as his mind raced to figure a way out of his newest dilemma. He could not think of a worse person to show up in his camp. Ike Adams had been the overseer on Cromwell Plantation—until Carrie had thrown him off for trying to rape Rose. Adams had always carried a hatred for Moses. It was a hatred that encompassed everyone around him. It was Ike's betrayal that had sent Captain Jones and his men to Carrie's plantation. Moses had confronted the scoundrel, knocking him out, disposing of his clothes, and tying him up before going to Carrie's aid. He regretted not killing the man when he'd had his chance. He knew nothing would stop Adams from killing him now if he found him here. Instinctively, he ducked farther back in the shadows as he struggled to find a solution, praying Adams would get back on his horse and ride off.

"You boys got some spare coffee?" Adams asked. "You're the last unit I was sent to give the message to. I sure could use a cup of something hot."

"Give him a cup, boys," Palmer growled. Then he looked around. "Where did Samuel go? I told him to get my food. What's that darkie doing? Playing around in the woods?"

"You got you a nigger out there, Palmer?"

"Yeah. He was looking for his master," Palmer said with a nasty laugh. "I figured I would give him a new one. He's been right handy to have around."

"Better keep an eye out for him. Them slaves been getting right uppity since this war started. The grapevine works real well around here. They know a lot of their kind are taking off and ending up in what the Yankees are calling Contraband Camps. Those Yankees are shielding them from their rightful owners. Even giving them an education and paying them for the work they do. The news is getting around. It hasn't done much to help the morale, if you know what I mean," Adams said with a sneer.

"Samuel is all right. He's big and strong—one of the biggest blacks I've ever seen. He sure made my life easier this week. I didn't have to do much digging," he said boastfully. "Yep, he came in real handy." Suddenly he looked around. "Where is he, anyway? I told him to come right back."

"You can't never trust them," Adams growled, as he took a sip of his coffee. "There's a boy I'm looking for right now. I reckon I'll stumble on to him one of these days. Real big fellow. Slave by the name of Moses. He's done turned himself into a Union spy."

Angry mutterings erupted around the fireplace.

"How do you know?" one man asked, leaning forward to catch the answer.

Moses watched as Palmer stared into the woods, shook his head in disgust, and then turned back to hear Adams' answer. Moses smiled at the idea of Adams providing a cover for him. His smile dimmed quickly as he realized the cover wouldn't last for long.

"I saw him with a unit of Union soldiers foraging our plantations after the Battle of Williamsburg. Foraging for food and stripping the countryside as they went."

"If you find him you let us know," a voice rang out. "We'll help you hang him up."

"Oh, I'll catch him eventually. I seem to have a nose for that one. For him *and* his wife," Adams said with a mean laugh. "I know right where his wife is. It won't be long before I head north to finish what I started. There are still plenty of ways to cross Yankee lines. It ain't so hard."

Moses clenched his fists at the thought of Adams getting near Rose again. He wished he knew how Adams had managed to get free after he had stripped the man of everything but his underwear and left him tied in the underbrush. He would probably never know.

"Yep. If that boy knew how close I came to having his wife, he wouldn't be down here spying for them Yankees. He would be getting his wife as far away as possible!"

"What are you talking about, Adams?" Palmer snapped. "I know you're dying for us to ask, so go ahead and tell your story. Then we have work to do."

Adams smirked. "You got plenty of time to pull your food together. You know as well as me you won't be sleeping much tonight," he said sharply. "Anyway, it's a great story. I was way up in the peninsula when I found a man's body floating in the Potomac. He'd been dead a right long time, but I found some papers on his body. Papers for a couple of slaves named Rose and Moses. I knew right away they were the ones who'd run off from the plantation I worked."

Moses leaned forward as Adams talked. How in the world had he found Mike O'Leary's body? Sorrow filled him as he remembered the cheerful Irishman who had been their conductor on the first stage of their escape through the Underground Railroad. He had been killed by two hunters, who had then dumped his body in the river to make sure no one discovered what they had done.

"Anyway, I was pretty sure those two had taken off for Philadelphia. I headed that direction as soon as I could. I only had to hang out there a week to find that wife of his. Caught her when she stopped to buy sweet potatoes from a street vendor I'd bribed to lure her over."

As he listened to Adams talk about his wife, anger roared through Moses, pounding in his ears and making his eyes pulse. Clenching his fist and gritting his teeth, he listened intently. Was Rose back in the South? Had she been hauled back to slavery? He had to know.

"Weren't no big deal to catch her," Adams sneered. "For a slave woman, she's a right pretty thing. I didn't see no reason not to have a little fun with her before I took her back for the reward money."

Moses leaned against a tree, gripping the bark till blood ran from his hands. It was all he could do to keep from bolting into the clearing and killing Adams. He should have done it when he had the chance.

Adams' voice continued from the clearing. "One of those Yankee nigger-lovers messed up my plans."

Moses held his breath and leaned forward farther.

"Big redheaded fellow heard her yell for help and knocked me out cold. When I came to they were both gone."

Moses shook his head. Who had saved Rose?

"Did you go back after her?" a voice called. "I hear those women make mighty fine lovers."

Adams shook his head. "I had some other slaves to carry back home. I figure I'll stay gone a while and let her think she is safe. When she least expects it, I'll pop back into her life," he said with a mean laugh. "When I set out to get a runaway, I don't give up so easy."

Once more the roaring in Moses' head made it almost impossible for him to see or hear. Fury became a living thing, threatening to destroy his reason. *God help me*, Moses finally managed to groan silently. He had to think. Rushing into the clearing would accomplish nothing other than assuring his death. There were any number of men out there who would gladly shoot him once they discovered he was the spy Adams had told them about.

Palmer's voice rose into the night. "Where is Samuel? Mike and Chad, go find him. Adams is right. They aren't to be trusted. Find him and bring him back. Maybe he needs some reminding of what his place is."

Moses had heard all he needed to. It would do no good to wait for Adams to leave. Turning, he melted back into the shadows.

With great relief Matthew Justin stepped off the plank leading down onto the dock at the end of Washington Street. He was glad to be home. The streets of Philadelphia seemed a continent away from the battlefields he had recently called home. He moved aside as a steady flow of stretchers carrying wounded soldiers streamed past him. He could only imagine the joy of the young men who were just arriving in Philadelphia after two weeks in the field hospitals of Virginia. Their moans and cries had filled the boat as they plowed up the coastline. Crowds of people were waiting on the dock to welcome them home and to care for them. Philadelphia had responded rapidly to the medical needs of their new army. Hospitals, capable of caring for over ten thousand men, were already established in the city.

Matthew watched for a few minutes, then broke away from the crowd to walk rapidly up the street. His lanky form was beginning to fill out again after six months of confinement in Richmond's Libby Prison. His beard remained, but he had cut his hair close to his head again. His work as a war correspondent for the *Philadelphia Tribune* demanded he maintain a respectable look. When he was in the city, anyway. There was not a single man on the battlefield who cared a whit how he looked. He was just another man doing a job.

"Hey, buddy! Watch where you're going!"

Matthew stepped aside as a wagon groaning under its burden of munitions rolled by on its way to the docks. Shaking his head, he laughed at himself. He'd better pay closer attention. He could allow his mind to wander when he'd gotten back to his office. Gripping his briefcase tightly, he hurried up the street. He had a lot of work to do before he could join Aunt Abby and Rose for dinner tonight.

He smiled as he thought of Aunt Abby. She was not related to any of the people she so lovingly opened her heart and home to. She had family down South, but they weren't very close. Even though she was a wealthy and respected business lady, she refused to let formality stand between her and those she loved. Matthew could hardly wait to see her again.

Philadelphia was a city at war. Soldiers and sailors thronged the streets—marching through on their way to Washington, wistfully enjoying their leaves, or waiting for ships being readied for war. The hot summer day released its stranglehold as dusk approached, casting off its warmth and allowing a cool breeze to blow in from the bay as Matthew moved farther away from the docks. Women in brightly colored dresses dotted the landscape, meshing with the flowers blooming in a myriad of windowboxes. If it weren't for the sight of ambulance wagons transporting wounded soldiers to hospitals, one could almost believe it was a normal summer day.

"Prisoners coming through! Prisoners coming through!"

A loud voice jerked Matthew's attention away from his surroundings. He watched as everyone within hearing distance stopped to stare and gawk at the manacled men being conveyed down the road in a large, open wagon. Matthew could feel nothing but sympathy for the dozens of men being transported to one of the various Northern stockades or to Fort Delaware on Pea Patch Island below the city. He knew firsthand the misery of prison life. Long after the crowds had turned back away to go about their business, Matthew stared after the wagons. Those soldiers might well be in prison for the duration of the war. He had been released only because he had been a civilian, a journalist, when he was captured. Most of the men with whom he had shared his confinement were still languishing in one of the Southern bastions.

Shaking his head, he moved on. Suddenly all he wanted was to be in the warmth of Aunt Abby's home. His soul longed for comfort and friendship. He would not go to the paper's office first. That could wait until tomorrow.

Rose was in no hurry as she sauntered down the street. She was tired from a long day at school, but it was a good tired. A tired that said she had learned much and been challenged to stretch herself intellectually. It was the kind of tired she had dreamed of after long days of work in the plantation house when she was so fatigued she could barely hold her eyes open to sneak in a few minutes of reading before succumbing to the exhaustion claiming her body. Taking in deep breaths of the cooling air, she allowed herself to relax. Suddenly her eyes opened wide as she saw a familiar face.

"Matthew Justin!" She was delighted to see the tall man striding toward her.

"Hello, Rose," Matthew said with a wide smile. "Heading home?" When she nodded, he asked, "Mind if I walk with you?"

"That would be wonderful. Aunt Abby will be thrilled to see you. You're early, aren't you?"

Matthew shrugged. "I couldn't face going to the office today. I much prefer the idea of being in the company of two lovely ladies."

Rose smiled, then searched his face. "Did you by any chance . . . ?"

Matthew shook his head. "No. I'm sorry. I didn't see Moses while I was there. But that doesn't mean anything bad has happened. There are over one hundred thousand men serving in the army of the Potomac under McClellan. He could have been any number of places."

"I know. I was just hoping . . . " Rose fought to control her disappointment. She knew mail did not always move easily from the camps. But she'd heard nothing from him at all since the first battles to take Richmond. Was he dead? Had he been injured? Had his cover as a spy been discovered by Southerners only too willing to kill him?

"How is school going?"

Rose struggled to pull her thoughts back. "Fine. School is going fine." She forced a smile. "Another teacher from the Contraband Camps at Fort Monroe came to talk to us today."

"I was there," Matthew replied.

Rose spun to face him. "You were at Fort Monroe? What's it like? How many blacks are there? What are the conditions? What . . . "

"Hold on there," Matthew laughed. "I can only answer one question at a time." He paused. "General Butler has taken in hundreds of fugitive slaves. My best guess is there are close to a thousand—counting women and children."

"That's what the man who came today said," Rose mused.

"The men are doing work for the army. So are the women. Cleaning, laundry, cooking. . . . The children go to school."

"How are living conditions?"

Matthew frowned. "Okay, I guess. There is a place they call Slab Town. The huts are made out of the rough outside of logs that have already been sawed into planks. There are houses being built in the burnt-out remains of Hampton. Some are living in big buildings built by the army." He paused again. "I wasn't really there long enough to pass much of a judgment."

Rose was watching him closely. "But you don't feel good about it."

"I don't really know how I feel about it," Matthew said with a frown. "They are certainly not living in conditions I would care to live in, but it might be a whole lot better than slavery. I guess what made me uncomfortable was the man who had been put in charge of the ex-slaves. I was asked by my paper to do an interview with him—a fellow by the name of Tallmadge. From what I can tell, he is uncaring and dishonest."

"I've heard about him."

"How in the world did *you* hear about him?" Matthew asked, astonished.

Rose smiled. "The man who came to talk to us today. His name is Mr. Lockwood. He's been down at Fort Monroe as a representative of the American Missionary Association. He seemed to feel the same way about Tallmadge. He returned to the North to talk with officials, to try and have something done about him. And to find more teachers," she added.

Matthew turned to watch her closely. "Have you changed your mind about going? I know you wanted to stay in school so that you can prepare to help your people."

"I don't know, Matthew," Rose said slowly. "I'm confused right now." She paused, suddenly glad to have him to talk to. "Have you ever heard of a woman named Mary Peake?"

Matthew thought for a moment. "I heard her name while I was down at Fort Monroe. Is she one of the teachers?"

"She *was* one of the teachers. In fact, she was the very first teacher in the camps. She's dead now. She had been ill with tuberculosis for quite some time. In spite of her bad health she continued to teach. She died a few months ago. More teachers have gone down but there aren't enough to meet the need."

"Matthew Justin. You're home!"

Rose looked up, startled. She hadn't realized they were almost to the house.

Aunt Abby, with a wide smile on her face, stepped from the porch and began to walk to meet them.

Matthew strode ahead and wrapped her in a big hug. "Aunt Abby. It's wonderful to see you," he said warmly.

Rose watched as the woman who had become like a mother to her smiled up into Matthew's face. Aunt Abby's huge heart had won her over the minute she laid eyes on her.

Abigail Stratton had taken over her husband's business when, still a young man, he died unexpectedly. Her struggle to make her way in a man's world had both strengthened her and deepened her compassion. She carried herself with confidence, not seeming to mind that she stood taller than most men around her. Soft brown hair, now sporting streaks of iron, framed a pair of startling bright gray eyes. Her voice, low and melodious, invited listeners into her world, her caring and warmth soon making everyone feel totally at home. Aunt Abby had welcomed Rose and Moses into her home—had made them part of her family. Rose loved her fiercely. Thinking about it only made what she was contemplating even more difficult.

Rose followed Matthew and Aunt Abby into the house.

"Dinner won't be ready for an hour or so," Aunt Abby apologized.

"I'm early," Matthew responded. "Your home has a much stronger pull than the office. I hope you don't mind."

"Nonsense. I'm delighted you're here. You can relax while I finish dinner."

Rose headed for the stairs. "I'll change and be down to help." As she climbed the steps she pondered the haunted look in Matthew's eyes.

It wasn't until they were finishing a dessert of fresh strawberries that talk turned to serious subjects.

Aunt Abby turned to Matthew. "Tell me about Richmond. I'm so worried about Carrie, Robert, and her father. I've read about the fighting, but I know I can trust you to tell me the whole story. I suppose there are benefits to having a war correspondent as part of my family, even if I do worry about you constantly."

Rose pushed aside her plate and leaned forward to listen. The dishes could be taken care of later.

Matthew leaned back in his chair. "From all I could tell, the battles at Seven Pines were a pointless killing of thousands of men. After two days, the lines were the exact same as before it started. Except that they were minus over six thousand men on both sides."

"So the papers didn't exaggerate the numbers."

"Not this time," Matthew said grimly. "They published it the way I sent it to them. I was hard put to decide which side I felt worse for. I'm just as concerned as you are about Carrie, Robert, and Mr. Cromwell. It must be horrible for the people in Richmond to be wondering every minute if their city is about to fall. But they had a major advantage. Their wounded soldiers were only a few miles at the most from hospitals equipped to care for them." He paused for a long moment. "It broke my heart to see thousands of Northern young men lying in the dirt, on straw, or makeshift mattresses, waiting for spaces in tents or buildings to open up." He shook his head.

Aunt Abby reached out and put her hand on his. "It must have been horrible."

Matthew sighed heavily. "It was like nothing I have ever seen. I wish to God I never have to see it again, yet I know this is just the beginning." He shook his head again and seemed to forget they were there as he stared off into the distance. "I was at the supply depot at White House when they started to bring them in. They came on boxcars, several hundred at a time. They were packed tightly in the cars, dead and alive together—many with no initial treatment of their wounds—but all hungry and exhausted."

His voice faltered. Aunt Abby squeezed his hand but he seemed not to notice. "So many of them had such awful wounds . . . they were crawling with maggots. And the smell—the stench was enough to make me vomit. All the hospitals were full. Some of them were carried aboard boats. Others laid by the tracks in the rain for hours until room could be made for them. Piles of amputated limbs were everywhere. Dead bodies were stacked on platforms." His voice dropped to a whisper. "It was like being in the midst of a long nightmare that would never end. The flow of wounded was endless. So much waste."

Tears streamed down Rose's face. She knew these were memories he could never erase from his mind—they would rise to taunt him all his life.

"I'm so sorry, Matthew," Aunt Abby said tenderly.

"What?" Matthew straightened suddenly, his eyes opening wide as if he were just remembering they were listening. "I'm sorry. Please forgive me. You shouldn't have to hear such things."

"Nonsense!" Aunt Abby exclaimed, blinking back her tears. "Trying to hide the truth doesn't hide the reality of what is. I only wish everyone could go down and see what you've seen. Maybe everyone would work harder to find a way to end this crazy war."

Matthew looked at her for a moment and then stared off again, a remote look in his eyes.

Rose and Aunt Abby exchanged anxious glances. Rose felt her heart squeeze with pity for the man who had been such a good friend to her. If it hadn't been for him, Ike Adams would have taken her back to slavery—after he had had his way with her. Matthew had never talked much about what he had endured in the prisons. He had seen some horrific sights in his life between these latest battles and his earlier time in prison. It was a wonder to Rose that he still managed to hold on to his sanity. Many lesser men would have snapped long ago.

Matthew started talking again. "When General Lee pulled his troops back, our soldiers moved back to where they had been. But first they had to bury the thousands of dead scattered everywhere. Graves were dug for both Rebels and Yankees. The smell of burning horses almost choked you." He paused for another long moment. "The dead they buried—they didn't do a very good job. I went there later—the smell was horrible. Rain had washed away the dirt over the graves. ... " His voice faltered as his eyes filled with tears. "There were legs and hands sticking out and heads pushing through the ground ... " He bowed his head as if the pain were more than he could bear. "So much death—so senseless," he finally murmured in a broken voice.

Aunt Abby sprung up and wrapped her arms around him. "I'm so sorry, Matthew. I know it must have been horrible." She stroked his head tenderly. "But you're home now. You're with Rose and me."

Rose brushed away the tears on her cheeks. Matthew took a deep breath and straightened. Tears were still shining in his eyes but the haunted look was dissipating.

"Thank you," he murmured, managing a shaky smile. "I'm sorry you had to hear that, but somehow it seems to help to say it out loud."

"Sharing pain always helps," Rose agreed. Her mind traveled back to the time Moses had stripped his shirt to let her see the criss-cross of whip scars on his back, when he had finally released the agony of seeing his father die. It had been the beginning of his healing. "You'll never forget what you've seen but it will lose some of its power to haunt you."

"You're very wise for one so young," Matthew said, smiling slightly.

Rose shrugged. "My momma was the wise one. I'm just lucky enough to have remembered much of what she tried to teach me."

"I so wish I could have met your momma before God took her home," Aunt Abby said. "I have heard so much about her from both you and Carrie."

"My momma was a saint," Rose said firmly. "I know she and my daddy are happy now. That's what counts." She would hold the memories of her momma close all of her life but she knew she was with God. Her momma would be thrilled that she was free and following her dreams. That had meant everything to her.

"What's going to happen now, Matthew?" Aunt Abby asked.

"McClellan will have to launch another attack against Richmond. I have a feeling it will be soon. President Lincoln didn't send over one hundred thousand men down there to just camp outside their gates."

"McClellan is being criticized for his actions," Rose commented.

"I know," Matthew responded. "I wouldn't want to be in his position. He is moving much too slowly and cautiously. The Rebels have surely had all the time they need to reinforce their troops and prepare for what is coming. I've heard the reports that our troops are hopelessly outnumbered. McClellan is using that as the reason he keeps stalling on pressing an offensive. I find it difficult to believe. The South simply doesn't have that kind of manpower."

"There are many people in the North who are getting impatient with him," Aunt Abby commented.

"Impatient is one way to put it," Matthew said wryly. "Infuriated might be a more accurate portrayal." He paused. "He and Lincoln have clashed several times. The more Lincoln tries to get action from him, the slower he moves."

"I heard McClellan was furious when Lincoln ordered McDowell's reinforcements back to protect the capital," Rose said.

"McClellan claimed to know all along that General Jackson's campaign in the valley the last two weeks was just a Southern ploy to give General Lee time to prepare for the battle. Maybe he did know. But I don't see how Lincoln could have done anything else. Just as the South can't afford to lose Richmond, we can't afford to lose Washington." Matthew turned to Aunt Abby. "I understand the Abolitionists aren't too fond of McClellan either."

Aunt Abby frowned. "I'm afraid you're right." She paused, then shook her head. "Balance seems to be an impossible thing to find in this war. You know I have worked with the Abolitionist Society for years. I want nothing more than to see every single slave in the South freed . . . "

"But . . . " Matthew prompted.

"There's not a but," Aunt Abby protested. "It's just that there are differences of opinion on how it can be done. There are many abolitionists who want to see McClellan strung up because he isn't dedicated to freeing the slaves. They extol General Fremont for issuing his own Emancipation Proclamation in Missouri."

"And you don't think he should have?" Rose asked.

"I'm not sure what I think. I know how much Lincoln hates slavery. I also know I get impatient myself that he won't make it an issue in the war, even though I think he should. His dedication is to preserving the Union of the country. I can't condemn that because I hold it dear to my own heart as well." She paused for a long minute and then shrugged her shoulders helplessly. "I think there are too many questions that don't have easy answers. There are plenty of people who *think* they know the answers, but Lincoln is the one responsible for making the decisions. I know I'm very glad I'm not in his place. I pray to God there is a way to accomplish both objectives."

Silence fell on the room for several long minutes. A cool breeze waltzed through the open curtains, pushing them aside in a carefree dance. Rose stared at the billowing fabric thoughtfully, allowing their conversation to filter through her mind, all the time trying to answer the questions her own heart was hurling at her.

Matthew was the first to speak. "I've thought so much about this issue. The hard reality is that if we are going to wage war to destroy a government based on slavery, I don't think it's possible to keep the war from revolving around the fundamental concept of human freedom. McClellan holds a deep sympathy for slave owners. He believes the whole purpose of the war is simply to reunify the states."

"I'm sorry to hear that," Aunt Abby said in a troubled voice.

"I am, too," Matthew continued. "He's infected his troops with this same belief. However inept a military commander he may be, he is indeed a leader and most of his men adore him. They would follow him anywhere."

Rose watched Matthew carefully. She knew him well enough to know he was leading up to something.

Matthew turned to stare out the window. "There are many people who want to proclaim that this war is not being fought to end slavery. Yet the truth is that the war is about slavery. Lincoln can deny it for as long as he wants, but sooner or later he is going to have to face it— and do something about it."

Rose felt hope soar within her. "So you believe Lincoln will eventually have to free the slaves?"

"I do," Matthew said firmly. "Already people are getting tired of the war. People will fight for a principle, but if they are expected to fight for a long time, I believe you have to put a human face on it. They have to fight for something more than just a principle." He paused. "Lincoln is a good leader. I respect him. His passion is to save the Union. But I believe he will have to declare war against slavery to do it."

Rose sat back in her chair and stared at him.

"What are you thinking about, Rose?" Aunt Abby asked gently.

Rose wasn't ready to put voice to her thoughts yet. She answered Aunt Abby's question with another one. "What do you think of Anna Dickinson?"

Aunt Abby sat back in her chair with a surprised look. "How in the world did we jump to that topic?"

Rose said nothing, just waited.

"Isn't Anna Dickinson the abolition movement's newest star?" Matthew asked.

"She is," Aunt Abby agreed, still looking at Rose curiously. "I've heard her speak on several occasions. She is only twenty years old and one of the most articulate speakers I have ever heard. Besides being a strong abolitionist, she is a staunch advocate of women's rights. She began her speaking career here in Philadelphia."

"I heard her speak a few weeks ago," Rose offered. "She strongly believes emancipation should be an official war aim of the North. She says that while the flag of freedom flies merely for the white man, God will be against the North." She paused, then pushed on, "She also said women should be equal with men. That we should vote. That we should share responsibility for what is going on in our country now." She took a breath, her mind spinning too fast to be expressed in words.

Aunt Abby watched her for a moment, then responded. "I believe God wants his people to be free," she said slowly. "If that means he will be against the North until we proclaim emancipation—I don't know. It wouldn't exactly make sense that he would instead decide to stand on the side of the South since they are the ones holding people in bondage. No, I think God gets blamed for a lot of things men bring upon themselves."

She paused. "As for the other—yes, I believe women are equal. I believe they should have the right to vote. Especially now. There are women all over this country who are carrying on for men who are on the battlefields. They are doing the job not only because they have to, but because they are perfectly capable. This war is a hideous thing, but I think it's going to be a step forward for the women's movement that started about twenty years ago. Women aren't going to be content to step back into their old roles." Suddenly she laughed. "Now please tell me how we got onto this subject. Am I missing something?"

Rose stared around the room for a moment then looked back. "A man from the Contraband Camps came to our school today. A Mr. Lockwood. He told us about the new schools being formed, about how hungry the ex-slaves are for education. Most of the slaves are completely uneducated of course, but Mr. Lockwood said they were doing a lot of things in the camps to prove that blacks are just as capable, industrious, and learn just as quickly as whites if they are treated fairly and given the same opportunities."

"Of course they are," Aunt Abby agreed.

"He also said that proving those things would give a great boost to the cause of emancipation. People in the North have many fears about what will happen if all the blacks are freed. He said relieving some of those fears would make it easier for Lincoln to make emancipation a reality."

Aunt Abby leaned forward. "What are you saying, Rose?" she asked softly.

Rose let out a deep breath and stared around the comfortable room again. "I'm not going to wait until I finish school to be a teacher. My people need me. They need me now. Mr. Lockwood asked me if I would come join their efforts. I'm going to go down to the camps," she said firmly. There, it was out. She'd been dreading saying those words all day. But she felt certain it was the right thing for her to do. Just saying it made her feel better.

"I see," Aunt Abby said slowly.

Rose went on, "It's not just because I'm black—not just because I was a slave. It's more than that. It's because I'm a woman, too. Anna Dickinson is right. We have to take responsibility. We have to be willing to step forward and do what needs doing. I have to go, not only for my people, but also for other women." She stopped, still overwhelmed with where her thoughts had taken her. She had been so uncertain when she had walked home. Somehow, in the midst of their conversation she had realized what she had to do.

$\mathcal{Seven}$

$\mathcal{M}$oses tried to flatten himself even farther into the ditch as a group of soldiers wandered by. Pressing his stomach, he ignored the pangs of hunger shooting through his body. He had more important things to worry about than food. He could hardly believe he had managed to elude capture for this long.

It had been two long days since Ike Adams had shown up in camp. It was almost impossible to believe the Rebels hadn't found him that night when they had come looking for him. One second sooner and he would not have been able to conceal himself, high in the thick leaves of a large oak tree. They had searched for over two hours in the dark until Palmer had called them back to camp.

From where Moses sat huddled in the tree, he could hear everything that had been said. He listened as Ike Adams described him in detail. He had groaned silently when Palmer put two and two together and realized a Union spy had been serving his every need, listening to everything he said. Palmer's anger would have been laughable if he had been somewhere other than thirty feet up in a tree with no way of escape. It had been almost dawn before he had crept down. He would have stayed up there longer except that his muscles were screaming from being cramped for so long. He could barely walk when he had first dropped from the tree. The guard had his back turned when Moses inched past the horses, praying one of them would not betray his presence.

Moses quit breathing as a voice sounded just yards from where he lay. "Get your gear ready, men. I have an order to prepare three days of rations. This looks like it's the real thing. It will be dark soon.

96

We move in the morning." Then the voices had simply retreated, leaving him to make his silent exit.

He had waited in vain the last two days for the sound of battle. Palmer had been so sure the order of three days of rations meant the next battle was at hand. For whatever reason, it had not happened. Now he had until tomorrow morning to make his way back to the Union side.

Moses forced himself to think calmly. He had basically been hiding for two days, the knowledge of what would happen to him if he were captured as a Union spy immobilizing him. The time for hiding was over. If he was going to get out of this alive he was going to have to take bold action and trust it would come out all right. Slowly his heart calmed as planning overcame the fear that gripped him. As the fear receded, words Rose had spoken to him before he left echoed through his mind and heart. He had promised her he would come home. She had put a finger to his lips and lovingly said, *"I believe you. I know you have to do this thing. I'm proud of you. I believe you're going to open up the way for many more of our people."* She had paused and looked deep into his eyes. *"One of the reasons I love you is because you're a leader. I'm sorry I let my fears get the best of me."*

Moses knew he had let his fears get the best of him. But no more. He had been so overwhelmed with his situation, so paralyzed by the supposed inevitability of capture, he had hidden from his fears. Another voice edged into his thoughts.

"Why, boy, you know what you got to do when you be afraid. You gots to act. That be the only thin' will make that fear demon run away. You gots to act and trust God will take you where he wants you."

Moses smiled as Old Sarah's voice rang clearly in his mind. His time with Rose's momma had been much too short, but she had told him many things he would never forget. With a clear head he formulated his plans.

Moses leaned wearily against a tree, mud pulling at his feet as water sloshed around his knees. If he never saw another swamp in his life it would be much too soon. He wasn't sure how many hours he had been surging his way through the stagnant, murky water.

"Who goes there!" a voice rang out.

Moses gritted his teeth and once more sank down below the surface, just his head clearing the swamp. He struggled to control his fear as he felt a snake slither by in the darkness. Resolutely he kept his mind focused. If he let his imagination take its course he would bolt and run. He would be captured within moments.

"I know I heard something, Captain," the same man insisted.

Another voice floated to him. "There's so many animals in this god-forsaken swamp you could have heard anything. I don't see anything moving now."

Moses waited for what seemed an eternity before he dared to stand back up. Staring into the darkness, he stood still until he had convinced himself there was no danger. He continued to move forward slowly, praying he was headed in the right direction. The cloudy sky made it impossible to use the stars for navigation or to maintain a straight course through the swamp. He had lost count of the number of times he had to crawl over logs and move around tangled trees and brush.

Ignoring the hunger and thirst racking his body, Moses moved on. As insects dropped on him from the trees, he flicked them away, gritting his teeth to fight his fear. Swarms of mosquitoes were simply to be endured. Blood clotted on his arms where tree limbs slashed and ripped at him as he pushed his way through the tangles. His legs ached from colliding with underwater stumps and logs. None of that was important. His mind was focused on a single goal—to reach the Union side . . . and safety. Rose was counting on him. He couldn't let her down.

Neither could he let his captain down. He was sure Captain Jones had to do some fancy talking to convince McClellan to send him over as a spy. He wasn't going to disappoint him. Somehow he had to get back. He could only hope his information wouldn't be too late to accomplish some good.

Dawn was just beginning to light the eastern sky when Moses felt solid ground rise up under his feet for the first time in hours. He held his breath, wondering if the ground would once more sink down into swampland. Had he finally reached the end of the murky death trap? A wide smile broke his face as the ground hardened and began to slope upward. He had done it! He had crossed the swamps of the Chickahominy in the middle of the night, and evaded capture!

The smile lasted for only a moment. It was much too soon to celebrate. He had escaped the swamp but now a wide open space waited for him. It was sure to be carefully watched by both sides. Gunmen, both Union and Confederate would be waiting for any unusual movement. They would shoot first and ask questions later.

Moses' heart sank as he watched the brightening skyline. He would no longer have the cover of darkness to camouflage his movements. Advancing to the edge of the clearing, he crouched down behind a thicket of blackberry brambles and stared out. The smell of fresh fruit tickled his nostrils, reminding him of his hunger. Mindless of the prickly thorns, Moses tore at the clusters of lush blackberries. As he stuffed them into his mouth he felt a new strength surging through his body. The moisture exploding in his mouth was like manna from heaven.

With his hunger somewhat abated, Moses leaned forward again to stare at the opposing line of trees. How many Union troops were stationed there? Would they start firing immediately if they saw someone moving toward them? Moses sunk down to the ground. He was not at all confident bullets would not start flying from every direction as soon as he broke into the clearing. Searching the land as far as he could see, he looked for a place that would offer him at least a little cover as he tried to sneak across. The sky continued to brighten.

A sudden movement on the Union side grabbed his attention. As he watched, a small unit of soldiers rode out of the clearing. Moses leaned forward to watch what must be an advance group. There was not much chance he would recognize anyone, but hope kept his eyes locked on them.

"Captain Jones!" he whispered in amazement. A wide grin split his face as his captain, Joe, and several others surged forward.

Bang!

Moses jumped as a gun sounded less than a hundred yards from where he lay.

"Get 'em, boys!"

Moses' heart sank in dismay as he realized a Confederate unit was stationed directly to his right. He knew he should slink back and look for another place to cross, but curiosity over the action taking place right before his eyes held him where he was.

Captain Jones raised his gun to his shoulder and fired off a round while waving his men back into cover. Joe matched his action, then spun back toward the woods.

"I got one!" a triumphant yell rose from the Rebel side.

Moses groaned as he saw his captain slump in the saddle and then begin to fall slowly sideways.

"Finish him off!"

Moses didn't even realize he was up and running until he was partway across the clearing and bullets were whizzing around his head. Zigzagging in a crazy pattern to avoid the shots, he dashed across the clearing, ducking instinctively as a bullet whistled just inches from his head. He felt another rip through the loose sleeve of his shirt but he kept running. He had only one thought. To reach the captain. From somewhere in his consciousness he realized his name was being called from the woods. Ducking his head lower, he ran even faster.

Suddenly, bullets erupted from the Federal side. Joe must have recognized him and was trying to provide cover. Bullets spit over his head from both sides now as he pressed forward. It seemed like an eternity before he reached the captain, scooped him up in his arms, and sprinted into the woods, his weakened body screaming under the extra weight of the wounded man.

"Keep going, Moses! Get out of here! Here they come!"

Moses heard Joe, managed to nod his head slightly, then kept running. Or at least he tried to run. Within moments he was stumbling under the weight of his captain, cursing his own weakness. A tree root rose up in front of him, reaching out to snag his foot. With a groan, Moses tripped under his extra burden and fell forward. The ground rose up before him, then crumbled away as they crashed down. Moses tried to shield the captain as they tumbled and slid down a brushy bank into a steep ravine.

Moses lay still for just a moment, pain piercing his body from the fall. Gingerly he moved his legs, praying they would still work. Even though every inch screamed in agony, his limbs obeyed his commands. Taking a deep breath, he stood and reached down to once more pick up the captain. He didn't know if Captain Jones was still alive. All he could do was get him back to a hospital tent as quickly as possible.

"Don't move!" a sharp voice commanded. "I've got you now."

Moses froze as the familiar voice sounded above him. Straightening, he stared up into Ike Adams' raging eyes. Was this how it was going to end? Adams must have been in the advance group of Rebels.

Adams, keeping his gun trained on Moses, laughed nastily. "I could hardly believe my luck when I saw you dash across that clearing. I reckon God is on my side, all right."

Moses looked up, suddenly resigned to his fate. There was nothing he could do. He had no protection and no way to put up a fight. Even if he tried to run up the side of the ravine, it was much too steep. Adams would have plenty of time to fill him with lead.

"I wish I had time to watch you cower down there like the cornered animal you are, but things could get hot around here. I reckon I'll have to have my fun quicklike," he sneered as he lifted the musket to his shoulder.

Moses wondered just for a second where the rest of the Union unit was. It made him sick to think they could be dead or wounded. How had Adams gotten through all those men? When he heard the click of the hammer on Adams' gun, life seemed to split into slow motion. He watched the man who had caused him so much misery prepare to kill him, his sneering face taunting Moses as he looked down the barrel of the gun. Everything seemed to split into slow motion. Then Rose's face appeared before him—almost real enough to reach out and touch. *"I love you, Moses. I'm proud of you."*

"I love you too, Rose," he whispered, continuing to stare into Adams' hate-filled eyes. He refused to look away. He would show no fear now that his time had come. He refused to give Adams the satisfaction.

Moses jumped when the gun exploded. He was amazed when he felt nothing. Maybe this was what death was like—a vague passing into another world. He waited for pain to spread through his body. Then his eyes opened wide. Ike Adams, a surprised expression on his face, slowly loosed his grip on his rifle, slumped forward, and fell to the ground. His rifle clattered down the slope toward Moses, but all he could do was stare at it.

He waited for long minutes, expecting one of the men in his unit to walk up to the edge of the ravine, but no one appeared. Finally he looked down at the unconscious man at his feet. "I'll be right back, Captain."

Grabbing hold of tree roots and exposed rock, he pulled himself up the side of the gully and peered over. "Joe!" he exclaimed. Hurriedly, he climbed the rest of the way out and ran to his friend who was leaning against a tree, his head cocked at an odd angle.

"I got him, Moses," Joe said with a weak grin, pain twisting his face.

"You shot Adams?" Moses asked in amazement.

"Sure did. I don't know what made that madman dash right through all of our soldiers. It was as if he had only one thing on his mind."

Moses shook his head. "He was a very sick man. Too much hate destroyed his heart and mind."

Joe grinned again, a bare flicker of movement on his lips. Then he sobered. "I've been hit, Moses." A pause. "It's bad," he gasped weakly.

Moses nodded grimly. "I know. I'll get you out of here."

Joe shook his head. "The captain . . . "

"I'll get the captain out of here, too."

Again Joe shook his head. "Too late for me . . . get the captain." His voice faded away as his eyes closed. Suddenly they sprang open. "My wife . . . tell her . . . tell her I love her . . . her and little Joey."

Moses blinked back the tears as the shadow of death settled on Joe's face. Gently he closed the staring eyes. Long minutes passed as he stared into the face of the friend who had saved his life. "Thank you," he said softly.

A distant gunshot jarred him back to reality. Touching Joe's arm one more time, he jumped up and ran for the ravine. There was nothing he could do for Joe now. But he might still be able to save his captain. Tears blurred his vision as he stumbled to the ravine. He stopped abruptly as he reached Adams' body. Time was critical, but he had to know. Leaning down, he grabbed Adams' arm and rolled him over on his back. Sightless eyes looked up at him.

Moses stared at the dead man, struggling between gladness that his enemy was dead, and sadness that a life could be so wasted.

Another volley of shots rang out—closer this time. After one final look, Moses turned and eased his way back down into the ravine. Without checking to see if his Captain was still alive, he hoisted the dead weight onto his shoulder, then struggled up the other side of the ravine. He paused just a moment to catch his breath, then broke into a steady run toward the rear of the lines.

Moses was gasping for air when he broke from the woods into the camps. He stared around him but didn't slacken his pace. No one stepped forward to stop him. Everywhere there was wild action as men sprang forward to accompany their units. Napoleon cannon and three-inch artillery guns rumbled by on their way to the front. The sounds of battle echoed through the air now, rolling forth on every puff of breeze the still day offered.

"What you got there?" a surgeon asked sharply as Moses ran up to the nearest medical tent.

"Captain Jones, sir. He was hit by an advance group of Confederates."

"Is he still alive?" he barked, motioning for an aide to bring a stretcher.

Moses shook his head as he laid the captain gently on the waiting canvas. "I don't know. I just got him here as quick as I could."

"We'll take care of him now," the surgeon said in a gentler voice. "If he lives, the captain will have you to thank for saving his life."

Moses stared after them until the tent door swung shut. There was nothing more he could do. Now that the captain was wounded he didn't know who to report to with his information. Setting his face and ignoring the fresh pangs of hunger, Moses went in search of McClellan's headquarters. It might be too late for his information to do any good, but he would still report.

~Eight~

arrie was numb as she moved slowly down the hill, fighting the stream of people flowing toward her. Somewhere in her consciousness she was aware a battle was being fought, but she had long ago lost interest in the actual event. There had been fighting for five days now. The long standoff had ended on June 25, when Lee attacked the Army of the Potomac at Mechanicsville. Every day brought fresh fighting—and a fresh flow of wounded into the hospitals. It seemed as if every building in the city was bulging with wounded and dying soldiers.

Carrie stumbled slightly as a heavyset woman, unmindful of her surroundings, pushed past her. She set her lips tightly and continued against the press of people. All she wanted was to get home. All these people, every day hurrying to the highest points in the city, could head for the hills to watch the battle raging outside the city if they wanted to. It seemed as if everyone wanted to watch the spectacle. Carrie had sickened of it.

Her father had convinced her on the second day to climb the steps of the Capitol, where a marvelous view could be seen from the roof. Carrie had been most fascinated by the people of the city. As if the hills were a great amphitheater, men, women, and children crowded the slopes, witnessing what they called the grand fireworks—the exploding of bombs and artillery, the rattle of gunfire. She had heard people proclaim how beautiful they were. She could only stare, a sickness gnawing at her stomach. There was nothing beautiful in the roar of battle—it was awful! What they saw as beauty were instruments sending death to the ones they loved so dearly. How could they forget the thousands of wounded filling their city, the thousands of dead waiting for burial? Carrie had watched for only a few minutes before she had turned and fled. Not even to please her father would she be a spectator to carnage.

"Watch out," a man snapped sharply.

Carrie shook her head, trying to refocus her thoughts. She was greatly relieved when she saw that she was just a block from her father's home. Turning off busy Broad Street, she hurried down 24th Street, the sound of cannon and gunfire pursuing her into the house. Carrie longed to stuff something in her ears to shut out the noise.

"General Lee has those Yankees on the run!"

Carrie managed a smile as she looked at the excitement on Manning's face. "That's nice."

Manning stared at her. "That's *nice?* All you have to say is that's *nice?*"

Carrie looked wearily at one of the boarders. "Yes," she stated simply. Then she turned and trudged up the stairs. She could feel his stare boring into her back but she simply didn't care.

Janie was sitting in her bed, staring at a book when Carrie reached their room. She managed a weak smile when Carrie entered the room, but other than a wave of her hand, she did not move from her bed.

Carrie nodded in return and then slowly removed her clothes. Clean clothes would boost her drooping morale. Crumpling her soiled dress and apron into a ball, she stuffed it in a bag to carry it down to May, who would wash it in hot water the next day. It never totally lost its odor but at least the scent was diminished. Wrinkling her nose, she tossed the bag toward the door, then slipped into a fresh dress. She had saved three to wear just at home. All the rest were designated hospital dresses. The remainder of what had once been an extensive wardrobe had been donated for transformation into bandages, uniform material, or whatever else the ladies of Richmond deemed it suitable for.

Once she was in clean clothing, Carrie collapsed gratefully onto the bed. Within minutes she was sound asleep.

It must have been the sound of silence that wakened her about an hour later. Blinking her eyes to make them focus, she looked toward Janie's bed. Her friend was wide awake, staring at the window. Carrie listened carefully. "Is the battle over?"

Janie shrugged. "I think so. At least for today," she said, then paused. "A new batch of wounded will be coming soon."

"I don't think it will ever end," Carrie responded, a deep despair threatening to overwhelm her. Would Robert be in this newest batch? Was he already lying wounded in one of the hospitals? Or would his name turn up on the list of dead soldiers?

"I don't know if I can take much more," Janie murmured, tears choking her words.

Carrie leaned forward, drawn by something she had never heard in her friend's voice. Janie was always the strong one. Always the one who held on to hope when Carrie was struggling to find something to hold on to at all. There was no strength in her voice now—only the helpless sound of a child who has lost her way, fearing she will never see home again.

Janie stared at her. "This war is too terrible," she whispered. "Four more soldiers developed gangrene today. I'm afraid they'll have to amputate. Two more died. And Jimmy . . . "

Carrie stood and moved to sit on Janie's bed. "Jimmy? Did something happen to him?"

Janie managed to nod. "He was doing so well."

Carrie frowned, waiting for her to go on. She had heard many stories about Jimmy. He had been brought in after the battle of Williamsburg and had fast become a favorite of Janie's. He was always laughing, always teasing—even when pain seemed to twist his pleasant face like a corkscrew. Janie had worked to treat all the patients the same, but Carrie knew Jimmy held a special place in her heart. "What happened?" she finally asked softly.

Janie shook her head and stared up through eyes swimming with tears. It took her several long minutes before she could speak. When she finally did, it was with a limp laugh. "I remember him pulling that gun he had hidden out from under his pillow when the surgeon said he was going to take his leg."

"I remember. He said if the surgeon tried to take his leg it would be the last thing he ever did."

"The surgeon left it, but there were some badly splintered bones in his thigh. We've made him lie still for over a month, afraid what movement would do. All we could do was splint the leg and hope it would heal." Janie's voice broke as once again tears filled her eyes.

Carrie waited patiently. Janie would tell her when she could. She could already guess the outcome, but Janie needed to talk—it would help release some of the pain.

"Jimmy just couldn't lie still any more. This morning he grabbed a pair of crutches and hobbled all around the ward, laughing and joking with some of the men just brought in. I was thrilled to see him up and about. He was so happy," she whispered. She shook her head, then forced herself to continue, "I was tending another soldier when one of the nurses rushed up to me. Said Jimmy was calling for me. When I got there, there was blood everywhere. I did the only thing I could think of—I grabbed my handkerchief and pressed it into the wound."

"He severed an artery?" Carrie asked, a sinking sureness in her heart.

"That's what the doctor said. Said it would be impossible to go in and repair it. He got that *look* on his face, just shook his head and walked away."

"What did you do?" Tears were rolling down Carrie's face as well.

"What *could* I do? I sat there holding the wound. As long as I held it, he would be okay." Sobs began to rack Janie's body then. "I held it for such a long time. Finally, Jimmy looked at me and said, 'It's okay, Miss Winthrop. I'm ready to go.'" Janie gasped and clutched at Carrie's hand. "He knew, Carrie. He knew he was about to die. I held on as long as I could."

Carrie listened, sympathy and horror clouding her mind. What would she have done? Could she ever have brought herself to let go?

"I passed out," Janie said helplessly. "When I came to . . . Jimmy was dead," she cried brokenly, then collapsed into Carrie's arms.

Carrie held her tightly, stroking her head gently. Janie finally gave one last gulping sob and straightened. "Thank you," she said thickly, her eyes swollen from the torrent of tears. "I guess I needed that."

"No one can stay strong all the time in the midst of such madness," Carrie said gently. "I've wondered how you managed to for so long."

Janie laughed shakily. "My momma always said my head was the hardest substance known to mankind. I guess she was right."

Carrie looked at her thoughtfully. "As long as our hearts don't become the hardest substance known to mankind, we might make it."

"I guess I was trying to numb my heart to the pain as well," Janie admitted. "But it was all a pretense. Every soldier who is carried through that door rips at my heart. I guess that's just the way it's going to have to be."

Carrie was waiting in the parlor when her father came in.

"They're on the run!" Thomas stated.

"Tell me about it," Carrie invited. The only way she kept up on what was going on was through her father. Part of her wanted to block everything out, but she knew she needed to stay informed. She had to know what was happening in her crazy world.

"McClellan is withdrawing his troops. Lee is going after them."

"If they're leaving, why not just let them go?"

Her father frowned. "An undefeated army will return."

"But you just said they were retreating. That would indicate a defeat."

"I suppose defeat is the wrong word. Lee is out to destroy the Army of the Potomac. He doesn't want them to be able to rise from the ashes of their former glory."

Destroy. Carrie mulled the word over. The idea of destroying an army seemed so sterile—until one realized an army was made up of men. How many men would have to die before the destruction was complete? She decided to keep her thoughts to herself. She knew her father's hope revolved around the bold actions Lee was taking to rid Richmond of the threat of invasion.

Lee, understanding his opponent well, had elected not to wait for McClellan's attack. While his enemy had been digging in, preparing for a long siege that would bring the capital to its knees, Lee had been laying out his plans for a bold offensive campaign. Finally, on June 25, he had been ready. That McClellan had been shocked by the Confederacy's boldness was affirmed by his retreat after the very first day of battle. Lee had been pushing after him, forcing the Federals to fight as they struggled to escape the net that was growing tighter every day. Richmond cheered their general's bravery and daring, but no one knew better than the men and women whose sons fought each battle what his exploits were costing.

"Did you check the lists for me today?" Carrie asked quietly, deciding to change the subject.

Thomas nodded. "Robert's name wasn't on there. I have every reason to believe he is fine, fighting hard with his men."

Carrie nodded, relieved. She didn't share her father's confidence. It was impossible to keep track of the wounded pouring into their city. At last count there were over ten thousand crowding every available space. Even the grounds around Chimborazo Hospital were covered with men.

Thomas broke into her thoughts. "I did read something today I think you should know," he said almost as a question.

Carrie looked up quickly at the tone of her father's voice. It was obvious he wasn't sure how she would respond to the news. "What is it?"

"I saw the list for soldiers killed in action. Ike Adams was on it."

Carrie gasped and leaned forward. "Ike Adams?" she breathed, her heart pounding with—what? "I thought overseers were exempt from fighting."

"He was no longer an overseer. He was a slave hunter. Conscription claimed him."

"And then death."

Thomas nodded grimly. "I can't say I'm sorry. Not after he betrayed you." His face whitened. "When I think of what could have happened to you . . . "

"But it didn't," Carrie said quickly. Then she grew thoughtful. "I suppose I should say I'm not glad he's dead. But to be honest, I am. He not only tried to hurt me—he hurt a lot of people I care about deeply." She didn't mention Rose and Moses. Her father had forgiven her for helping so many of his slaves escape, but there was no reason to throw it in his face. "I feel sorry for his wife and kids."

"Don't bother," Thomas said abruptly. "I ran into Eulalia the other day on my way to the Capitol. I stopped and talked with her for several minutes. Adams deserted his family months ago—left them to survive on their own."

Carrie frowned. She had been angry with Adams for so long, but now that he was dead she felt a sort of sympathy for a man who would waste his life in hatred and then throw away the one redeeming thing he possessed. "He was a miserable man. I would not wish the kind of eternity he'll have to face on anyone."

"I'm afraid I have not one noble thought in my head for a man such as him. He deserves whatever he gets. I, for one, feel nothing but relief that he is gone."

Carrie sat silently for a few minutes. It seemed unreal that Adams was really dead; the man could no longer pose a threat to her. Not to her. Or Rose. Or Moses. A slow smile spread across her face. "I'm not feeling particularly noble right now either," she said with a smile.

As Thomas chatted on about other things, Carrie continued to think about Adams. Suddenly, words Old Sarah had said about Adams flashed into her mind. *"Why, that be one man who ain't got nothin' but hate poison in his blood. But there ain't been no one born that be that way from the start. No, somethin' done put that poison in him. We prob'ly won't never know what put it there, but it been put there sure 'nuff. You gots to pity a man like that. Now, I be hatin' the things he be doing just as much as anybody else, but it won't be doing my heart no good to be hatin' him. That won't do nothin' but put poison in my own blood. No—I reckon I'll just keep on pitying that poor empty shell of a man."*

Old Sarah, who had more reason to hate than most people, found room in her heart to pity the man who had tried to rape her daughter. Thomas' voice settled into a background drone as Carrie searched her heart until she found what she was looking for. A tiny kernel of pity. As she contemplated Adams' life, the kernel of pity took root and began to grow—crowding out the bitterness. She wouldn't allow bitterness to overtake her. Letting hatred grow would only make her exactly like Adams—a sad, pitiful person. Carrie smiled to herself as she realized Sarah, even though she was dead, had taught her yet another valuable lesson.

"Carrie. Carrie—did you hear what I said?"

Carrie jumped.

Thomas was looking at her, a concerned expression on his face. "Are you all right, dear? I'm afraid I have kept you up far too long. Why don't you go on up to bed?"

Carrie nodded, hugged her father and retreated to her room. She wanted time to think about the new revelation born in her heart.

The sun was already causing a steamy mist to hover over the ground when Carrie walked up the hill to the hospital. She liked the mornings best. For the last week they had proven to be the only time of the day that was quiet. If the familiar pattern repeated itself, the sounds of battle would soon destroy the peaceful day.

Today was proving to be the hottest day of the summer so far. It was barely eight o'clock and there were already rivulets of sweat streaming down her back. Pushing her hair back from her head, she fought down the yearning she had to be home on the plantation with a cool breeze flowing over her. Suddenly she stopped just short of the hospital bridge, stared east for several long moments, then closed her eyes.

Into her mind sprung a picture of her special place. It felt like a lifetime since she had last retreated to the tiny clearing on the James. It came to life in her mind in minute detail. She could almost reach out and touch the water gently lapping at the banks. The low-hanging branches of her oak tree offered protection from the searing sun, while a gentle breeze caused the wildflowers to sway lazily. Waiting for her was her special log where she always thought out her problems.

The rattle of wagon wheels arrested her attention and the picture dissolved. When she opened her eyes she saw an ambulance rolling up the hill bringing another load of wounded soldiers. Carrie shook her head and pushed on. The world was still full of trouble, yet somehow she had been given a brief respite. She hoped it would carry her through another long day.

The scene at the hospital was chaotic. Long into the night wagons had continued to roll in, bringing the newly wounded from the battlefield. Carrie tightened her lips and hurried into her ward. How thankful she was that Dr. McCaw had insisted on adequate ventilation. Even though the heat of the day was already intensifying the odor of infection and putrification, there was at least a tiny breeze flowing in the ample windows. Her ward was on the outer ring of buildings within the compound. Pity swelled in her for the soldiers who had no benefit of even the small breeze. Carrie hurried toward the newest patient, careful not to slip on the gritty sand they used to clean the floors.

"Hello, soldier."

"Hello, ma'am."

Carrie was relieved to hear the answer come back so clearly. She examined him carefully. From the waist up, with the exception of filth and mud, he seemed to be unharmed.

As if reading her mind, he said, "Lieutenant Cabby Marsh, ma'am. One of those Yankees managed to catch my knee with his minie ball. I still got it, though," he grinned. "It may never work again but I kind of like being able to look at it."

"Do you by any chance know Lieutenant Robert Borden? I know it's improbable, but . . . " For some reason, Carrie couldn't fight the compulsion to ask the question.

"Lieutenant Borden? Why, of course I know him," Cabby said with a wide smile. "My family's plantation is just a few miles upriver from Robert's. I've known him all my life."

Carrie was delighted. "Have you seen him—I mean, recently? Do you know if he . . . if he . . . " She couldn't bring herself to say the words.

Cabby grinned up at her. "As of yesterday afternoon your lieutenant was just fine, Miss Cromwell."

"You know who I am?"

"Certainly. Robert talks about you at night when things have calmed down a little and we're trying to get our strength up for the next battle. I'd have known you anywhere. When he found me wounded on the field he told me he hoped I ended up in Chimborazo with the prettiest nurse anywhere. I guess I did."

Carrie laughed, her mind racing. Robert had still been alive yesterday. Just that little bit of news was like a healing balm to her raw nerves. "Thank you, Cabby. That's wonderful news."

A low moan swung her attention to the next bed. Her eyes widened as she took in the pool of blood forming on the sheets. In an instant she was at the soldier's side, her eyes examining the wound.

"The poor fellow caught a ball in his side," Cabby informed her. "They stopped the bleeding earlier, but it looks like it's not going to cooperate."

Carrie set her lips, then walked briskly to find the head nurse. "We have a man bleeding over here. He needs attention."

"Everyone needs attention," the nurse snapped, not unkindly, his tired eyes reflecting the strain he was under. "All the doctors are busy now." When Carrie opened her mouth to protest, he added, "I'll get someone there as quick as I can."

Carrie returned to the soldier and pressed a glass of water into his hand. "Help is on the way," she said gently.

"That's real nice of you, ma'am. I don't reckon I've ever had anything hurt quite so much as this ball in my side. It's making a right smart burning." He stared for a long moment at the blood pooling under his side. "Am I going to bleed to death?" he asked in a deceptively casual tone.

"Of course not!" Carrie answered quickly. Yet, she wasn't so sure. She knew how busy the doctors were. She had no idea how long it would take for someone to come help the man. Resentment chaffed at her as she strained against the restrictions she had been given. She was to offer absolutely no medical help. Her job was to provide comfort and companionship. But how could she provide comfort to a man who was dying right in front of her eyes? That he would die if help didn't arrive soon was obvious. His breath was coming in shallow gasps and his face was turning a chalky gray. A light touch on his clammy arm confirmed her suspicion that shock was rapidly setting in. It appeared that assistance was not imminent.

"You can help him can't you, Miss Cromwell?"

Carrie turned to look at Cabby.

"Robert told me you are going to be a doctor. Why don't you help him?"

"I'm not supposed to," Carrie responded through gritted teeth.

"I don't suppose rules have as much priority as life," he stated in a calm voice, his eyes daring her to defy the authorities.

Carrie stared at him for just a moment, glanced back at the dying man, then sprang into action. Dashing to the table beside the door, she grabbed a handful of linen and sped back to the bed. The soldier offered no protest as she pulled down the sheet and inspected his wound. The two-inch gaping hole was deep and vicious looking. "Have they taken the ball out yet?" When the soldier shook his head, she said gently. "The pressure is going to hurt badly, but we have to stop the bleeding."

"Do what you have to, ma'am," he said weakly.

Carrie folded the linen quickly into a thick pad, placed it directly over the wound, then applied an even pressure. "Can you hold it there for just a moment?" she asked the wounded man. When he complied, she sprang to a nearby shelf and grabbed several blankets. "I know it's hot, soldier, but your body temperature needs to be brought back up." Quickly she tucked the blankets in as much as she could without covering the wound. Then she moved back to his side and continued to put pressure on the wound.

Carrie lost track of how long she had sat there, or how many times she changed the compress after it had become soaked with blood. Finally the bandage she held against it didn't immediately turn bright crimson. Anxiously, she looked at the soldier's face. It was beginning to regain some of its color, and his breathing had become more even. He was still on the edge of shock, but he seemed to be stabilizing.

"What exactly do you think you're doing?"

Carrie started at the sound of the harsh voice over her head.

"I do believe I'm the doctor in this unit. Have you forgotten?"

Carrie flushed, but spoke quietly. "No, sir. This soldier has a wound that was bleeding badly. It needed to be stopped."

"I don't see anything to indicate you are a doctor, Miss . . . "

"Miss Cromwell. No, sir. I'm not a doctor. But I couldn't see letting a man die because someone was too busy to tend to him."

"You thought a man would die from a little bleeding?" the doctor asked in an amused voice.

"People die from shock and loss of blood," Carrie responded firmly, her temper beginning to boil.

The doctor, one she hadn't seen before, regarded her with a patronizing air. "My dear, I'm sure you think your hours in the hospital have equipped you with medical information." His voice hardened. "We have enough to do around here without women meddling where they don't belong. I never wanted women in the hospital anyway, but it seems there was no choice."

Carrie opened her mouth to speak, but he ignored her.

"I'm going to let this go this once. But I don't ever want to hear of you trying to play doctor again. If I do, I'm afraid your services will no longer be welcome here."

Carrie flushed hotly, but before she could say anything, a sharp voice came from behind her.

"See here, doctor. Miss Cromwell was acting out of care and compassion. She believed the man was bleeding to death. He looks so much better since she controlled the bleeding, I believe she was right."

The doctor turned to Cabby angrily. "Thank you for your input, soldier, but it's not needed. Medicine is no place for women. I don't suppose you would want some flighty woman working on your wounds, now, would you?"

"I wouldn't mind any woman who had enough sense to save my life," Cabby retorted.

The doctor snorted and turned his back on him. He renewed his attack on Carrie. "I mean what I said. Any more medical attention and you'll need to find yourself another position. Am I understood?"

Carrie nodded, struggling to stem the tide of angry words waiting to erupt from her mouth. She couldn't trust herself to be civil, so she chose to remain silent.

The doctor nodded sternly, satisfied he had made his point, leaned forward to inspect the wounded soldier, then stalked out. Minutes later the young soldier was on a stretcher, headed for surgery to remove the ball.

"Thank you, ma'am," he whispered, reaching for Carrie's hand. "I sure appreciate what you did."

Carrie nodded and squeezed his hand. "Good luck," she said tenderly.

The long morning passed slowly. Around two o'clock the familiar sounds of battle wafted in the open windows. Carrie sighed in resignation and continued working. Her heart felt bruised from her encounter with the doctor that morning. Questioning had revealed his identity to be a Dr. Dole from Mississippi. From all she could tell he was a competent doctor. Sternly, she pushed away the hurt she felt. It had been clear from the beginning that being a doctor was going to be a long, hard, uphill battle. If she let every obstacle she came up against hurt her, she would soon be immobilized.

As the day wore on, heat and humidity draped a blanket of misery over the hospital. Black flies swarmed over everything, creating misery for patients and staff alike. Cries for water rose like a cloud. Men already dehydrated from dysentery and typhoid fever, contracted after drinking bad water in the camps, could not get enough liquid. Carrie prayed for a storm to bring relief to the tortured men.

The sun was setting when Carrie stepped outside for a few minutes. Hunger pains were stabbing at her, but she chose to ignore them. All she wanted was a few minutes of fresh air. Or at least a change from the stale, reeking odors of the ward. There was very little fresh air in Richmond anymore. Moving to the edge of the clearing, she glanced down at the river and the boats crowding it. She ran her hands up her face, massaging her throbbing temples, then stopped to stare at her filthy fingernails in disgust. She washed her hands often, but there was no way to keep blood and dirt from becoming embedded in them.

"Ma'am?"

Carrie spun as a weak cry sounded behind her. An ambulance wagon with four young men had been parked under a shady oak tree. Black flies were crawling everywhere. Quickly she sprang to the side of the wagon.

"Can you help us, ma'am?"

"The doctor will be here in a few minutes," she said soothingly.

The soldier grimaced. "I sure hope so. We been out here for a bunch of hours. Not sure how many."

"A bunch of hours?" Carrie gasped, looking around frantically. "What did they tell you?"

"Just that they were real busy but would get to us as soon as they could. I think they were trying to find somewhere to put us. I guess things are pretty full. I reckon they could have forgot about us."

Carrie stared at him, trying to think. "I'll be right back," she said abruptly. Finding a doctor, she told him the dilemma. His face crinkled in sympathy but he merely shook his head. "I'm on my way into surgery, miss."

"But surely those men don't have to just lie outside in that wagon," she protested. "Have they been forgotten?"

The doctor shrugged. "I don't think so, but I don't really know. We're all doing the best we can," he said wearily. "Someone will get to them. That wagon isn't so bad. At least they're not crammed into a ward."

"But what about their wounds? What if one of them dies?"

The doctor nodded grimly. "Then the poor beggar will probably be better off." His face softened. "I'm sorry, ma'am. I can't help now. Ask someone else." Having said all he was going to, he moved on.

Carrie looked around desperately, wondering what to do. Several more attempts netted much the same result. Finally she made her way back to the wagon.

"Is someone coming, ma'am?"

"They'll be here as soon as they can," she said, trying to sound encouraging. "In the meantime, I've brought you some water." Hands reached forward eagerly. Carrie gave them their fill, then looked off toward the hospital, willing someone to notice and come help. The sky turned a darker blue as the sun slipped beneath a bank of purple clouds on the horizon.

"Are we going to be out here all night, ma'am?"

Carrie shook her head but she had no idea if she was telling the truth. Her earlier look into the wagon had told her there was much she could do to help. She didn't know the full extent of their injuries, but surely she could alleviate some of their suffering. As she contemplated the possibility, it was as if a great fog settled on her mind.

Somewhere, in the midst of all the fatigue and pain, Carrie had begun to doubt herself. Anyone who gets lost in the fog rarely even notices its encroachment. It comes on gradually, the sum total of many small uncertainties that hardly seem worth a second thought. There is a little patch of mist here, another patch farther over. There is a slow thickening of the haze along the horizon as the sky turns gray and sags lower toward the trees. Sunlight fades out imperceptibly, until suddenly there is a fog everywhere, blanketing everything within its reach. The noises coming from the shrouded landscape are unidentifiable, confusing and full of menace. Carrie was losing herself in the fog. Little doubts had crept into being, had grown, waiting for some quick shock to jar all of them into one disastrous uncertainty.

Carrie trembled as the doubts rampaged through her mind. She had been so sure she had helped that young soldier earlier in the morning. Yet he had died several hours after surgery. The doctor— striding through in the afternoon—had stared at her as if it were her fault. Maybe it was. Maybe she was never meant to be a doctor. Maybe she could not really help people. Doubts assailed her, threatening to crush her confidence.

The young spokesman for the group persisted, his voice weaker this time. "Are you sure someone is coming?"

Carrie turned to look into his eyes again. She saw hope, a hope that refused to die even in the midst of horror and pain. Time seemed to stand still as the frail hope seemed to reach out for her, seeking a way into her own heart. Struggling against her fear, Carrie let his hope become hers. She clung to the courage it offered. Suddenly she knew what she had to do. She might not save these men. She might even make things worse. But at least they would know someone cared. At least they would not die alone and frightened in a wagon.

"I'm going to help you," she said firmly. "I don't know when anyone will be coming," she admitted, stepping closer. "Will you let me help you?" Her voice was strong now.

The soldier nodded gratefully. "Anything you can do would be much appreciated."

Carrie asked pointed questions, discovering that between the four men there were two broken legs, a broken arm, eight bullet wounds, and two cases of dysentery. Two of the men had raging fevers. One was completely unresponsive, even though he was conscious. She thought longingly of the herbs at home, knowing she could not just waltz into the hospital to request medicine. "I'll be right back."

More wagons rolled up the hill as the bedlam of war kept its frenetic pace. No one even noticed when she grabbed bandages, a pail of water, some blankets, and splints. She hoped she looked like she was just carrying them to a ward. In minutes she was back at the wagon. Tossing the supplies inside, she climbed in and set to work.

She started with the man who had called her over. "What's your name?"

"Angus McFarley, ma'am."

"Well, Angus McFarley, we need to get some of these wounds cleaned up." Dipping a bandage in water, Carrie gently washed the grime and dirt away from the bullet wounds. She winced at the red flesh; signs of infection were already surrounding the area. It did no good to wish for powdered charcoal and turpentine spirits to treat the injuries. That would have to be done by someone with access to the medicine. In the meantime, she could make sure they were clean.

Once done with that, she turned to his leg. By its awkward angle she knew it was badly broken. She probed gently with her fingers, trying to ascertain the kind of break. "It feels like a clean break, Mr. McFarley. I can set it for you." She paused, looking at him squarely. "Or you can wait for a doctor."

Angus returned her look evenly. "Well, ma'am, I have to tell you I've never had a woman doctoring on me before, but you've done a fine job so far. There's no telling how long I'll have to wait for a real doctor. I reckon you better go ahead. It's hurting me pretty bad."

Carrie nodded crisply and repositioned herself in the wagon. If she was going to get tossed out of the hospital she might as well go out with a bang of glory. She had just grabbed hold of his foot and braced her back against the side of the wagon when a voice exploded in her ear.

"What the devil is going on here?"

~Nine~

*C*arrie didn't even look up. "I would say it's rather obvious that I'm getting ready to set a leg." With a mighty heave, she pulled with all her strength. She heard a satisfying snap at just the same moment Angus cried out in pain. Only then did she look up. "Would you like to help me splint it—doctor?" She almost groaned when she saw the surgeon's insignia on the young doctor's shirt, but she had known when she began that she was taking the chance of being discovered and tossed from the hospital. It was a risk she had chosen to take. At least now the remaining men would get the attention they needed.

"You seem to know what you're doing. I'll watch."

Carrie glanced up in amazement, then tightened her lips and went to work. He was probably waiting for her to make a mistake. Well, he was going to be disappointed. Positioning the splint carefully, she wrapped bandages around it until it was secure. Only when she was certain the bone wouldn't shift did she settle back. "They'll set it in plaster of paris later, Angus. This will do for now."

"Thank you, ma'am," Angus said fervently. "What can you do for the other fellows?"

Carrie sat quietly, waiting for the watching doctor to speak. When he said nothing, she decided to press on. This may be her only chance to treat patients until this war was over and she could go North to medical school. She was not going to waste time wondering what some doctor was thinking.

"Those two with the dysentery—they've been real sick, running a real high fever. Can you do something?"

"I'm afraid not, Angus. Not without the proper medicine. All I can do is make them more comfortable until they get inside the hospital."

"What kind of medicine would you be prescribing?"

Carrie finally turned and took her first good look at the doctor. Grudgingly, she had to admit she liked what she saw. He wasn't handsome, but the life in his eyes made him attractive. A thick thatch of red hair framed a pair of dancing green eyes. That explained the slight Irish brogue she detected. Tiny lines around his eyes betrayed the man's penchant for laughter. "I hope you're asking because you intend to help these men." She paused. "I would suggest a powder composed of five grains of the mercury and chalk of the pharmacopoeia, six grains of Dover's powder, and two grains of sulphate of quina. It should be administered several times a day until they begin to recover."

"I'll get it," he said with a smile. "You set the other leg." Turning, he walked quickly back to the hospital.

Carrie suppressed her amazement and went back to work. She would try to figure it all out later. Right now she had a job to do. Her hands were tender but strong as she probed the leg of the man who was completely unresponsive. Somehow he was managing to keep his eyes open, but they were the eyes of a staring zombie. The pain of his fractured leg, combined with two bullet wounds and dysentery, had obviously overwhelmed him. Carrie's heart swelled with sympathy. Her examination revealed that his leg was badly fractured, a jagged, splintered break that would not respond well to setting. It would be too easy for a piece of bone to cut into muscle or a blood vessel. Straightening the leg as best she could, she placed a splint around it and wrapped it carefully. It would take a skillful surgeon to save his life. With the workload surgeons were under now, he would no doubt lose his leg. Even under the best of circumstances it would be difficult to save.

She had just finished the bandaging when the young doctor once more appeared at her side. He watched her quietly for a few moments as she carefully cleaned the soldiers' wounds.

"Would you like some help?" he finally asked in an admiring voice.

"Yes. Thank you," she said in surprise. "Did you get the medicine?" When he nodded, she smiled in relief. "This soldier needs some. So does the one leaning against the back. He has two bullet wounds in his left arm. They look pretty bad."

The two worked silently until all the men had been treated and stabilized. Carrie had just settled back against the wagon when a group of men with stretchers moved toward it.

"I told them we should be done about this time. They are here to take the men into the hospital. I arranged for some beds for them."

Carrie's heart swelled with gratitude. "Thank you, Doctor . . . ?"

"My name is Dr. Wild. Michael Wild." He managed a tired smile. "And you are?"

"Carrie Cromwell." Stepping out of the wagon, Carrie moved to the side to make room for the men who were approaching the wagon. They looked with surprise at the blood splattering her dress, but no one said anything.

Except for Angus McFarley. "Thank you, ma'am. You make a mighty fine doctor."

Carrie smiled at him gently. "Thank you, Angus. I hope you get well soon." Then they were all gone. She looked up at the sky, the first stars beginning to twinkle. On the horizon was a dark bank of clouds. Carrie hoped it meant rain.

"Where did you learn how to do all that?" Dr. Wild asked quietly.

"I learned some of it from my mother. Some from a slave on our family plantation. Some from medical books."

"How did you know about the medicine for dysentery? That's a fairly recent discovery. Not even all the doctors here know it."

Carrie shrugged, feeling a small thrill of satisfaction. "Most things can be learned by reading."

"Yes . . . " Dr. Wild said thoughtfully. "For those who care enough to want to know. You obviously care a great deal."

Carrie decided to be honest. She was much too tired to play games. "I want to be a doctor, Dr. Wild," she said, looking him straight in the eyes. "I realize what most of the country thinks of women in medicine. I know especially what the South thinks of women in medicine. That doesn't change the fact that I'm going to be a doctor. People will just have to get used to it," she added bluntly.

She was astonished when Dr. Wild threw back his head and laughed. "I like you, Carrie Cromwell. You remind me of a friend of mine—Ann Preston."

"Ann Preston?" Carrie gasped. "Why, she is a professor of physiology at The Female Medical College of Philadelphia. She has had a tremendous impact on the school since graduating from there in 1852."

"Right on all counts."

Carrie could feel herself relax. She may still be dismissed from her work, but it probably was not going to be by Dr. Wild. "You went to school in the North?"

"They had the best schools in the country at the time. I practiced medicine in Raleigh, North Carolina, until the war started. Dr. McCaw asked me to join him here." Dr. Wild leaned back against the wagon, stretching his arms over his head. "Once this war is over, I hope to never again have to treat the kind of things I've had to treat here," he said brusquely.

"I've never seen anything so horrible," Carrie stated. "It breaks my heart to think it's Americans who are mutilating other Americans."

"Do I detect a lack of sympathy for our noble cause?"

Carrie paused. She knew many Southern citizens had been jailed for their anti-war feelings. "Let's just say I'm very sorry there are powerful men willing to sacrifice the lives of so many fine men to fulfill their own selfish aims."

Even in the darkness, she could see the surprise on the doctor's face. Maybe it was the shroud of night that was giving her such boldness. Or maybe it was because she was too exhausted to care.

"You're a woman who speaks her mind, Miss Carrie Cromwell."

"Guilty on all counts," she said, laughing slightly. Suddenly all she wanted was to go home. "Now, if you don't mind, Dr. Wild, if you are going to throw me off the hospital grounds and tell me never to come back, I wish you would go ahead and do it."

This time Dr. Wild laughed out loud. "Why would I do that?"

Carrie told him the story of what had happened that morning. "And yet you still treated those men?"

"I couldn't see letting them suffer any longer. I decided I was willing to take the consequences."

"Even if the consequence is moving to another ward?"

Carrie looked at him closely but the darkness made his face indistinguishable. "What are you talking about?"

Dr. Wild was all seriousness now. "Miss Cromwell, this war is going to go on for a long time, I'm afraid. The medical community is simply going to have to lose its distaste for women in medicine. They'll be forced to when there are no longer males to do the job. I prefer to think of myself as a little more progressive than the rest of the men around me. My years in the North helped give me that advantage." He paused. "I'd like to request that you be moved into my ward. I could use your help."

Carrie sat silently, too stunned by this new course of events to know what to say.

"You won't, of course, be able to operate as a full doctor. But you will find you have many liberties, while still working under my orders. There are a great many doctors who are a mockery to their profession. I would welcome you as an addition to my staff."

"Thank you," Carrie finally stammered.

"You'll do it, then?" Dr. Wild sounded relieved.

It was almost laughable to think that she would turn down such an opportunity. "I would love to, Dr. Wild. Thank you," she repeated.

"Good!" Dr. Wild exclaimed. "By the way, how long has it been since you've taken a day off?"

Carrie shrugged. "A few weeks, I guess. I haven't really considered a day off important when so many are suffering."

"Nonsense! You can't give your best when you're completely drained. I learned that a long time ago. I don't want to see you back here until day after tomorrow. Now go home and get some rest. You must be exhausted."

Carrie knew just exactly how exhausted she was. Every part of her body ached. Yet none of it mattered now. She was taking a giant step in pursuing her dream. She had gambled and won—won something she had not even imagined.

Carrie had not seen her father for two days when he burst through the door, excitement exploding on his face. She had been asleep when he had come in for a few hours of rest the night before.

"It's over!" he exclaimed. "McClellan has been beaten back. His whole army is in full retreat now. Richmond is safe."

"What grand news!" Carrie exclaimed.

"How far are they from the city?" Janie asked from where she was lounging in a chair directly across from Carrie.

Thomas frowned at that question. "McClellan has set up a base at Harrison Landing."

"Harrison Landing?" Carrie asked. She thought for a moment. "That's at Berkeley Plantation, isn't it?" Her heart sank at the thought of what destruction a hundred thousand men could wreak on the lovely plantation situated high on a hill overlooking the James River.

"I'm afraid so, Carrie."

There was something in his voice that caused Carrie to look at him closely. "Are you worried about home?" she asked.

"I would be foolish not to realize Cromwell Plantation may be harmed by the Federals. They don't seem to have much regard for property belonging to men in Confederate leadership." He paused, then continued in a bitter voice, "Edmund Ruffin and I have not seen eye to eye for a while but I would never wish on someone what has happened to his beloved plantation."

"What are you talking about?"

"The Yankees have destroyed it. His home has been burned, his trees cut—even his fences have been pulled up and burned. But it's what they have done to his fields that has hurt him the most. His lovely fields have all been salted. After years of using them for agricultural experiments that benefited us all, they have been destroyed."

"Salted?" Janie gasped. "Why, it will be years before they will be suitable for use again. Are they doing that everywhere?"

"Thankfully, no," Thomas replied grimly. "At least not yet. I'm sure the Yankees were well aware of who that plantation belonged to. I imagine it was their way of evening the score."

"But why would they target Mr. Ruffin?" Janie asked.

"He was a very outspoken secessionist," Carrie replied. "He also claims to have fired the first shot of the war. Even at age seventy-eight, he is still eager to join the battle." She turned back to her father. "Surely they won't do the same thing to Cromwell. You have no such notoriety."

"I have long ago given up trying to guess what the Federals will, or won't, do. I never thought they would actually invade our country and try to rob us of the freedom that is rightly ours."

Carrie gazed at her father, saddened at the bitterness oozing from his voice. Now was not the time to remind him that the South had been robbing millions of slaves of the freedom rightfully theirs, for years. She was learning that people found it very easy to only be concerned with the part of the picture that affected them. The rest didn't matter so much if it didn't touch their pocketbooks directly. "Our home is many miles from Berkeley. The Union army has already stripped it of food. Maybe they won't even go near it." She paused, searching for a way to take her father's mind off his home. "What happened in the battle today?" She immediately regretted the question when she saw his face darken.

"They fought at Malvern Hill. McClellan is indeed in full retreat but I'm afraid the cost of victory has been incredibly high today."

Carrie felt the familiar sickness tighten her stomach.

"How many?" Janie asked quietly, her voice reflecting the agony Carrie was feeling.

"The Federals were firmly entrenched on Malvern Hill, fighting hard to give the rest of the army time to retreat. Our artillery was simply no match for theirs. "

"We heard the guns," Carrie said. "They seemed much louder today, yet I know the battle was not any closer."

Thomas shook his head. "You heard the Union gunboats joining in the fight. Their immense guns make field artillery seem like nothing. I heard men saying they were so loud they literally shook the water."

"So how many?" Janie repeated quietly.

"They were too entrenched," Thomas said again, the pain evident in his voice. "Lee's attacks were cut down time and time again." He paused a long moment. "There were over five thousand casualties."

Carrie groaned and covered her face with her hands. "In one day? Several hours?" Five thousand men—dead, wounded, or missing. The horror of it washed over her in waves. Once again stark fear for Robert raised its head, mocking her earlier confidence. Would this tug-of-war never end?

"And you call that a victory?" Janie asked in a strained voice.

Thomas shook his head again wearily. "It can be counted as nothing but a defeat, but McClellan is still in full retreat. The danger is over."

"Why is McClellan retreating after winning the battle?"

"I have no idea, Janie. I can only theorize based on what I have heard. McClellan never expected Lee to go on the defensive. I believe Lee's actions completely demoralized him. He could no longer have the glorious victory he had envisioned for so long, so he decided to just give the whole thing up."

"Do you think he'll be back?" Carrie managed to ask.

"I don't think the Union will give up its goal of taking Richmond, but I don't believe it will be McClellan leading the army. I have gotten my hands on enough Northern newspapers to realize President Lincoln, along with much of the North, is fed up with their general. No, I think Richmond is safe for a time."

Carrie stared out the window for a long minute. "Do you realize the last seven days have cost the South almost twenty thousand men? Why, from what you have told me that is more than twenty percent of Lee's entire army."

A weary acknowledgement washed over Thomas' face. "The cost has been horrible," he agreed. "But, for now the city is safe."

Carrie suddenly realized her father was hanging on for dear life to the one reality that gave him hope. No matter what the cost, Richmond had been saved. The dead would be buried, the wounded treated—and the South would fight on. If the war was to continue it was necessary for those leading each side to see the casualties as numbers—not young men who would never return home to be fathers, husbands, and sons. "I need some fresh air," she said abruptly.

Rising from her chair, she hurried outside. She could understand what her father was feeling, but it still left her sickened. She wished he would come spend a few days in the hospital. Maybe then he would feel differently, yet somehow she doubted it. It was impossible to live in Richmond and not be aware of the suffering. The streets were crowded with the wounded, and stacks of dead soldiers lined the train platforms. You had to be deaf, dumb, and blind to not see the cost of the war.

Carrie stared out into the darkness. How did people become so immune to suffering? How could any cause be worth what was being seen every day? Slowly, an understanding crept into her heart. The time for a quick end to the war had long passed. The passions that had fueled the initial explosion might be waning, but the fire was pushing on, fed by the growing hatred and bitterness of a war that was devastating forever the face of the nation. The war had taken on a life of its own—the people were simply being pulled along in its trail of fire—trying to survive in the charred remnants of its path.

Her father was simply doing what everyone else was doing—struggling to survive. Carrie's heart tightened at the helplessness her father must be feeling—he was losing everything he had worked all of his life to build. His pain from Abigail's death might have kept him away from Cromwell Plantation for the last year and a half, but his heart was still firmly entrenched there. The plantation was his home, his life. Gradually, as fog retreating before the rising sun, her anger at her father dissipated, compassion taking its place. They didn't have to agree with each other, but love demanded she at least try to understand him. Suddenly she was eager to be back inside. She hadn't even told him about her encounter with Dr. Wild. Smiling, she turned toward the door, stopping at the window for a moment to study his anxious face as he sat talking quietly with Janie.

"Carrie!"

A sudden shout from down the road arrested her in her tracks. She turned slowly, then burst into laughter and flew from the porch, her blue dress flying behind her. "Robert!"

Robert pushed Granite into a fast gallop, vaulting off as soon as he reached the gate leading into the yard. In an instant Carrie was in his arms, laughing and crying all at the same time. Just to feel him, just to know he was alive, was enough. There was no need for words.

"Robert. You're home safe!" Thomas' voice boomed out into the night.

Carrie pulled away, staring up into Robert's face. "Come inside. You must be exhausted." Robert obeyed with no comment. Not until Carrie reached the light of the house was she able to see him clearly. The same haunted, pain-stricken look she had seen before was still in his eyes. Her heart constricted as she gently led him to the couch and sat down next to him. He looked tired—and older than when she had seen him last. Carrie knew she had no way to fully understand what he had endured in the last week. She heard ghastly stories from the soldiers she cared for, but hearing a story and being there were two very different things.

Thomas stared at him for a long minute. "You're exhausted," he said simply. "I was going to ask questions. They'll keep."

"I'm very glad you're home, Robert," Janie said softly. "I'm going up to bed now."

Carrie turned to Robert as Thomas nodded, then followed Janie up the stairs. Robert's hands were trembling slightly as Carrie gathered them in hers and gazed into his tortured dark eyes. He stared at her until, with a moan, he laid his head on her shoulder. Carrie wrapped her arms around him, holding him close. She had no idea how long they sat there before a low rumble of thunder and a brisk wind blowing through the open windows caused him to draw back. Still he did not speak. Instead, he cradled Carrie's head between his hands, devouring her with his eyes.

Carrie wanted to cry at the anguish she saw stamped on every feature. Instead, she poured all the love she could into her eyes. Slowly, very slowly, she saw some of the pain begin to ebb. Only then did she speak. "I love you, Lieutenant Robert Borden. Thank God you're home."

"And I love you, Carrie Cromwell," Robert said huskily, tears causing his eyes to shine. "Knowing I have you is all that keeps me going sometimes," he said softly, the shadows in his eyes deepening.

Carrie understood. He was afraid she was going to ask him questions and he wasn't ready to talk. "Your friend Cabby is doing well."

Robert stared at her. "Cabby? Cabby Marsh? You've seen him?"

"Seen him? Why, he's one of my favorite patients," Carrie said cheerfully.

"Did he . . . I mean, does he . . . ?"

"Still have his leg? You bet he does!" Carrie smiled at the look of relief on Robert's face. He needed some good news. "His knee will never be the same, but the doctors managed to save his leg. He's already moving around on crutches. At least he was when I last saw him two days ago."

"You mean he was up the same day they brought him in?" Robert asked in amazement.

"He's a remarkable man. He said he wasn't going to give the Yankees the satisfaction of keeping him down."

Robert smiled at that. "Sounds like Cabby, all right." Then his eyes darkened again. "It was terrible . . . " he said slowly. "Every day when the fighting was over, the battlefield turned into a scene straight from hell. Bodies were writhing and convulsing as far as the eye could see. Screams and cries could be heard all through the night . . ."

Carrie held his hands tightly, letting him talk.

"I don't know why I'm still alive. So many friends died. I watched them die," he muttered thickly.

Carrie squeezed his hands tightly. Robert looked up at her but his eyes weren't seeing her; they were seeing memories too awful for words. "No more," she said softly. "You're here with me now."

Robert started slightly, then his eyes seemed to focus on her again. His breathing slowed and his face regained some of its color. "I'm sorry."

"Don't be sorry. You'll carry those memories all your life. But when they reach up to grab you, you have to remember where you are. Pain can pull you down so far it will destroy your hope and your reason to live."

Robert pulled back. "And just where did you get such wisdom?" he demanded in a genuinely surprised voice.

"From Aunt Sarah," Carrie said. "That lady carried more pain than most people."

"One of your father's slaves?"

Carrie nodded, relieved to hear Robert's tone of voice. There was no anger; it was more a curious statement of fact. She had determined to let God work on Robert's heart when it came to the divisive issue of slavery. "I have wonderful news," she went on, changing the subject.

"I could use some good news about now," Robert said, smiling.

Carrie was thankful for his smile. Trying not to leave out any details, she told him everything that had happened at the hospital the day before. "I'm going to be working with Dr. Wild when I return tomorrow," she finished.

Robert stared at her in amazement, then shook his head. "I knew you were going to make it as a doctor," he said admiringly.

"Well, I'm hardly a doctor yet!" Carrie protested.

"It's the step you needed," Robert said firmly. "Now you'll have the opportunity to show them what you know."

"And the opportunity to learn even more," Carrie agreed with a laugh, her heart suddenly light. How she had wanted to share the good news with Robert. She hadn't even had a chance to tell her father.

"I want to do something fun."

Carrie was surprised by the sudden change of topic. "What do you have in mind?" she asked, amused.

"There's a party tomorrow night. They're calling them starvation dances. Would you like to go?"

Carrie struggled with her answer. The idea of a party in the midst of such suffering seemed a ludicrous thought. Yet, Robert surely needed something to divert his mind. "I'd love to," she finally said.

"Wonderful!" Robert leaned forward and kissed her gently. "Do you mind if I answer any questions tomorrow after I've had some sleep?"

"You don't ever have to answer questions if you don't want to," Carrie said softly, remembering the haunted look in his eyes.

Robert gazed down at her for a moment, then drew her into his arms. "I'm not sure what I did to deserve you," he said gruffly. Then he lowered his lips to hers gently.

Carrie was the one to draw back first even though she longed to stay forever in his arms. "Go get some rest, lieutenant. That's an order."

Ten

*C*arrie was dressed and waiting when Robert arrived the next evening.

"You look lovely," Robert said, his eyes lighting with approval. "Someone told me the ladies in Richmond no longer had party dresses."

"It's the only one I saved," Carrie admitted. "It's the one—"

"You were wearing the night we first danced," he interrupted. "At the Blackwell Ball. I remember."

"I just couldn't bring myself to have it turned into bandages or something. It is too special."

Robert leaned down to kiss her softly. "I'm glad." Then he stepped back. "You don't look as if you spent a long day at the hospital."

"I'm glad I don't look it. Unfortunately, I *feel* very much like it. But it's a different kind of feeling," Carrie said with a bright shine in her eyes. "Now I actually feel as if I'm making a real difference. Oh, I know the soldiers appreciated everything I did before, but . . . " She paused trying to think of the right words. "Dr. Wild is wonderful about giving me real responsibilities. He seems to trust me. There's just something about looking at a wounded soldier and knowing that because I did the right thing he probably is going to live." Then she laughed self-consciously. "Not that I did any major life saving today. It's just knowing I have the freedom." Suddenly she laughed again. "I don't know how to put what I'm feeling into words. All I know is that I loved it—every single minute of this long, exhausting day. I loved it!" Abruptly, she clapped her hand to her mouth.

"What is it, Carrie?" Robert asked in an alarmed voice.

"Did you hear what I said?" Carrie was horrified with herself. "How can I say I loved it when every man I saw today was suffering terribly. How completely selfish!"

"What rubbish," Robert snorted. "You weren't loving their suffering. You were loving the ability to help them. If it were up to you this war would have ended yesterday."

Carrie looked at him quickly. "Does that bother you?"

"You mean, do I think you are disloyal? No. I know where you stand, Carrie. You know where I stand." He paused. "Only I'm not sure where I stand anymore. I still think the Southern cause is a just one and I will fight this war with everything in me, but . . . " He paused for a long minute, staring off into the distance. "Hindsight is twenty-twenty I guess. I think if anyone could have seen what all of this was going to mean there would have been much greater effort to insure it never happened in the first place. I guess you don't fully understand the horrors of something until you're in the middle of it. The sad thing is that too many times it's too late to back out." Robert took a deep breath. "No, I'm afraid the only way out of this is forward. We must press on to victory or we have indeed lost everything. It is impossible to go backward and undo the past. All you can do is live with the present and try to make the best of the future."

Carrie watched him thoughtfully as he spoke. "You have been doing a great deal of thinking," she observed.

"There is little else to do when you're lying in camp during the nights. When there is nothing distracting your thoughts it is much easier to think clearly. One thing I have decided—never again will I allow myself to be so caught up in the events of my world and my activities that I lose contact with my own heart and mind. All of my achievements mean nothing if I lose myself in the process." Robert looked at Carrie. "What is that funny look on your face?"

"That funny look is my attempt to contain the swelling of my heart," Carrie said softly. "It is expanding with love right now."

Robert took her in his arms. "I recognize that feeling," he said tenderly. He held her for a long moment, then stepped back. "Are you ready to go dancing?" he asked with a quick grin.

"Absolutely!" She had decided for this one night to push back all thoughts of the men in the hospital. She had a very much alive soldier here, right now, who needed some rest and relaxation before he headed back into battle. "Father is going to be there as well. Janie is accompanying one of the doctors from the hospital. It seems like the whole town is in a celebrating mood now that McClellan is not camped outside our gates."

Robert laid a finger on her lips. "Not a word about the war," he said firmly. "Tonight I am simply a Southern gentleman escorting the most beautiful woman in Richmond to a dance."

Carrie curtsied gracefully. "And I am merely a demure Southern belle meekly accompanying my dashing Southern gentleman," she responded sweetly.

Robert shouted with laughter. "There is, I'm afraid, nothing either demure or meek about you, my dear."

"Just so you're not surprised," Carrie said impishly.

Their laughter and banter continued all the way to the Hobson mansion. Carrie was surprised at the number of people mounting the steps to the graceful home on Franklin Street. Relieved smiles and cheerful talk rose as testimony to the vanquished Union Army. At least for tonight everyone would pretend the war was over.

Carrie had long admired the three-story structure surrounded by oak trees and dogwoods. An explosion of flowers bordered the yard and the sidewalk leading up to the stately stairs framed with wrought iron. She had been to a party here before, just after the war had started. Sumptuous buffets of food and beverages had flowed as liberally as the music and dancing.

She and Robert performed their greetings, then wandered inside, pulled along by the music emanating from the large ballroom. Robert nodded genially to several people as they passed through but he didn't stop. Carrie gazed around as they eased through the crowd. What she had heard about the starvation parties was true. There was not a morsel of food in sight and the only beverage looked to be a very watered-down lemonade. She could feel herself relax even more. It was a relief to know valuable resources weren't being lavishly wasted. Tonight she would let herself enjoy the party.

"May I have this dance, beautiful lady?"

Carrie moved willingly into Robert's arms. "I thought you'd never ask." The old magic rose up to capture them as soon as they glided onto the dance floor. Faces blurred as they waltzed gracefully around the room. All she could see was Robert. All she could feel were his arms. All she could hear was the music carrying them, lifting them to heights she had been hungry for. Everything else faded from her mind—the war, the hospital, the future. There was just now—and Robert.

They had danced through several songs before Robert leaned down to talk softly. "Now do you know why I wanted to come?"

Carrie smiled up at him. "Yes, sir. I do." She grew thoughtful. "When you can find no reason to celebrate—you need to find one anyway."

"You learn well, Carrie Cromwell," Robert laughed.

"I've always said my daughter was extremely bright," an amused voice broke in. "Might I have this dance, my dear?"

"I would be delighted, Father," Carrie replied, stepping back from Robert and raising her arms to her father.

"I do believe the Virginia Reel is next," he teased. "Do you need a break?"

"Hardly!" she retorted. "Unless of course you're afraid you can't handle it."

Thomas winked over her shoulder at Robert and swept her onto the floor. "Just try to keep up, my dear!"

Carrie was laughing and out of breath when the music finally slowed and stopped. "Drink! I need something to drink," she begged.

"Not bad for an old man, eh?"

"That was no old man I was dancing with," she replied. She was thrilled to see laughter and light in her father's eyes again. As her father disappeared to get some lemonade, she glanced around for Robert. She finally saw his dark hair rising above a knot of uniformed men standing near the fireplace. Just then he looked up and caught her eye. A thrill rushed through her at the look of love he shot across the room. She could still hardly believe this man loved her. Suddenly she tensed. There was something on his face that had not been there a few minutes ago.

"Here you are, my dear."

"Thank you," Carrie murmured, tearing her eyes away from Robert. They could talk later. She searched her suddenly anxious mind for something to talk about with her father. He saved her.

"I hope you don't mind if I join some of my colleagues on the porch."

"Of course not. I was just thinking I would like some time to engage in people watching," Carrie replied quickly. She was relieved when her father melted into the crowd.

"Well, if it isn't Carrie Cromwell."

Carrie tried to control a groan from escaping her lips as she pasted on a smile and turned. "Why, Louisa Blackwell. What a surprise!" She was sure her feigned pleasure was not extremely successful. Why tonight of all nights? Oh, she had known Louisa was in the city, pushed from her plantation by invading Union troops along with everyone else. Their childhood pretense of friendship had faded long ago. They would be cordial if protocol demanded, but they made no effort to seek out each other's company. Carrie didn't know why Louisa had become so bitter and ill-tempered, but she *had* learned it was to her benefit to stay out of her way.

"I had heard you were in Richmond," Louisa simpered, her blond hair immaculately styled as always. "Whatever are you doing with yourself?"

Carrie was sure from the look in Louisa's calculating blue eyes that she knew already. "Just doing my part for the war effort," she said casually, trying to figure out a way to escape. A quick look over Louisa's shoulder told her Robert was still engaged in deep conversation.

"Why, I'm surprised to hear that!" Louisa exclaimed.

Carrie regarded her evenly, but didn't respond.

"Really, Carrie, how can you help the South when you've done so much to harm it already?" Louisa's tone sharpened. "Setting your daddy's slaves free was hardly a way to help the war effort!"

Carrie could feel her temper rising along with Louisa's voice.

Louisa wasn't done. "I understand your daddy's plantation has not been harmed. Poor Edmund Ruffin has suffered such a terrible loss. Imagine that. Your daddy's plantation is so close to his." She paused, letting the drama build, then she dropped her finale. "I don't suppose, though, that the North would hurt someone who is helping their own cause. Lucky for your poor daddy that he has a Yankee traitor in the family."

"That is ridiculous!" Carrie gasped angrily, suddenly aware of people leaning forward to catch the conversation. She was so furious she couldn't think straight.

"It certainly is ridiculous," a stern voice boomed over her shoulder.

Carrie felt a rush of relief as Robert's hand settled on her shoulder.

"I'm sorry, Miss Blackwell, that you have so little to do with your time that you find it necessary to spread erroneous propaganda." Robert's voice was calm, but the edge in it made Carrie shiver. "I'm sure your little sewing circles keep you busy, but I think you'll need to find someone else to devour with your gossip. Carrie happens to spend all of her days and most of her evenings at Chimborazo Hospital ministering to the needs of the wounded. I hardly think those are the actions of a traitor."

Carrie watched as the anger in Louisa's eyes turned to red-faced embarrassment. She was being made to look ridiculous—in the past that had only served to make her more dangerous.

"Oh, really," she drawled. "And do you call setting all her daddy's slaves free the act of a genuine Rebel? I even understand she wants to see *all* slaves set free."

Robert ignored the rising swell of comments from the growing circle of observers. "I understand," he replied firmly, "that when you own slaves you are free to do with them what you want. Is that not why we're at war, Miss Blackwell? To guarantee ourselves the right to run our lives and affairs the way we see fit—without intervention?" He paused, but gave her no opportunity to reply. "What Miss Cromwell does with her family's slaves is hardly any concern of yours. And her personal feelings about slavery are not anyone's business. She is giving everything she has to alleviate the suffering in our city. I would think that is all anyone would need to know." Robert smiled slightly and took Carrie's hand. "Now, if you'll excuse us."

Louisa wasn't done, however. "Well, of course. I would never want to stand in the way of anyone who wishes to escort a slave lover!"

Carrie gasped and straightened, the sudden surge of fury clearing her thoughts. "Louisa Blackwell, I'm ashamed of you. You can accuse me of loving anyone you want to. I will consider it a compliment. God forbid I should ever be consumed with as much hatred as you!" Then, calming her rising temper, she said, "I'm sorry for you, old friend." She watched the sudden look of surprise battle the fury on Louisa's face. Carrie smiled up at Robert. "May I have this dance, sir?" The quick light in Robert's eyes told her he was proud of her.

"I would be honored ma'am," he said gallantly.

Carrie fought to control the pounding of her heart as they swept across the floor. Part of her wanted to beg Robert to take her home. But she knew that if she left she would be granting Louisa the victory she wanted. Determined to not give Louisa the satisfaction of running her off, she plastered a smile on her face and danced.

Three songs had followed them around the floor before Robert stopped and pulled her to the side. He took her hand without a word, and the two of them walked down a hallway. Carrie followed willingly, glad to escape the suddenly stifling confines of the ballroom. She breathed a huge sigh of relief when he swung open a set of double doors onto a balcony overlooking the city. Carrie moved to the edge of the wrought iron railing and leaned out, taking in deep breaths of fresh air. Towering trees blocked any view of the stars, a gentle breeze caressing her hot face. Long minutes passed before Robert turned her to face him.

"I was very proud of you back there."

Carrie pulled back, astonished. "Proud of me? I thought I looked like a fool. I could barely think of what to say."

"Exactly. I wouldn't have been surprised if you had slapped her in the face. She certainly deserved it."

Carrie giggled at the idea of slapping Louisa in the face. Then she sobered. "Why is she like that? What have I done to make her hate me so much?"

"Nothing," Robert said firmly. "Some people are just like that. It's easier to be hateful and jealous of other people."

"But why in the world would Louisa be jealous of me?" Carrie asked in genuine surprise.

Robert smiled softly. "That's one reason I love you so much, Carrie Cromwell. You don't know how incredibly beautiful you are. Oh, Louisa is attractive too, but her beauty is all on the outside. Your beauty goes down to the very core of your being. It's who you are."

Carrie gazed up into his eyes, warmed by the admiration she saw there. "Thank you," she finally murmured. The scene in the ballroom faded away as the night reached out to wrap them in its embrace.

Suddenly she remembered the knot of men standing next to the fireplace. "You're leaving again, aren't you?"

"How in the world did you know that?"

Carrie shrugged at his look of astonishment. "The look on your face earlier. When you were talking with the other officers. I've seen it before."

Robert nodded heavily. "I leave in the morning. All I know is I'm heading out with General Jackson. Beyond that, I have no clue. General Jackson is not one to reveal his plans to anyone. Most of the time his closest staff have no idea what is about to happen. He tells them just enough to move them from one point to another."

"I see." Carrie could think of nothing else to say. She supposed she should be getting used to the uncertainty war brought, but it didn't seem to be getting any easier. Each parting was like a ripping of her soul. She knew countless thousands of women were dealing with the same thing every day, but knowing it didn't make her own pain any easier to bear.

Robert stood quietly for a long time, staring out into the darkness. Finally he turned. "I'm going to do something I vowed I wouldn't."

There was something in his voice that made Carrie's heart race. Breathlessly, she waited.

"I told you I was not going to speak of marriage until this war was over." His voice took on a note of desperation. "But I have no idea when this war is going to end. It could go on for years. I suppose it's selfish to want to marry you while I am still fighting, but . . . " his voice trailed off.

Carrie moved closer and took both of his hands in hers, her heart swelling with tenderness. "But the knowledge someone loves you enough to commit their whole life to you is a wonderful thing. It can carry you through a lot of hard times."

Robert stared down at her. "Exactly." He paused. "You don't think I'm selfish?"

"I think when you finally ask me I will be the luckiest woman in the world. Whether we're married or not, my love for you will not change one iota, nor will the amount of time I spend worrying and wondering about you."

Speechless, Robert swept her into his arms. "I love you, Carrie Cromwell. Will you marry me?"

"Yes, Robert Borden, I will marry you." An explosion of joy made her laugh with delight. "May I ask when this wondrous occasion will take place?"

"Right now!" Robert laughed. Then he sobered. "How about when I come back from this mission? I don't know what is happening but I haven't heard anything about General Lee moving the entire army. I have hopes I won't be gone too long."

"I will count the days until you return, lieutenant." Carrie opened her mouth to say more but she was silenced by a long kiss.

With relief Thomas watched Carrie and Robert disappear down the hallway. He had seen and heard Louisa Blackwell's attack. He thought they had handled it beautifully. He had been angry of course, but pity was a much stronger emotion. Louisa was such a beautiful girl. What had happened to turn her into such a shrew? Surely she could not love Robert Borden that much—could not be that jealous. He had seen her with swarms of admirers ever since she had arrived in Richmond. Perhaps it was just that she was hungry for the kind of love his daughter and Robert shared, and she feared she would never have the same.

"So is it true, Thomas?"

Thomas turned his attention back to the group of men he was conversing with. "Is what true?" he asked pleasantly, even though from the look on their faces he suspected what was coming.

"Did your daughter let all your slaves go free?"

"No, it is not true," he stated simply. He was relieved to be able to tell the truth. He knew many were free, but he also knew some had chosen to remain on the plantation.

One man edged a little closer. Edgar Jackson had moved to Richmond a few months ago from South Carolina. Thomas respected the job he did in the War Department, but he had no taste for the man personally. He couldn't pinpoint why exactly, except that the man left him feeling slightly dirty after each encounter.

"You mean to say there is no truth to the things that young lady said? Why would she make accusations like that if there were no basis for them?"

Thomas could feel his anger rising, but managed to maintain a pleasant smile. It would do no good to rise to the man's bait. He had struggled with his own anger over Carrie's actions. Their love for each other had been strong enough to help them weather their differences, but when he was honest with himself he acknowledged there was still some hurt over the matter. "There is no understanding why people say the things they do sometimes," he said with a slight smile, then turned to the man next to him. "I understand you saw a full report of the meeting between Colonel Key and General Cobb. I'd very much like to know what happened between them. I've only heard rumors."

"Yes, I did see it. I think you'll find it very interesting."

Ignoring the angry look on Jackson's face, Thomas felt a surge of relief as the conversation began to flow in another direction. He had known Carrie's anti-slavery feelings might become known in the city. He hoped it would not cause trouble for her, and he would do what he could to help, but she was a woman now. He knew she would have to handle the consequences of her own actions. That was one reason he loved her so much. She was willing to take responsibility for her own deeds. He turned to listen to his friend Allen Bristow.

"Evidently McClellan got the notion that President Davis and General Lee might be willing to participate in a truce. He thought the time might be right for settling the war by conference."

Thomas frowned. "Didn't McClellan arrange the meeting just after General Stuart made him look like a fool by riding all the way around his army?"

Bristow laughed. "Yes. I think it made him a little anxious. Anyway," he continued, "he led us to believe we were discussing an exchange of prisoners. Davis sent out General Cobb. McClellan sent his aide-de-camp, Colonel Key. They met on the bridge crossing the Chickahominy on Mechanicsville Turnpike. McClellan had his troops throw up a little hut for them to talk in."

"How hospitable," someone laughed.

When the laughter died down, Bristow continued. "Key told Cobb he was pleased they could meet on a peaceful mission, then told him he desired nothing more than a permanent peace. Cobb's response was that peace could be established at any time in half an hour if the North were to give the South our freedom. He made it very clear that the Union invasion, which has resulted in so much slaughter and waste, has created such animosity and resistance that the end will only come when the North either gives us our freedom or destroys us."

Thomas listened carefully. He was aware of a growing uneasiness within his heart. He agreed that there would be no backing down by the South. It was too late to undo all that had been done. However, his confidence was diminishing. Yes, Lee had pushed back McClellan—at the cost of twenty percent of his army. Bristow broke into his thoughts.

"Key's response was typical of the Northern sentiment. He hopes the Confederate leaders are realizing our struggle is hopeless because of the greater numbers, money, and resources of the North. He believes there is great pro-Union sentiment throughout the South. He rattled on about the hopelessness of foreign intervention, the blockade, the losses we have suffered recently in the west, and the invincibility of McClellan's mighty army."

"The same mighty army we just sent running with their tails tucked between their legs," one of the group hooted. "I guess we showed them what their big numbers and money can do. Let them come down here. We've got enough spirit to fight off anything they can send our way."

Thomas merely listened as the ring of men muttered their angry agreement.

"Cobb straightened him out," Bristow said grimly. "Told him there was no Union sentiment left in the planting region."

Thomas hid his frown. Was that true? Surely they couldn't have jailed everyone not in agreement with the war. He staunchly supported the Confederate cause, but realism said the strong pro-Union sentiment present before the war had not been washed away.

Bristow continued, "He let that Yankee know that our slaves have never been as retractable as now—that their labor is directed almost exclusively toward the production of food." He barked a laugh. "Told him food and arms made sufficient material for war. He made it very clear that our military strength is far from broken and that the only way McClellan was going to enter Richmond was if we decided to abandon it." Another whoop of laughter met this last statement. Bristow raised one hand. "Cobb told him that even if they were to take Richmond and every other stronghold in the Confederacy, it would require total military occupation to suppress the organized resistance."

"Not that we have to worry about that," one said gleefully.

Thomas remained silent, deep in thought. "What else was said?" he finally asked.

Bristow shrugged. "Key went on for a while about many in the South not being in agreement with the war. He said that secession originated among the arrogant planter's class who thought themselves socially superior and wanted to frame a government in which they could hold all the political power." He paused for a moment. "One of the last things he said was that it seemed to be appearing more obvious that slavery would have to be abolished in order to reform the Union."

"That argument is hogwash," one man sputtered angrily. "I've never owned a slave in my life. I'm fighting this war because I'm not going to have anyone come down here and steal my rights from me. States have their rights. That's what our entire Constitution was built on. The North seems to have forgotten that."

Thomas was deep in thought as he listened to the explosion of sentiment around him. He hated to admit how close Key's words had been to the truth. He himself had objected strongly to the fire-eating secessionists. It was only when Lincoln had tried to send men from Virginia into battle against their Southern brothers that he had cast aside his Union sentiments and given his heart to the Confederacy. He was as joyful as anyone that Richmond had been saved. Realism told him the loss of the city would have been a serious blow. Not only would they have lost their capital—they most likely would have seen their principal army either surrender, or be destroyed. Thomas had seen the generous terms Lincoln was offering any states who returned to the Union. Many of them would have been seriously tempted to accept them if Richmond had fallen.

"I, for one, will never degrade myself by crawling back to the Union," Bristow declared angrily. "They started this war. I aim to do everything within my power to help end it. With a just Southern victory!"

Thomas squelched his doubts and raised his voice to join the cheers of the other men. It was too late to turn back now. The die had been cast. There was nowhere to move but forward.

Eleven

Rose ambled down the road, drinking in the sights of the city that had been her first home of freedom. She did not deny the racism evident in Philadelphia, but at least she had not been accosted and sent back to slavery. Most people in the city had no quarrel with her being free as long as she remained in the subjugated position they believed proper—her time in Philadelphia had taught her that valuable lesson. Gaining her freedom had been just the first step; now she had to fight for equality and dignity.

Receiving Moses' letter telling about Ike Adams' death had done wonders to restore her feeling of safety. She no longer looked into every face, wondering when she would encounter the man so determined to drag her back into slavery. She was trying to find forgiveness in her heart for the man who had caused her so much heartache, but she knew a seed of bitterness remained. Her momma had told her getting rid of unforgiveness was like weeding a garden. *You gots to keep pullin' at them weeds till they just ain't there no more. You think you got 'em licked—then they just spring right back up. You just gots to keep pullin' till you win the battle. Then there ain't nothin' to stop your growin'. You gots to forgive folks the same way.* Rose knew it would take time.

It had been hard to say good-bye to the people at the Quaker School. She had made many close friends in the months she had been there. Leaving was difficult but the adventure of working in the Contraband Camps was luring her forward. The rumble of a train easing past the road brought her back to the present. She was sure the thermometer had soared over ninety degrees today. The heat and humidity were stifling in the close city streets. She wiped her face to stop the trickle of salty moisture in her eyes.

"Might I interest you in a ride home?" a merry voice inquired.

"Aunt Abby! What are you doing here?" Rose asked as she climbed into the carriage. "What a welcome sight!"

"I went by the school but I didn't get there before you left. I've been searching the streets for you ever since."

Rose laughed. "It's a good thing you know all my routes home."

"It's a better thing that you have only three," Aunt Abby retorted. "Otherwise, I wouldn't have even tried, and there would be nothing left of you but melted chocolate on the pavement."

Rose laughed even harder as Aunt Abby mimicked a lady they had overheard the other day saying negroes must become melted chocolate in such heat. "Heaven forbid that should happen!"

"How was your last day?"

Rose hesitated. "Bittersweet," she finally said. "I'm excited about what lies ahead, but I hate to leave where I am now."

Aunt Abby nodded. "It's always hard to leave the shelter of a secure harbor and head for the insecurity of the open sea. You want to reach your destination—you just wish you could do it from the dock."

"Exactly," Rose agreed. "I've been remembering so many things my momma told me."

"Such as?"

"She used to always tell me, *'It ain't fear that stops you, it's lettin' the fear stop you that stops you. You gots to just press on through and do that thin' that scares you so much. The doin' will wring most of the fear right out of ya.'* " Rose paused, remembering. "I feel so silly being afraid. Why, I used to hide in the woods and teach school when it was against the law. Now I'm being *invited* to come down and do the very thing I've always dreamed of. Teach black people in a regular school. Why am I so afraid?" she asked in a disgusted voice.

"I think your momma was right. There is nothing wrong with fear."

"Not as long as you don't let it stop you," Rose finished.

"Exactly. You're not letting your fears stop you. Or have you decided not to leave tomorrow?"

"Of course I'm leaving tomorrow!" Rose exclaimed.

"Then you have nothing to feel bad about. Anytime you have to make a change there is some fear involved. Even if it's a good change, the unknown can be a little scary." She paused. "I think I'm the one who should be feeling bad about my feelings."

"Whyever for?"

"I don't want you to go," Aunt Abby admitted with a small smile. "I know that is a terribly selfish thing, but it's the truth. Oh, I'm glad you're going to be teaching, and I'm happy for the people who will have you as their teacher, but . . . " Her voice trailed off into a whisper. Finally she looked up, swiping at the tears in her eyes. "I'm going to miss you, Rose."

Rose reached forward and took her hand. "And I'm going to miss you more than words can ever say. You've become like another mother to me. A mother and a special friend. I wish I could stay right here in Philadelphia and teach refugee slaves. You gave me the first free home I've ever known, Aunt Abby. I'll never be able to thank you enough."

"Thank *me*! I should be thanking you. You have made a miserable, lonely old lady very happy."

Rose laughed, glad to see the shine back in Aunt Abby's eyes. "I could never even think of you as a miserable, lonely old lady." She meant it. Rose knew how respected Aunt Abby was in the business community, how many friends she had who dropped by often to see her.

"I'm afraid I may be soon!" Aunt Abby said lightly—too lightly.

Rose leaned forward. "What do you mean?" she asked quietly.

Aunt Abby shrugged and laughed. "I seem to be making myself unpopular with my view on women's rights."

Suddenly Rose remembered where Aunt Abby had been that day. "You went to the rally Susan B. Anthony held on Abolition today! How did it go?"

"It was wonderful. There were more women there than I thought would come. I even knew a few of them. I heartily endorse what the speakers were saying. If the country expects women to pay taxes then we should have the vote! It's high time people recognized the capability and equality of women," she said firmly.

Rose was confused. "Why did you say you're—?"

"Making myself unpopular?" Aunt Abby finished. "There was a crowd outside the auditorium when we left. It was mostly men, but there were a few women. Can you imagine that!" she exclaimed in an indignant voice. "They let us know their views on women getting the vote."

"I thought you said it was going to be an abolitionist meeting."

"Well, yes, it was that too." Aunt Abby paused, evidently trying to gather her thoughts. "Susan Anthony has been overruled in her desire to hold wartime women's rights conventions. The Abolitionists believe women should wait to press the issue of suffrage until after the war. They think women will be compensated for their wartime abolition work by congressional support for our rights when the war is over. So while it was overtly an abolitionist meeting, there was still talk of women's rights."

"What did the crowd do?" Rose asked anxiously.

"Oh, they yelled some rather nasty things about the proper place of women. Said we should go home and quit trying to be men."

Rose continued to stare at her. "There's something you're not telling me."

Aunt Abby laughed. "Sometimes your perceptiveness amazes me. Yes," she admitted, "there was something else. Years ago when I was taking over my husband's business and fighting the men so well established there, one man in particular was a thorn in my side. His name was John Standard. I have no way to prove it, but I'm sure he sent the thugs who tried to scare me to death in a dark alley one night."

"The night Matthew came to your rescue and you became such good friends?"

"Yes," Aunt Abby said with a fond smile. It quickly faded. "Standard was one of the men outside the meeting hall today. I didn't see it, but I'm fairly certain this is his spit drying on my dress," she said, looking down at her skirt.

"He spit on you!" Rose was aghast. She could not imagine anyone spitting on such a dear, refined lady of high social standing.

"I'm afraid so," Aunt Abby sighed. "He yelled some threats but I couldn't really catch what he said."

"Are you sorry you attended?"

"Sorry I attended?" Aunt Abby mused. "No," she said firmly. "The time is here for women to have the vote. In the beginning the women's movement showed little interest in obtaining the vote. They wanted control of property and earnings. They wanted the right to divorce and equal opportunity for education and employment. They were fed up with their lack of legal status and they wanted to change the concept of female inferiority perpetuated by established religion." She paused. "Many have finally come to realize we have no avenue to affect change until we have the vote. Mrs. Anthony has reluctantly agreed to let abolitionism hold the front seat during the war, but she is determined to keep the flame lit for equal rights."

"So we all have something in common," Rose murmured. She was not glad to hear that Aunt Abby had been spit on today, but somehow it renewed her courage to know there was another segment of the population that was having to fight for what they wanted and deserved. It let her know that she wasn't alone.

"We are not so very different, Rose," Aunt Abby agreed. "There are certain rights we should have as people. Rights that were granted by our Constitution. Rights that I believe were planned for us by God. It is too bad we have to fight for them, but since reality deems we must fight—so be it—we will fight!"

Rose laughed at the light of battle in her friend's eyes. "I feel sorry for anyone who gets in your way."

"And I feel sorry for anyone who gets in *your* way.

Rose reached for the hand stretched across the carriage. It was not a hand held forth in comfort; it was a hand signifying unity in battle. Rose clasped it firmly. White or black, they were women. Yet so much more than just women. They were children of God fighting for all he had meant them to have in the first place. Battle might not be a pleasant thing, but it was so much better than sitting idly on the sidelines while injustice flaunted itself. There would always be plenty of spectators. Rose intended to be a leader.

Dinner had just been set on the table when there was a firm knock at the door. Rose knew they were not expecting any callers, but it would be nothing new for someone to stop by unannounced. Humming lightly to herself, she walked to the door. When she looked outside she released a horrified scream at what she saw there.

Aunt Abby came running. "Rose! What is it?" she asked sharply.

Rose stood stock still with her hand over her mouth, staring.

Aunt Abby pushed by her to look onto the porch. "Oh, my Lord!" she exclaimed. "What coward would do such a thing?"

Rose stood frozen, transfixed on the spasmodically twitching body of a headless chicken. A pool of blood was forming under its body, soaking the welcome mat. "Who would do this?" she whispered. "Is it because of me?" Stories she had heard from other negroes in the city filled her mind. Had someone finally gotten tired of her living with a white woman and was giving a brutal warning?

"I don't think so, Rose," Aunt Abby said grimly. "This type of thing has happened before—when certain men were trying to scare me away from taking over my husband's business. I suspect this is related to the meeting I went to today."

"What are you going to do?" Rose whispered.

"I'm going to do absolutely nothing," Aunt Abby said angrily. Leaning down, she grabbed the chicken by its feet and carried it into the house. "I can either let this chicken be a symbol of fear or I can turn it into something good. I think I will turn it into chicken soup." Just before she closed the door, she leaned out and called loudly, "Thank you so much for providing tomorrow's dinner. It was quite generous of you!" Then she slammed the door.

Rose stared at her. "You're going to eat it?"

"Certainly." The angry look faded as Aunt Abby moved forward to take hold of one of Rose's hands. "People who want to control other people usually try to do it by fear. The only way to beat them at their game is to make them think it's not working. Remember what your momma said. It's not wrong to feel fear, but we have to work hard not to let it control us."

Just then a knock sounded at the door again. Rose froze, unable to move. What if the person who had left the chicken was back?

Aunt Abby moved forward at once, an angry light in her eyes. "Maybe we can catch the coward this time!" she said as she flung the door open, the chicken still tightly clutched in one hand. "Matthew!"

Matthew stepped in, a look of deep concern on his face. "What in the world is going on here? Why is there a pool of blood on your porch? Why are you holding a dead chicken?"

Aunt Abby laughed weakly. "All very good questions. Will you give me a moment to put this chicken in the kitchen?"

Matthew leaned against the counter and listened grimly as Aunt Abby filled him in on what had been happening. "What are you going to do?" he finally asked.

"Nothing," Aunt Abby said firmly.

"Don't you think she should do *something*?" Rose asked anxiously. "I'm scared for her to be here alone."

Matthew frowned. "That's right. You're leaving soon."

"I'm leaving in the morning." Rose paused. "At least I was."

Aunt Abby whirled to glare at her. "I will not listen to such nonsense. I will be fine. I've had this game played on me before. Whoever left this chicken is just trying to scare me. You most certainly are going to get on that boat and leave here tomorrow. I will not hear of your staying because of me."

"And I could not live with myself if something were to happen to you," Rose protested. "What if Matthew hadn't been around when those thugs came after you?"

"And what if your boat had turned over when you and Moses were forced to cross the Potomac on your own?" Aunt Abby retorted. Her voice softened as she walked over to put her hand on Rose's shoulder. "Listen, if we allow the *what ifs* of our life to control us we would never do a thing. The not knowing would paralyze us. You and Moses got in that boat because it was the only way you could reach your goal. You made the decision to take the risk and trust God with the outcome. I have to do the same thing. Most of my adult life has been spent fighting for basic human rights—for women and for blacks. I counted the cost a long time ago."

"But . . . " Rose protested.

"But—nothing," Aunt Abby said firmly. "I know you love me and are concerned about me. I give you my word I will not go out looking for trouble—but neither am I going to run from it. I have to trust God with my life, just like I have to trust him to take care of you while you're down in the Contraband Camps. We cannot let our fears for other people keep them from doing what they are meant to do. It would be selfish and unloving."

Rose bit her lip and stared at the woman she loved like a mother. She knew Aunt Abby was telling the truth but it didn't make leaving her any easier.

"I'll keep an eye on her as much as I can, Rose," Matthew promised. "God sent me to her when she needed me before. If that time comes again, God can send someone else to help her if I'm not around."

Rose shook her head. "I'm not sure I'll ever become very good at this *trusting* thing," she sighed.

Aunt Abby laughed heartily. "It takes years, my young friend. I've been at it much longer than you, and sometimes I feel I've gotten nowhere. I can trust God so easily with one thing, but five minutes later something else has me anxious and worried. Sometimes I have to ask myself if I believe God loves me. If the answer is yes, then I have to choose to trust him. It's a daily decision, and it doesn't depend on your feelings."

Rose listened hard. She knew she was going to have to hang on to these words very hard in the months ahead.

Aunt Abby turned to Matthew. "Enough about me. Spit and dead chickens are certainly unpleasant, but they are trivial compared to what you have been experiencing," she stated. "Please do fill us in on what is happening in the war."

Matthew nodded. "I'll be happy to do that, but do you think we can catch up over that scrumptious roast I smell cooking in the oven? I'm starved," he said with a smile.

Not until the hot meal had disappeared did Matthew turn to the topic of the war. "I'm sure you know Richmond is still secure as the capital of the Confederacy."

"I know McClellan retreated many miles from the city. I usually stay up-to-date, but I have been dreadfully busy the last two weeks. I heard enough to know Carrie and her family were probably still safe," Aunt Abby replied. "That was enough at the time."

"And I got a letter from Moses," Rose added. "He hears a lot of things. He told me a lot of the military leadership feels the loss of Richmond is McClellan's fault."

Matthew shrugged. "Trying to get the real story is difficult. McClellan is very gifted at manipulating the news he allows to leak through to the war correspondents. Many of my fellow reporters have lambasted the President because they feel McClellan has not been given enough support. It took a lot of sneaking around while I was down there, but the picture I received was a very different one."

"I would love to hear a little truth!" Aunt Abby exclaimed. "Please don't take this personally, but sometimes the press makes me so mad I could scream. It's impossible to really understand what is going on when the news you receive is so biased. One paper says one thing. Another says something else. Whatever happened to good old honesty?"

"I don't take it personally," Matthew assured her with a smile. "I realize the press has a lot of power to dictate and sway popular opinion and actions. As in any profession you have individuals who are committed to the truth. And you have those who will write whatever they are told, whatever sells the most papers, or whatever promotes their own personal agendas. I happen to believe this war could have been avoided if the press had not been busy inflaming public opinion on a daily basis." He paused. "All I can do is try to be one who tells the truth. Or at least the truth as I can best determine it."

"The press does a lot of good things," Rose interjected. "I know there is still a long way to go before my people are free, but the Northern press has done much to bring the true conditions of slavery to light."

Aunt Abby smiled. "Once again you bring me back to a position of balance, Rose." She paused. "Not that I don't have some arguments with the way the paper has handled the issue of abolitionism, either. The way they idolized John Brown made me feel ill." She shook her head firmly. "Enough of this kind of talk. I want to know what happened outside of Richmond."

"It was really very simple," Matthew stated. "McClellan was outmaneuvered by General Lee. I'm sure there are many times Lincoln has wished he could have convinced Robert E. Lee to stay with the North. I think this war would be over."

"Because he's such a wonderful general?" Rose asked.

"Because he's not afraid to take the offensive and fight!" Matthew said. "I don't think McClellan thought Lee would come after him. I believe he had convinced himself the Confederate troops would just hang around and wait for him to finish his ongoing preparations. He simply failed to respond well when he was put on the defensive." Matthew shook his head in disgust. "During most of the fighting, McClellan was sitting in his headquarters tent, miles from the action. He thought he could manage an army of over one hundred thousand men with a telegraph machine. Toward the end he just left the army to fight on their own."

"Surely not!" Aunt Abby exclaimed, her eyes wide with disbelief.

"I'm afraid so. I managed to slip down to the river and watch McClellan head upriver with some of his staff to the *Galena,* a navy gunboat. The Union army basically fought without a commanding general the last two days. I have it on good authority that the general enjoyed a lavish spread with white linen tablecloths while thousands of his men died in the Confederates' desperate attempt to take Malvern Hill."

"Is it true that the South suffered more casualties that day than the North?" Rose asked.

"It's true," Matthew affirmed. "While McClellan was trying to retreat down to the James River, a large portion of the army bunkered down on Malvern Hill. The position was virtually impregnable. I have talked to men who said that day was not a battle—it was a wholesale slaughter of Rebel soldiers. They admired the Rebels' courage, but no matter how many times they charged they were relentlessly driven back."

"So what happens now?" Aunt Abby asked quietly.

Matthew shrugged. "McClellan is already covering himself. He is laying the blame for the losses squarely on the shoulders of the government. He claims the Secretary of War has wanted him to suffer a defeat from the very beginning."

"What?" Rose asked incredulously. "Why would anyone want that?"

"McClellan claims they wanted him defeated and overthrown so that disunion would prevail and they might be free to rule unhampered in the North. He believes they saw him as their paramount enemy who must be destroyed."

"Ridiculous!" Aunt Abby snorted. "Lincoln has met his demands time and time again."

"I agree," Matthew replied. "It's a pity, really. From all I can tell McClellan is a fine leader. His men love him, and he has an uncanny ability to rouse their enthusiasm and support. He is simply not a military leader. I have even heard the fine general now believes that everything that happened to him on the peninsula was God's will."

"You told me earlier he believed it was God's will for him to be victorious in taking Richmond," Aunt Abby commented.

"So I did." Matthew laughed. "It's amazing to me how people can change their perception of God's will as the circumstances change. I guess it's easier than admitting you were wrong, but it sure does make God look fickle."

"Do you see any end in sight?"

"I'm afraid not, Aunt Abby. McClellan has failed. President Lincoln will keep looking till he finds someone who can do the job. He is determined that our country will not be torn apart."

"But is it not already being torn apart? Even if the South is defeated, do you really think they will return to the fold humbly? What of all the bitterness and anger over the Union's attempts to pull them back?"

Matthew shook his head. "As usual, Mrs. Livingston, you ask the difficult questions much brighter men than I are unable to answer." He spread his hands. "I simply don't know. But the mold seems to have been cast. When this war ends, the job of putting our country back together again will indeed be a difficult one."

"Is there any good news in this country?" Rose asked plaintively. "It seems all I ever hear about anymore is this horrible war."

Matthew turned to her with a smile. "There is always good news, Rose. There are always great acts of kindness, sacrifice, and courage in times like these."

"Such as . . . "

"Such as a young lady I met just yesterday. She was barely seventeen years old, I would guess. She has left home to serve the medical needs of wounded Union soldiers. The boat I arrived on was crowded with very sick men. I never once saw her lose her good cheer. She moved around the ship like a bright light, singing the whole time. It was really rather amazing. I was doing my best to hold my stomach in place; she was doing her best to hold hope out to the men who needed it so much."

"I bet Carrie is like that," Rose said softly, her throat tightening with the familiar ache of missing her dearest friend. She seldom thought of the fact that she was actually in reality Carrie's aunt since Carrie's grandfather had been her own biological father. She was simply her closest friend. How glad she would be when this war was over and they could be together again.

"This war has also been the instigator of many firsts," Matthew continued. "I just finished an article that will be coming out in the paper next week."

"Firsts?" Aunt Abby questioned.

"Yes. It seems the war is bringing out the inventor in many people." Then he frowned. "Too many of them are inventions I think our country would do well to have never heard of. Things like land mine fields, flame throwers, naval torpedoes, revolving gun turrets, and long-range rifles."

"Isn't this the first time there have been organized medical and nursing corps?" Rose asked.

"Yes, along with hospital ships and army ambulance corps. Of course, we also have our very first bread lines down South." He stopped and grinned. "It's also the first time there has been a wide-ranging corps of press correspondents in battle areas. I guess I have the war to thank for my job."

"Not that you wouldn't gladly give it up in a heartbeat," Aunt Abby wryly observed.

"Very true," Matthew agreed. "I long for the days when I can wander all over the country, reporting the news of a nation at peace. I never imagined, when I first began studying journalism, that I would be covering the story of America at war—against each other." His voice became pensive. "I also never thought I would be searching the faces of prisoners looking for Robert or one of my other Southern friends." His voice became angry. "I hate this whole stupid war," he growled.

Aunt Abby reached over and laid her hand on his arm without saying a word.

Rose watched sympathetically as Matthew struggled to regain his composure. She understood so well how he felt. How she longed for a time when she and Moses could build a life together in freedom. Matthew broke into her thoughts.

"Enough about the war," he said briskly. "You are leaving tomorrow. Surely we can find a more pleasant topic to discuss."

Rose picked up the conversation. "I have two lovely ladies to travel with. A Miss Carter Lepley and Miss Teresa Farnsworth. Both are from Boston and seem to accept me completely."

"They certainly should," Matthew snorted.

"Thank you," Rose said with a laugh. "I don't anticipate any trouble down in the camps." She paused, not wanting to mention her feelings of trepidation. Talking about them would only bring back her jitters. She wanted to enjoy her last evening in Philadelphia. "Could I interest anyone in a game of croquet?"

Aunt Abby clapped her hands together. "That's a wonderful idea, Rose! There is still plenty of light and the day has cooled off nicely." She stood and smoothed down her dress. "You two go set it up. I will bring out some cold lemonade and cookies."

The next hour passed in laughter and good-natured teasing. Rose was the ultimate winner. "I'm going to take that as a good omen," she declared. She was going to miss everything so much—her beautiful home, the wonderful school, Aunt Abby, Matthew . . . Suddenly she felt hot tears sting her eyes.

"Why don't we do some singing?"

Rose smiled in spite of herself. Once again Aunt Abby was reading her mind. She was longing for anything to do that would keep her from having to climb the stairs to her room for the last time. She wanted this night to last forever. "That sounds wonderful," she exclaimed.

"Let's sing the song my friend Julia Howe wrote," Aunt Abby suggested.

"The *Battle Hymn of the Republic?*"

"That's the one, Matthew. It has become a favorite of the country since she wrote it last year. And I must admit I like these words set to this tune much better than *Old John Brown's Body!*" Aunt Abby's fingers flew over the keys of her grand piano as their voices poured forth into the night.

Mine eyes have seen the glory of the coming of the Lord;
He is trampling out the vintage where the grapes of wrath are stored;
He hath loosed the fateful lightning of his terrible swift sword;
His truth is marching on.

Glory, glory, hallelujah!
Glory, glory, hallelujah!
Glory, glory, hallelujah!
His truth is marching on.

In the beauty of the lilies, Christ was born across the sea,
With a glory in his bosom that transfigures you and me;
As he died to make us holy, let us live to make men free,
While God is marching on.

He has sounded forth the trumpet that shall never sound retreat;
He is sifting out the hearts of men before the judgment seat;
O be swift my soul to answer Him! Be jubilant, my feet!
Our God is marching on.

Twelve

*M*oses felt nothing but sorrow as he gazed around what had, at one time, been a beautiful plantation. He had come to Berkeley Plantation once when he was still a slave. He remembered a stately, elegant mansion surrounded by huge trees and immaculate grounds. It had been the high point of social life in the area—drawing people all the way from Richmond to its elaborate parties and balls.

Berkeley Plantation, along with adjoining Harrison Landing, was now the camp for McClellan's defeated army. Moses wandered through the camp, wrinkling his nose in distaste. There were now over one hundred thousand men in muddy blue uniforms. Tents stretched as far as the eye could see. Rain had been falling the day McClellan's army had reached the plantation. The plains spreading out from the house had been reduced to paste by men's boots, horses' hooves, and wagon wheels. The wheat and corn fields, the vegetable gardens and the flower garden all disappeared within hours. No matter where he looked, Moses could see nothing but desolate waste. He shivered at the thought of how Carrie's heart would break if the same destruction was wrought on Cromwell Plantation.

Moses turned to look at the river glistening in the sunlight and filled with hundreds of boats bobbing in the harbor. The plantation, and the miles along the riverfront, had once been graced by magnificent old trees—oaks, pines, maples. But that had been before Union soldiers set to work with their axes, producing fuel for cookfires. With the exception of one big poplar left to shade the cook's stove outside the house, not one tree was left standing on the three-mile riverfront.

Moses had been inside the house only once in the last four weeks. He had gone to visit Captain Jones only to discover he was still too ill to have visitors. The elegant manor house had been completely denuded of fine furniture in the army's effort to feed the fires. The rich, old carpets were covered with mud, their former glory extinguished.

"It's a shame to see the old place destroyed."

Moses turned to the soldier who had stopped beside him and was looking at the house. He wasn't sure what to say. Any expression of Rebel sympathy could be viewed as traitorous. He knew there were any number of men who would love to send him packing back to Philadelphia.

The soldier continued. "I was at a party here once. Years ago. I can't believe it's the same place." His voice was genuinely regretful.

Moses spoke carefully. "I know what is being done is necessary to support the army and so preserve the Union, but I can't help wonder about the future of the people we are trying to restrain."

The soldier looked at him in surprise. "I thought you would have nothing but hate for these people! I heard you came from a plantation nearby."

"I did, but I don't hold a hate for the people. I hold a hate for slavery. I believe my people will be free someday—hopefully before this war is over. I guess the whole country will have to go to work rebuilding their lives."

The soldier stared at him for a long moment, then moved on. Moses shrugged. He had seen no animosity there—just a complete inability to understand what he was saying. Turning away from the house, he looked over the vast camp. Even with the safety offered by extensive fortifications and gunboats, it was a miserable encampment. Moses was somewhat accustomed to the heat and humidity of July. The Northern soldiers had no such advantage. Besides the discomfort of incredibly cramped conditions, the water was bad and the sanitation deplorable. Swarms of black flies plagued both man and animal. Dysentery had become epidemic. Every morning more dead were laid out. Moses wondered how much longer the army could remain in this position. In spite of plenty of food, new uniforms, and equipment, the men grew weaker every day.

"Moses!"

Moses spun to see who was calling him. It was one of the nurses from the hospital, a rather homely, middle-aged woman with kind eyes.

"The captain is asking for you," she said with a smile.

"Captain Jones?" Moses exclaimed. He didn't stop to wonder what his captain wanted. It was just wonderful to know he was having visitors. "Thank you."

Captain Jones was sitting up in his bed when Moses entered the room he was sharing with about thirty other officers. The air in the room was stifling. Moses wondered how anyone could get well in such conditions. "Hello, Captain Jones, sir. I'm glad to see you're feeling better."

"I understand I have you to thank that I'm feeling anything at all."

Moses shrugged, suddenly embarrassed. "I didn't do anything special, sir."

"As far as I'm concerned you did," Captain Jones retorted. "You saved my life, young man. The doctors told me if I had gotten to the hospital much later I wouldn't have made it. As it is, it's been touch and go, but my doctor assured me this morning I am past the worst and should recover fully."

"I'm happy to hear that, sir!" Moses said fervently. He had developed a genuine liking and respect for his superior officer.

"Come closer, Moses. I want to talk to you."

Suddenly apprehensive, Moses moved next to the captain's bed, then slowly sat down where his commander indicated. The captain spoke so quietly he had to lean forward to hear him.

"You saved my life, Moses. I'm grateful." He raised his hand when Moses opened his mouth to interrupt. "Let me finish. I'm doing better, but I still don't have a lot of strength."

Moses nodded. "I'm listening."

"Good. Like I said, I'm grateful to you for saving my life. Now I want to know if there is anything I can do for you?"

Moses just stared at him, his thoughts spinning. Could he . . . ? He shook his head firmly. "There is no need for you to do anything for me, sir. I'm just glad you're going to be okay. Besides," he added, "you've already done so much for me. You've given me a chance to be part of your unit. I know most of the other officers didn't want anything to do with a colored spy. I'd say we're even."

"I think not," Captain Jones said decisively. "You have more than earned your keep in this army. I understand the information you brought back from the Confederate camps was clear and detailed. It's no one's fault our commanding general chose not to act on it."

Moses blinked his eyes in surprise. He had not expected such candor from the captain. Maybe coming close to death gave him more freedom to speak his mind.

"There must be something I can do for you," the captain continued.

Moses looked at him more closely. The captain seemed to be insinuating a lot more than what he was actually saying. "Do you have something in mind, Captain?"

"Possibly," Captain Jones replied with a slight smile. "I had a conversation with Joe one night."

Moses flinched from the still-fresh pain he felt from his friend's death. He pulled his thoughts away from Joe's dead face as the captain continued.

"Don't you have some family around here?"

"Yes, sir," Moses said softly, not willing to believe the captain was headed where he seemed to be.

"I don't imagine you want them to be slaves any longer than necessary, now do you?"

"No, sir. I sure don't," Moses answered clearly.

"Well," the captain drawled. "The way I figure it, you've got about five weeks coming to you before you're going to be needed again."

"Excuse me?" Moses could hardly believe what he was hearing. Dare he really believe it?

Captain Jones' voice dropped even lower. "Lincoln has called for McClellan to retreat all the way up the peninsula. The campaign to take Richmond is over. Now, I know McClellan. He will follow Lincoln's orders but he'll be in no hurry to do it. The way I figure, you've got five weeks to find some of your family. Do you think you can do it?"

Moses tried to control the trembling in his voice. "Yes, sir. I can do it."

Captain Jones reached under his cover and pulled out a sheet of paper. "I took the liberty to write you a pass to get out of camp. You're on your own after that." His voice grew suddenly stern. "I expect you back in five weeks. Once you get your family to the Contraband Camp at Fort Monroe, you can rejoin the army. I trust you won't let me down."

Moses made no attempt to hide the smile exploding on his face. "You'll see me in five weeks, Captain." He paused a long moment, trying to find words to express what he was feeling. There were none. Captain Jones extended his hand. Moses gripped it firmly. "Thank you, sir."

Rose leaned against the railing of the boat, ignoring her churning stomach. Fort Monroe had just appeared on the horizon. As it loomed larger and larger she was no longer sure if the agitation in her stomach was due to the choppy seas, her nerves, or excitement. It was probably all three. Her eyes widened as they drew closer to the huge hexagonal fort constructed from huge blocks. It was as impressive as Moses had written. It comforted her to know Moses had been at just this same place. Somehow it made her feel a little more connected to him.

"It's beautiful, isn't it?" Carter Lepley asked in an awed voice. "They told me it was big, but I didn't expect anything quite so grand."

"Don't be too impressed, Carter," Teresa Farnsworth replied. "From what I've heard, we'll hardly get near the fort. Our job is in the outlying settlements."

"Oh, I know, but it's still comforting to know there is such a strong Union presence to protect us. I just don't know what I would do if the Rebels were to come in."

"I hardly think you have that to worry about!" Teresa snorted. "They gave it up without a fight in the first place because they knew our force was too powerful. That hasn't changed."

Rose watched her two companions with amusement. She could not have imagined two more different people.

"I'm glad to hear that," Carter replied softly. "I hate to think of my poor students living forever in fear that their freedom will be snatched away from them." The stiff breeze ruffled the blond tendrils escaping her bun and caused her brown eyes to water. Her sweet face was anxious as she gazed at the approaching shore.

"I think your students are used to living with that kind of fear," Teresa stated, her long red hair bouncing freely around her shoulders, her bold green eyes missing nothing. Her voice was strong and confident.

Rose had grown genuinely fond of both of them. Sweet Carter was easy to get along with, yet she could be strong when she needed to be. Rose had seen her stand up for her beliefs more than once when Teresa had tried to ramrod an idea of hers through. And Teresa had a heart of gold, but sometimes her youthful idealism could make her a bit obstinate. Rose expected she was in for some lessons in reality when they finally reached the camps. Both women seemed not to notice the color of Rose's skin; to them she seemed another sister. Their treatment of her as an equal had given her a greater excitement for the future, having already made such wonderful friends.

Carter turned to her now. "Rose, do you think our students really are used to living with fear—that it doesn't bother them anymore?"

"You never get used to living with fear," Rose stated quietly. "You learn to survive. You learn to endure it. You learn to move forward in spite of your fears. But it always bothers you."

The other two women fell quiet as they contemplated her words. Suddenly Rose was anxious to get off the boat. The long journey was over. There would be no more seasickness. She had grown to love the open sea and the feeling of freedom the vastness granted her, but there was a new adventure in sight. She found herself yearning to begin.

Their boat had just settled in at the dock when Rose heard her name called. Her face exploded in a smile as she looked up and caught sight of the matronly looking woman striding down the dock, the sun catching in her ebony hair and angling off the bony structure of her somewhat homely face. "Marianne!" she called. Then she remembered she was not in the Quaker School where it had been expected to call everyone by their first name. Many would think her presumptuous if she addressed her new superintendent like that. "Miss Lockins!" she amended hastily.

Rose was the first down the gangplank when it dropped. Swiftly she made her way to where Marianne was waiting. "It's wonderful to see you again," she cried.

"And it's marvelous to see you, Rose. I didn't dare hope I would have the privilege of working with you so soon."

Rose felt herself drawn to the caring and warmth in the older woman's eyes just as she had been when they first met. "Mr. Lockwood came to our school. When he talked about how the camps could advance the cause of emancipation, I knew I must come. I still intend to pursue my education, but I believe I'm to be here for now."

"I'm just glad you're here," Marianne said fervently. "There is so much need—so many students who are starved for learning." Then she glanced toward the boat. "Did you bring the books?"

"I'm surprised the boat didn't sink under their weight," Rose laughed. "The response to Reverend Lockwood's pleas was incredible. He told me he thought you would be well pleased." Suddenly she remembered her two friends. "Miss Lockins, I'd like you to meet two more of your new teachers." Quickly she introduced Teresa and Carter. Within moments the foursome was moving back up the dock.

Rose was silent, torn between despair and hope as they made their way through the outskirts of the Contraband Camps. Matthew's description had not prepared her for the stark reality.

Marianne read her thoughts. "Slab Town is probably the worst of our camps. These people are fairly new. They arrived, for the most part, with just what they had on their backs."

Rose nodded slowly. "There are barrels of clothes with the boxes of books," she stated quietly. She stared around at the rude log huts and shabby structures made of old pine slabs. It had rained the night before, turning the dirt into a sucking mud. Children were playing in the streets, many of them showing the effects of not enough food.

"I know the conditions aren't wonderful," Marianne said apologetically. "We are doing everything we can to improve them. The government has just put one of the men in our missionary society in charge of the contrabands. We have found ourselves in a constant fight with the government."

"Yes. Reverend Lockwood talked about it. I'm glad the quarter-master from the army is no longer in control."

"He cared no more for the contrabands than he did the rats running around the fort," Marianne said angrily. "Things will be different, but it will take time."

"Are the people healthy?" Carter asked.

Marianne frowned again. "The conditions here are ripe for sickness and disease. The children are especially hard hit, I'm afraid. Reverend Lockwood is pressing the government to provide a doctor for the camps."

Rose felt the despair rise from her heart. The conditions might be deplorable and sickness might be rampant, but certainly the conditions were no worse than what some of them suffered on the plantations. The Cromwell slaves had been treated well, but Rose knew that was not always the case. And even though their physical needs had been well cared for, they had been denied education and freedom. Suddenly she laughed loudly.

"Rose?"

Rose turned to Marianne with a wide smile on her face. "Conditions can be changed and improved. The important thing is that these people are free. They have the opportunity to learn. Their children have a chance to live a different life than they were living. We have fought to survive for years. We will continue to fight."

Marianne turned to Teresa and Carter. "Rose is right. Some of our new teachers have not been able to handle the conditions. They have chosen to leave. I hope you two will be able to see beyond the poverty and into the hearts of a people who have too long been denied the most basic human rights. I believe you will find them strong, industrious, and bright. But only if you look with your heart—not merely your eyes."

Carter was the first to speak. "We have learned much from Rose on the way down here. We simply want to help."

"Good," Marianne said firmly. She stopped in front of a ramshackle hut. "This is your home, Carter. You will share it with two other teachers." She opened her mouth as if to apologize for the conditions, then shut it again. "It should only be temporary. We are working to prepare another home in the main camp."

Carter stared at what was going to be her new home and paled. Long moments passed before she was able to speak. "Thank you," she finally said quietly. "When will I meet my students?"

Rose wanted to cheer her resolve. Carter had told her some of her background during their boat trip. She knew the petite blond came from a wealthy Bostonian family. Tired of what she perceived as a useless life, she had gone to school to be a teacher. She had been teaching at an exclusive school for girls when she decided to travel to the Contraband Camps.

"I'll be back when I get Rose and Teresa settled in," Marianne said cheerfully. "I think you'll like your housemates. You'll meet your students tomorrow."

Rose glanced back as Marianne led them down the road. Tears sprang to her eyes at the sight of Carter's tiny frame outlined by the roughness of the cabin. She tried to push down her feeling of foreboding. She had seen a strength in Carter on the way down, but was her new friend strong enough to handle such conditions? For that matter, was she? She had never known a life of anything but relative luxury compared to this. Her tiny room in the big plantation house had always been secure and warm, with plenty of good food. Life with Aunt Abby had been like a dream. With the exception of the brutal months during the escape, she had never truly known want.

"We call this the Grand Contraband Camp," Marianne stated proudly.

Rose looked around in surprise. She had been so deep in thought she had lost track of where they were going. "What was this before?" Evidence of a dreadful fire was everywhere—charred remains of houses resting on foundations, unsightly dilapidated walls, and blackened chimneys reached for the sky.

"It used to be the city of Hampton—before the Confederates burned it during their retreat. They heard rumors we were going to use it to house Contrabands. They decided they would rather have it destroyed than used for such purposes."

"They destroyed a whole town just because negroes were going to use it?" Teresa asked incredulously.

"You'll find prejudice and sentiments of hatred run rather high in the South," Marianne said grimly. "Of course," she mused, more to herself than them, "such sentiments are not exclusively the domain of Southerners."

Rose looked at her quickly, making a mental note to ask her what had caused such a sad look in her eyes.

Marianne continued, "Look beyond the charred buildings. What do you see?"

Rose looked again, and was immediately impressed. A large number of neat cottages were springing up among the ruins. Gardens were prolific, lending a bright green life of their own.

"The houses have just gone up since this spring. Most of these people lived in horribly crowded conditions all winter. The government has given us some lumber, the rest has come from the buildings evacuated by troops after their winter encampment ended. They have been constructed very quickly." The pride in her voice was evident. "The Grand Contraband Camp is becoming quite a thriving community. The people here are fishing, oystering, huckstering, gardening, and farming. Why, there are farms outside of town that negroes have taken over. There are even a number of dairies now being run by ex-slaves."

Rose looked around, her excitement growing. "I understand many of the Contrabands are working for the government and being paid."

Marianne nodded. "The refugees are making themselves invaluable to the army. They work as cooks, servants, stevedores, carpenters—oh, all kinds of things. Whatever needs to be done, they're able to do it."

Rose watched her closely, once more struck by the sad look in her eyes. "Is there something wrong?" she asked quietly.

Marianne looked at her for a long moment. "I would prefer you not get too bad of an impression."

"I'm here for the long haul," Rose responded. "My people need me." She paused. "I would prefer to know the truth."

"Yes," Marianne nodded. "The truth is always best." She took a deep breath. "It could be worse I suppose . . . " She shook her head. "I'm afraid the government is not being particularly prompt about paying the refugees for their work."

"They're not getting paid at all, are they?" Rose asked, anger darkening her eyes.

"Oh, they're getting paid something, at irregular intervals." Marianne's voice was heavy. "Reverend Lockwood is trying to do something about it, but I'm afraid . . . "

"That the North doesn't do a much better job of seeing coloreds as humans than the Southerners do?" Rose asked tensely. "It sounds to me like being a contraband is not too much different from being a slave."

"Things will get better, Rose," Marianne protested. "It takes time to change people's attitudes. Many of the soldiers show great respect and appreciation for the Contrabands. At least the slaves are free to learn and build their own homes."

"So that the Northerners can have free labor," Rose stated flatly. "How noble of them!" She fought to control her growing anger. Were things never going to be any different for her people?

"I'm sorry," Marianne said softly. "We're not too far from your quarters. You'll need to get settled in."

Rage seethed in Rose's heart as she followed Marianne and Teresa. Suddenly she remembered something Aunt Abby had said before she left, when she was talking about women's rights and how they were realizing that until they had the vote—had the power to legislate change for themselves—life was going to remain much the same. Slowly the anger raging through her steeled into determination as she realized true change was not going to occur until her people were free and had the ability to make decisions and changes for themselves.

Of course the Federal government had the idea they owned the contrabands. Without the protection of the government, most of them would have been captured and returned to their owners. But someday . . . someday they would all be free. Then things would be different. A slight smile played on Rose's lips. She knew why she was here. Just as she had prepared the Cromwell slaves for freedom before they escaped, she would do her best to prepare her students for the freedom lurking below the horizon. When it finally appeared and beckoned them all forward, it would be those with education and knowledge who would know best how to embrace it—how to cultivate change for their whole race.

Torn by indecision, Moses pushed aside the bushes and peered out. His resolve to rescue his momma and Sadie was wavering. All he knew about them was that they had been sold to a man named Johnson who lived on the James River. That was precious little information to go on, with so little time to accomplish his mission.

Moses had been on foot for two days now. Captain Jones had offered him a horse but he had refused. It was going to be hard enough to stay out of sight on foot; riding a horse would have made it impossible. Not to mention the suspicion it would have aroused to see a colored man on a well-cared-for horse. It would have taken only seconds for someone to put two and two together and then the gig would be up. He had no intention of landing in a Rebel prison.

Moses sank back into the bushes and pondered his situation. He could just make out the tallest steeples protruding above the trees surrounding Richmond. Even if he were able to get past the city, he would have to take a wide, circuitous route north. Proceeding up the river was out of the question. He knew it would be well guarded, not to mention clogged with naval boats. Besides, it would be next to impossible to get past the rapids. No, if he were to go to his momma, he would have to go around the city.

His eyes darkened as he considered his options. Even if he were able to maneuver his way around Richmond and head north, it would take him at least a week to go a hundred miles. And what would he do once he rescued them? His momma was too old and Sadie too crippled to make it back to Fort Monroe. He could possibly take them far enough north to reach sympathetic people who would take them on to freedom, but if he did he would never have time to make it back to the fort to rejoin his unit. He had promised Captain Jones he would return in five weeks.

Tears filled his eyes as he once more relived the last day he had seen his momma and then seventeen-year-old Sadie. Their eyes, wide with terror, had begged him to save them, to keep the family together. All he could do was watch as they were led away from the auction block, seething at his own impotency. He had vowed that day to find them and set them free. His mind turned to fifteen-year-old

June. Seventeen, he corrected himself, trying to imagine his little sister a grown woman. He had been forced to watch as she was sold off to a man named Saunders who lived south of the city. He had no idea how far south. He thought he had overheard someone say Saunders had a plantation on the river, but he wasn't certain.

Quiet sobs shook Moses' broad shoulders as he made his decision. It was better to save one than none. "I'll be back, momma," he whispered. Tears streamed down his face as he turned south and began to walk swiftly.

~Thirteen~

Rose's heart was beating fast with excitement as she accompanied Marianne and Teresa down the road. She had spent a very restful night in her tiny room, pleasantly surprised by her quarters. The image of Carter standing in front of her dilapidated shack had hit her hard when she saw the stately old mansion she was to share with ten other teachers. It bore the scars of the recent fire, but remarkably it was still standing. Days of hard work by the refugees had made it livable. The room she was sharing was small by any standards—having been made by partitioning a larger room—but it was quite sufficient. Rose hadn't imagined it would be much more than a place to sleep.

"This is it," Marianne said proudly. "This is our school. We have close to three hundred students in just this building. They come in shifts, of course, or we would never be able to fit them in. The day's first class will be here in about thirty minutes. I wanted to show you everything before they get here."

Rose stopped, unable to believe her eyes. She smiled, even as tears streamed down her face.

"Rose? Are you all right?"

Rose nodded as Marianne's worried face appeared in front of her own. "Yes," she murmured. She tried to explain what she was feeling. "I had a dream one time. In the dream I was free. Teaching black children eager to learn. My school was a simple white building with a small covered porch . . ."

Understanding dawned on Marianne's face. "A building just like this one," she said.

Rose nodded again and wiped her tears. "I'm sorry, it's just . . ."

172

"It's just that you've carried that dream a long time, not ever knowing if it could really come true."

"Yes," Rose whispered, appreciating Marianne's understanding. Her voice strengthened. "And now that it's a reality, there is a lot of work to be done. We'd better get started. I don't want to meet my students with swollen eyes."

Marianne had barely begun her tour of the small building when Rose heard a slight noise and looked up quickly. A tiny face peered around the door frame. Rose smiled and walked over. "Hello. What's your name?" She knelt down to put herself on the same level with the little girl.

"My name be Pearl," a shy voice whispered back.

Rose fought to control the emotion welling in her. She was meeting her first student as a free teacher. Love swelled in her for the little girl. Pearl could not have been more than six years old, with little pigtails and huge, dark eyes. Her simple blue dress had holes in it, but it was clean. Her bare feet were caked with mud and dust from the road. "Hello, Pearl. My name is Rose."

"Be you one of the new teachers?"

"Yes, I'm one of the new teachers."

Pearl continued to gaze at her with a curious expression. "But you be colored like me. I thought teachers be white."

If Rose hadn't been sure she was where God wanted her, all doubt was erased in that one moment. "No, Pearl. There are colored teachers, too." Then she remembered something. "Didn't you ever meet Mrs. Mary Peake?"

"Pearl came after Mrs. Peake passed away," Marianne said. "She's never seen anything but white teachers. Which is another reason I'm so glad you're here."

Rose nodded and turned back to Pearl. "Colored people can be anything they want to be, Pearl."

Pearl stared at her. "You mean I could be a teacher like you?" Hope lit her features for a minute, then her eyes clouded with tears.

"What is it?" Rose asked, reaching out her hand to touch the little girl's shoulder.

"Do you think I could maybe be a healer person one day—instead of a teacher? My big brother done got real sick. . . ." Her voice choked.

"He done went to be wid the Lord two days ago. There weren't nobody to make him better."

Rose eased forward and took the sobbing girl in her arms. "I'm so sorry," she whispered. She lifted the little girl's face so she could look into her eyes. "But, yes, Pearl, one day you could be a doctor. Soon our people—coloreds like you and me—are going to be free to do whatever we want. But we have to learn all we can now."

A sudden commotion at the door caused her to look up as a young boy dashed into the room. "Pearl! Momma be worried sick about you. What you run off for?"

Pearl drew her tiny frame up proudly and sniffed back her tears. "I didn't do no runnin' off!" she cried in her little-girl voice, slightly muffled from her crying. "I come to school early to meet the new teachers."

The little boy barely glanced at Rose, then turned toward Marianne and Teresa. "How do, ma'ams," he muttered. "I'm sorry to be running in here like this, but my momma sent me after my little sister."

Rose hid her smile at the important look plastered on the little boy's face. She guessed him to be eight years old. Then she sobered. For all she knew the little boy had been protecting his family for a long time. If he still had a daddy, he was probably working with the army.

"This here be a new teacher, too," Pearl cried, surprising Rose by turning and throwing her arms around her neck. "Her name be Rose."

A muffled cough behind her caused Rose to turn and look at Marianne. She read the look in her eyes instantly and turned to correct the little girl. "Yes, that's right, Pearl. My name is Rose. But I think it would be better if you called me Miss Rose." She knew Marianne wanted the children to call the teachers by their last names, but that was one of the things she and Moses had not gotten around to doing. Slaves never had last names of their own—they were simply given the name of their master. They talked about choosing a new last name that would belong just to them, but they hadn't done it yet.

"Okay, Miss Rose," Pearl agreed brightly, then turned to her brother. "This here be Gabriel. He be eight!" Pride for her big brother shone in her eyes.

Rose smiled and reached out a hand to the suddenly suspicious little boy. "Hello, Gabriel. It's nice to meet you."

Gabriel took her hand but continued to stare at her. Finally he found the courage to speak. "You be a real teacher?" When Rose nodded, he stood silently, apparently thinking hard. "You be one of them free coloreds from up North that feel sorry for us?"

Rose was curious as to what Gabriel meant by his question. "No, Gabriel, I don't feel sorry for you. You have a whole exciting life of changes and opportunities ahead of you. My job is simply to help you do that. And yes, I am free. And yes, I came from the North—from Philadelphia." She paused and smiled at him. "But until a year ago I was a slave just like you and your family were until you ran away. I spent my whole life on a plantation less than one hundred miles from here."

Suspicion faded from Gabriel's face, replaced with the same wonder she had seen earlier on Pearl's. "You done been a slave . . . and now you be a teacher?" Without warning he turned to run out the door. "I's got to tell my momma 'bout having a colored lady for a teacher!" he cried over his shoulder, dodging through the swarm of children advancing toward the school.

Rose looked at Marianne apologetically. "I'm sorry. I seem to have messed up your schedule for the morning."

"No apology needed," Marianne responded with a warm smile. "What I have suspected all along is right. White teachers can make a big difference here, but your impact here will be far greater because the people won't have to move beyond their suspicion. You will be one of them—able to understand them."

Rose merely nodded, hoping she could live up to the trust God had bestowed on her.

The room quickly filled with children of all shapes, sizes, and ages. Excited chatter bounced off the rafters of the building until Marianne held up her hand for quiet. Instantly, all noise stopped. Rose was impressed. Marianne was obviously respected and loved.

"Good morning, school."

"Good morning, Miss Lockins," their voices chorused back.

"Why don't we start the day with a song? Then we'll meet our new teachers."

In the back of the room a boy, about twelve, tall and lanky, stood up. He opened his mouth and began to sing, a pure tenor exploding from his vocal cords.

Swing low, sweet chariot
Coming for to carry me home
Swing low, sweet chariot
Coming for to carry me home.
I looked over Jordan
And what did I see
Coming for to carry me home
A band of angels coming after me
Coming for to carry me home.

Rose smiled, holding back her tears, as she raised her voice to sing along with the children. Images of Moses, tall and strong, filled her mind. That had been their song during the long months of escape. Many a time it had given them strength to carry on. Oh, how she wished she could share this moment with Moses. Where was he? What was he doing? When would she see him again?

Moses wiped the sweat from his face and swatted at the mosquitoes attacking the exposed parts of his body as he pushed through the overgrowth along the river. Even in the darkness, the murky humidity pulled at him, soaking him and leaving him drained. Tree limbs whipped his face and body, while thorns pierced his flesh. His face was set with determination as he forged on.

Moses had not planned on traveling just at night, but it was the only way he felt safe. There were too many Confederate soldiers scouting the area. The first few days heading south he had spent hiding in the bushes, never knowing when a small scouting party would appear around a curve. So far he had been lucky. Whether it was the strike of a horseshoe against a rock or a muffled snort, he had always been able to duck from sight. The Rebels must be reconnoitering the area to determine McClellan's next move. Captain Jones was right—the general was in no hurry to follow Lincoln's order.

Still, he would have to move his army soon. Moses wasn't sure if that would complicate his life or make it easier.

He was just as leery of running into Union troops. Like before, he had gotten rid of his Union identification. It was simply too dangerous to have on him. But there was no guarantee of how the Federals would treat him either. His chances were better, but he wasn't interested in playing the odds.

After three days of hiding in the bushes, he realized he would have to limit his traveling to night hours. His frustration mounted daily. His supply of hardtack had run out after a few days, and finding food at night was much more difficult. He had grown tired of blackberries.

Moses had no idea how much ground he had covered before the sun began to lighten the horizon. It would be time to find his hiding place for the day soon. Stretching his aching back and legs, he slid down the bank into the river, closing his eyes in ecstasy as the cool water closed over his body. He lay in the water quietly, allowing it to restore some of his energy.

The sun had pinkened the sky when he pulled himself onto a tree trunk stretching out over the water. Reaching into his haversack, he pulled out a tin cup and dipped it in the water time and time again, gulping it down thirstily. Then he carefully filled his canteen, knowing he might not have water again until dark. He would have to hoard it. He turned toward the bank, then stopped, the spectacle before him rooting him in place.

As the sun slipped its way onto the painting of a new day, it spread its signature in bold strokes across the sky. Clouds exploded in oranges and purples, the surrounding sky turning a bright azure blue. A low-lying mist over the river caught the colors and threw them back at the sky, swirling in a dance of greeting for the sun. A soft breeze rippled the water, while a chorus of birds sang to the new day.

"Good morning to you, too, Lord," Moses said quietly, reverence filling his heart along with a fresh sense of peace. If God could create a painting such as the one he was looking at, then surely he could handle helping him find his little sister. His body relaxed as he stared at the sky. He didn't move an inch until the colors began to fade.

A shout from downriver caused him to stiffen, then move silently toward the bank. He had just slipped into the cover of the brush when the first boat appeared around the curve of the river. The sound of men's voices floated clearly across the water.

"McClellan is on the move!" one man crowed.

"Yep. That dirty Yankee and his army of scoundrels are tucking tail and running for good. I reckon those folks in Richmond will be able to sleep a lot more peacefully now."

Moses leaned forward, determined not to miss a single word.

"The man I talked to said Harrison's Landing looks like a giant mud flat."

Anger tinged his companion's words. "Yeah. They said the old manor house might as well be burned. It won't ever be the same."

"The owner is ready for some Yankee blood, that's for sure," one chortled. "Seems when he evacuated he left orders to have the place burned, but his slaves didn't do it. He hates thinking the Yankees used his home for their hospital."

Their words floated on the breeze, then were gone. Moses watched as the boat eased from sight, the paddles flashing in the sun. McClellan's army was gone. Moses had been gone a little more than a week. The peace he had been feeling just minutes before evaporated with the mist. His fists clenched in frustration. He had to figure out a way to determine where he was. He had no way of knowing where Saunders' plantation was. He was going to have to take the risk and ask someone.

Suddenly the idea of hiding in the bushes for a whole day seemed impossible. If he was going to rescue June, he would have to take the chance of being caught. Five weeks had seemed like an eternity when Captain Jones had offered it. Now he was seeing it in the light of reality—it would be a struggle to make it back in time. Besides, he had to find something to eat besides fruit if he was going to be able to keep going. Muttering a prayer under his breath, Moses continued his way down the river, ignoring his fatigue. At least it was easier going in daylight. He could see the branches before they slapped him in the face, and there were not as many mosquitoes.

Moses planned as he walked. He would get as far as possible in the daylight. Then he would creep inland, looking for some slaves to give him information. He looked down at his clothes and grinned. No one would confuse him with a Union soldier anymore. His clothes were stained with mud and dust, and torn in several places from the brambles.

Suddenly Moses jerked to a halt, staring around him. His pulse quickened as he realized what he was looking at. Cromwell Plantation! A wide grin spread across his face as he turned inland. He thought he had passed it during one of the long nights. His brow creased as he realized he had not been making the good time he thought he had. He knew he had been moving slowly, but he hadn't thought his floundering in the night had cost him that much. His lips tightened as he strode forward. He had wasted too much time.

Caution kept him in the trees. He had no idea what to expect. Union troops had destroyed other homes along the river. Had they set fire to Cromwell? Would he find any of his old friends, anyone who could help him? Pushing down the questions, Moses concentrated on approaching the slave quarters undetected. It seemed like just minutes before he was pushing aside the brush and peering out onto his old home. What he saw made his face split into a wide grin. Opal!

Moses stood slowly and eased from his cover, standing quietly in the shade. It was just moments before Opal looked up. Time stood still as she stared, shook her head, rubbed her eyes, then stared again. "Hello, Opal," Moses said, smiling.

"Moses! Glory be! Moses!" Opal cried, running forward. "I can't believe my eyes. Is it really you?"

Moses put a finger to his lips. "I'd just as soon the whole world not know I'm here!"

Opal slapped a hand to her mouth. "Of course not!" she whispered. Then she wrapped her arms around him in a big hug. "Glory be. It's great to see you!" She stopped suddenly, her eyes wide. "What are you doing here? Are you in trouble? Some kind of spy mission?"

Moses shook his head. "Are there any soldiers here?"

"What kind?"

"Any kind!" he exclaimed, then relaxed as he saw the smile playing on Opal's lips. She was teasing him—she hadn't changed a bit.

"There aren't any soldiers here, Moses. You're safe. The soldiers took all the food they needed in the spring. The only food we have here now is what we're growing ourselves. But we're doing fine. A lot better than the folks in Richmond," she said, then frowned. "Have you seen Carrie? Is she all right?"

"I don't know. I haven't seen her since I left her in the tunnel."

"You think she made it to Richmond?"

"Carrie is a resourceful young lady. If anyone could have made it, she could." Changing the subject, he asked, "Is Sam still here?" He was pretty sure the old butler was the only one who could help him.

Opal nodded. "We've all decided the whole world has gone so crazy we might as well stay put. At least we know we can eat, and the Union army doesn't seem to want to harm us."

"Most of them are good men," Moses agreed. "Just be careful. Some of them hate coloreds as much as any Southerner does."

"That's what Sam told me," Opal said with a wise look. "Said hatred isn't just North or South."

Moses smiled at the mention of the old man and was suddenly eager to see him again. "Is he in the house?" When Opal nodded, he took off at a jog. Memories flooded him as he ran up the driveway— riding up the night Cromwell had bought him, cramped in the back of an open wagon; seeing Rose for the first time; Old Sarah helping him let go of his hate . . . When the big house broke into view, he slowed to a walk.

An old man appeared on the porch, his bearing erect, his eyes sharp. Moses continued to walk forward until a wide grin appeared on the man's face.

"Moses! It's good to see you, boy."

Moses laughed loudly. Sam's voice was as casual as if they saw each other daily. Only his eyes revealed his pleasure. "Hello, Sam. It's good to see you, too." He paused. "I don't have much time."

"Somethin' tells me you didn't just show up for a social visit," Sam drawled.

Moses sank down on the steps. "I'm looking for a man named Saunders. Actually I'm looking for his plantation. All I know is it's about fifty miles south of Richmond."

Sam nodded. "That would be old Joshua Saunders. Owns Millstone Plantation."

Moses' pulse quickened. He'd come to the right place. "You know where it is?" he asked eagerly.

Sam nodded again. "You don't look like you've eaten for a while, boy. Why don't I be tellin' you how to get there over some food?"

Minutes later Moses was shoveling hot food into his mouth. He didn't think he'd ever tasted anything so good. After days of hardtack and beans, then nothing but fruit, the steaming vegetables and hot cornbread were delicious. He could feel life pouring back into his body as plate after plate disappeared beneath him. Not until he was full did he look around. The elegant plantation house looked just the way he remembered it. "How do you like being lord of the manor?"

Sam shrugged, a smile playing at his lips. "'Bout as well as I thought I would," he replied. "I know it can't last for good but I'm enjoyin' it sure 'nuff for now." He paused. "Opal even taught me how to read."

"That's great, Sam." Moses' voice turned serious. "Keep learning, Sam. There's a lot of people up North who want to see us free. I can feel it coming. I can feel it coming."

"Yep," the old man said easily. "It's coming. Now each person gots to figure out what they're goin' to do with it—use it, or waste it."

"You haven't changed," Moses laughed. "You always know how to say it the way it is."

Sam changed the subject. "Why you need to know where Saunders lives?"

Moses changed to all business. "I'm going after my little sister June."

"The army know you're doing this?" When Moses nodded, Sam continued, "How you aim to get her out of there?"

Moses shrugged. "I haven't figured out all the details yet. First I have to get there."

"It'll come to you," Sam agreed. He pulled out a sheet of paper and began to draw a crude map.

Moses leaned forward to watch him. Concern flooded his mind. Sam knew the roads, but he couldn't travel on them. It would be too easy to get caught. Would he be able to continue down the river and then pick up on the map when he thought he was far enough south? His mind raced as he tried to formulate a plan.

He sat back and studied the map for a long time. Finally, as if reading his thoughts, Sam spoke. "I don't imagine the roads are too safe for you."

Moses just shook his head, still staring at the map. A long silence passed as both men pondered the problem.

"You gots to take the boat," Sam stated quietly.

"The boat? What boat?" Moses asked.

"Marse Cromwell's boat. It was hidden pretty good when the soldiers came through. Figured we might need it some day, so we hid it real good."

"I don't want to take it if you're going to need it," Moses protested.

"I figure this is what we needed it for," Sam observed quietly. "I ain't plannin' on gettin' in any boat and floatin' down that river. If you want it, you're welcome to it."

Moses considered his options. He could continue to flounder down the river on shore, or he could take his chances floating downstream under the cover of night. According to Sam's map, he still had a good thirty miles to go. He had to find June and get her out of there, or he would never make it back to his unit on time. "I'll take it," he announced.

Sam stood and headed back toward the kitchen. "I reckon you're goin' to need some food."

Moses followed, once more confident in God's leading.

Moses had been so exhausted from traveling all the previous night and day that he took a few hours' nap before resuming his journey. He was amazed at how refreshed he felt from the short respite—it was as if he'd had a full night of sleep.

It was almost dark when Sam stopped in front of a jumbled pile of brush and limbs. "There's your boat."

Minutes later Moses had uncovered the simple rowboat.

"The Union soldiers took Marse Cromwell's big boat, but they didn't get this one," Sam said proudly.

Moses stared at it in delight. "It's just like the one Rose and I rowed across the Potomac," he said quietly. Once again memories poured into his mind. Memories—along with an aching of longing for his wife. He would give anything to see her—to hold her in his arms and feel her soft lips. Resolutely he pushed the thoughts away—they would bring him nothing but torment right now.

Sam helped him carry the boat to the edge of the water, then stepped back. "God bless you, boy."

Moses exchanged a long look with him, then embraced him warmly. "Thank you, Sam."

"We gots to stick together, boy. That's how we all gonna make it. I learned that a long time ago."

Moses watched until Sam's figure was swallowed by darkness. Then he settled into steady rowing. He figured it would take him two nights to travel the thirty miles. He would have to estimate his distance the best he could. Sam had studied the river, then told him by his figuring he could make between three to four miles an hour.

Memories assailed Moses as he pulled at the oars. He could almost see Rose in the bow of the boat, could almost feel her hands massaging his shoulders to ease his bunched muscles, could almost hear her beautiful voice singing out into the night. Once again the ache of missing her swelled up in him, tightening his throat and constricting his stomach.

He groaned, and leaned harder into the oars. Sweat poured down his face, his breath coming in quick gasps. Finally he gave a short laugh and stopped rowing. If he kept up this pace he'd be too exhausted to paddle by midnight. He knew how important it was to maintain a steady rhythm. Moses searched his mind for something to take his thoughts off Rose. There was only one thing that came to him. He kept his voice low as his deep bass floated toward the heavens.

Sometimes I feel like a motherless chile,
Sometimes I feel like a motherless chile,
Sometimes I feel like a motherless chile,
A long ways from home,
A long ways from home.

True believer, true believer,
A long ways from home,
A long ways from home.

Sometimes I feel like a moaning dove,

Sometimes I feel like a mo'ning dove,
Sometimes I feel like a mo'ning dove,
A long ways from home,
A long ways from home.

True believer, true believer,
A long ways from home,
A long ways from home.

When Moses finished singing that song, he launched into another. Just like generations before him, the words poured hope into his heart. The songs he sang were not merely songs, they were life itself—the life of the human soul. They had been all that kept his people going at times. He recognized them as a rich heritage. He poured out his soul—the songs in return poured life back into his soul.

When he was finally quiet, the inky night embraced him in fellowship and brotherhood. The soft breeze caressed his aching muscles and kept the mosquitoes at bay. Twinkling stars whispered great secrets of the universe. Hooting owls joined with croaking frogs to form a background symphony for the gentle lapping of the waves. A shooting star grabbed his attention as it flashed across the sky, then faded into oblivion. Moses continued to hum quietly as the boat glided across the water.

Two mornings later, Moses pulled the boat ashore at first light, found a place to hide it, then carefully covered it with limbs and a pile of brush. If anyone looked closely they would know something had been hastily concealed, but it would have to do. If he moved quickly he might find someone in the area who could tell him how to locate Millstone Plantation.

Once the boat was hidden, Moses settled down on a log and finished off the last of the cornbread and sweet potatoes Sam had sent with him. He washed it down with a canteen full of water, then returned to the river to refill it. He stood on the bank of the James River for several minutes, staring out into the early dawn. He would miss the river. It had become his friend during the last two long nights. He had shared secrets, memories, and hopes with the great expanse. In return, it had taught him one of the lessons of life.

Life will always flow on, it had whispered gently. *You might try to stop it, but no one can alter the flow of life. You can only learn how to move with it gracefully, tumbling through the rough times, restoring yourself during the smooth times—knowing that wherever it takes you a mightier hand than you is guiding you—always directing your path.*

Moses raised his hand in farewell, then disappeared into the woods. Thirty minutes of hard walking brought him to a narrow dirt road, dusty from the heat. The morning air was still cool, but the sun promised another searing day. Moses stood still, pondering his options. The road seemed little used, but that didn't mean anything. He was so close to June! Dare he risk walking down the open road? A clatter of wheels in the distance made his decision. Turning quickly, he dove for cover in the bushes, then peered out, watching to see who was coming.

The sounds of an approaching wagon drew closer, then finally materialized into a rickety open wagon, drawn by an equally rickety mule. Moses waited quietly, watching closely as the wagon drew nearer. Not until he could tell that the driver was an elderly colored man did he step from his cover in the woods.

"Whoa there!" the driver called in a startled voice. "What you want, boy?" came the suspicious question.

"I mean no harm," Moses assured him.

"Hmph. Don't reckon as how I could stop you if you did," the man drawled. "What can I do for you?"

"I'm looking for Millstone Plantation."

"Millstone, eh?" The man examined him for a long moment, then barked. "What for?"

Moses hesitated, then chose honesty. "I'm looking for my sister."

The driver looked puzzled. "You be a free man, boy?"

Moses smiled. "I am unless the wrong people find me." Instinctively he knew he could trust this man.

The driver threw back his head and laughed heartily. "My name be Bartholomew. My friends call me Bart."

Moses moved forward and shook his hand firmly. "I'm Moses."

"And you're lookin' for Millstone Plantation. Well, you ain't too far away, boy."

Moses' heart quickened in anticipation. "How far?" he asked quickly.

"Oh, I reckon you can be there in less than an hour if you want to climb in this wagon with me."

Moses thought quickly. Regretfully he shook his head. "I don't think I better be doing that. I've come a long way without anyone seeing me. I think I'll just walk."

"Suit yourself," Bart said casually. "Your sister know you're coming?"

"No." Moses didn't see the need to say any more. He was sure Bart could be trusted but the less said, the better.

"Well, you tell me who she is, and I'll let her know you're on the way."

"You're from Millstone?" Moses asked incredulously.

"Lived there all my life," Bart said with a grin, then became very serious. "Moses, you listen to me. You stay to the woods and you'll be just fine. Follow this road up a couple of miles till you reach a stand of tall pine trees—you'll know 'em when you see 'em. Take the right fork—it'll take you right into the plantation. The slave quarters ain't too far from the big house." He paused. "Old Marse Saunders high-tailed it for Richmond when the Yanks came through. Had the place to ourselves for a while. Now the overseer is back. He's a pretty good man—treats us okay, but he ain't gonna take kindly to someone coming for one of his slaves."

Moses waited quietly. He hadn't said anything about taking his sister, but he knew he didn't have to. Why else would he be sneaking onto the plantation?

Bart continued, "You wait till it's good and dark. That overseer of ours likes a drink or two at the end of a long day. Keeps him quiet most of the night, if you know what I mean."

Moses nodded.

"Come around to the right of the house. You'll find a narrow trail through the woods. It'll bring you right back to the quarters." He hesitated a long moment. "I hope your little sister is still around. Not too many of the young ones left," he mused.

"What do you mean?" Moses asked anxiously.

"Those Union men made it real easy for folks to leave when they came through a few months back. Lots of Marse Saunders' people headed for them Contraband Camps."

Moses fought to control his panic. Had he come all this way for nothing?

"Now, me," Bart continued, "I reckoned I would stay on. I don't reckon I'll be living too much longer. This be all the home I've ever known."

Moses nodded understandingly. Old Sarah had been the same way. He didn't blame them. Suddenly his trust for the old man hardened and became solid. "I'm looking for my sister, June. She should be seventeen now. Saunders bought her a couple of years ago."

Bart's face split with a wide grin. "You be June's big brother? Why, she's told me all about her family, sure 'nuff. You in luck, boy. June still be here."

When he paused for a long moment, Moses stepped closer. "Is somethin' wrong with my sister?"

"No, no! Least I wouldn't say it be somethin' wrong. Could be somethin' might make your plans a little harder."

Moses struggled to figure out what the man meant. Suddenly, understanding dawned on his face. "My sister is pregnant," he stated quietly.

"Goin' on six months," Bart agreed with a nod. "Her husband is a fine man, but he was sent to Richmond to work on the fortifications. Been gone about five months now. Doesn't even know he's gonna be a daddy. Nobody got no idea when he'll be back."

"That's why June didn't go with the soldiers?"

"Yep. Wanted to be here when her man got back."

Moses stood silently, taking in all the information. He stepped back from the wagon. "Please don't tell her I'm coming. I'd like to surprise her."

"Oh, you'll surprise her, all right." Bart laughed, his gap-toothed mouth opening wide. "She be in the cabin right next to the maple tree." Bart gathered up the reins. "Good luck, Moses."

Moses raised his hand. "Thank you, Bart." He watched until the wagon rolled from sight, then merged back into the woods. His sister was less than three miles away. He would see her. She would choose what she wanted to do. She was a grown woman now. Moses chuckled at the idea of June being a wife and momma. His little sister had grown up. His heart sped up at the idea of seeing her again. He could hardly wait till dark.

Fourteen

$\mathcal{M}$oses awoke refreshed from his long sleep. A deep draught from his canteen cleared his mind and roused his still-sleeping stomach. A deep growl reminded him it had been morning since his last meal. Stretching to loosen the tight muscles in his back, Moses peered out from the clearing he had selected for his hiding place. Clouds were scudding in from the west and a brisk breeze was blowing, carrying with it the scent of rain. Moses welcomed the coming storm. It would settle the dust, as well as provide cover for him as he approached the plantation. Satisfied no one was in the vicinity, he stepped out from his covering. It was time to hunt more fruit.

Dark clouds had deepened the approaching nightfall, and a stiff wind tossed trees wildly as Moses searched for the trail Bart had told him about. He had missed it once already, realizing his mistake as soon as he spotted the brick manor house in the distance. He had retreated quickly, retracing his steps. His frustration mounted as the sky darkened. If he didn't find the trail before dark, he wouldn't dare move forward. It would be too easy to be caught by the overseer.

Suddenly, the wind calmed for just a moment, giving him a glimpse of the opening. As soon as he stepped onto the small trail, the skies released a deluge of water. Moses laughed as water danced off the leaves and washed the dust and dirt from his body. He welcomed the crash of thunder and lightning—it would cover his movements. He was confident no one would be roaming around on a night like this.

It took only a few minutes to break through into the clearing surrounding slave quarters. Moses stopped, waiting and watching. Now that he was so close to seeing his sister again, his heart was racing so hard and fast he could hear it pounding in his head over the storm. "I'm keeping my promise, Daddy," he called softly, staring up at the raging sky. "I'm keeping my promise!"

Ducking his head, he raced through the raindrops to the door of the tiny cabin next to the maple tree. He paused once again to catch his breath, then knocked firmly.

"Come on in," a musical voice called. "Ain't no reason to stand out there getting soaked."

Moses opened the door and stepped inside. June was seated by the window in a straight-back chair, calmly shelling peas, a bowl of cornbread sitting on the table beside her. Her mouth fell open when she saw him, her eyes wide with astonishment. "Hello, little sister," Moses said softly.

"Moses," June whispered. "Moses!" The air was rent with her cry of joy as she tossed aside the bowl of pea pods, scattering them everywhere. "Moses! It's really you!" Laughter and sobs shook her body as she ran to him and threw her arms around him. "It's you. It's really you," she kept repeating.

Moses held her tightly, his own tears mingling with laughter.

Only once did June pull away. With a look of disbelief she reached up to touch his face, then threw herself back in his arms. "Thank you, Jesus! Thank you, Jesus!" she cried over and over. Finally she pulled back and stared up into his face. "How did you . . . ? Where did you . . . ?"

Moses laughed and led her back to the chair she had been sitting in. "Sit down. I'll tell you all about it," he said, chuckling while he brushed his own tears away. "Mommas-to-be shouldn't get too excited, you know."

June laughed. "I think my baby is as happy as me. It's sure enough bouncing around in there." She patted the chair next to her. "I still can't believe it's you. I didn't know if I would ever see any of my family again." She paused. "Momma . . . Sadie . . . ?"

Moses shook his head. "I haven't seen them. I came after you first." The storm raged, offering them its protection as he told his story. "Enough about me," he said, finally. "What about you? How is it here?"

June shrugged, leaning forward to pull the bowl of cornbread over. "You can eat while I talk," she said with a smile. "My big brother was always hungry."

"Your big brother hasn't changed much," Moses grinned.

"Now, that ain't true," June said slowly. "I recognize the body but the talk is sure 'nuff different. Why everythin' about you is different. You've gotten learning and you been living free up North. Why, you've turned into a grown man."

Moses read the concern in her eyes. He leaned forward and took her hands. "I'm still the same Moses, June. I never forgot about you, or Momma, or Sadie. As soon as I had the chance I came to get you. Just like I promised."

June nodded slowly. "I was so scared that day Marse Saunders bought me. I ain't never been scared like that. Not even the time the men came after us with whips right after they killed Daddy. At least we were together then. But that day," she stopped and shook her head, "I wanted to die that day."

Moses nodded grimly. How well he remembered. He, too, had wanted to die, and he had wanted to kill someone. He had not been able to tell which emotion was the strongest. "I know, little sister."

June took a deep breath. "I survived. Just like others before me. When I got here people were real nice. They knew what I'd gone through. It ain't so bad, Moses. Marse Saunders is a good man. He don't ever beat anyone and up till the Union came through, we had plenty of food. Even the overseer ain't bad—long as we do our jobs. The most he ever does is yell real loud. I ain't never seen him hurt anyone."

"It's not like being free, June."

"No, I reckon it's not," she murmured. "I try not to think about being free. I gave up my chance when the Yanks came through. I'm married, you know. To a wonderful man named Simon. Marse Saunders sent him to Richmond to work on building them walls of dirt around the city. I heard through the grapevine, though, that slaves aren't coming back. There's too much to be done and the government is paying the owners." She stopped, tears welling in her eyes. "I didn't want to leave. Simon wouldn't know where to find me."

"And what about now, June? Do you still want to be free?" He leaned forward and grabbed her hands. "That's what I'm here for, June," he said fiercely. "To help you get free."

June pulled back, startled. "How?" she asked in a bewildered tone.

"I'm going to take you to the Contraband Camps at Fort Monroe. You'll be safe there. We'll tell people here where you're going. They can tell Simon when he comes back. I can try to get word to him," he added. "It will be hard, but it might be possible."

June sat silently, seeming to struggle with her feelings. "I was afraid to leave before," she said slowly. "Afraid to be without family again. But now I got me more of a family to think about. I got me a baby growin' inside." She paused. "I want my baby to be free. I want my baby to have a chance to be diff'rent." She peered into Moses' eyes. "You really think Simon will be able to find me?"

"We'll make sure he does," Moses promised. He ached to take away the fear lurking in his sister's eyes, but he knew it was a battle she would have to fight on her own. He could not take such a huge step for her. It would have to be her own courage and will that would take her through the struggles ahead. Her being pregnant would only add to the hardships they would face as they made their way to Fort Monroe. She had to want freedom enough to endure whatever came.

Silence filled the room for a long while as June stared out the window, slowly patting her stomach. Finally she turned to him, her face beautiful with a glowing smile. "When do we leave?"

Moses grinned. "We leave before daybreak," he said firmly. "We don't have a lot of time, and we'll have to travel slow."

June nodded slowly. "All right," she murmured.

Moses took her hands again and tried to prepare her for what lay ahead of them. They talked long into the night, the storm continuing to offer its covering.

Rose was humming softly as she walked down the dusty road toward the school. Was it possible she had been here less than a month? Sometimes she felt as if she had been in the camps for years. At other times it was as if she had arrived just yesterday.

"Good morning, Miss Rose!" a little girl called, waving frantically.

"Howdy, Miss Rose," one elderly woman greeted as she paused in the middle of her sweeping.

"Have a nice day," a young mother called, balancing a baby on one hip.

Rose smiled and waved to everyone. However long she had been here, she had fallen in love with the people trying to forge a new life for themselves. Their stories were all similar to hers. Having spent all their life in slavery, they were now determined to make things different for themselves and their children.

"I been reading that book you gave me," one boy, about twelve, called out.

"I *have* been reading that book you gave me," Rose called after him, chuckling. She had loved teaching in the little secret school in the woods of the plantation, but those feelings didn't compare with the love she had for her little white school and its eager-eyed students.

Rose had never seen such a thirst for learning. It seemed like everyone, young and old, had one thing in mind—they wanted to read and write. Scores of children crowded into the building during the day, all ages and all levels mixed together. Teaching them all was a challenge beyond any she had imagined, but they were learning. She loved watching the little eyes light up with sudden understanding when they first made sense of the jumbled letters swimming across the page, or finally comprehended some concept she was teaching.

The adults came at night, exhausted from their long days of work but determined to learn to read and write like the youngsters. Rose was amazed at how fast they were catching on. They seemed to soak knowledge up like dry ground during a heavy spring downpour. Rose pondered her thoughts. For too long these people had been held captive in a dry land of ignorance and bondage. Now they were free and absorbing all they could.

"Miss Rose!"

Rose turned toward the stooped old man waving at her from his porch. "Good morning, Ezekiel," she called.

"Come here, please," he called in his quavery voice.

Rose complied willingly. Ezekiel had become one of her favorite students. Seventy-five years old, he was the oldest student in the school. While many older slaves were opting to live out their remaining days on their plantations, Ezekiel had been determined to be free for once in his life.

"You got another book for me, Miss Rose?"

"You've already finished the last one I gave you?" Rose asked, astonished.

"Ain't got nothing much to do besides read," Ezekiel replied. "Besides—I got me a lot of making up to do." His voice turned deadly serious. "I been thinking, Miss Rose. I can forgive the white man for making me a slave all my life. I don't reckon I'll ever forgive him for stealing education from me." His voice softened. "You run on. Looks like your students are going to beat you to school this morning."

Rose looked up, then hurried to the school steps. It was like this every morning. The people in the camps, thrilled to have someone of their own race as a teacher, had embraced her wholeheartedly. She, in return, was giving them everything she could.

"Miss Rose, you still coming to our house for supper tonight?" one little girl asked shyly as soon as Rose appeared on the porch.

Rose knelt down and smiled at her. "I wouldn't miss it for anything, Annie. Is your momma sure I can't bring something?"

"No, ma'am," Annie replied anxiously, her long black braids bobbing as she shook her head. Her thin face, made thinner by giant black eyes, revealed her excitement. "My momma said you was just to come. I reckon she'll be cooking all day—in between doing wash for the army, that is."

"I'm looking forward to it," Rose promised. "Did you read your book last night?"

"Yess'um! I read everything you told me. Did you know the world ain't flat, Miss Rose? I been looking at that ocean for a few weeks now and figured sure enough those boats must just drop off the end if they go too far. According to this book you gave me, though, the world ain't flat. You really think that's true? That the world is round?"

"Yes, Annie. I think that's true. The world is round. Just like the book says."

"Well, what keeps things from dropping off when they get to the bottom side?" Her voice was deadly serious. "I watched a bug crawl around a plum the other day. He dropped off when he got to the bottom. I reckon people must live on the top part of the earth." She seemed relieved to have solved her problem.

Rose smiled. "People live all over the earth, Annie. A thing called gravity keeps them from falling off."

"Gravity? What that be?" Annie's eyes were wide with the joy of discovery. This was the very reason Rose had come here. She smiled down at the bright-eyed imp as they made their way into the schoolhouse.

Rose was tired but happy as she moved down the lane toward Annie's house. There were not many nights she did not share a meal with one of her students. There was a great competition to see whose invitation she would accept next. The white teachers ate with their students, too, but not nearly as often.

Annie's family lived in a small plank structure on the outskirts of the camp. The superintendent had managed to find ten acres of land for Annie's father to farm. Rose knew the association was fighting for more land for the refugees to raise crops on. As she neared the simple home, Annie ran from the door and raced down the road toward her.

"Miss Rose! Miss Rose!" Soon her whole family was gathered on the porch.

Rose looked around appreciatively as she hugged Annie, then took her hand as they walked the rest of the way together. The rich, dark soil had been well worked, and a variety of vegetables were already exploding toward the sky. Rose's mouth began to water.

"Hello, Amos. Hello, Harriet." Rose smiled and then examined the faces of her hosts. They were smiling, but their faces and eyes were clouded with tension. "Is something wrong?" she asked quietly, her heart suddenly heavy with foreboding.

Amos was the first to speak. "Those soldier fellows are at it again," he stated bitterly.

"Now," Harriet protested, "ain't all the soldiers bad."

"Didn't say they were," Amos snapped. "But they be enough of the bad ones to cause a passel of trouble."

"What happened?" Rose asked, then glared at the children.

"The children know what's going on. Ain't good to hide trouble from kids. They won't be ready when it comes close to them," Amos said.

It was one of the truths of slavery—everyone, even children, had to be prepared for hurt and pain.

"A friend of mine—fella who ran off from the same plantation as me—been farming not too far from here. He and some other fellas used their own money to work and plant 'bout sixty acres. This afternoon some Union general—I think his name be Burnside—came through with his troops. Those soldiers done destroyed nearly all their crops!"

"But why?" Rose exclaimed, guessing the answer before Amos gave it.

"There be a powerful lot of hate in them Union folks, too," Amos growled bitterly. "I reckon there ain't never going to be a time we ain't gonna have to fight for things."

Rose wished it wasn't so, but the truth of his words couldn't be denied. Anger threatened to overwhelm her as she thought of all that hard work needlessly ruined. How many people would go hungry because those crops were destroyed? "I'll talk to the superintendent," she promised.

"Oh, I done went and talked to him. He'll do what he can. Trouble is, you can't control all them soldiers." He looked around his farm with a sigh. "I been lucky so far. I wonder how long it will last?"

Annie sidled up to Rose. "Do people really hate me just 'cause I'm colored?"

Rose knelt quickly, her heart constricting. "Yes, honey, there are some people who will hate you just because you're colored. Some people are ignorant and just don't know better. But there are a lot of good, kind white people out there, too," she hastened to add. "White people who are fighting for us to be free. White people who are sending books down here so you can learn and raising money to help you eat. Why, it was a white person who made it possible for these very camps to exist. He was a general, just like the men who destroyed the crops."

"We got white teachers, too," Annie observed thoughtfully.

Rose breathed a sigh of relief. More than anything, she did not want the negroes in the camps to learn to distrust all Northern whites because of the activities of some. She nodded. "That's right, honey. Being good or bad isn't a color thing. It's a heart thing. We all have to work on our hearts."

"I'll work on my heart. But I'll also work on some Yankee soldiers if they come near my place. I spend all day working for that army. I don't reckon I'm going to let them walk all over me. I ran away from slavery so's I wouldn't have no one walking on me," Amos said, still angry.

Harriet just gazed at her and shrugged her shoulders.

Rose didn't answer. She understood his anger. Placing her hand on Annie's shoulder, she said, "Now, how about we go inside and taste your momma's good cooking?" Perhaps the meal would help them forget today's bad news.

Annie smiled and took her teacher's hand, leading her into the humble home.

Annie had been right. Her momma had been cooking all day. Dish after dish of hot vegetables graced the table, and mounds of fresh cornbread spun their delicious fragrance into the air. Rose was stuffed when she finally pushed back from the table. "Harriet, that was wonderful," she groaned, patting her stomach.

Annie jumped up. "You said we could sing tonight, momma!"

"So I did, young'un. Go get your daddy's fiddle. I reckon he can rustle us up some songs."

Rose felt her worries and cares drift away as song after song flowed into the darkening night, drifting up to dance with the stars. She had discovered long ago that it was impossible to carry burdens while singing. The very act seemed to lift the worries right out of the soul.

Finally Amos put down his fiddle. "I reckon I better be getting you back to your house, Miss Rose."

Rose hated to leave, but she knew he was right. She thanked Harriet, hugged the children, and walked with Amos down the road. Neither talked, content to let the magic of the night hold them. They were perhaps a half mile from the house when a distant shout caused them to turn and look back.

"Was that Harriet?" Amos asked with a puzzled look on his face, leaning forward to try to penetrate the darkness with his eyes.

Craning to listen, Rose was suddenly aware what she was hearing—the thud of horse hooves and the distant shouts of men. Soldiers!

Amos realized it at the same instant she did. "Soldiers!" he growled, his voice tight with fear and anger. "I got to get to my family," he cried desperately.

"I'm coming with you!" Rose declared, trying to push aside the pictures crowding into her mind.

"No!" Amos said fiercely. "Go get help!" Then he turned and fled.

Rose gazed after him for just a moment, then ran the other direction. She would go to the superintendent. Mr. Crosby would help. It seemed like forever before she was pounding on his door. It opened almost instantly, the kindly man staring out at her with a concerned look on his face.

"Rose? What's wrong?"

"Amos ... Harriet and the kids ... " Rose gasped, her words tumbling together. She took a deep breath. "Soldiers are there. Amos was gone—walking me home. He's gone back. . . . I'm afraid. . . . " she gulped, unable to say more.

"I'm on my way," Mr. Crosby promised. "I'll get some men to help."

"I'll come with you."

"No, you go back to your house. It's simply not safe for you to be out right now," he said firmly, then turned to talk to someone in the house. A man Rose knew well appeared behind him. "Walk Miss Rose home. Don't leave until you see her into the house. I'm on my way out to Amos' place. I'll let you know what's happening," he quickly promised Rose, then turned and disappeared.

Rose was sitting in the living room when the long-awaited knock finally came. She sprang toward the door. Marianne, who had waited up with her, followed right behind. She pulled the door open expectantly. At the look on Mr. Crosby's face, her whole body tightened with fear. She held the door open wordlessly, then followed him into the living room.

He stood at the mantel for a long while, staring down at the empty fireplace. His tall body sagged with fatigue, and his face was lined with what she could only guess was sorrow and anger. He seemed to be struggling with what to say.

"What happened?" Rose finally asked. It was better to know than to continue to hang in the torment of wondering.

"Amos didn't make it in time," Mr. Crosby finally managed. "Harriet and Annie . . . " he choked on the words. "They were raped," he finally said, his eyes filling with tears. "They're still alive," he added. "They will be okay."

Rose groaned and hid her hands in her face. Images of Annie's bright face and ready laugh filled her mind. She could still see Harriet proudly carrying bowls of vegetables to the table and singing loudly, her round face creased with smiles. "No," she cried softly.

"How is Amos?" Marianne asked, her cracked voice revealing her own pain.

There was another long silence.

"The soldiers beat him up pretty badly," Mr. Crosby finally admitted. "He tried to stop them. There were just too many. By the time we got there, the soldiers were riding off into the darkness, laughing."

Fury blazed through Rose. "We have to catch them!" she cried. "They can't get away with this!"

"We're going to do everything we can," the superintendent promised with a heavy voice.

"But there's not anything we *can* do, is there?" Rose yelled angrily. "Is this what freedom is going to be like? If this is the way the refugees are going to be treated, they might as well be in slavery!" Rose knew her emotions were getting the best of her, but she didn't care. The thoughts of Annie and her family were driving her mad.

Mr. Crosby walked over to put a hand on her shoulder. "I know you're upset, Rose. We'll do everything we can," he repeated. "Annie and her family are going to need you. They trust you."

Rose stared up at him, searching his face, then dissolved into tears.

Marianne was at her side in an instant, gathering her up in her strong arms.

Moses and June crept out of her tiny cabin while it was still pitch dark. The storm had blown by, leaving the air cool and fresh, heavy with the sweet smells of summer. Honeysuckle assaulted their senses, mixing with the aroma of fresh-cut grass from nearby hay fields.

Moses knew the fresh mud would reveal their tracks to anyone looking, but a late-night conference with Bart had convinced him Saunders' overseer wouldn't come looking. There was no one else to keep an eye on the rest of the slaves if he took off, and besides, there were so many slaves running away, the area overseers had become rather indifferent to it. They would do the best they could with the slaves they had left. No planter could expect more of them than that.

Moses moved steadily, but at a much slower pace. June's pregnancy wouldn't permit them to go as fast as Moses would've liked to. After much thought, he had decided to do the only thing that seemed reasonable. They would go as far as they could in the boat. When he deemed it unsafe, they would return to land. He knew he was taking a chance. The closer he got to Hampton, the more boats and people he would find. On the other hand, the closer he got, the greater the chance the Union would accept them as contraband. Once they arrived, he would figure out a way to convince them he was a Union spy, needing to join McClellan.

Neither one spoke a word as they eased through the tangled underbrush. Moses prayed silently. He was not at all sure he could find the boat he had left behind, but his whole plan hinged on him doing just that. He had been afraid to take the road, sure he would never recognize where he had broken out of the woods and met Bart. If he was going to find the boat, he would have to stick to the shoreline. Finally the sun began to make the moving easier. At the pace they were going, it would probably take another two hours to reach the boat.

"Are we almost there?" June asked quietly, fatigue radiating from her voice.

"We have a little farther to go," Moses admitted. "But we're making good time," he lied. "Why don't we stop and have something to eat?"

"That would be nice," June agreed. Seconds later she sagged against a log, her hands resting on her swollen stomach. "I won't always be this tired," she said with a weak smile. "Not getting any sleep last night—along with all the excitement . . . "

"I know," Moses replied soothingly. "We're doing just fine. Once we find the boat, you can have a nice long rest. We won't be moving again until dark."

He allowed her to rest for almost an hour, then they pressed on. When he was sure they must be close, he searched until he found a shaded, sheltered clearing in the woods. Moving quickly, he gathered huge armfuls of long grass and mounded them on the dirt and pine needles. "You can rest here until we're ready to leave."

"But where is the boat?" June asked, looking around bewildered.

Moses looked at her tenderly, seeing his mother in her face. He knew she was exhausted. "I'm going to find the boat now. I'm sure it's not too much farther. I'm going to leave the food and water," he said, hoisting a big bag off his shoulder. "I'll be back soon."

"You sure nothing will get me out here?" June asked anxiously.

"Nothing more than some mosquitoes," Moses replied with a grin.

June smiled, then laughed out loud. "I'm sorry. Of course I'll be fine. Good luck with the boat."

Moses heaved a sigh of relief, waved, and plunged into the woods. Now that he was alone, he would make much better time. And he wouldn't have to work so hard to hide the anxiety he was feeling at the idea of not finding the boat. That morning had convinced him June could never walk all the way to Hampton in her condition. If he didn't find the boat—if someone had taken it—he didn't know what they would do.

The sun continued to climb, once again laying its sultry grip on the countryside. Moses was soon glistening with sweat and breathing hard. He searched the woods with his eyes. He had not pulled the boat up too far before he had hidden it. But where was it? Every stand of brush and undergrowth was beginning to look like the hiding place he had hastily constructed.

Suddenly his face cleared and he bounded forward with a glad shout. "It's here!" he cried, then looked around fearfully, realizing that someone could've heard him if anyone was nearby. Now was not the time to become careless. He had made it this far by exercising great caution. He had June to be responsible for—he would need to be even more careful. Peering into the pile of brush, he satisfied himself that the boat was really there, scoped out the area for landmarks, then turned back to rejoin his sister. He would leave the boat hidden until dusk.

Fifteen

Carrie looked into the mirror and tucked a few loose strands of hair into her bun. Not that it would matter. She knew the intense humidity would tease them back into rebellion in just a few minutes when she stepped outside. A quick, critical gaze in the mirror told her she looked as well as she could, considering the pasty pallor of her skin—the result of long hours in the hospital. Quite suddenly she longed for the mirror in her bedroom at home on Cromwell. She had watched herself grow up in that mirror. She had told secrets to, and had had secrets revealed to her, by that mirror. All her life it had stood as a symbol of courage and fortitude. Was it still intact? Had the Union soldiers discovered the ultimate secret it held?

"Are you coming, Carrie?"

Carrie shook her head, bringing herself back to the present. There was little time for idle thought now. She missed her days of daydreaming. "Grow up!" she hissed to the mirror. Then she raised her voice. "Coming, Janie!"

Carrie gazed around her as the carriage rolled through the streets. She had not been downtown for almost a month. Not since the night Robert had proposed to her. Her skin tingled now as she thought of it.

"Any word when Robert will be home?" Janie asked, as if reading her mind.

Carrie shook her head. She knew her friend was just giving her an opportunity to talk about him. "The fighting at Cedar Mountain seems to be over. Father told me Lee was moving his army north to join with Jackson. He thinks there is to be another big battle at Manassas." She shuddered thinking about it. Robert had been wrong.

He had not returned quickly from another short mission. He had been gone a month, with a return nowhere in sight.

"Well, you'll be ready for him when he comes," Janie said firmly.

Carrie tried to draw hope from her friend's words. Surely now that she and Robert were on the verge of marriage he would come home to her. Surely God would not take him from her now. It was so hard to keep hope alive. So hard to see soldier after soldier die from wounds inflicted during what they were now calling the Seven Days' Battle. The battle for Richmond was over for the time, but could Robert possibly continue to live in the midst of such carnage? Most of the time she was able to silence her fears with busy activity. But the times when her fears haunted her were still too frequent, causing the shadow in her eyes her father had commented on the night before.

"Your daddy was right," Janie observed. "You need to spend some time away from the hospital. I think going shopping is just the remedy for you."

"I thought you said goods were scarce," Carrie protested.

"Let's just say you won't have the choice you had before the war," Janie admitted with a grin. "And be glad your daddy still has some money left."

Carrie frowned. She knew her father was sinking most of his fortune into support of the Confederacy. She had seen the ledger book he left opened on his desk one night. He had mortgaged Cromwell Plantation before the war started, confident in his belief it would be a short, successful struggle. What was reality doing to his hopes now? Carrie shook her head firmly. It would do no good to wonder. She was supposed to be having a good time. "Where are we going?" she asked, forcing a cheerful note into her voice. Janie's quick glance said her friend knew she was playacting, but she played along anyway.

"I thought we would see what Thalheimer's has."

"I won't buy anything fancy," Carrie warned. "Not when so many people are in need."

Janie shrugged. "Quite frankly, I think you could show up in rags and Robert would be thrilled."

Those words caused a genuine smile to warm Carrie's face. It was still incredible to her that she was to be married soon—just as soon as Robert returned. Basking in the glow of his love, she allowed herself to believe it would really happen.

The carriage was just pulling up in front of Thalheimer's when Carrie heard her name called. She turned quickly, a wide grin springing to her face. "Pastor Anthony!" she cried, jumping from the carriage and moving quickly to join him. "It's wonderful to see you."

"And you, as well, Miss Cromwell. I suspected you were in the city."

Carrie nodded, examining the man standing in front of her. He was still the same well-dressed, middle-aged man she remembered, but she could not miss the haggard expression and dark circles under his kindly eyes. "I'm so sorry I haven't been to see you," she said. "I arrived in the city about the middle of May and have been working in the hospital ever since."

"Say no more," Pastor Anthony interrupted. "I understand only too well. There are very few buildings not full of wounded soldiers now. I have seen the heroic care the women of the city have given."

"How are you, Pastor?"

"We can talk about me in a few minutes. How are your friends? Did they make it home?" It was obvious he was choosing his words carefully in front of Janie.

Carrie nodded her head joyfully. "So much has happened . . . " Then she turned toward the carriage and said, "Please let me introduce you to a very dear friend of mine." After the introductions had been made, she said, "I have plenty of time to do my shopping. Why don't we go sit in the Capitol Square and talk for a few minutes. Do you have time?"

"Certainly," he agreed.

The shade from the trees covering the benches offered a welcome respite from the searing August heat. After finding a seat somewhat out of the flow of heavy traffic, Carrie turned to Pastor Anthony. "Rose and Moses made it to Philadelphia. I know very little about how it went. I got a short letter one night telling me they had reached their destination safely. Rose wasn't free to write more. I can't begin to tell you how thankful I am that you helped us connect with the Underground Railroad." She glanced at Janie. "She knows everything. We're free to talk."

"I'm so glad they made it!" Pastor Anthony said fervently. "The Underground Railroad has pretty much faded out of existence now. There are huge numbers of slaves simply walking away from their owners and heading North to freedom. The war has given them cause to believe freedom is just around the corner."

"Do you think it is?" Janie asked hopefully.

"I hope so, but I have no way of knowing. All I know is I'm thankful for whatever gives them the courage to make those decisions."

"Do you know anything of Eddie?" Carrie asked. She had not been able to get near the prison where Eddie, Opal's cousin whom Opal had lived with for a while, was incarcerated on charges of spying and anti-war activities. All she had been able to do was offer Opal and Eddie's children a safe place on the plantation when he had been imprisoned and his wife was killed in a factory explosion.

"Castle Thunder is an awful place," Pastor Anthony said grimly. "I have heard Libby Prison is like a haven compared to it."

Carrie shuddered. "There's nothing that can be done to get him released?"

"I'm afraid not. The Confederate authorities are cracking down hard on anti-war activities. The man they have in charge of the prison is a brute. The best we can hope for is that Eddie doesn't get hung in the midst of all this. Are Opal and the kids safe?"

"They were the last I knew," Carrie replied. Her frustration mounted as the number of unknowns in her life grew. "I haven't heard anything about Cromwell Plantation being destroyed. While they are there they will at least be able to eat. And there are always the Contraband Camps," she added. "They know they're free to go."

"How is your work in the hospital going?" Pastor Anthony changed the subject.

"Exhausting, but rewarding," Carrie said simply. "I have nightmares every night and wake up every morning wondering which of my patients is going to die that day, but I am learning, and I hope I'm making a difference."

"Carrie is being modest," Janie interjected. "She is the only woman carrying any real medical responsibilities."

Carrie shrugged. "I'm just doing my job."

Pastor Anthony leaned forward. "Could you add one more job to your list?" he asked intently.

"What do you have in mind, Pastor?" Carrie would do whatever she could for the kind pastor. Without his help, Rose and Moses would not have been able to escape. She owed him a great deal and respected him highly.

"There is a hospital in the colored part of town," he began.

"I didn't know that," Carrie responded, surprised. "Not that I know every hospital."

"It isn't well-known yet. It's really a rather loose use of the term, just my attempt to help the negroes of Richmond. It can be almost impossible for them to obtain medical help anywhere else."

Carrie listened closely, drawn by the compassion in his voice. She knew he cared deeply for the colored people in his church. "Where is it?"

"Not too far from my church, down by the riverfront. In fact, it is just three buildings down."

"Who is running it?" Carrie inquired.

Pastor Anthony smiled slightly as he shrugged his shoulders. "I'm afraid I am."

"I didn't know you knew anything about medicine!" Carrie couldn't hide the surprise in her voice.

"I don't," he said apologetically. "But I couldn't stand seeing the people . . . I mean . . . I had to do something."

Carrie nodded. She understood Pastor Anthony's heart. She looked at Janie and knew they were thinking the exact same thing. Turning back to the pastor, she asked, "Why don't you take us there?"

"When?" Pastor Anthony responded in amazement, disbelief on his face.

"No time like the present," Carrie said. "Shopping can be done anytime." Her voice grew serious. "I don't know what I can do, but I'll try my best to help."

"I will, too," Janie agreed.

"Supplies are becoming very limited all over the city," Carrie continued. "The blockade is working too well, I'm afraid. There are many medicines becoming harder to obtain." She shook her head. "Until I see the place and some of your patients, I won't know what we can do."

"I would appreciate anything," Pastor Anthony replied fervently.

"Is there a doctor?" Janie asked.

Pastor Anthony just laughed a mirthless laugh.

"I'm not a doctor, Pastor Anthony," Carrie said quietly. "But Janie and I have seen a lot since we began at Chimborazo." She stood. "I'll have my father's driver take us down there. Spencer has become somewhat used to my strange requests."

Just then a loud laugh down the street drew her attention. There was something familiar in it, and Carrie glanced up. When she saw Louisa staring back at her, she almost groaned out loud. She was in no mood to put up with her old nemesis today. "Hello, Louisa," she said as pleasantly as she could.

"Well, if it isn't Carrie Cromwell," Louisa replied with a hateful sneer. "Look, girls," she said to the young women accompanying her. "Do you remember me telling you about my old neighbor who humiliated her father and her friends by becoming a nigger lover?"

Carrie took a deep breath as she struggled to control her anger.

Janie reached out to touch her arm. "She's not worth it," she said quietly.

"Thank goodness there are still those among us who know how to love all of God's creation, miss," Pastor Anthony said with a gentle smile. "I think it's possible you don't understand the love he has for you."

Louisa stared at Pastor Anthony, her lips curling in scorn. "And who are you, old man?"

Carrie gasped, shocked at Louisa's disrespect. "Louisa Blackwell!" she said indignantly. "This is Pastor Marcus Anthony."

Louisa, obviously not impressed, edged closer, her eyes narrowing. "I've heard about you," she said to the pastor. "You're the pastor of that colored church down by the river."

"That's right," Pastor Anthony agreed, a gentle smile on his lips.

Louisa pounced. "I think you ought to be ashamed of yourself. A healthy man like you ought to be fighting this war, not playing God to a bunch of negroes who don't have a soul anyway." Her voice was strident, causing a number of people to turn their heads and stare.

Carrie had heard enough. "Louisa Blackwell, I'm ashamed of you."

Louisa merely laughed. "Oh, fiddle, Carrie Cromwell. You must know by now I don't care one iota what you think of me. You made it clear long ago that you had taken leave of your senses. Thank heavens there are still people who can think—who can see people like you for what they really are. A South-hating, nigger-loving traitor."

Pastor Anthony stood, his voice controlled but firm. "Miss Blackwell, I have just met you, but I feel the need to say something. The word 'nigger' is completely reprehensible to me. The word means ignorant—if you care to look up the meaning for yourself. It has absolutely nothing to do with race or societal status. I have discovered it is most used by people who are much more ignorant than the people they are trying to malign." He turned to Carrie and Janie. "Would you care to be going now, ladies?"

Carrie glanced back and smiled at the sight of Louisa standing with her mouth open, silent for once.

"A rather pitiful young woman," Pastor Anthony remarked. "Has she always been so unhappy?"

"I'd say she brings most of her unhappiness on herself," Carrie retorted, still seething with anger.

"That may be," Pastor Anthony responded. "But unhappiness is still a miserable thing. I would not want to have to live with the poison in her heart, no matter what caused it."

Carrie was quiet, pondering his words, but still angry at Louisa.

It was not until they were in the carriage that Pastor Anthony spoke again. "May I share a thought with you?"

Carrie nodded somewhat reluctantly.

"Carrie, no matter what you do, someone is not going to like it." He turned to Janie. "The same thing goes for you." He looked back at Carrie. "Both of you girls are different. A good different—but a lot of people won't see it that way. They are threatened by your love and acceptance of negroes because they perceive it as a threat to their own image and position."

"But it's not!" Carrie cried.

"Of course it's not," Pastor Anthony agreed immediately. "But fear is not governed by reason. It is governed by the emotions of the heart." He paused. "That's not what I wanted to say, though. It's true that no matter what you do, there will always be someone who doesn't agree with you. I've learned that all I can do is make my decisions the best I can, then resolve to live with the consequences. Once you're quite sure of how you feel about yourself, it's easier to find humor in situations when people attack you. You're not so busy trying to decide how to defend yourself because other people's opinion of you simply is not important anymore."

Carrie stared at him. "I understand about making your decisions and living with the consequences, but I'm afraid I see nothing funny in what just happened with Louisa."

"She sure did look funny standing there in the middle of Capitol Square with her mouth wide open," Janie said slowly.

Pastor Anthony smiled. "And it seemed to me the people who were looking, were looking more at her."

"Louisa's ears always do turn a little red when she gets angry," Carrie put in, smiling.

The three looked at each other for a few moments, then dissolved into laughter. When they stopped laughing, Carrie discovered she was no longer angry. "You're right, Pastor Anthony," she said thoughtfully. "I do feel sorry for her."

Pastor Anthony nodded. "She must be a truly lonely person. It is very hard to receive love when you have none to give out."

Carrie pondered his words as the carriage rattled through the streets. He was right. All anyone could do was make their decisions and live with the consequences. She had made her decision about slavery. She could accept the consequences with bitterness—or with humor and loving acceptance. She knew it would probably always be a battle for her. Her temper was too hot and quick when people attacked something she believed in. Suddenly she realized she was no different from the people whose hot tempers had started the war. She just happened to be hot-tempered about something different. The realization was sobering.

"Why the heavy look?" Janie asked.

"I'm just realizing human nature is a very difficult thing to escape. We can be self-righteous—or realize much of what we hate in others is what we have inside ourselves."

"Kind of dissolves your anger, doesn't it?" Pastor Anthony said.

"Yes, it does," Carrie agreed. She looked at the pastor. "I guess it's easier to give when you're not so busy condemning the other fellow."

"Sure does free up a lot of energy," he agreed with a smile.

Carrie laughed suddenly, feeling as if a burden had been lifted from her heart. She may have to learn this lesson over and over, but she felt as if, for a brief moment, she had been given a bird's-eye view of the human race. She found people much easier to love from this angle.

"Here's my hospital," Pastor Anthony announced suddenly.

Carrie looked up quickly. She had been so absorbed in her own thoughts, she hadn't even been aware of her surroundings. Now she looked around. She remembered the street well from when she had come in search of Pastor Anthony when she needed help with Rose and Moses. It looked much the same, with men loitering around shabby buildings. Across the river she could see tents spreading out like a wave on Belle Island. Her heart ached for the men who were living there as prisoners.

Pastor Anthony led her and Janie into the ramshackle building. Carrie stared around her. The structure itself was really not bad. There were plenty of windows, and the ceilings were high enough to allow for adequate circulation. But there was not a single bed in the place. Rows of patients lay on coarse mattresses resting on the dirt floor, and swarms of black flies feasted on the bodies of the infirm.

"Hello, Pastor Anthony," a woman called, raising her hand in greeting.

Carrie suddenly noticed a number of women moving between the rows of sick people.

Pastor Anthony saw where she was looking. "The women come to help whenever they can. I'm afraid we have no regular nurses."

Carrie shrugged. "There are scores of hospitals and sick houses in the area that don't have nurses. It is impossible to meet the demand." She watched the women closely. Their caring and tenderness were evident as they held water glasses and cooled hot faces with wet rags.

"What illnesses do these patients have?" Janie asked.

"Mostly typhoid. Some of the men have been hurt building fortifications. A few have been injured working in the munitions plants."

"No one offered them care?" Carrie asked indignantly.

Pastor Anthony shook his head. "If a slave is injured, the owner takes responsibility. The patients here in the hospital are free."

Carrie looked again at the patients, then turned to Pastor Anthony. "What can we do to help?"

A great sigh of relief exploded from Pastor Anthony's lips. "Whatever you can," he said helplessly, spreading his hands. "You're the doctor."

Carrie opened her lips to contradict him, then shut them again. To a people with absolutely no medical care, she could be whatever they needed her to be. There would be no one studying her credentials here. The only thing they would be interested in was whether or not she could help them. She turned to Janie with a question in her eyes.

Janie nodded. "I can't think of anything better to do with my spare time," she said with a slight smile. "I'm in this with you."

Carrie smiled back and turned to the pastor. "We'll take a look at the patients now. We'll do what we can. Chimborazo is still crowded but the critical cases have stabilized. We will have more free time— at least until the next battle."

Carrie and Janie moved from patient to patient, examining them and talking with them quietly. They met back at the front of the building. "There's not much wrong here that can't be treated with the right medicines. The people here seem to be suffering mostly from bad water and malnutrition."

She called Pastor Anthony over. "Do all of the people in your church have gardens?" she asked crisply. When he shook his head, she continued. "Well, they need to. There is still time for some crops to be grown before summer is over. Every single person in your church who has any land at all around their house should put a garden in. Many of your patients are suffering from malnutrition. They have no defenses to fight disease. They need good food." She saw him open his mouth to interrupt, but stopped him. "I know good food is hard to come by because of the prices, but you simply must find a way. These people are going to have to take care of themselves since there is no one else to do it."

Pastor Anthony nodded slowly, deep in thought. "There is some land behind these buildings. It is horribly overgrown, however."

"Get people to clear it," Carrie said in a firm voice. "Plant food everywhere you can find a place." She paused. "I'm going to need about fifteen people to come with me next week for one day," she continued.

Pastor Anthony blinked, but nodded again.

"Have them bring bags. I wish I could say there is medicine for these people, but the truth of the matter is, there is a shortage in all the hospitals. Even if I could get my hands on some, there is no money to pay for it. We'll make our own."

"Make our own?" the pastor echoed.

"Yes," Carrie continued, blessing Old Sarah once again for all she had taught her. "I'll need to take the women out into the woods. It's not too late to gather herbs that will help with much of what ails these people. In the meantime, I want you to make sure these people get plenty of fresh water. There are still wells that have pure water. They are not to drink anything that doesn't come from them." She paused. "One more thing. I want every single piece of bedding in here washed in hot water." From the looks of things, it has been a long time since they had seen *any* water.

Pastor Anthony nodded yet again, then turned to Janie. "Should I salute?" he whispered.

Carrie joined in the laughter, but knew her orders would be followed. "We'll be back as soon as we can," she promised.

Carrie and Janie stared at each other in excitement as they rode back toward the center of town.

Janie was the first to speak. "Can you believe it?" she finally said.

Carrie smiled. There would be no medical school until after the war was over, but that didn't mean she couldn't help people now. There would be no one staring over her shoulder as she tried to help the colored people lying in that building. Grim determination took hold of her. It was up to her and Janie. They would have to learn all they could—absorbing knowledge as they worked in Chimborazo and scouring all their medical journals. The people in that hospital were counting on them.

Dinner was already on the table when Thomas strode in the door with a grim expression on his face. He nodded to everyone, then settled himself in his chair. "I'm sorry I'm late," he said apologetically.

"Bad news?" Carrie asked quietly.

"There will be another battle soon," he said shortly. "Forces are once more gathering at Manassas. From what I hear, General Pope is much more forceful than McClellan."

Carrie whitened, but remained silent. She would never get used to the idea of Robert in battle—she would never lose her fear of losing him—but expressing her fears served no purpose. They were being shared by hundreds of thousands of women all over the country. She had much to be thankful for. At least they were only fears and not a reality.

Thomas shook his head. "General Lee is an excellent commander. Only time will tell," he said with a heavy sigh. "General Pope has quite a record in the west."

Carrie waited quietly, sure her father had more to say.

He finally looked up with a heavy sigh. "General Cobb sent a message to Secretary of War Randolph. As you know, he's one of our nations most eminent political leaders. The note was quite to the point." Thomas paused, remembering. "It said, '*This war must be closed in a few months, perhaps weeks, or else will be fought with increased energy and malignity on the part of our enemies. I look for the latter result.*'" He focused on Carrie again. "I'm afraid I agree with him." His eyes darkened with anger. "General Pope certainly has that attitude," he said angrily.

"What do you mean?" Carrie asked.

"Evidently Pope has decided it is his job to teach the inhabitants of occupied Virginia that secession is a rocky road to travel. I have seen a copy of his orders. Citizens of occupied territory will be held responsible for all damage done by guerrillas. Any guerrillas who are caught will be executed, along with those who aid them. If shots are fired at Union soldiers from any house, that house will be destroyed and the people arrested. Anyone they deem as disloyal will be driven outside the Union lines, and will be treated as spies if they return. If they choose to stay, they must take an oath of allegiance to the United States. If they take it and then violate it they will be shot!" Thomas' voice rose steadily, ending in a shout as he slammed his fist on the table. "The man is a monster!"

A long silence filled the room. Carrie ached for her father, but knew there was nothing she could do. Except perhaps take his mind off of it for a little while. It was he who had told her that in order to win the war all other considerations must be put aside and the total energy of the country concentrated on victory. Was that not what the North was doing? She was quite sure he would not appreciate an objective viewpoint.

She had decided not to tell him about her confrontation with Louisa today, and her news about working in the colored hospital could wait too. He would only worry about her safety, and it would also bring up uncomfortable questions about how she knew Pastor Anthony. She searched for something to talk about.

"I got a long letter from home today," Janie said, reaching for the piece of paper beside her plate. She opened it up and read through some of it, then looked up with a smile. "This is the part I was looking for."

"Heard from your sister in Alabama today. You know there is a strong Union presence in her area. She wrote and told me there has been great resistance by the people there. Guerrillas have been firing into Union trains as they go along the tracks through the forests. The commander there finally got tired of it and ordered that ministers and other leading churchmen be arrested and put on the train one a day to try and stop the guerrillas. Your sister says our men are wonderful shots, so they continue to shoot the Yankees, while the pastors sit there unharmed. I'm sure the Union commander is frustrated that his wonderful plan isn't working."

Carrie smiled halfheartedly, unable to find any real humor in anyone else being shot. "How long has it been since you've seen your family, Janie?" she asked, even though she knew the answer. She had watched Janie's loneliness for her family grow in the last few months.

"Almost two years," she admitted with a slight catch in her voice.

"Why don't you go home for a visit?" Carrie couldn't imagine not seeing her father for almost two years. "Raleigh isn't really that far if you take the train."

"It's not that easy," Janie replied. "I've looked into it."

Carrie opened her mouth to protest, but her father spoke up, having gained control of his earlier anger.

"Janie's right, Carrie. It's possible, of course, but travel is becoming more and more difficult."

"Why?" she demanded. "It's not like she wants to go north."

"She still has to have a passport," Thomas responded. "I'm afraid the Confederacy has found it necessary to impose rather strict travel restrictions."

" A passport?" Carrie had never heard of such a thing. "That's ridiculous!" she snorted.

"I'm afraid it's not," Thomas said heavily. "However ineffective it may be, it's seen as a defense against spies carrying valuable information north." He paused. "You can get them, of course, but there is a backlog of paper work. You'd have to plan far in advance. Then there is the problem of the trains," he continued. "Our troops have first priority on every train. It is especially hard to get a seat on a train leaving Richmond; most are occupied by soldiers."

Carrie sighed with frustration. "Is there any part of our lives this war isn't touching?" No one answered.

Sixteen

oses pulled the boat ashore and turned away. He and June had come as far downriver as they could. They had managed to slip by the myriad of large boats in the river the night before, but it was getting too risky. He had spent every second of the long night wondering when a shot was going to blast forth from one of the silent watchdogs. He knew June was almost sick with fear, not to mention the heaving of her stomach as the wind had tossed the little boat back and forth on curling white-caps. It was time to continue on land.

Moses turned to June. "We'll walk from here."

June sagged with relief against a tree. "I'll make it, Moses," she promised. "I know we made good time in the boat, but if I never see water again that will be just fine with me!" she declared passionately. She held her hand to her stomach. "My baby agrees," she said, smiling now.

Moses smiled back at her, trying to hide his concern. He just wished he had some way of knowing where they were. June had been wonderful—as brave and strong as he remembered her. But she was going to be a mother soon. She had experienced sharp pains the night before, leaving him terrified she would have the baby right in the boat. The pains had eased, but his fear had not. He had to get her somewhere she would be safe—both she and the baby.

He turned to where she was resting, sitting on the ground with her back against a tree. "I'm going to look around. Maybe there is a road."

June struggled to her feet. "I'm coming with you," she announced calmly.

"You need to rest!" Moses protested.

"I need to be with you," she corrected him. "You said yourself we might be near the fort. If you are captured by soldiers, I want to be with you. I am *not* going to be left in the woods by myself." Her voice left no room for argument.

Moses nodded reluctantly, then took her arm to help her through the undergrowth. "Let's go, little sister."

Twenty minutes later they broke out of the woods onto a road. It looked to be well-traveled. Moses did his best to remember the map he had pored over before leaving. He had followed the river southeast, careful to hug the western shore. He was somewhere near the end of the long peninsula that protruded into the Chesapeake Bay. Fort Monroe perched on the very end of the peninsula. In order to reach it he would have to travel northeast. Moses studied the road they were standing on. It seemed to head due east. He shrugged. At some point he would have to head north, but at least the road didn't veer farther south. They would take it. It was better than crashing through the woods.

A sound in the distance caught his attention. Moses snapped his head up and listened closely. Grabbing June's arm, he pulled her back into the bushes until he was sure they were invisible from the road. A few minutes later a knot of soldiers came riding around the curve, laughing and talking.

"Finally, we're going back North," one man said joyfully.

"Thank God," another growled. "If I have to breathe this wet stuff they call air even one more day, I think I'll scream. I can't wait to get off this peninsula with all its mosquitoes. I'm fed up with being eaten alive."

"Yeah," another man laughed. "I understand why these people want slaves to do all their work. You couldn't pay me enough to farm around here. Give me my little place in upstate New York any day."

Moses waited for their voices to fade into the distance before he pulled June out to the road again. "No talking," he said quietly. "I have to be able to hear if anything is coming." June nodded and started off in the direction he pointed. She was smiling with eyes full of trust. Moses found himself a bit unnerved. He wished he trusted himself as much.

They had walked for nearly two hours before they heard another noise and dove back into the bushes. Moses was peering out at the road when he heard June suck in her breath sharply. He spun around to stare at her. She was settled back against a tree with a pain-filled expression on her face. "June?" he whispered anxiously.

"I'm okay," she whispered. "It's just . . . " Another spasm of pain snatched her words as her face contorted in agony.

Moses tried to calm the panic rising in him.

Slowly, June's face relaxed, and she opened her mouth to speak again. "It's . . . " She raised her knuckles against her mouth and closed her eyes in a tortured expression.

Moses looked around frantically, panic-stricken at the thought of June having her baby in the middle of the woods. He should never have taken her from Saunders' plantation. At least she had been safe there. Had he rescued her only to have her and her baby die? The nearing clatter of wagon wheels made him duck behind the bush once more to peer out. He prayed June would not scream and reveal their hiding place.

Desperately, he began to pray for a way to get her to Fort Monroe. Even if she felt better, there was no way she was going to walk through this heat with him scavenging food along the way. He should have stayed in the boat, he realized. "God, help me!" he whispered.

Just then an approaching wagon slowly rounded the curve. Moses watched as the sturdily built conveyance, pulled by a handsome bay horse, drew nearer. His eyes opened wide when he realized the man and woman perched on the seat were colored, their light skin evidence of a mulatto heritage. Two children sat quietly in the back of the wagon. As they drew almost even with him, Moses could see a troubled look on their faces. Every few seconds the woman would peer around as if she were watching for pursuers. Runaways. Moses remembered well the furtive glances and sick feeling he had had when he was on the run, never knowing if the next bend hid a slave catcher who would take him back to his life of captivity or, worse, to be hung. Should he ask them for help? He was wracked with indecision.

A muted scream from behind him made the decision for him. The wagon plowed to a stop as the man jerked back on the reins. "You hear that?" he asked in a deep voice.

The woman nodded, her eyes as large as saucers. "Just keep going, Wally. You know we can't be stopping!" she cried. "There might be somebody after us."

Moses spun around just as June screamed again. His decision was made. Taking a deep breath, he stepped from the woods.

The woman gasped when she saw him materialize in front of their wagon, and the children's heads disappeared in a flash.

Moses held his hands up. "Please. I mean no harm. I'm sorry to frighten you."

The man she had called Wally glared at him suspiciously, his lean, lanky body coiled for attack. "Who are you, man? What's that screaming I here?" He looked fearfully at the bushes as another cry rent the air.

"It's my sister," Moses said, knowing he sounded desperate.

"She hurt?"

"No—I mean, I don't know—she's pregnant! I'm trying to get her to Fort Monroe." He was pleading now. "Can you help me get her there?"

Wally started to shake his head, but his wife stared hard at Moses, her earlier fear seemingly gone. "You say your sister is pregnant? What's she doing out here like this?"

Moses shook his head. "We didn't think she was due for another couple of months." He decided to be completely honest. "She just ran away from a plantation upriver. I'm trying to get her to safety. There's no way she can walk from here."

Wally broke into the conversation. "How do we know you're not just trying to trick us?"

Moses shrugged. "I guess you could come look at my sister." He took a deep breath. "Please. I just need to get her some help."

The wife was climbing down from the wagon, her stout form making the wagon appear oversized. Moses breathed a sigh of relief at the look of concern on her round face.

"Where you going, woman?" Wally protested.

She spun on him, her eyes flashing. "How would you have liked it if I had been out here like this having one of our fine babies? Lord, Wally, I can't just leave her out here." With those words she turned to Moses. "Where is she?"

Wally was climbing down from the wagon to follow them as Moses led her back through the woods. June was huddled against a tree, her face glistening with sweat, her breath coming in quick gasps. She stared up at them, her eyes wide with panic.

"Lord of mercy!" the woman breathed as she dashed to June's side. Squatting down in front of her, she said quietly, "It's gonna be all right, honey. You just try to breathe a little easier. Squeeze my hands when the pain comes."

June locked her eyes on the lady's kindly face. "Who are you?" she gasped.

"My name is Deidre. What's yours?" Her voice was calm and soothing.

"June," she managed, her face twisting again.

"Well, June, you just keep on squeezing my hands. Looks like your baby might be coming a little sooner than you expected."

Moses ground his teeth as he clenched his fist. This wasn't the way it was supposed to happen. June was supposed to be safe at Fort Monroe when the baby came. He stepped forward. "What can we do?"

Deidre looked up with a calm smile. "How about bringing a blanket from the back of the wagon?" Now that she had decided to help, it was obvious she was going to be in control. "Wally, best be moving the wagon off the road," she ordered. "We're going to be here a little while. Send little Carla over here. She can help. She may only be ten, but she's seen babies born."

Moses sprang into action, glad to have something to do. He was just coming back with the blankets when he heard June.

"My baby . . . Will it be . . . ?"

Deidre patted her hands. "There isn't any way of knowing what the good Lord has in mind right now. But I'd say our coming along when we did is a good sign."

Moses took hope from her words.

"Hurts . . . " June mumbled.

"There's never been a baby born yet that didn't make its momma miserable in the process. This one seems to be a little more determined than most, but that doesn't necessarily mean trouble." Deidre looked over her shoulder as Carla ran up, her pigtails bobbing behind her. Then turning to the men, she said firmly, "I'll call you when you're needed."

Moses opened his mouth to protest, but Wally grasped his arm firmly.

"The woman has been a midwife for years. Your sister couldn't be in better hands."

Moses allowed himself to be led away, but he felt sick inside. He glanced back for one final look at June. Their eyes locked and she flashed a quick smile before she doubled over in pain again. He knew she was trying to make him feel better, but he felt he was to blame for the fix they were in.

Wally had pulled the wagon deep into the woods. A little boy about six years old was sitting on the driver's bench. "This here is Andrew."

"How do, mister," Andrew said shyly.

Moses nodded but couldn't speak.

Wally looked at him closely. "You're headed to Fort Monroe?"

Moses just nodded again.

"Look, man, it ain't gonna do you any good to stand around and torment yourself. You said yourself the baby was early. Well, it ain't nobody but God that can tell a baby when it's time to be born. Stop beating yourself up. You done the best you could."

Moses stared at him, the truth of Wally's words finally pene-trating his guilt. "I don't know what I'll do if something happens to her." He found himself telling Wally the whole story—about their being separated, just finding her, and trying to spirit her away to freedom. "I got to get there soon!" he added desperately.

"You sound like you got something more on your mind than just making it to freedom," Wally observed perceptively.

Moses hesitated for a long minute, then took a deep breath. "I ran away from slavery last fall. Been living up in Philadelphia. I'm working as a spy for the Union army."

"Say what!" Wally exclaimed, skepticism loading his voice.

"It's true," Moses said. "My commander knew about my sister and gave me the time to help her escape. But I have to rejoin my unit in just two weeks. I promised."

Wally must have believed him. "I reckon you can still make it," he said calmly. He looked at Moses more closely. "You mean they're letting negroes serve in the Union army?"

"There's only a few of us right now," Moses said. "We're not allowed to carry guns. But I believe that is going to change. The North needs us. This is the colored man's war, too!"

Wally nodded. "I heard they're taking men on the ships." He paused, then evidently decided Moses could be trusted. "I'm headed for Fort Monroe to get on board one of those ships. I'm going to be in the United States Navy." There was no mistaking the pride in his voice.

Moses' heart quickened with hope. So they were headed to Fort Monroe, too! Wally must have read his mind.

"When my wife finishes helping your little sister out there, I reckon we'll all just keep going. We'll make it in time."

Moses took a deep breath, searching for the words to express what he was feeling. "Thank you," he finally said, knowing the words were woefully inadequate.

"We got to stick together, man," Wally said with a quick grin.

Suddenly a sharp cry sounded from the brush.

"June!" Moses exclaimed, leaping up.

Wally grabbed his arm. "That weren't June, Moses."

Moses was bewildered. "Then, who . . . ?"

"I reckon the Lord done dropped another little baby in our world. I guess he ain't giving up on it just yet." A smile played across his lips.

Moses stared at him for a moment, then spun back toward the woods. Another wail broke through the brush, floating toward them with the promise of new life. Moses gazed in the direction it had come from, torn with wonder and uncertainty. Was June all right? Would the baby make it?

After what seemed an eternity, Deidre appeared between the trees. Her face was peaceful, her smile beautiful. "Your sister and nephew would like to see you."

Moses sprang up instantly and dashed through the woods. He slowed, then stopped as soon as he entered the clearing. June was leaning against the tree, a tiny bundle in her arms, a look of awe on her face.

She glanced up and broke into a weary grin. "It's a boy," she whispered. "His name is Simon. I named him for his daddy." Her eyes glistened with tears as she gazed down at his tiny face.

Moses edged closer, then knelt beside them. "He's beautiful," he said quietly, his eyes never leaving the puckered face of his nephew. "Your husband will be very proud." Then he stared into June's face. "You okay?"

June nodded calmly. "I'm fine," she assured him. "Just tired."

Wally and his family appeared in the clearing. They watched for a minute, then Wally cleared his throat. "I pulled the wagon in a ways farther. I reckon we'll stay here through the night, then move on in the morning. June needs to get some rest, and that baby needs at least one night before he starts bumping and rolling. He's already had a pretty rude welcome to the world."

June looked up, gratitude radiating from her eyes. "Thank you so much," she said fervently. Just then little Simon opened his mouth and began to cry. June smiled tenderly and shifted him into position to feed him.

Moses watched for a moment, then began to gather armloads of fresh grass. The mother and new baby would at least have a soft place to rest. Wally appeared soon with another blanket to lay on the makeshift bed. June lay down gratefully. Within minutes mother and newborn were sound asleep.

Moses moved to where Wally had stashed his wagon, several yards away. "Are you running away, too?" he asked curiously.

"Trying to figure out how a slave got a wagon?" Wally grinned. "No, we ain't slaves. We are free," he said proudly. "My daddy was given his freedom after saving his owner's life. We been working a little farm not too far from here."

Moses was puzzled. "Why did Deidre seem scared someone might be coming after you?"

Wally scowled. "Bunch of Union soldiers rode through a few nights back. I reckon they were some stragglers of McClellan's. Ruined our crops, then set fire to our house. They rode off laughing before it caught good. I was able to put it out."

"They did it because you're colored?" Moses observed sourly.

"Didn't have nothing to do with being colored," Wally said firmly. "Them soldiers were just out looking for trouble. They never saw us. Had no idea what color we are." He chuckled. " 'Course it's funny when you're mulatto. The half of you that's colored is a heck of a lot more important to folks than the half of you that's white."

"I'm glad you can laugh about it," Moses said in amazement.

"You got to laugh, man. There's way too much in this life to make you cry." He paused, looking into the distance. "I reckon lots of people are going to think those soldiers are just after negroes. Ain't so. They're just after trouble. I heard them talking. Trashed as many white people's places as they did coloreds'. I guess war just does that to people. Sets loose the devil in them. Know what I mean?"

"Yeah," Moses responded. "I know what you mean."

Wally leaned forward in excitement. "When I saw my house burning I decided I was gonna join the Navy. I figure you're right. This ain't just a white man's war. Just 'cause I'm free doesn't mean I don't want freedom for the rest of my people. And being free in the South ain't so much different from being a slave anyhow. White people still treat you like trash," he said with contempt. "I want the day to come when all of us be free. If we're all working for the same thing, I figure we'll have a lot more power."

"The day is coming," Moses said solemnly. "I met some of the folks up North who are fighting to make it happen. Even saw Frederick Douglas speak one night."

Wally's eyes popped open. "You saw Frederick Douglas?" he breathed. "That man's really something. I've even read some of what he done wrote. He has a way with words, that one does. I bet hearing him speak must be something. Hard to believe he used to be a slave."

"He's a fine man," Moses agreed. "Wants nothing more than what we want. To see all his people free. It's coming, I tell you. It's coming." He paused, deep in thought. "The way I see it, the end is inevitable. The very fact the Union army is fighting in the South means the doom of slavery."

"How you figure?" Wally asked doubtfully.

"You should be with the Union troops. They don't think twice about taking a Southerner's property. That includes his slaves. The Union doesn't necessarily want anything to do with them, but if letting them go will hurt the Southerner, then they're all for it. Slaves are escaping in hordes. I reckon that Contraband Camp we're heading to is going to be pretty crowded." He paused again. "I tell you, the more slaves go free, the more are going to follow. The power of fear that's been holding them in slavery for so long is being broken. Even if the South were to win the war, I think slavery is dying!"

"Hallelujah!" Deidre cried with a loud laugh.

Moses stood ramrod straight in front of the laughing officers. He showed no emotion. He had known proving he was a Union spy was going to be difficult after destroying his papers.

"This boy look like any Union soldier you know?" one officer laughed. "He looks like something dragged in from one of the swamps around here."

Moses had told the men his story. He didn't blame them for not believing him—it wasn't as if there were hordes of colored spies in the Union camps.

"I think it more likely this boy has been sent down here to spy on the Union!" another soldier laughed. "Of course, he doesn't appear to be too good at it." The laughter grew louder.

Moses knew his time with the Union army could be over, at least until he could figure out a way to get in contact with Captain Jones. He would stay here in the camps until he could devise a plan.

One officer broke into the laughter. "What if he's telling the truth?"

Moses inspected the man who spoke. Not much older than Moses himself, he was sunburned and had massive muscles in his arms.

"You can't be serious, Captain Jenkins," one man protested.

Captain Jenkins shrugged. "Why not? There are a few other negroes serving as spies. I have fifty coloreds on my ship right now. They've done a fine job."

"But look at him!" another protested. "He's filthy."

"I suppose you'd be dirty, too, if you'd just done what he claims to have done." His voice grew even more serious. "And I *am* looking at him. I see a man with honest eyes. A man with a strong body that could be put to good use for our cause."

The room was taut with tension. Moses waited silently.

Captain Jenkins walked forward. "Tell me about Captain Jones, Moses."

"Captain Jones is about six feet tall, sir. He has dark hair and brown eyes. His build is very muscular. I believe he told me he comes from Bethlehem, Pennsylvania. Before the war he was a construction contractor. The Captain is a fine commander. He is strict, but he cares about his men. And he has a birthmark on his left wrist," he added firmly.

Captain Jenkins stared at Moses for several long minutes, then nodded his head abruptly. "He's telling the truth," he declared. "No one could know that much about a man, and not really know him."

"How do we know he's not making it up?" an officer cried.

Captain Jenkins spun to glare at them. "I went to college with Captain Bill Jones," he snapped. "We were roommates." The room lapsed into stunned silence, while Moses fought the desire to sag with relief. The captain turned back to him, this time with a kind expression on his face. "Didn't you tell me Captain Jones wanted you back in eight days?"

"Yes, sir!" Moses said strongly.

"We better get you on your way," Captain Jenkins replied. "There is a ship leaving tomorrow morning. You can go aboard tonight if you want. You'll have to go overland after that to connect with McClellan." He scribbled out some orders on a sheet of paper and thrust them at Moses. "You leave at first light."

"Yes, sir!" Moses said with a grin. Saluting, he turned and left the room, careful not to throw a gloating look toward the bewildered officers still staring at him.

"I'm going to be fine, Moses. Quit worrying," June chided. "I'm staying right here in this camp until my Simon comes for me."

Moses tried to push down his concern. "I hate to leave you with no family. I know Aunt Abby would welcome you. And you would be with Rose, too."

"Wally and Deidre said they would keep an eye on me. And what do you mean saying I have no family? Simon is the most beautiful son there ever was! I'm sure Aunt Abby is a wonderful person. And I can hardly wait to meet Rose. But I am not leaving this camp without my husband. That's final," she added in a voice that meant business.

He knew that voice from way back. It was the same one his momma used when he had pushed her too hard on an issue she wasn't planning to budge on. Moses finally nodded, knowing he would just have to trust God to take care of his little sister. "You win," he mumbled.

June rushed forward to throw her arms around him. "You've done what you promised Daddy you would do—you've taken care of me. I'm free now, Moses. I'm free! Everything else be gravy." Her eyes shone. "I'm gonna get me a paying job, and I'm going to school so I can read and write just like you."

"I wish Rose could teach you," Moses muttered, still wishing he could take June to Philadelphia and leave her and baby Simon where he knew they would be safe.

June stared up into his face. "One day I'm gonna meet that wife of yours. And when I do I'm going to tell her she got the best man in the world for her husband—next to my Simon, of course," she added with a mischievous grin.

Moses laughed, hugged her tightly, then picked up his small bag. "You'll be hearing from me," he promised.

He stepped off the porch, then turned right toward the ship landing. His walk was brisk and purposeful. He was heading back to his unit and his commander. When he reached the outskirts of the camp he turned to wave one more time. Suddenly he froze, staring hard into the distance. There was something familiar about a woman walking in the midst of the crowded street. He felt oddly as if he should know her. He stood still, staring, trying to bridge the distance with his eyes. What was impossible to span with his eyes, somehow was accomplished with his heart. Without knowing why—he just knew. His heart was pounding as he slowly retraced his steps, his eyes never leaving the woman moving with the crowd, talking and laughing.

Moses drew closer until finally his eyes confirmed what his heart had told him. His pulse was beating so hard he could not force words from his mouth. He was no more than thirty feet away when the woman finally looked up. Their eyes locked, followed by total disbelief—then an explosion of joy.

"Moses!"

"Rose!" Moses closed the last thirty feet with a few mighty bounds. Great laughter rolled up from deep within him, spilling into the evening air. Lifting her easily, he spun her in great circles. She was so light; he'd forgotten how light she was, how beautiful.

Rose was laughing as hard as he was when he finally put her down. "Moses!" she cried again. "What . . . ? How . . . ? Where . . . ?"

Moses silenced her questions with a kiss. It was only the laughter of the people watching that made him look up. He grinned at them all, kissed his wife again, then stepped back. "Maybe we should tell all these people I'm your husband."

"We figured that out ourselves," one woman called out. "Miss Rose has been telling us about you ever since she got here. You should be real proud of your wife, Mr. Moses. She be the finest teacher we have here."

Moses looked lovingly at his wife. Lifting an eyebrow, he said, "A teacher . . . ?"

Rose smiled. "I couldn't get a letter to you. I knew Aunt Abby would tell you I was here. I just couldn't wait. The need here—"

Moses silenced her with a finger to her lips. "We can talk about it later. I'm just glad you're here now. Where are you staying?"

"There's a house not far from here. A group of us teachers live there together."

Suddenly he groaned. He had completely forgotten that he was shipping out in the morning.

"What is it, Moses?" Rose asked anxiously.

Moses shook his head, took her hand, and turned to the crowd. "I'm glad to hear my wife has won your hearts. I have a boat to catch early tomorrow morning so I can report back to my army unit. Now which of you fine people are going to loan us your house for a night?"

"Moses!" Rose gasped, trying to hide her wide smile.

"I reckon my family can move over next door," an elderly woman volunteered. "There be only four of us." She continued on with a sparkle in her eyes. "You're lucky, Mr. Moses. There ain't nobody here who wouldn't want to do something for Miss Rose."

"But, Mabel," Rose started to protest.

"That is mighty nice of you, Mabel," Moses interrupted. "We will be happy to accept. Which one is your house?" Mabel pointed it out. "Thank you. Will it be all right if we return in an hour?" When she nodded he turned to the rest of the crowd. "Now if you'll all excuse us..."

Laughter followed them as they moved down the street. Crowds of excited children ran in front of them, leading the way. Moses took Rose's hand when they reached the little clapboard house he had just left minutes ago.

"Why are we stopping here?" Rose asked. Her hand was gripping his tightly as if she were afraid he would disappear.

Moses grinned down at her. "There's someone I would like you to meet."

Just then June appeared on the porch, holding Simon in her arms, a curious expression on her face. "Moses? What you be doing back here?" Her eyes were resting on Rose, glancing suspiciously at the linked hands.

Moses couldn't wipe the grin off his face. "Rose, I'd like you to meet my sister, June. And this is her new baby, Simon." Rose looked from Moses to June, then back to Moses. She opened her mouth, but no words came out. Moses laughed loudly, then pulled Rose up onto the tiny porch. "Let's all go inside. We have a lot of talking to do."

Day was giving way to night when Moses and Rose stepped back out onto the porch. Rose turned and gave June a big hug. "This has been so wonderful," she said warmly. "I never thought I would have family here in the camp." Her head was spinning from the events of the day. Just yesterday Mr. Crosby had offered to have a house built for her before the end of summer so she could live closer to her students. She had declined, having no desire to live alone. She had not yet gotten over her fear from the attack on Annie's family. It had been easy to choose to remain with the other teachers. Now it was different. She would tell Mr. Crosby she had changed her mind. Plans would be made for June and the baby to move in with her.

June hugged Simon closer. "Neither did I," she said softly, her eyes filling with tears again. "I was making myself be brave for Moses so he would go, but my insides were like jelly."

Moses stepped forward and gave her one final embrace. "I have to leave early in the morning. You and Rose take good care of each other."

Thankfully it was not far to Mabel's house. Rose nodded and smiled when people called her name, but her eyes never left Moses' face. He looked down at her often, his eyes warming her with the love she saw there.

The door had barely closed behind them when Moses pulled her into his arms. "Rose," he murmured softly, his lips caressing her hair.

Rose melted into his embrace, still hardly able to believe she was actually with her husband. All her questions had been answered in the two hours they had spent with June, but the magic still held her in its grip. "I love you," she whispered, reaching up to touch his cheek. "Oh, how I love you."

Moses grabbed her hand and held it against his cheek, then turned it over to kiss it tenderly. "You're all that's kept me going sometimes," he said gruffly.

Rose felt a sudden wave of longing wash through her whole body. She had never seen such a vulnerable expression on her strong husband's face. She knew in her heart he had been through awful times. Maybe he would want to tell her tonight. Maybe he wouldn't. It didn't matter. All that mattered was filling his heart with enough love to stand whatever else was coming. She pulled his face down to hers and kissed him with a deep, lingering kiss.

Moses grabbed her close, then lifted her so her feet dangled above the floor. He held her cradled in his arms for a long time, staring down into her face, before he carried her over to the newly made bed. Never taking his eyes from her face, he lowered her carefully, then sank down beside her.

Through the window above the bed, stars were blazing in the sky, the full moon casting a milky shadow on the floor. It seemed that even the heavens were serenading their reunion when they finally pulled away to talk.

"I'm proud of you, Rose."

"And I'm so proud of you, Moses," Rose whispered back.

Moses groaned. "I know both of us are doing the right thing, but it's so hard to be apart."

Rose understood the aching in his heart—it was a pain she battled every day. She had found the strength she needed to keep going in the love they had just shared. But somehow she knew Moses needed more. Reaching over, she grasped both of his hands. "It won't be forever. Someday we'll be together the way we want. In freedom. Knowing our children will never know the humiliation of slavery. We'll be helping lead the way for millions of people who are trying to figure out how to live a new life." She paused. "And they will have you to thank. People like you who have put aside their own wants and desires so others can have what they are already experiencing." She squeezed his hands tightly. "I am so proud of you."

Moses gazed into her eyes hungrily. Slowly he nodded, the shadow completely disappearing from his eyes. "I was getting so tired," he murmured, pulling her close again.

"There's nothing wrong with getting tired. Fighting evil is always draining. But you've got to keep fighting. That's the only way you're going to be happy, because that's who God made you to be." Rose understood about fighting. She had wanted to flee the camps after the attack on Annie's family. But God had taken her one step at a time, even when she thought it was impossible to deal with such pain and anguish.

"I remember something your momma told me," Moses said. "She told me you can't ever run from being a leader—'cause you're not going to be happy being anything else."

"She was right," Rose replied fervently. "I believe one day we'll be together. Until then we both have to be what we have to be."

Moses took her in his arms again hungrily. They might only have one night, but they would make it a night they would never forget.

Seventeen

obert rubbed his hand across his bearded face as he stared wearily into the night. His whole body ached from fatigue and the ever-present diarrhea brought on by a steady diet of apples and green corn. Searing heat strove to sap what remaining energy he had. He raised his hand and gave the order, "Forward—march!"

Granite pricked his ears forward and stepped out proudly. Robert's heart ached as he looked down at the once-beautiful thoroughbred. He still had plenty of spirit, but too little food had turned him into a bony caricature of the impressive horse that had pranced out of Richmond over two months earlier. Robert pulled grass for him when it could be found, but grain rations had run low when the Army of Northern Virginia had left the Confederacy and moved into Maryland. Robert was glad Carrie couldn't see him. It would have broken her heart.

She would have much the same reaction if she could see him, he was sure. His face cracked a slight smile. It had been weeks since anything resembling a bath had passed his way. His hair and hands were covered with an ever-present grime. Robert had dropped weight steadily till he finally had to exchange his belt for a rope to knot around his waist. His clothes had been torn and ragged when his men had found wagons full of Federal supplies after the Union defeat at Manassas. He never thought he would be thankful to be dressed in Union blue. The supplies had been welcome but had not been enough to clothe and feed his men and horses adequately.

His face twisted in a grimace as he looked over his men. He had nothing to complain about. He was riding a horse, and he still had boots on his feet. Many of his men were plodding down the dusty roads barefoot. Their clothes, mostly rags, hung from their emaciated bodies. There was not a one of them who had escaped the diarrhea brought on by their diet and the extreme heat. More and more disappeared each day—he'd given up taking roll call. He had heard all the excuses.

"Uh, Mitchie didn't really figure on fighting on Yankee soil. He figured he'd signed on to protect the South against invasion, not go after the Yankees."

"There weren't nothing left to Marley. He just couldn't make his beat-up body go another inch."

"Well, you see, Sammie got a letter from his wife. She's having a right rough time feeding the kids and the littlest one was real sick. He went back to take care of his family. Said he never figured on his family suffering when he came to fight. McClellan's army went through and wiped out all their crops."

Robert knew Lee was losing thousands of worn-out soldiers on a daily basis. He vacillated between rage and understanding. All he knew was that the mighty Army of Northern Virginia was the weakest it had ever been. And they were marching into Northern territory, daring McClellan to come after them again.

Lee was risking everything in order to win everything. Robert struggled to share the confidence of his commander. He understood what the general was thinking. Lee was not planning on capturing major Northern cities—he knew his army was not equipped to hold them. But the move into Maryland would harass the Northern government and relieve Virginia from fighting for a time. Robert knew the general had more on his mind, however. With a Confederate army in Maryland, the Federals would certainly move away from the fortifications of Washington to attack them. Manassas had been a Southern victory, but the cost had been high—nine thousand Rebel casualties. And though Pope's army had been pushed back, they had not been destroyed. McClellan was once again amassing a strong force to attack them. The decisive victory Lee had been looking for might finally be won here in Maryland.

"Hey, Lieutenant, some of the men need a rest."

Robert looked down at Hobbs and nodded. They needed to be making better time, but the men had almost reached their limit. "Tell them we will rest for one hour. Then we move on."

Hobbs nodded and moved away to report. With great affection, Robert watched him leave. He and Hobbs had developed a strong bond. It was more than him having saved Hobbs' life in the first battle at Manassas. It was more than Hobbs helping Carrie escape the plantation. Robert had developed a genuine love for the boy with such a great devotion to his country and a total loyalty to his lieutenant. Hobbs was a true Rebel.

Robert swung down from Granite and led him over to a thick bunch of grass off the side of the road. He looped the reins loosely over the saddlehorn, giving the horse plenty of rope so he could forage. Then he slumped down against a tree and watched his men collapse into whatever pockets of shade they could find. They gazed with disgust at the rotting apples they pulled from their haversacks, but began devouring them anyway. They would need the strength to keep going.

The Army of Northern Virginia was not much to look at, yet Robert knew it was something special to meet. They might not have food and clothing, but they still had their muskets and ammunition. Some of the old muskets had even been replaced with new smooth-bored rifles confiscated from Federal supply wagons. And the men knew how to use them. Extreme hardship had sifted out all but those who were dedicated to the cause and could stand anything. But how much more could they really stand?

As the sun sank low in the sky, Robert went over the battle plan. He still marveled that someone of his rank would be privy to the general's confidence. Lee was marching his army north, headed for the sheltering rampart of South Mountain. He would take advantage of its covering to split his army, sending Jackson first south to destroy the army at Harper's Ferry, then back north joining him in battle against McClellan—trusting Jackson's speed. It was a risky move but Robert knew Lee was counting on McClellan's slowness to make it successful. They had left Frederick that morning. Smith Mountain was their day's objective.

Robert stood and stretched. "Prepare to march!" he called. All around him soldiers struggled to their feet, but there was no word of complaint—they were the Army of Northern Virginia.

"Forward—march!"

"Reporting for duty, Captain!"

Captain Jones glanced up from what he was reading, then put it down, his face splitting into a wide smile. "Moses! It's good to see you again."

"It's good to see you, sir."

"I trust your mission went well."

"Yes, sir. My sister is at the Contraband Camp at Fort Monroe. Thank you."

"Excellent!" Captain Jones paused. "The score is a little more even."

"The score never needed evening," Moses protested. "I'm just glad my sister is free."

Captain Jones nodded, then turned back to what he was reading. "I've just been informed of something very interesting."

Moses had never seen his captain's eyes sparkle with such excitement. He stood quietly, waiting for the captain to continue. Captain Jones was obviously absorbed in what he was reading. Moses watched his face as he studied the documents before him.

"Lee hasn't got a chance!" Captain Jones chuckled after a long silence. "You're a spy, Moses. You should appreciate this." He stared again at the note in his hand. "Seems Lee lost something rather valuable. His army was in Frederick just this morning. One of our soldiers was inspecting the area Lee's men left, when he spotted a cigar. Of course he picked it up, then noticed something wrapped around it." He grinned. "Guess what it was?"

"A love letter to his wife?" Moses asked, taking a wild shot in the dark.

Captain Jones doubled over in laughter. "That would be highly entertaining, but hardly the reason for his destruction." He sobered. "No, it seems the general, or most likely one of his officers, left behind a copy of the orders concerning his battle plan."

Moses sucked his breath in sharply, taken by surprise.

Captain Jones slapped his leg in delight. "Our men took it straight to McClellan. One of his aides was able to identify the writing as belonging to Lee." He stood up and began to pace around the tent.

"Do you know what this means, Moses? McClellan knows every move Lee is going to make. That should make even *him* move forward with confidence. I predict Lee will be smashed soon. He will be lucky if he even has an army to take out of Maryland."

Moses' heart pounded with excitement. How he wished he could be in the swarm of soldiers who would destroy Lee. He was grateful for any part in the army, but his desire to be on the front lines was growing.

Captain Jones stopped his pacing. "Join our unit, Moses. We leave tomorrow to attack one of the passes through South Mountain. We are going to catch Lee in his game!" He paused. "You won't be in the battle, but you'll be in the group of scouts who will determine their defense." He paused again, then walked over and placed his hand on Moses' shoulder. "I believe someday soon there will be colored soldiers in our army. It's men like you who are going to make it happen."

"Thank you, sir." Moses turned and left the tent, his head high.

Robert knew it was going to be a long night. Things weren't going the way Lee had planned. That had been obvious when McClellan sent his army forward to smash through the Smith Mountain rampart in two different places. No one knew what had caused the cautious Union general to act so out of character. If McClellan had been just a little more aggressive, he could have destroyed the Army of Northern Virginia. It was only McClellan's normal hesitation—his delay in sweeping forward—that had kept Lee from retreating back to Virginia. In the meantime, Jackson had captured Harper's Ferry—along with eleven thousand Union prisoners and hordes of supplies. Instead of retreating, Lee had ordered his army to concentrate on a little town called Sharpsburg.

"I ain't feeling so good about this, Lieutenant." Hobbs voice was quiet, his face pinched with strain.

Robert turned to him, trying to hide his own uneasiness. "Why not, Hobbs?" He already knew the answer.

"Well, I know we're in a pretty strong place up here on this high ground overlooking that muddy creek down there . . . "

"But we're not exactly invulnerable."

"Yeah," Hobbs muttered. "The way I figure it, the Yankees got a lot more men than we do. Not to mention they probably all have shoes and are eating decent meals." He paused. "Not that I'm saying we can't beat them soft Yankees," he said fiercely, "but . . . "

"You'd feel a lot better if the Potomac wasn't right at our back door," Robert finished. If McClellan *was* to break through their defenses, there was only one ford for a crossing. There would be nowhere to go if a hasty retreat became necessary. Lee's army would simply be destroyed.

"Yeah," Hobbs muttered. He managed a weak grin. "Maybe the general thinks we'll fight harder if defeat just ain't an option."

Robert managed to return his smile. He had been struggling with his doubts all day. Of course, he could not voice them to any of his men. On the face of it, Lee had every reason to depart quietly without a fight. Robert knew the general well. Lee was choosing to stay when he did not have to stay, choosing to fight when he did not have to fight. Since he was not out of his mind, the only conceivable reason for staying was that he believed they could win. Robert had been trying all day to develop the same confidence, but it continued to elude him. There was a deep unrest in his heart. Something in him warned of tragedy. He had made every effort to shrug it off, but it clung to him like a pesky mosquito, biting at every positive thought he tried to dredge up.

He turned to look out over the muddy creek in the distance. It was called Antietam. He was surprised anyone would bother to name such a tiny thing. Open, rolling fields panned out as far as the eye could see, with the exception of a corn field almost directly in front of their position. The corn was mature, standing taller than any man. It made Robert homesick for his own plantation. Towering over the serene landscape were mountains, the same color as the Blue Ridge Mountains in Virginia. Robert never ceased to be amazed that such carnage could take place in such beautiful locations.

"What's that white building in the distance, Lieutenant?" This question came from another of his men who had walked up to join him and Hobbs.

Robert shrugged. "All I know about this place is that they call themselves Dunkers."

"I know about them," the man volunteered. "My daddy lived around here before he came South a lot of years back. He told me Dunkers is another name for German Baptists. That building must be their church."

"German Baptists . . . " Robert probed his mind for something he remembered Matthew telling him years before. Suddenly he had it. "Dunkers are a pacifist Christian sect." He grimaced. They might not have wanted to fight, but there was no way to stop the fight from coming to them. Their little community would never be the same after what was about to transpire.

"You think we can take them, Lieutenant?"

Robert shoved down all his doubts and turned to the knot of men who had gathered to hear the answer to Hobbs' question. He would rather be shot than allow these brave soldiers, who had already endured so much, to go into battle without full confidence. "Those Yankees don't stand a chance," he said with a broad grin. "Thankfully, one Rebel is as good as two Yankees. I figure the odds are about even!"

A cheer rose around him as determination replaced doubt on the men's faces.

"Those Yankees are finally going to give up!" one man crowed. "They've got to get tired of losing soon."

"Yeah! They'll think twice before they come down South to bother us again."

"I just want to beat their pants off of 'em and get back where I can eat something besides apples and corn," one soldier called plaintively, then grinned.

With a smile, Robert watched them wander off. They were good men. As soon as they were out of sight, his smile faded. He was worried. He could play whatever game he wanted to, but the truth was that this would be their hardest battle yet. He looked out over the ridge where he could see a veritable ocean of bluecoats. It didn't look like McClellan was in a hurry to attack. That gave him a small measure of relief. At least some of Jackson's army would have time to join them before morning.

Morning rolled in with a heavy blanket of fog. Robert and his men stood ready all day, but still McClellan's guns remained silent. More of Lee's army reached the field but they were still seriously outnumbered.

At sundown there was sound of a brief skirmish off to the left, but the main force kept out of the fray. It was simply not in McClellan's nature to start a serious fight at night. Robert's men brought him reports of even more soldiers pouring in for the fight, and he kept up his vigil, encouraging his men with visions of victory, building their hope, while his own dwindled.

Night finally claimed the field for another day. A drizzling rain offered welcome relief from the heat, and a queer silence fell over the field. It seemed the whole world was holding its breath, waiting in dread for the coming day of slaughter and death. The dark clouds that had already claimed the country settled low over the battlefield of Antietam, infusing men's hearts, filling them with deadly determination and a cold fear.

Robert lay on his back, resting his head on his haversack as he stared up at the drifting clouds. Why could he not escape the feeling of gloom invading his heart and mind? He had been in plenty of hard battles already. Each one had been entered with a certain amount of fear, but never with the feelings assailing him now. Unbidden, his mind floated to Carrie. It seemed somehow sacrilegious to see her beauty in such a place. Yet, it was her face that gave him his only glimmer of hope, her ready laugh and loving smile that gave him the determination to fight. He had to make it through this battle. He had to go home.

A slight smile played on his lips as he lost himself in the memories. She was such an incredible woman—full of goodness and courage and integrity. She had proven that over and over. He could hardly believe she had agreed to be his wife. The knowledge of her waiting for him filled him with wonder. She was his bright light in the darkness.

Hobbs materialized beside him. He sat down and at first seemed content just to sit there. After a long while he spoke. "I know you're trying to make the boys feel better, but you're not too sure about this, are you?" His voice was almost a whisper.

Robert didn't try to deny it. Hobbs knew him too well.

The silence stretched out between them. Then Hobbs continued, "If I don't make it, will you tell my momma? Write her a letter and let her know I died fighting?"

"Of course," Robert replied. Hobbs had never made such a request, and it left Robert feeling uneasy. Hobbs was not just one of his unit—he was a friend. The battlefield had proven the great equalizer. "If something happens to me . . . will you tell Carrie?"

"You bet, Lieutenant," Hobbs promised. "I'll tell her."

The two men sat quietly, waiting for dawn.

The new day had not fully made its way onto the world's scene when the first shots rang out, muffled by the misty drizzle and low-lying clouds. Robert sucked in his breath and craned to see in the half-light. Flashes from firing rifles appeared due south of his position. McClellan was going after Stonewall Jackson's men. Robert knew Jackson was waiting with artillery massed around the Dunker church, and solid ranks of infantry in the cornfield. The gunfire was sporadic, indicating McClellan was sending skirmishers to test the lines.

"Get your men ready, Lieutenant!"

Robert spun around as a sharp call came from behind him. "Yes, sir, Colonel Masters," he responded. He barely knew the colonel, but he liked his steady eyes and ready smile. This morning he was all seriousness, his eyes scanning the horizon.

"Is your horse ready?" Colonel Masters snapped.

Robert hesitated. He had assumed he would be on foot with his men, but nonetheless Granite was saddled and behind the lines. "Yes, sir."

"If you need him, don't hesitate."

Robert exchanged a long look with the colonel. The only reason he would need Granite would be if all the other commanding officers for his unit fell in battle and he had to lead the charge. "Yes, sir," he said more slowly. The colonel saluted and rode away.

Robert turned back to stare at the battlefield. Moments later the early morning exploded as the cannon burst into action. Robert watched in horror as the guns launched a methodical, murderous bombardment on the cornfield, flattening the tassled corn. Scores of fallen men lay amidst the cornstalks. When the bombardment finally stopped, the Federals once more surged forward. There were still enough of Jackson's men to fight, but most of his line had been blown to bits. They held their ground but finally gave way before the superior force, and the Federals swept up toward the Dunker church.

Robert waited impatiently for the order to advance. Now that the battle had started, all fear and uncertainty had been pushed aside. He knew his men were watching him, waiting for his signal. Suddenly a cheer rose from among his unit. He spun back toward the battlefield in time to see another line of Confederate soldiers erupt from the woods behind the church.

"Hood's men!" the cry rose around him.

The tattered men in gray quickly formed a line that was immediately ablaze with musketry fire. The deadly assault broke the Federal line apart. Filling the air with the Rebel yell, Hood's soldiers charged, deadly in their intent. The Federals faltered, then began a desperate retreat, frantic to escape the fatal barrage. Robert watched grimly as men tried to climb fences, only to hang where they were shot. The cornfield had turned into a grisly obstacle course as fleeing soldiers stumbled and tripped over the dead and wounded. The stout Union artillery once more beat the Confederate advance to a standstill.

"Here come some more!" Hobbs yelled.

Another division of Union soldiers poured from the woods, intent on beating back the Confederate assault.

"Lieutenant Borden. Order your men right and forward!"

Robert sprang into action. Their moment had come. "Ready, men! Right—march!" His voice rang out clearly. His unit sprang into action. Staying low, Robert led his troops around the hill, then down into the woods bordering the cornfield. Hood's men were being pushed back before the furious Federal assault.

"Forward!" Robert yelled. Once again the murderous Rebel yell burst forth as his men surged through the trees, along with other Confederate units rushing to stop the Union advance. Robert kept up with his men, firing, reloading, and firing again.

"Aahhh!" he heard a man just feet from him scream. Robert looked just in time to see him fall, shot through the head. He tightened his lips and continued to drive onward. The shooting from the advancing Federals grew more intense. All around him, men threw up their arms, crumpling to the ground or pitching forward in a strange dance with death. The yells of the Union mixed with the screams of wounded Confederates.

A flash out of the corner of his eye grabbed his attention. He watched as Colonel Masters toppled from his horse, dead. Blood had turned his uniform crimson before he hit the ground.

"Forward! Forward!"

Robert recognized the voice of Major Botler. His men hesitated for a moment, stunned by seeing their colonel fall. Robert knew if they faltered all would be lost. He joined his voice to the command. "Forward!" His men regrouped and continued to surge ahead, jumping over the fallen bodies of their comrades. The fire from the Federals continued to blast them, the whistling of exploding shells adding to the surreal effect as smoke, trapped by the low clouds, swirled around them, making visibility almost impossible. Robert nearly fell several times as he tried to race through the smoky haze over the men who had already succumbed to the gunfire.

Another scream jerked his attention to the side just in time to see Major Botler grab his stomach, his face a stunned surprise. For just a moment he locked eyes with Robert, then tumbled from his horse, dead before he hit the ground.

His men panicked, turning back to flee into the relative safety of the woods. "Forward!" Robert yelled. His voice was swallowed by the melee. His men continued to run, beaten back by the superior force. Robert glanced over his shoulder at the advancing Federals and turned to join his men. He would have to regroup.

"Get 'em, boys!" Another long line of Confederates shot out of the woods, racing through Robert's fleeing men.

Robert breathed a sigh of relief. The reinforcements would give his men time to regroup before they had to charge back into battle. Once he had reached the woods, he looked around frantically for Captain Dickens. Now that Colonel Masters and Major Botler had fallen, it would be up to the captain to lead the assault. But he was nowhere to be seen. Robert would have to lead the charge.

Robert spun to look back at the battlefield. The fresh wave of Confederate soldiers was pushing back the Union assault. Suddenly he groaned. A unit of Union soldiers was pouring from the woods. He watched in amazement as they yelled and laughed hysterically, firing as they rushed forward. His blood chilled.

"Lieutenant!"

Robert turned around to see Hobbs standing beside him, Granite pawing the ground expectantly. He took the reins reluctantly. He knew he was in command now. Giving Granite a quick pat, he vaulted into the saddle. "I'm sorry, Carrie," he muttered. He wished he had any other horse to ride into the carnage being played out before him.

Raising his hand, he made a grand sweeping gesture and yelled at the top of his voice. "Forward! Charge!"

His men hesitated for just a minute, then rushed in behind him, their yell splitting the air.

"Forward!" Robert yelled again. Their guns exploded in a wave of flame as his men poured fire into the advancing Federals.

The Union faltered but continued to sweep on. Robert's men continued their furious attempt—firing, reloading, and firing again. Finally, after what seemed an eternity, the Federals seemed to be moving back, but their firing never ceased.

"Give it to them, boys!" Robert yelled. It was the last thing he remembered.

~Eighteen~

*H*obbs watched in horror as Robert toppled from Granite's saddle. He could see blood pouring from the lieutenant's forehead as the front of his uniform turned dark red. He groaned and tried to break through the wall of people to reach Robert's side.

Suddenly, the wave of Confederate soldiers turned and began to stream back toward the woods. Robert's men had seen him fall and had lost all appetite for battle. It had been too much to watch their commanding officers die one after the other before their eyes.

"No!" Hobbs yelled. "I got to get the lieutenant!" He fought the tidal wave of men but was swept along with them. Tears streamed down his face as he stumbled into the cover of the woods, another contingent of Rebels surging past to stop the newest Federal assault. Hobbs collapsed against the nearest tree, staring out onto the battle-field. He could see Robert lying where he had fallen. More men were falling around him. He groaned loudly, burying his face in the rough bark of the tree.

"Come on, Hobbs! We gotta get out of here!"

Hobbs shook his head and jerked away from the soldier pulling at him. "No!" he yelled.

"There ain't anything you can do for the lieutenant now," the soldier insisted, ducking as a bullet whizzed past his head.

"He saved my life, Walker!" Hobbs hollered. "He saved my life! I can't just leave him!"

"He's dead!" Walker screamed back. "You can't do anything for him."

Anguish tore at Hobbs' heart. Walker was right. He spun around for one last look at his lieutenant. Suddenly he froze. Robert's hand fluttered upward as if he were grasping for life. "Did you see that?" he yelled above the firing. "The lieutenant moved. He moved! He ain't dead!"

Walker pulled at his arm. "You're seeing things, Hobbs. Anyway, if he ain't dead now, he soon will be!"

Rage tore through Hobbs' anguish. He jerked away. "So we just leave him?" he cried contemptuously. "Go on, you coward. Run away. The lieutenant saved my life. He would have done the same for you. I ain't leaving him."

Walker hesitated, then his face flamed with shame. He turned around to stare out at the chaos. "You're right," he finally admitted, though the fear never left his face. "What do we do?"

Hobbs turned to search the field with his eyes. He needed time to think. Off to his right, a wounded soldier tried to struggle to his feet. He managed to reach a crawling position, then his body was suddenly jolted by more bullets. He flung one arm in the air, gave an unearthly scream, then collapsed. Hobbs shuddered, then stared out at the lieutenant again. "We got to shield him from the bullets," he yelled suddenly. "We can't get him off the field now, but we can at least keep him from getting shot again. We got to give him a chance!" he yelled desperately.

"Sure," Walker agreed. "But what do you have in mind?" His face was ashen as he stared out at the fighting.

Hobbs scanned the area. "The logs," he said suddenly. "All those fallen logs. We'll build a barricade around him."

Three more men appeared beside them. Walker grabbed their arms. "The lieutenant ain't dead," he yelled. Quickly he outlined Hobbs' plan.

Hobbs dashed toward the nearest log. Grabbing it up into his arms, he ran out, mindless of the bullets whizzing around his head. Ducking low, using the log as a shield, he flew to Robert's side, and placed it directly in front of where he lay. From all appearances, Robert was dead. Walker materialized beside him, laid a log on top of Hobbs', then turned and fled for the woods.

The four men made many trips until Hobbs was satisfied they had done the best they could. If Lieutenant Borden wasn't dead, he would at least not catch any more bullets. When this horrendous battle was finally over, the medics would move in to do their job. Hobbs turned with the other men and ran for the rear of the lines.

Robert was vaguely aware of a burning in his side, but his head was hurting too badly to identify its source. He reached out his hand once and touched what felt like the rough surface of wood. His mind spun in confusion, trying to make sense of the noise surrounding him, rolling toward him in wave after wave of fury. Heat pressed down until the temperature in his body rose in rebellion to match it. Smoke swirled around, then finally settled on him like a thick cloud. "Carrie . . . " he whispered just once before he slipped into the oblivion of unconsciousness.

Moses was called forward to join the medics when night finally fell on the gruesome fields of Antietam. There were too many wounded to be handled by the normal medical staff. It would take everyone working together to reach the men still desperately clinging to life.

Moses had not seen his unit during the long chaotic day of battle. He had listened, hope soaring—then plunging as cannon boomed and shells screamed across the sky. Union-charge cheers would fade away, replaced by the piercing Rebel yell, then the roll of musketry would float toward him on the breeze. He had watched as wave after wave of the wounded stumbled into camp, followed by men on stretchers. They were laid out now like waves upon the sea.

"Let's go, Moses," one of the medics ordered.

Moses nodded, picked up his end of the stretcher, grabbed a lantern, and made his way out onto the battlefield. The medics had been working all day, transporting wounded men on the periphery. Now that the day was over, they were scouring the field itself.

"First, we take the ones with the best chance of making it," the medic said matter-of-factly.

Moses said nothing, stunned by the grisly sight that opened before his eyes. The moon breaking through the clouds outlined the already swollen corpses impaled on the fences they had tried to climb to safety. Bodies lay across the upper rails, mouths gaping open in death, while piles of their comrades littered the ground around them. The once-lush cornfield had become a cemetery. Uniforms of blue and gray mingled, thousands of them, arms and legs of the dead tangled together—united in death. The ground was soaked with blood and gore, the stench of mortality rising up to mingle with the smoke still hovering over the surreal scene.

Moses fought to control nausea. He stared in amazement as the medic he was with calmly picked his way through the corpses, his eyes sharp for any sign of life. "How do you stand this, Burl?" he finally muttered, his voice thick and heavy.

Burl looked up sympathetically. "You learn how to shut off your feelings, Moses. It's the only way you can stand it. That, and the hope you may find one man whose life you can save."

Moses wasn't sure he would ever be able to shut off the horror and pity threatening to choke him. He bit his lip to keep from groaning as he tripped over a soldier clad in gray. The blackened and bloated body rolled slowly, until the sightless eyes stared up at him, beseeching him even in death. Tears sprang into Moses' eyes as he took deep breaths to control his emotions.

"Here's one," Burl called quietly.

Moses leaped forward and helped him lift the wounded man onto the stretcher.

"Didn't think you boys were ever going to get here," the boy managed to whisper. "Got any water?"

Moses uncapped his canteen and held it to the boy's parched lips. He guzzled it thirstily, then fell back onto the stretcher, his red hair tumbling around his shoulders. "This morning I thought this place kinda reminded me of my family's farm," he murmured. "I don't think so anymore." Then he lapsed into unconsciousness.

"Best thing for him," Burl muttered as he turned and began to pick his way back to the medical tents.

Moses held his end of the stretcher, watching carefully as they plodded on, but trying to block out the images of the dead men they walked over. It was going to be a long night.

Once they had delivered the hapless soldier to the hospital camp, they turned and retraced their steps.

"Here's one!" Moses called.

Burl appeared at his side, then shook his head regretfully. "That one stays for now," he said shortly.

Moses stared at him in astonishment. "But why? He's still alive!" The man lying before him must have been in his early twenties. Both legs had been blown away below the knees, and he had a gaping hole in his left shoulder, but somehow he had managed to hang on to consciousness.

"Help me," he gasped.

"We'll get him later if he's still alive," Burl said in a thick voice. "I've got my orders, Moses. We're only supposed to bring the ones in who have a good chance of making it. Then we can go back after the long shots." He reached over and touched Moses' shoulder. "Those are our orders," he said firmly.

Moses gazed at the man staring up at him with mute appeal.

Burl knelt beside the wounded man. "Someone will be back," he said gruffly. "Hang on!"

Hope seemed to die in the man's bleary eyes, as he heaved a sigh and closed his eyes. He had held on through the long, hellacious day, waiting for help. Seconds later he gave his final gasp of breath. Moses lowered his head; the cruelties of war never ceased.

Moses stumbled on, continuing his search. Gone was his desire to be a soldier. He would do everything he could to help the Union, but the past few hours had sucked all the idealism of battle out of him. There was nothing glamorous about war. It was horrid, grisly, and inhuman. Confusion spun through his mind. Was it really possible that the South was so afraid of his people being free that they would send countless young men to die such horrible deaths just to keep it from happening? He shuddered to think of the passions, on both sides, that had ignited a war resulting in what he was experiencing tonight. He had thought the battlefields around Richmond were horrible. He hoped to never again see anything to compare to Antietam.

Moses lost count of how many trips they made back to the hospital camp. Burl was right. His feelings were becoming numb. There was only so much the human mind and heart could stand before it simply refused to endure any more.

It was long after midnight when they finally reached the far side of the field that edged along the woods. Union medics merged with Rebel medics, all thought of fighting gone. They were all on one mission—to save as many as possible. Moses had stopped more than once to offer water to men waiting for their ride. It made no difference to him what side they were on. The uniforms had stopped registering in his mind—the men were no longer Union or Confederate. They were simply human beings suffering beyond all endurance.

Moses had become aware of another phenomenon playing itself out on the field. Rebel soldiers were picking their way through the bodies. They would stoop to offer water to a wounded man, then turn away and move on—intent on their search for booty. Moses watched as dead Union soldiers were relieved of their boots, coats, and even their pants. Rifles were picked up and caressed like new babies. No one made a move to stop the plundering.

"What's this?" Burl called.

Moses turned to see what he was looking at. Over to his left, he could see a pile of logs built up like a barricade. Curious, he picked his way over.

Burl reached it first. "Poor devil," he muttered. "I guess his men were trying to save him. Maybe he died a little easier at least." He shook his head and moved in the direction of another man who was calling him.

Moses stood and stared down at the still form. His heart pounded in his head. Even in death, he recognized Robert Borden, the man Carrie loved—the son of the man who had killed his daddy. Turning sharply to hide his tears, he moved toward Burl. "Coming," he muttered in response to his call.

It was almost two in the morning before Burl and Moses were replaced with a new crew.

"Get some sleep," the officer ordered. "You'll be back at it in four hours."

"Let's go, Moses," Burl said wearily. "You'll feel like you haven't slept at all when they call us."

Moses shook his head. "You go ahead. I'm going to have one more cup of coffee." He watched Burl trudge away, then finished his drink. Taking a deep breath, he stood and strode back onto the battlefield. He knew no one would notice him in all the confusion. Quickly he picked his way around the sea of dead bodies, resolutely ignoring the feeble cries that still filtered through the night. The skies had once more trapped the moon as a light drizzle began to fall.

Robert lay where Moses had first seen him. The barrier built around him seemed a mockery—even a wall couldn't keep death from snatching its prey. Holding his lantern high, he inspected it closely. Close to a hundred bullets were either embedded in the soft wood, or were scattered on the ground around the makeshift shelter. His expression changed to one of admiration. Robert's men had kept him from being shredded by musketry fire.

Moses had decided what he was going to do. He could not bear the thought of Robert Borden being tossed into a mass grave of Rebel soldiers. He knew from past experience that not all the dead, especially now that the Confederates had left the South, would receive a proper burial. Taking Robert behind the lines of the Rebel camp would at least assure him a burial. That was the least he could do for Carrie. Someday he would be able to tell her what had happened to the man she loved.

A quiet whinny caused Moses to look sharply into the woods. A horse would be very helpful about now. He jumped up and began to edge toward the shadowy figure in the woods. The horse stood quietly, allowing him to grab the broken bridle reins and lead him forward. It wasn't until he was once again in the circle of lantern light that he got a good look at the towering animal. "Granite!" he exclaimed. It just wasn't possible. Slowly he walked around the thin, gray thoroughbred. The horse stood quietly, his ears pricked, then lowered his nose to sniff the still form on the ground.

Moses shook his head in disbelief. It *was* Granite! There were still horses roaming around, not yet collected after the battle. It seemed Granite had returned to where he had lost his master. There was no telling how long he had been standing in the trees. "You're going to make things a lot easier, big guy," Moses said softly. He had been wondering if he had enough strength to carry Robert behind the lines. Now all he had to do was drape him across the saddle and lead Granite.

But Moses didn't relish the idea of going behind Confederate lines again. It was a risk he had decided he would have to take for Carrie's sake. Just then a sudden idea sprang into his mind. A smile split his face for the first time that day as he patted Granite on his thin neck. "You might have just saved my hide," he murmured. He would tie Robert securely to the saddle, take him just short of the lines, then let Granite carry him on in. It would keep him out of the Rebel camp and assure him that Robert would receive a proper burial. Moses nodded. It was a good plan.

Stooping, Moses gathered Robert carefully in his arms and lifted him. Suddenly he noticed something. Robert had not taken on the bloated, blackened condition of the rest of the corpses he had passed that night. He must not have been dead too long. Moses grimaced as he felt Robert's blood-stained clothes soak through his own.

"All right, Granite . . . stand easy, guy. I've got a job for you." Moses moved next to the big horse, and shifted Robert's weight. He would try to angle him across the saddle as gently as possible, but it wasn't going to be easy. He wasn't sure why it mattered—it just did. He counted quietly to himself and heaved on the count of three, giving a grunt of satisfaction as Robert's shoulders settled on the top of the saddle, his arms flung across the sides. His head flopped awkwardly, banging against the saddlehorn. "Sorry," Moses grunted.

Moses' right hand held Granite's bridle as he eased around the front to grab Robert's arms and pull him the rest of the way over. Suddenly he froze. Had there been movement in Robert's hand as he grabbed it? Horrified, he stared at the dead man. Finally he shook his head. The long night was getting to him. He was imagining things. He moved away and searched until he found an abandoned haversack. Opening it quickly, he discovered two short lengths of rope. He grabbed them and dashed back to Granite's side.

This whole escapade was taking too long. If he wasn't back at camp when someone came to waken Burl and him, he would be in big trouble. He understood his position as a negro man. As long as he did whatever they wanted him to—and did it well—he would be okay. There was no room for actions of his own, however. Captain Jones was different; he seemed to trust Moses. But he hadn't seen the captain all day and had no idea where to find him. He had to get back.

Moses grabbed Robert's hands and quickly tied them to one of the stirrups. There was no movement. He knew he had been imagining things. Granite continued to stand quietly, seeming to understand what Moses was doing. Moses circled him and pulled Robert's feet together. Once they were tied to the other stirrup, he would be secure in the saddle. At least secure enough to be carried back to his camp.

The job finished, Moses moved back to Granite's head. "All right, boy. I've got a job for you to do. But you aren't doing it for me. You're doing it for Carrie." Granite looked at him with huge eyes.

"Aahh."

Moses sprang back from Granite and stared at Robert. Then he looked around frantically, trying to identify where the noise had come from.

"Aahh . . . "

Moses' eyes flew open wide with disbelief. He pressed his ear close to Robert's head.

"Aahh . . . "

"I'll be!" Moses exclaimed. "You're alive!"

One of Robert's hands fluttered the tiniest bit, like a leaf in a spring breeze, then lay still. Suddenly his mouth opened again. "Carrie . . . " he whispered faintly. Then his head lolled back against the saddle.

Moses stared at him. What was he going to do now? He couldn't just take Robert to the lines and let Granite go. He stood still, gazing at Robert's wounded body, trying to think. *His father killed your daddy.* His eyes hardened as the voice in his head reminded him of the truth he was trying to push down. Why should he do anything for this man? *Carrie gave you your freedom and this is the man she loves.* His face twisted as he faced the other truth.

The night spun around him as confusion battered his soul, the two voices trying to tear him apart. Finally Moses straightened, his eyes clear. He would do the right thing. It had nothing to do with what he owed anyone. It had everything to do with love. He loved Carrie Cromwell. It was as simple as that.

He would have to take Robert into the Confederate camps. Then he would try to devise a way to get out. He pushed away the nagging problem of being discovered missing from camp. He would face that when the time came. The way was clear before him. Confusion had fled from his heart once he had made his decision. It would be up to the doctors once he got Robert back.

Moses grabbed Granite's reins and began to lead him through the woods. He picked his way carefully, pulling back limbs that would have hit Robert, giving trees a wide berth. Just then an idea sprang into his mind. He shook his head and pushed on. The idea persisted. Moses heaved a sigh of disgust and stopped.

"It's crazy," he muttered up to the sky.

They're good people.

"Sure, they're good people. That doesn't mean they want this man dumped on them." Moses didn't care that he was talking out loud. The very idea was so ludicrous he was beginning to think he was crazy just to be thinking it.

Take Robert to them.

"Look, God," Moses said angrily. "If this even is God. Which I seriously doubt," he added. "I think all this has finally gotten to me and I'm losing my mind." A soft breeze sprang up, blowing gently across his hot face. Once again he was gripped with confusion and turmoil. Moses groaned and buried his face in Granite's mane. "What am I supposed to do?"

Do the right thing.

Moses stood still for several long minutes, then turned and began to head due east. It was crazy. It could mean Robert would die for sure. His heart was telling him God was leading him. His head was telling him he had taken leave of his senses. He knew only one thing for sure. The confusion had stopped swirling in his head as soon as he changed direction.

Nineteen

ight was just beginning to dim when Hobbs, carrying a stretcher, led a medic through the woods. "Thank you for helping me," he said, his face taut with worry and fear.

"You can't possibly think this man is still alive," Manson protested, his florid face lined with fatigue. He shook his head. "I'm plumb crazy to be doing this. I could be catching a few hours of sleep."

Hobbs grabbed his arm and pulled him forward. "The lieutenant might be alive," he insisted. "Come on, Manson. We've known each other since we were kids. Don't you remember when I pulled your little sister out of the river?"

" 'Course I remember," Manson growled. "You won't let me forget! It's the only reason I'm out here on this wild-goose chase."

"Lieutenant Borden saved my life," Hobbs reminded him for what must have been the tenth time. He still couldn't believe he had talked Manson into coming out here with him. He had scoured the lines all night, searching for his commander. He knew that Robert could be lying anywhere, but one of his final conversations with a medic had given him hope. "That fellow I talked to remembered seeing the barricade of logs we built. Said there was still a man lying there."

"If he was alive, they would have gotten him," Manson protested.

"You said yourself they have orders to bring back the ones with the best chance first," Hobbs reminded him. "That don't mean he's dead for sure."

"Yeah, yeah!" Manson growled, his face sympathetic. "I'm coming with you, aren't I? How much farther?"

"We're almost there," Hobbs responded. He gave a cheer when they broke through the woods. The mountains stood like silent ramparts over the grisly scene. Hobbs stopped and stared, his face turning white. It had been horrible to see yesterday when the battle was raging. Now the cornfield had become something even his worst nightmares could never have envisioned. His stomach heaved and his mouth turned to cotton.

Manson put his hand on Hobbs' shoulder. "I told you it was bad."

Hobbs shook his head and turned away. "Let's find the lieutenant," he growled. He had taken no more than a few steps before his insides went into full rebellion. He bent double as dry heaves wracked his body. The horrors of the last twenty-four hours exploded from his body. When he finally stood, it was only Manson's steadying hand that kept him from falling. He took several deep breaths. "Sorry." He took another deep breath. "The lieutenant should be this direction."

They had gone several hundred feet before Hobbs could make out the crude barricade in the distance. "There it is!" He picked his way quickly over the dead bodies, rushing up to the spot he had last seen Lieutenant Borden. He stood stock-still, staring at the empty space behind the logs.

"He's gone," he said in disbelief.

"Great. We came all the way out here for nothing," Manson said in disgust. "One of the boys probably got him."

"He's gone," Hobbs said again, his mind trying to convince his eyes they were playing tricks on him. "How could he be gone?" Disappointment gripped his heart.

"Good lord, man!" Manson exclaimed. "Be glad he's off the field. He's probably lying on the ground somewhere being tended to right now."

Hobbs looked up quickly, his disappointment giving way before a desperate hope. "I'll find him in one of the camps."

Hobbs spent all the next day scouring the buildings and tents holding the Confederate wounded. He had stared into the faces of thousands of wounded men but he could not find his lieutenant. No one had seen him—it was as if he'd vanished.

It was almost midnight before he finally retreated to the rest of his unit and collapsed on the ground. Hopelessness had settled on him like a heavy mountain fog in the early spring. It clung to him, pulling from him what little energy he had left. He walked slowly up to the nearest fire and sank down, staring into its curling flames.

"Didn't find him, huh?" Walker asked sympathetically.

Hobbs shook his head. "No," he said dully. He looked up, from somewhere a faint hope reaching through the fog. "I ain't done looking, though. There's still them buildings in town. I heard the people around here have taken in a lot of our men. Robert could be there."

"That could be," Walker agreed.

Hobbs stuffed down his anger at the look of skepticism on his comrade's face. What did it matter what he thought? It was his life the lieutenant had saved. It was he who had made the promise to let Carrie know what had happened to him. He stood, walked to his haversack, and reached for his grimy, worn-out blanket. He would welcome the comfort it would give him tonight. In the morning, he would continue to look.

Someone was shaking Hobbs' shoulder.

"Get up, man! We're getting out of here."

Hobbs struggled to focus his eyes. It was still dark, the position of the moon telling him he could not have been asleep for more than a couple of hours. "Huh?"

"Lee has called for a retreat. We're getting the heck out of here," Walker insisted. "And not a minute too soon. I heard somebody say we lost more than ten thousand of our men yesterday. I'm ready to go home."

Hobbs stared at him, fully awake now. "Ten thousand?" he repeated in a stunned voice.

"Yeah! Now get moving. Some of the boys have already started heading out."

Hobbs shook his head slowly. "I can't go right now."

Walker stared at him as though he had taken leave of his senses. "What do you mean you can't go right now? We've got our orders!"

"I've got to find the lieutenant."

Walker cursed and grabbed Hobbs by his shirt collar. "Have you gone completely loony, man? Lieutenant Borden is dead! You hear me? He's dead. You've got to face it." He shook him, then pushed him back. "We're soldiers, Hobbs. We follow orders. Lee has given the order to retreat. We retreat!"

Hobbs stared at his friend, knowing the anger suffusing his face was caused more by fear than anything. Both of them knew the Confederate army was not strong enough to withstand another onslaught of Federal forces. They had to git, while the gitting was good. "Yeah, Walker. I hear you," he said slowly. "We have to retreat."

Walker settled back on his heels, relief flooding his face. "That's more like it," he growled. He stood and moved away. "Our new commander, Colonel Jordan, said we pull out in fifteen minutes."

Hobbs nodded and watched him walk away. He waited until the darkness had swallowed Walker before he stood, stuffed his blanket into his haversack, then turned to disappear into the woods behind him. He still had a job to do.

As Hobbs trudged through the woods, moving toward the houses a couple of miles away, he realized he was acting completely out of character. He had not once in his army career disobeyed a direct order. And he knew Walker was probably right—Lieutenant Borden was dead. Even as the thought fought its way into his mind, Hobbs rejected it. Something in him told him the lieutenant was still alive. He could not face Carrie Cromwell until he had tried everything he could to discover her missing fiancé.

Hobbs gazed around as he pushed on toward the houses sheltering wounded Rebels, ignoring the flow of Confederate soldiers in full retreat. He shoved aside the annoying voice whispering that he should turn around and go with them. He shuddered at the thought of being caught behind enemy lines.

It was still pitch dark when Hobbs finally found the houses he was looking for. Wounded men were being cared for here by local civilians who had risen up to meet the need. He watched quietly for several minutes. Lights bobbed through the windows and across the green yards. He could vaguely discern the outlines of men lying on the grass, forming long rows that disappeared into the darkness. Every few seconds a cry or moan floated toward him on the breeze. His heart ached for their agony. He had been there. He knew the pain—understood the fear.

A woman, dressed simply in a long gray dress, stopped in her movement from soldier to soldier. She raised her lantern high and straightened, staring into the dark woods. Hobbs shrank back, though he knew it was impossible for her to see him. What was she looking for? Suddenly he stood and moved forward. The longer he stayed where he was, the greater the chance he would be caught by McClellan's men. "Hello," he called softly.

The woman gasped and spun to face him, her hand going to her throat. "What do you want?" she called sharply.

Hobbs moved forward slowly, hoping to alarm her as little as possible. "I'm sorry. I didn't mean to frighten you."

"I hardly think you frightened me," the lady responded crisply. "After the last few days I'm afraid I'm rather numb to fear."

Hobbs smiled appreciatively, moving closer. The lady staring at him was perhaps in her mid-forties, rather slender, with steady eyes and a face that spoke of kindness. She reminded him of his momma. He pushed down the sudden pang of homesickness that shot through him. "I'm looking for a friend of mine. He was wounded in the battle."

"What makes you think he's here?" she snapped suspiciously.

"I've looked everywhere else," Hobbs said with a small shrug. "This place is my last hope."

The lady lowered her lantern just a tiny bit and held it closer to his face. "Who is this friend?"

"My commander, ma'am. His name is Lieutenant Borden." Hobbs paused. "He saved my life during the first battle at Manassas. I got to find him."

"Aren't you a Confederate soldier?"

"Yes, ma'am." Hobbs saw no reason to deny it.

"In case you're not aware of it, young man, your army is retreating."

"Oh, I'm aware of it all right!"

"Yet you're still here looking for your lieutenant?"

Hobbs just nodded.

The lady moved a little closer. "What's your name?"

"Warren Hobbs, ma'am. I'm with the 25th Virginians."

The lady smiled suddenly. "Well, Warren Hobbs. My name is Kathy Parker. Come with me. We'll see if we can find your lieutenant."

Hobbs sighed with relief. "Thank you, Mrs. Parker."

Dawn was touching the sky as Hobbs followed Mrs. Parker down yet another row of stricken soldiers. He had learned not to look too long at the faces, not to allow himself to wonder whose heart would be broken if this man didn't return. Frustration ate at him as row after row of men passed before him with no evidence of Lieutenant Borden.

"We only have three more buildings to go," Mrs. Parker stated.

Hobbs nodded wearily. "Yes, ma'am."

Suddenly she stopped and turned to him. "Do you like being a soldier?" she asked suddenly.

Hobbs frowned. "Like being a soldier?" he repeated. He shook his head. "Ain't nothing to like about it."

"Then why be one?"

Hobbs stared at her. "Ain't got much choice, ma'am. My country needs me."

"Your country needs you to slaughter other people who live in your country?" Her tone was disbelieving, yet kind.

Hobbs struggled to explain what he barely understood himself. "The South had to form a new country," he said slowly. "It seems kinda strange to think of those fellas we fought yesterday being from a foreign country, but they are."

"Nonsense!" Mrs. Parker said firmly. "How many slaves do you own, Hobbs?"

"Slaves? I don't own no slaves, ma'am. My family don't have that kind of money."

"Would you like to own slaves?"

"Well . . . " Hobbs shook his head. "I don't reckon so, ma'am. I kinda like doing my own work myself."

Mrs. Parker studied him, then shook her head. "Then why in the world are you fighting to support slavery?"

Hobbs stopped, fatigue making thought difficult. "I don't reckon I'm fighting because of slavery, ma'am. Those Yankees are trying to come down and run our country."

"Those Yankees are trying to keep America *one* country," she snapped, then shook her head. "Don't get me wrong. I think the Yankees are just as wrong as the Rebels are. Fighting is never the answer," she said firmly.

"You sure about that, ma'am?" Hobbs remembered the lieutenant telling him the people in this area were German Baptists.

"Of course I am!"

"Ain't you glad you're living in a free country? Ain't you glad you can practice whatever religion you want to?" He didn't wait for her answer. "My great-granddaddy had to fight in the American Revolution. I reckon a lot of people had to die so we could be free now."

"War is a horrible thing," Mrs. Parker insisted.

"Yes ma'am, it's a horrible thing," Hobbs agreed. "I ain't necessarily saying this war is right. There's a lot I don't understand about it. I'm just saying that things aren't as simple as they look sometimes. It'd be nice if they were—but that just ain't the way it is."

Mrs. Parker looked at him closely, then nodded her head. "You have a lot of wisdom for one so young," she muttered. Holding the lantern high again, she moved forward. "Let's keep looking for that lieutenant of yours."

The sun was exploding over the horizon when Hobbs noticed movement on a hill overlooking the town. He had just turned back toward the woods, disappointed, but convinced Lieutenant Borden was not there either. He stopped, trying to discern what was happening.

Mrs. Parker stepped up next to him. "That's Douglas Hill. What's going on?"

Hobbs' heart began to beat harder. "I'd say McClellan ain't planning on letting General Lee just trot off without some trouble. Looks like he's planting a battery of guns up there."

"Guns?" Mrs. Parker's voice was startled. "Surely he won't shoot those guns where they could hurt the town."

Hobbs shrugged. "Ain't no way of knowing what that Yankee is thinking." His own fear was growing. From where he was standing, he could see a lot of Confederate soldiers still on this side of the river.

Most of them had crossed over, but there was a large contingent still waiting its turn. He turned to look at the town. The small settlement was a virtual hospital. Every building was being used to minister to wounded soldiers, both Union and Confederate. Would McClellan really shell the town?

As if in answer to his unspoken question, a shell burst forth from one of the guns, screaming across the sky with a whistle before exploding onto the early morning. Hobbs watched as it flew over the town and blew up well beyond the last building.

"He's attacking our town," Mrs. Parker yelled angrily.

Hobbs shook his head. "I don't think that's his intent," he yelled above the shelling. "He's going after the rest of the army."

"Some of those shells might fall short," Mrs. Parker yelled back, her face red with rage.

Hobbs nodded reluctantly. "Yes, ma'am. I reckon they could." His mind was spinning, trying to figure out how he was going to get away. The lieutenant wasn't here, and he had to rejoin his unit now. He watched in dismay as the Confederate retreat turned into a stampede.

"Yellow flags!"

Hobbs turned to stare at Mrs. Parker. "Yellow flags?"

She nodded excitedly. "I've heard yellow is the color for hospitals. Perhaps if we raise the color above our houses . . . " She turned and began to run through the rows of soldiers.

"What's happening?" one of the soldiers yelled, struggling to raise himself into a sitting position.

"McClellan is attacking the town," another yelled back, his voice laden with fear.

Hobbs moved forward. "No, he's not! He's shelling over the town after our soldiers. You're safe."

Just then a shrieking shell fell on the main road of the town, exploding and spraying fragments in every direction. Fear turned into panic. Everywhere, yellow flags and rags were being hoisted above buildings in a vain effort to gain protection from the shelling. Nonetheless it continued, an occasional shell falling short, leaving the residents in a state of panic.

Hobbs watched in amazement as the whole town erupted into wild and uncontrollable chaos. There was not a single building ablaze, but already the town was reacting as if the entire place were engulfed in flames. From his position on a rise above the town, Hobbs had an excellent view. People poured from the buildings, holding whatever household goods they could in their arms, dragging their children behind them. Within minutes the roads were thronged, many of the streets blocked and impassable. Shrieks and cries filled the air.

Hobbs had never witnessed such hysteria before. The stampeding Confederate army seemed somehow calm and orderly compared to the townspeople. He was not sure what was holding him in place. Part of him screamed to run, but the scene unfolding before his eyes gripped him—held him where he was. Men were cursing and yelling, women were crying, the children screaming their bewilderment and fear. Wagons, horses, and ambulances all jammed together into one shouting, writhing mass. And still the shelling continued, stoking the panic to a feverish pitch.

Like a disrupted ant colony, the people fled in all directions. Hobbs saw several children disappear under the stampede. They were all heading for the open country, running to escape McClellan's guns.

"I'm getting out of here!"

Hobbs spun around as he heard one of the wounded yell.

"I'm coming with you!" another yelled. "I'm not going to lie here and let those Yankees blow me to bits. I lived through the battle; I don't aim to perch here like a sitting duck."

A portly nurse appeared suddenly. "Stay where you are," she cried. "You're safer here than if you try to run. You're too sick. You'll never make it."

The men settled back for a moment, exchanging looks of doubt and fear. A shell exploded just fifty feet from the end of their line.

"Those Yankees are gonna kill us all!" a frightened man yelled, leaping to his feet. One arm hung loosely in a sling. His right eye was bandaged, a rag wrapped all the way around his head. He staggered, then lurched forward.

Hobbs watched in horror as more and more men struggled to their feet and began to move in an unsteady line.

Some of the women who were attending them stepped out to stop them. "It's suicide!" one yelled.

A tiny lady moved in front of a towering Rebel officer. "Please, sir. Don't you see this is folly? Stop your men from following this course."

The officer hesitated. Another shell exploded nearby. "We're getting out of here," he hollered. Stepping forward he picked up the lady and set her aside. "Excuse me, ma'am."

"Take me with you!" one soldier pleaded.

"Don't leave me here to die!" another badly wounded man cried.

Hobbs felt nauseous as he watched the swarm of men fleeing McClellan's attack. And still the shelling continued unmercifully. He had seen enough. He looked around quickly, trying to determine the best route of escape. Ducking his head, he dashed to the right, hoping to make the cover of the woods before a shell fragment found him. The screaming and shrieking followed him as he ran for all he was worth, his heart pounding so hard he was having trouble breathing.

Finally he reached the woods. Now, to join up with the army and get across the river. Taking a deep breath, he continued to run as hard as he could, jumping over tree stumps and rocks and dodging falling limbs cut from their trees by shells.

It seemed like an eternity before he broke free from the trees into the field edging the Potomac River. Ducking his head again, he flew toward the crossing, merging with other Confederate soldiers fleeing for their lives. "We're gonna make it!" he yelled to one limping soldier.

"You might make it!" he hollered back. "I'm a goner."

Hobbs couldn't explain what made him stop. Reaching out he circled his arm around the man's waist. "We're getting out of here," he said firmly, and the two of them broke into a faltering run. They were only yards from the river when the ground exploded in front of them.

"Look out!" Hobbs yelled. He threw the man to one side, then leaped to land on top of him. He felt fire explode in his leg, then . . . nothing.

Twenty

arrie was in her room when she heard the front door slam shut. Heavy footsteps climbed the stairs and approached her room. Something in the sound caused her heart to catch in dread. She was at the door before her father knocked, opening it just as he raised his hand.

"Hello," Thomas said heavily.

Carrie moved aside, watching him carefully. Her father walked in, stared around for a moment as if he were dazed, then turned to her.

"The reports from Antietam are coming in," he said slowly.

"How bad is it?" Carrie asked, trying to put off what she knew was coming. Somehow she had known it all day.

Thomas grimaced. "Over ten thousand Confederate casualties."

"In one day?" Carrie groaned. Thomas nodded, then walked forward to take hold of her hands. Carrie braced herself, knowing no amount of preparation could make whatever he was going to say easier.

"I saw the lists."

"Robert is dead," Carrie said woodenly.

"No!" Thomas said strongly. "He is listed as Missing in Action."

Carrie felt her heart resume its beat, albeit much slower. "What does that mean?" she asked quietly. She had been feeling a sick dread all day. Now she felt as if her heart had been cut out.

Thomas frowned. "It could mean a lot of things," he admitted. "He could be wounded in a Union hospital. He could be a prisoner. Or..."

"He could be an unidentified body," Carrie stated simply.

265

Thomas nodded reluctantly. Then he looked at her sternly. "It also means he could be one of the wounded who have not been identified. Obviously our medical corps is overwhelmed." He released one of her hands and tilted her chin until her eyes met his. "Missing in Action means no one knows. *No one knows,*" he repeated firmly. "You can't give up hope. Robert has made it through a lot of battles."

Carrie stared at him, then turned toward her window and sank down to her knees, pressing her hot face into her hands. She had imagined this moment so many times, yet no amount of imagining could have prepared her for the stark reality.

You don't know he's dead! a stern voice in her head reminded her. *You must not give up hope!* Carrie heard the voice and tried to reach out to grab the faith it offered, but fear kept it floating illusively. Just as she thought she had it in her grasp, it would drift away, carried by the images of Robert lying dead on a blood-soaked battlefield. Carrie groaned as grief and fear rushed in, threatening to suffocate her. Had she given her all to hundreds of wounded soldiers just to see the man she loved snatched away? *Robert . . . Rose . . . Moses . . . Aunt Abby . . . Sarah . . . her mother . . . Granite.* The weight of her losses pressed down like an anvil on her bruised heart, squeezing the life from her until she was gasping for breath. She remained where she was, rocking slowly, surrendering to the grief and fear.

"Carrie!"

Carrie pulled away from her father's touch on her arm. "Leave me alone," she whispered.

"I won't leave you like this," Thomas' voice was a mixture of firmness and fear. "You must not give up hope. There is a good chance Robert is alive."

Carrie knew he was trying to offer her some hope, but dark clouds of fear were making it impossible to grasp. She moaned and shook her head from side to side.

"Carrie! This is not like you," Thomas exclaimed frantically. "You have to be strong."

Carrie pulled herself farther away as she heard the exasperation in his voice. Without understanding why, a hysterical giggle rose within her and leaked into the room. On its heels came a surge of tears. She was losing control of herself, of her ability to cope. She opened her eyes and stared at her father. "Everyone is gone," she said numbly.

"Who is gone?"

"Everyone. Robert. . . . Rose . . . Moses . . . Aunt Abby . . . Old Sarah . . . Mother . . . Granite." Her voice faded away, then strengthened. "Rose is gone. I miss Rose so much." Suddenly, more than anything in the world she wanted to see Rose.

"I know Rose was your good friend, but . . . " Thomas paused, confusion filling his face.

Carrie straightened as a surge of anger became a flood, pushing aside all barriers as it poured forth. "I know the truth about Rose," Carrie said coldly. Somewhere in her mind she knew she was being unreasonable, but she didn't care. "I know who she really is."

Thomas stared at her, his face turning white.

"I know my grandfather raped Sarah. I know Rose is really your half-sister. I know she is really my aunt!" Carrie cried. "I know it all! I know you lied to me for all those years!" She stopped, gasping for breath, the torrent of her emotions leaving her exhausted.

"How?" Thomas sputtered. "You weren't ever supposed to know . . . " his voice trailed away.

Carrie's voice was calm and distant now. "Of course I wasn't ever supposed to know. You expected Sarah, just because she was a slave—just because you owned her—to never tell her only daughter the truth about who she is. To never tell her she has a twin brother somewhere. You thought because they were slaves it wouldn't matter that their family was ripped apart and Sarah would have to live without her husband for eighteen long years." She took a deep breath. "Well, it mattered. It mattered to them just as much as it would matter to you. It mattered so much that Sarah couldn't die without Rose knowing the truth." Spent, she sagged to the floor. "They're people just like you and me, Father. Just like you and me," she repeated. "You tried to take that away from them—only you couldn't. You can't steal a person's humanity just because you think they're less than human."

Thomas was still staring at her with a dazed expression on his face.

Carrie wasn't done. "I'm proud Rose is my aunt. She is my closest friend. It wouldn't matter to me if she was purple or green. She happens to be colored—she also happens to be white. I miss her." A sudden wave of compassion surged through her. "You should be proud of her, too, Father. She is a beautiful, intelligent young woman."

Silence fell on the room as Thomas stared blankly at her.

Carrie gazed into his eyes, her emotions spent. She supposed she should be sorry for yelling at him, but she wasn't. She had merely spoken the truth. The shock of hearing Robert was missing had vanquished the last of her self control.

Thomas finally spoke, his face still ashen. "I'm sorry I lied to you," he said slowly. He opened his mouth to say more but nothing came out. His face twisted in a look Carrie couldn't discern.

"Father . . ." she said imploringly.

Thomas shook his head. "I—I guess I never saw it before. Rose—she was just one of my slaves. A product of my father's passion. I never really thought of her as my—half-sister," he said haltingly. "But I suppose she is." His voice was surprised, understanding slowly dawning in his eyes. "It has been so easy to see her as less than human—just another slave." Suddenly he groaned. "My father lives in her, too. I know she is just as much a person as I am."

Carrie sat quietly, watching her father. She recognized the pangs of self-discovery.

Thomas sank down heavily on the chair next to her dressing table and stared at himself in the mirror. "I've been such a fool," he whispered. Then he straightened. "But I'm still a Southern plantation owner," he said in a low, fierce voice. "I was just doing my duty."

Carrie knew better than to say anything. This was a battle her father would have to fight himself. Just like she had had to. She ached for him. She had fought habits from eighteen years of prejudice—he would have to fight over forty. Forty years of deeply ingrained prejudice and ignorance.

Thomas turned away from the mirror. "Thank you," he said heavily. "I think." He managed a small smile.

Carrie stayed seated on the floor, but smiled back.

Once more silence descended on the room. All Carrie could hear was the sound of the clock ticking, mingled with distant sounds of the city. A breeze fluttered in, making the curtains sway gently. A fly buzzed around her head, then darted out the window. Suddenly all she wanted was to curl up in a ball on her bed and dream the world away. The wild rampaging of her emotions had left her completely exhausted, but somewhere in the last chaotic moments the beginnings of peace had edged their way into her heart. She made no attempt to understand it—she simply accepted it. Anything was better than the black hopelessness and despair that had captured her.

"Are you as tired as I am?"

Carrie looked up at her father. "Yes," she said simply.

Thomas stood and held out his arms. "Come here," he commanded gently.

Carrie stood and moved into his arms, laying her head against his chest as he pulled her close. "I love you."

"I love you, too," he murmured.

"I'm sorry I got so angry." Carrie could feel Thomas shaking his head.

"Don't be." He laughed shortly. "Your father is just like you. Sometimes it takes a brick to make a dent in my head—or my heart, for that matter." He pushed Carrie away from him and looked down. "Don't expect me to change overnight. I have a lot to think about. A lot of strongly held beliefs to challenge." He paused. "I'm not sure what side I will come down on."

Carrie gave him another hug. She knew her father was a man of integrity. He would examine his beliefs honestly. She was confident the truth would win in time. There was no need to say any more.

"How often do reports about the soldiers come in?" she asked quietly, relieved to change the subject.

"Twice a day. I'll check every one."

Carrie nodded. "I have to go to the hospital. Would you like to eat something with me before I go?"

"Certainly."

Carrie almost smiled at the relief in her father's voice. She hooked her arm through his. "Well, I think that storm is over. But that doesn't mean there won't be more. I'm a woman, you know. I'm entitled."

Thomas chuckled. "So you are. So you are."

Carrie breathed a sigh of relief as she hurried up the hill to the hospital and watched the first of a long line of ambulance wagons turn into the yard. Her work in the hospital had become her salvation during the war. Now, with news of Robert missing, it would have to be even more so. All the way up the hill she had prayed silently for Robert. Her father had been right. She didn't know for sure if Robert was dead or alive. As long as there was a chance, she had to believe Robert was alive.

Carrie was swept up into mad activity as soon as she stepped into her ward.

Dr. Wild appeared at her side. "There is a new wagon coming in. Will you help me?"

"Certainly." Carrie's admiration and respect for Dr. Wild had grown with each passing day. He was an excellent doctor, but it was his compassion that never ceased to amaze her. There were endless drains on his time and energy, but he always seemed to have a smile and an encouraging word for each soldier he worked on. She had watched frustration cloud his face time after time when patients died. Too many of the Chimborazo doctors saw their patients as just another body in the count. Dr. Wild saw each one as a person to care about.

"I think we're going to see worse conditions than we have so far," Dr. Wild said as they strode across the yard.

Carrie looked at him, startled. "I'm not sure things could get worse."

"Oh yes, they can," he replied grimly. "These men were injured three or four days ago, where field surgeons and doctors were able to do only the bare minimum to keep them alive. The patients we have received so far were fresh from the battlefield."

As they arrived at the first wagon, Carrie looked down and felt nausea gripping her throat. The man staring up at her had several wounds crudely wrapped, his eyes glazed with the raging fever of infection. His bandages were loosely wrapped, providing little barrier against the swarm of maggots crawling over and under the linen.

"Get this man into the ward," she called to one of the attendants. "Take the bandages off and clean his wounds. I want every one of the maggots gone."

"Help me with this one, Carrie," Dr. Wild called.

Carrie dashed to his side. When she saw the patient her mouth gaped. "Hobbs!" she whispered.

"You know this man?" Dr. Wild asked sharply.

"Yes. His name is Warren Hobbs. He is one of the men in Robert's unit." She had long ago told Dr. Wild all about Robert and their wedding plans. "They are very close."

"It looks like he's going to lose his leg. I don't think it's possible to save it."

Carrie grimaced, glad Hobbs was unconscious. She looked at his leg closely, reluctantly agreeing with Dr. Wild's assessment. His right leg had caught several shell fragments, shattering the bone in several places and ripping the skin. "If only he had gotten treatment sooner."

"We'll be lucky if we can save his life," Dr. Wild said grimly.

Just then Hobbs' eyes fluttered open. "Leg hurts," he muttered. He fought to focus his eyes. "Miss Carrie . . . ?" he whispered.

Carrie reached for his grimy hand and held it tightly. "Yes, Hobbs. It's me. We're going to take good care of you." She fought her desire to bombard him with questions. Surely he knew what had happened to Robert; they were never far from each other on the battlefield. She held her tongue as she watched the ravages of pain settle on his young, tortured face.

He opened his eyes again. "My leg . . . ?"

"Dr. Wild will do the best he can," she said reassuringly.

Hobbs' face twisted. "Promise me . . . don't let them . . . take leg," he finally gasped.

Carrie stared at him, wishing for his own sake that he would lapse into unconsciousness again. How could she make a promise like that? If they didn't take his leg, he would probably die. Hard reality reminded her he had little chance to live regardless of whether he kept his leg or not. It was obvious infection had settled in and was destroying his body—sapping his life slowly but surely.

"Promise . . . " he whispered, his voice barely audible.

Carrie glanced up at Dr. Wild.

He stepped up next to her. "I promise you, Hobbs," he said firmly. He smiled and reached out to take Hobbs' other hand. "We won't take your leg."

Hobbs gave a gasp of relief, then went slack.

Dr. Wild looked up at Carrie. "Sometimes hope is all that will take them through. This man has little chance of living. If knowing he can keep his leg will give him the will to fight, then he'll keep his leg." He frowned darkly, shaking his head. "But it doesn't look good for him."

Carrie stared down at Hobbs, tears filling her eyes. "He helped me escape the plantation," she murmured. "Robert loves him very much." A lump swelled up in her throat as she thought of never seeing Robert again. And suddenly making sure Hobbs was okay for Robert's sake was the most important thing. "We have to save him," she said fiercely.

Dr. Wild reached out and touched her arm. "We'll do all we can. Hopefully Robert will be able to visit him soon."

"Robert is missing in action," Carrie said flatly. "My father saw his name on the list today."

There was a brief silence. "I'm so sorry."

Carrie pushed aside the emotion threatening to overwhelm her again. "Thank you," she said briskly, knowing Dr. Wild would understand. She couldn't afford to think of that now—if she sulked over Robert all day she wouldn't be able to give these soldiers the care they deserved, the care she hoped Robert was getting somewhere else. She would look after Hobbs as if he were Robert. Gazing at his unconscious form, an idea sprang into her mind.

"What are you thinking?" Dr. Wild demanded. "I've seen that look before."

"It's something I read this spring. A way we might save his leg ..." She hesitated, not sure she should even say what she was thinking.

"Go on."

"Instead of taking the leg, we could just cut out the part of the bone that has been destroyed," she said slowly. "Then we bandage it and allow the bone to fuse together."

"That would make his right leg several inches shorter than his left," Dr. Wild said slowly.

"At least he would still have a leg. And if you can take the infected part out, it might give the rest of his body a chance to recover."

"If *we* can take the infected part out," Dr. Wild corrected.

"We?" Carrie echoed. She had never before assisted in surgery.

"Any other doctor here would laugh at me for even attempting such a thing. You'll have to help me. Do you still have the book detailing the operation?"

Carrie shook her head. "I had to leave it behind on the plantation."

"Do you remember it well?"

"Yes."

"We'll operate as soon as the others are tended to, then," he said firmly, a slight smile on his lips. "We'll give this man the best chance we can."

Carrie nodded, excitement and dread mingling together. She had dreamed of one day being in the surgery room. She would only be assisting, of course, but at least she would be there.

Hobbs had to wait while other patients were tended to. Reality demanded they first care for the patients with a good chance of making it. Finally, two hours later, Hobbs was carried to the operating table on a stretcher.

"You know how to administer the anesthesia?" Dr. Wild asked.

Carrie nodded, reaching for the chloroform. She was thankful there was still plenty available. She knew many doctors operated on unconscious patients without it. Carrie had always wondered what happened if patients awoke in the middle of an operation. She was thankful she wouldn't have to make such a discovery with Hobbs.

Dr. Wild carefully cut away the rest of Hobbs' pants near the wound. Carrie managed to keep herself from groaning at the sight of the splintered bone, its jagged edges pressing into red, inflamed tissue. How had Hobbs stood such agony for three days? Carrie set her lips firmly and bent down to assist.

She had no idea how much time had passed when she finished wrapping Hobbs' leg and stepped back.

"Excellent job, Miss Cromwell."

Carrie smiled. "It was incredible to watch. I can only hope that one day I will have the skill you possess."

"I have no doubt you will," Dr. Wild said firmly. Then he looked down at Hobbs. "I'd give him less than a thirty percent chance to make it. We've done all we can."

Carrie laid her hand on Hobbs' arm. "I believe he'll make it." Why else would he have been in the first wagon she stepped up to? In spite of the situation, she smiled.

"What is it you find humorous?"

"Not humorous, really," Carrie replied. "Earlier today I was doubting the existence of God. Doubting whether he really cared. He has ways of reminding us."

A sudden shout grabbed Dr. Wild's attention. "Looks like we have more work to do."

Carrie gave a final look at Hobbs, then turned quickly to join the doctor. There was no more she could do until Hobbs regained consciousness. If he did.

"How is Hobbs?" Thomas asked, taking a sip of coffee as he settled down at his place at the dinner table.

Carrie shook her head wearily. "He is still unconscious." She stared at the plate in front of her. Would she ever get used to eating dinner at ten o'clock at night? The only positive thing about it was that the other people living in the house had eaten by then, and she and her father could spend some time alone. Janie was still at the hospital.

Her mind traveled back to dinner time on the plantation. Her mother had insisted dinner always be served promptly at five o'clock. Only an act of God could change it. They always had an elaborate spread, even if it was just the family but those were the times when she felt closest to her family, sharing stories as they sipped coffee and ate dessert. Pushing aside the memories, Carrie managed to keep from sighing. It seemed like another lifetime—surely another person had experienced that.

"You saw the list again today?" she asked bluntly.

"Yes. Robert is still listed as missing in action."

Carrie stared down at her plate, biting her lip.

"General Lee has pulled his men out of Maryland."

Carrie nodded, glad her father wasn't going to talk about Robert. "I see." She didn't know what else to say. It was impossible to feel interested in the developments of the war. She hated the war beyond her wildest imagination. Would it ever end?

"General Lee is a hard man to discourage," Thomas said admiringly. "He set out to defeat the Army of the Potomac on Northern soil. Evidently even the shock of Antietam has not made him abandon his goal."

"Why should he?" Carrie blurted. "He still has thousands of men left to slaughter," she said bitterly.

Thomas looked at her compassionately, but didn't respond. He took another long drink of coffee. "To his way of thinking it was McClellan's army that brushed the edge of disaster—not his."

Carrie took a spoonful of soup, her anger dissipating under the load of fatigue. Let her father talk. It did him good and she didn't really care.

"He actually thought he might continue to press the offensive, but he just wired Davis that the army is too weak. Thousands are deserting, heading for their homes," Thomas said in disgust.

More power to them, Carrie thought. Who in their right mind would want to continue to fight when all around them their friends were being killed and mutilated? Suddenly it was all too much again. The long day had camouflaged her pain, but now there was nothing to numb it. Pushing aside her plate, she shoved her chair back and stood. "I'm very tired. I'm going to bed."

"Carrie. Wait," Thomas said contritely. "I'm sorry. I know you couldn't care less about General Lee and his army. I'm just talking— avoiding what I really need to say."

Carrie settled back into her chair, looking at her father expectantly. The silence stretched out as her father fidgeted with his spoon. His eyes darting to hers, he began, "About what happened this morning...I need to tell you...about my father. He was...well... we weren't alike. He was ..." Thomas paused. "He felt differently about our slaves. He thought they were there just for his pleasure."

Carrie listened closely. He'd never talked about this before and she wondered what he was driving at.

"I still think it's our ordained duty to have slaves, but I think it is our responsibility to care for them, not just use them selfishly."

Carrie remained silent, but wondered what it would take for her father to see that the very act of slavery was a selfish use of humanity.

"Your grandfather was a proud man. Carving Cromwell Plantation out of the wilderness was a very difficult thing. It was a great accomplishment." Thomas stared off into space. "It was almost as if it used up all the greatness he had in him. At the end he was a bitter, tired old man. I believe he felt as if all his work had been for nothing."

"How could he feel that way?" Carrie protested. "Cromwell Plantation is a very successful, beautiful plantation."

"Yes," Thomas agreed. "But," he continued thoughtfully, "I believe my father lost himself in the creation of Cromwell Plantation. He poured himself into creating something and then there was nothing left for him—maybe I should say there was nothing left *of* him. Not of the man I knew as a child, anyway."

"You mean he was so busy doing things, he lost contact with his own heart and soul."

Thomas gazed at her, startled. "That's exactly what I mean. How did you . . . ?"

"It was something Robert told me the night he asked me to marry him," Carrie said quietly.

Silence fell on the room for a few minutes as both of them lost themselves in their thoughts.

"I felt horrible about what my father did to Sarah," Thomas continued. "I didn't know what to do." He paused. "I know now I did the wrong thing. It is my responsibility to care for my slaves. Sending John away—giving away Rose's brother—they were selfish acts. I'm so sorry."

Carrie reached out for his hand. "I know." She wanted her father to see so much more. She wanted him to understand that slavery was an awful thing. She wanted him to recognize the horrible wrong it had inflicted on millions of people. But she knew she couldn't force it on him. She had reached her own conclusions after months of struggle and soul-searching. She simply had to trust God to show him the truth. "I love you," she said tenderly.

Carrie was sitting next to the window, staring out into the warm night when Janie entered the room. She had heard voices downstairs a few minutes earlier. Her father would have told her about Robert. Janie closed the door behind her softly, then walked over and laid her hand on Carrie's shoulder without saying a word.

Carrie was grateful Janie didn't say anything. Carrie felt so lost, so alone. This was the very thing she had feared and now it seemed even more horrible than her nightmares. Was God playing a cruel trick? Robert held her heart. She longed to share the rest of her life with him. Where was he? Would she ever see him again? Was he suffering? The not knowing once again rose up and tried to swallow her.

"Carrie?"

Carrie registered Janie's voice. Only then did she become aware she was trembling all over. She stared up at Janie wordlessly.

Janie knelt and wrapped her warm arms around Carrie's shaking shoulders. "I'm so sorry," she whispered. "I'm so sorry."

Great sobs tore through Carrie's body. "Robert!" she cried. "Robert . . ."

Carrie was up before the sun the next morning. Janie was still sound asleep when she slipped out of the room. The two friends had talked until late into the night. Once Carrie had released her emotions, she had been able to communicate what she was feeling. The act of talking had helped deplete the suffocating helplessness.

Carrie strode purposefully up the hill toward the hospital. Janie was right. There was just as much reason to believe Robert was alive as there was to believe he was dead. Hope was all she had to hang on to, so she was going to hang on. For now she was going to give all she had to the people who needed her—who counted on her.

Hobbs was awake when she approached his bed. Most of the other men were still asleep, the sound of their quiet snores rising and falling.

"So it *was* you yesterday. I thought maybe I'd imagined it." Hobbs' voice was weak, little more than a whisper.

Carrie reached for his hand. "It was me," she agreed, smiling. "How are you feeling?" She reached out and touched his forehead. It was still burning hot.

"Not so good," he admitted. He hesitated for a long moment. "Do I . . . ? Were you . . . ?"

"Able to save your leg? It's there for now," Carrie replied. "We did the best we could. Your right leg is now several inches shorter than your left, but we saved it—at least if infection doesn't destroy it." She was determined to be honest with him.

"Thank you," he whispered. "Miss Carrie?" His eyes held hers as if he had something important to say.

Carrie's heart started pounding. Suddenly she was afraid to hear what he was going to say. "You need to get some rest. We can talk later."

Hobbs shook his head. "I promised the lieutenant," he said, his voice stronger now, his eyes desperate. "If I don't make it . . . "

Carrie dropped down into a chair beside his bed. "What happened?"

"The lieutenant got shot pretty early in the day. We couldn't get him off the field. There were too many bullets flying." His voice was filled with pain.

Carrie reached out and took his hand but didn't say anything.

"Me and some of the men—we put a barrier of logs around him. We figured it would at least keep him from getting shot up any more." He stopped. "We didn't know what else to do. I went back with one of the medics that night to get him, but . . . "

"But what?" Carrie asked desperately.

"He was gone, Miss Carrie."

"Gone?" Carrie echoed. "Gone where?"

"I don't know. I looked for him everywhere. That's how I got hurt—trying to find him." Then he told her about being trapped in the town.

Carrie could tell Hobbs was fading quickly. But his story had only confused her more. "But what could have happened to him? Is it possible you missed him in one of the hospital camps?"

"It's possible," he said slowly, his expression saying he didn't believe it.

Carrie knew how much Hobbs loved Robert. She knew how hard he would have looked for him.

Hobbs continued on, his exhaustion causing him to falter. "I don't reckon our lieutenant is a prisoner. I don't think the Union medics would have taken him before we could get to him."

Carrie was confused.

"Some of the fellas said maybe he deserted—got out of there while he could."

"Not Robert! He would never desert!" Carrie was sure of that. She might have wanted him to, but she knew he never would have.

"That's what I told them," Hobbs agreed. His eyes pooled with tears. "I reckon our lieutenant is dead, Miss Carrie. I reckon somebody carted him off and buried him."

Carrie stared at Hobbs for a minute, then shook her head decisively. "I don't believe it." When Hobbs stared back she knew what he was thinking—he was pitying her. She shook her head again. "I don't know where Robert is—but I refuse to believe he's dead." Carrie knew her belief made absolutely no sense.

But she believed it; she had to.

~ Twenty-One ~

A unt Abby was waiting for Matthew at the top of the stairs. "Welcome, Matthew. It's wonderful to see you. I thought you would never get back to Philadelphia." She looked into his blue eyes, relieved to see that the haunted look that had lurked there the last time she had seen him was gone.

Matthew hugged her warmly. "I was beginning to wonder if I ever would. I can't believe I've been home for over a week. The paper has kept me working so hard, I hardly have time to breathe."

"I'm just glad you could come for dinner. I have so wanted to talk to you. I sometimes despair of finding a rational, balanced person in this whole town!"

"I hope I don't disappoint you," Matthew laughed.

"Nonsense!" Aunt Abby scoffed. "You haven't let me down yet. It's not that I think we should agree on everything. It's merely that I want the freedom to express my views without fear of condemnation from those who disagree with me—or fanaticism from those who *do.*"

"You have my word I will give you that." Matthew strode into the hallway eagerly and gazed around. "I've missed this place."

Aunt Abby put an arm around his waist. "It will always be your home," she said quietly. She knew it must be lonely for Matthew to constantly come home to an empty boarding house room. "Dinner is ready. Are you hungry?"

"Will the sun rise tomorrow?" Matthew teased. "Lead me to it."

Aunt Abby had taken only a few bites before she could not control herself any longer. "There is so much I want to talk to you about." She put down her fork, the food quickly forgotten.

"Such as?" Matthew mumbled around a mouthful of food.

Aunt Abby knew he was teasing her. "Such as the outrageous amount they wanted for silk in the store today. I told the manager he could keep his silk and stalked out." Matthew put down his fork and stared at her. Aunt Abby laughed. "You want to ask silly questions, young man, that's fine—you'll get silly answers back." She glared at him. "You know very well what I want to talk about."

Matthew stared longingly at his plate of food, shoveled in a few quick bites, then laid his fork aside. "Only for you would I hurry such a wonderful meal."

"I could have waited to feed you until after we talked," Aunt Abby threatened.

"Now there's an idea," Matthew exclaimed. "I'll talk, but you have to warm up my meal and feed me again."

"You have a deal!"

"Would you like to start with Antietam?"

Aunt Abby paused. She didn't want to subject Matthew to reliving the horrible memories of Antietam.

"It's all right. It's been almost a month. I don't know if I'll ever sleep another night without vivid nightmares of the battlefields I've been witness to, but during the day I can manage to converse quite objectively about it. Rose was right. If you share it, it's not so horrible. I'm keeping a daily journal. It helps," he said simply.

Aunt Abby gave a sigh of relief. "I would very much like to know your perspective on it. President Lincoln is quite angry with General McClellan."

"With good reason," Matthew said darkly, a heavy scowl on his brow. "I imagine any other general would have ended the war by now." He shook his head. "General Lee was up against impossible odds at Antietam. If McClellan had ever once thrown all of his army's might at him, it would have been over shortly. I couldn't believe what I was seeing as the day progressed," he continued. "McClellan continued to send single unit after single unit in—each one being driven back after thousands were slaughtered. By day's end, McClellan had committed less than thirty thousand of his troops. He had over eighty thousand men there!"

"But why?"

"There is no way to understand our fine general," Matthew said sarcastically. He paused. "Actually, that's not true. Not if what I heard recently is accurate, and I have every reason to believe it is; my sources are quite good."

"What did you hear?" Aunt Abby leaned forward, relieved beyond words to have him there to talk to. She had missed him sorely the last six weeks. Being completely alone again, after Rose left, had taken some adjusting. There were still days she felt she lived in an empty tomb, but it was getting easier.

"President Lincoln called one of McClellan's officers into the Oval office. A fellow by the name of Major John J. Key. He serves on McClellan's staff—or at least he did. Lincoln had overheard something Key was purported to have said and wanted to know if it was true." Matthew paused, a look of disgust on his face.

"What was it?"

"Key had been asked by another officer why Lee's army was not captured at Antietam. His response was, *'That is not the game; the object is that neither army shall get much advantage of the other; that both shall be kept in the field till they are exhausted, when we will make a compromise and save slavery.'*"

Aunt Abby stared at him. "A Union officer made that statement? What did Lincoln do?"

"He promptly dismissed Key from the army," Matthew said with grim satisfaction. "I hate this war!" he growled. "To think men are trying to draw the suffering and agony out in an insane effort to save slavery makes my blood boil."

Sounds from outside filtered into the room—the clip-clop of horses pulling carriages, the distant whistle of a train engine. Laughter and talk floated in on the breeze. Aunt Abby would soon close the house up for the winter, but the cool fall nights invigorated her. Fall was her favorite time of the year. But she could find no joy in this one.

"I'm afraid sentiment is rather strong here in Philadelphia, as well. With elections coming up, they seem to be reaching the boiling point."

Matthew nodded. "I talked to a fellow about that this week. Enthusiasm for the war is fading everywhere, but it seems to be giving way to especially bitter dissension here."

"The city has long held a tradition of sympathy for the South," Aunt Abby replied. "Likewise, they have clung to a prejudice and antipathy toward the colored man. The combination is clouding its dedication to the Union."

"With a few men helping cloud that dedication," Matthew stated. "I interviewed Legislator Biddle a few days ago. He is quite opinionated."

"That's putting it rather lightly," Aunt Abby laughed. "The Democrats are going to give the Republican Congress a run for their money, I'm afraid."

"The Republicans will be lucky if they can hold onto the majority," Matthew agreed. "Biddle and the Democratic party claim to be merely trying to preserve the Constitution and the Union the way the founding fathers conceived them. They are solidly against this war."

"I'm afraid it's too late for that," Aunt Abby said sadly. "My daddy would have said that was like beating a dead horse. You can beat it all you want—but it's not going to get up and walk. No matter how this war ends, our country will never be the same."

"If only more people saw things the way you do, Mrs. Livingston."

"If only they had seen it before the war started," Aunt Abby retorted. "There is no way to undo the damage this war has done, and I'm afraid the only way for a raging fire to go away is for it to burn itself out." She paused. "I remember seeing a burning house one time. I was just a little girl. When the firemen first got there they tried to put it out, but it was already too hot. They eventually stopped pouring water on it. They said when it got that hot the only thing they could do was let it burn out and hope it didn't take everything around with it." She shook her head. "How much of what our country holds dear is going to be burned up in this war?" she asked sadly.

Aunt Abby rose to light the fire in the fireplace, then moved to shut the windows for the night. A stiff breeze was making the room chilly. As she gazed out the window, she noticed the trees swaying in the wind, leaves dancing, then dropping to swirl to the ground. "Many families in Philadelphia did not accept revolution gladly in 1776. Many feel the same way now."

"Biddle and other democrats are keeping things stirred up," Matthew agreed. "He certainly is not quiet about his beliefs. He is asserting that the South probably would have returned to the Union if her people had been offered complete security concerning the slave issue. He blames the continuation of the war on the North and says that slavery has been rooted in America by the Providence of God and that only gradual action can safely uproot it." Matthew shook his head. "He also told me that repugnance to negro equality is as strong in the middle states as it is in the South. He fears emancipation will inundate Pennsylvania with coloreds."

"Yet emancipation is coming!" Aunt Abby exclaimed. She turned around, excitement shining in her eyes. "That's what I want to talk to you about more than anything. What do you think of the Emancipation Proclamation?"

Matthew hesitated. "It's a step in the right direction," he said slowly.

"You don't believe it will accomplish anything," Aunt Abby stated flatly, disappointment rising to choke her. She had so wanted Matthew to share her excitement.

"I didn't say that. I've been trying to figure out what I think about it ever since I first heard of it. I knew Lincoln had written one long before he made it public. He was waiting for a glorious Northern victory to set it forth." He laughed abruptly. "I hardly think Antietam was a glorious Northern victory. We suffered over ten thousand casualties in one day, but in the end the South suffered worse than we did. Lincoln took what he could get."

"Why do you not feel good about it?"

"How do your abolitionist friends feel about it?" Matthew asked, instead of answering her question.

Aunt Abby frowned. "They are grateful that some kind of stand is being made, but—they fear it is too little. That the compromise within it will render it ineffective." She paused. "I have to believe any step will eventually take us where we want to go."

"Did you know Lincoln met with several colored leaders this fall?"

"That's probably a first!" Aunt Abby exclaimed. "What did they talk about?"

"Colonization. President Lincoln told them this war wouldn't have started if it wasn't for their presence in this country. He said that equality between our races just wasn't possible. Told them he was sorry they had been subjected to slavery but that even once they were free, they would still be far from equal. Basically, he told them it was best for our races to be separated. He offered money to send anyone who would lead the way in colonizing an area outside of our country."

"That's awful! Of course they turned him down."

"No one took him up on his offer," Matthew agreed blandly.

Aunt Abby could feel anger and frustration rising in her. Was there any way for all this madness to end? "The very idea of telling them that if they weren't here this war wouldn't be raging. It was hardly their choice to be dragged to this country and thrown into slavery! If blame is to be laid, it needs to rest on the first Americans who allowed slavery to pollute our nation."

"Have you talked with Rose about this?" Matthew asked.

"Certainly. We talked about it while Moses was still here. Of course they hate slavery, but they are Americans, the same as you or me," Aunt Abby said firmly. "They simply want the chance to live in their own country in equality." She paused, then added defiantly, "That's all most women want, too." She knew she was jumping to another subject, but she was too angry to think straight. "I tell you, Matthew—women aren't going to give up fighting until we have the right to vote. I refuse to simply sit back and let men make all my decisions for me. I firmly believe that if women had had a say in this, we might not have a war on our hands right now. We have a voice. We're not going to give up until it's heard."

"I hope you don't," Matthew said sincerely. "I agree that our country needs the perspective of women. I believe it could have a significant moderating effect." He paused and looked at her closely. "Speaking of that—have you found any more dead chickens on your doorstep?"

"Thankfully, no. I think my refusing to be afraid—plus the fact that you showed up on my doorstep minutes after it happened—made whoever did it think twice." She clenched her fist. "Just let them come back. I refuse to let some cowardly person intimidate me. I've come too far—fought too long—for that! I'm no longer a frightened newly-widowed weakling!" Aunt Abby suddenly laughed. "Sorry. I didn't mean to go off on that tirade. Now, weren't we talking about the Emancipation Proclamation?"

"Lincoln has made himself pretty clear from the very beginning how he feels about slavery," Matthew mused. "He believes it is morally wrong for man to hold his fellow man as property, but from the time he took office he has made it clear he had no intention of freeing the slaves. He believed the Constitution did not give him the legal right to interfere with slavery in the states where it existed."

"The South didn't believe he felt that way."

"No. They were convinced he was out to destroy slavery. Yet, I think the reasons for the war run much deeper than just slavery. I think slavery is the surface issue that ignited enough passion to spark the war, but there are other deep issues that contributed just as much."

"I know states' rights played a key role," Aunt Abby observed. "That, and the South felt they were being robbed of their way of life by the industrial North."

"All of that played a role," Matthew agreed.

Aunt Abby rose to stir the fire. "I suppose it's never possible to truly understand why people act the way they do. Human beings are so complex. What might be a compelling reason for one person, could mean absolutely nothing to the next. And in the end, I don't believe many people were thinking at all. At least not the ones making the decisions. They were simply being swept along by their passions and feelings." Sparks flew from the fire as she turned back. "So why do you think Lincoln published the Emancipation Proclamation?"

Matthew chuckled. "Lincoln is a complicated man. I don't think anyone has the ability to get inside his head—not that anyone can truly get inside anyone's head. But I have thought about it long and hard. With the Southern states claiming independence, he was no longer bound by the confines of the Constitution in his dealings with them. I think the reason was primarily military in nature. It was also politically astute."

"What do you mean?"

"Armies need a reason to fight," he said simply. "Men need a reason to keep throwing themselves into battle. The war has steadily grown more deadly. Each battle is more violent than the rest. This war has become what it really was from the beginning. A revolution. Men fight revolutions because they are passionate. The South has much to be passionate about. They are fighting for their homeland, for their way of life." He paused and took a long drink. "Up until now the North has mostly been fighting for a principle. They have been fighting to preserve the Union of our country. I believe Lincoln knows that dedication to a principle soon fades. He decided to put a human face on it. In order to keep the army fighting, he had to turn it into a moral war."

"Do you think it will work?" Aunt Abby asked anxiously.

"I don't know," Matthew said slowly. "The North is very divided on the issue of slavery. You see that here. I'm afraid there is very little moral mixture in the antislavery feeling in the North. Some of it is abstract philanthropy—part of it is hatred for slave owners." He paused. "Just as much is jealousy for white labor." He shook his head. "I'm afraid very little is a consciousness of wrong done—or the wish to correct it."

"But surely that is changing?" Aunt Abby protested.

"Yes, it's changing," Matthew agreed instantly. "The work of the abolitionists has done much to change the way people see slavery. But in the end, people are passionate about things that affect them every day, that reach into their world. To many of our citizens, slavery is something that happens to someone else."

"But they are the ones having to fight because of it. Women sending off their husbands, sons, and fathers to fight against slavery."

"Which is exactly why I think Lincoln has issued the Proclamation. He is counting on the time being right."

Aunt Abby frowned. "He has gotten much negative reaction."

Matthew waved one hand in the air casually. "No matter what someone does—including the President—someone isn't going to like it. It isn't going to fit their own personal agenda. I would say Lincoln has gotten much more positive reaction, especially from Europe."

"But I understood the statesmen there were outraged."

"True," Matthew laughed. "But the people love it, and the government has to listen. England has decided once and for all not to recognize the Confederacy. That alone will make it much more difficult for the South to succeed."

Aunt Abby stood and walked over to stare out the window again. Darkness had fallen, but she could still see the leaves swirling in the light of the street lamp, much like the stirring in her own heart. She spun around. "I still can't believe Lincoln told the colored leaders they should take all their people out of the country. How can a man who claims to know God believe negroes are not our equals?" She shook her head, searching for the words to describe what was going on in her heart. "Can he really believe God would create a race who would never have the chance for equality? Create a whole group of people who would forever have to live feeling inferior and unworthy? Why, the very idea is ludicrous!" she exclaimed angrily.

Matthew stood and walked to where she was staring out the window again. "I don't think Lincoln believes that."

"Then why would he do such a thing?" Aunt Abby cried.

"I think Lincoln is a man who understands human nature." Matthew paused and reached into his pocket. "I knew we would be talking about this tonight. I brought something Lincoln wrote." Unfolding the piece of paper he was holding, he began to read. *"Let me say I think I have no prejudice against the Southern people. They are just what we would be in their situation. If slavery did not now exist among them, they would not introduce it. If it did now exist among us, we should not instantly give it up. This I believe of the masses North and South. Doubtless there are individuals on both sides who would not hold slaves under any circumstances, and others who would gladly introduce slavery anew if it were out of exis-tence.*

"We know that some slavery men do free their slaves, go North and become tiptop Abolitionists, while some Northern ones go South and become most cruel slave-masters. When Southern people tell us they are no more responsible for the origin of slavery than we are, I acknowledge the fact. When it is said the institution exists, and that it is very difficult to get rid of in any satisfactory way, I can under-stand and appreciate the saying. I surely will not blame them for not doing what I should not know how to do myself."

Aunt Abby stared thoughtfully out the window. "He's right," she finally agreed. "I have met many Northerners who are jealous of the Southern right to own slaves. But," she said fiercely, "it doesn't matter how people feel. The simple fact is that slavery is wrong! No one has the right to own another person. And like it or not, our country is going to have to learn to live with the negro race in equality. God did *not* create an inferior race. He created a wonderful people whose skin is darker than our own."

"It will take people like you, Aunt Abby, to make it happen," Matthew said quietly. "It will take people with the ability to be color-blind, as well as the ability to see the heart before they see any-thing else." He paused. "I believe Lincoln knows our country is a long way from accepting coloreds as equals, maybe it never will. Perhaps he is trying to save them from more pain and humiliation." He paused. "Or he is trying to salvage his political future," he added wryly.

Aunt Abby nodded slowly. From somewhere, hope was springing up within her heart. Moving away from the window, she walked back to the fire and stared into the flames, welcoming their warmth. Suddenly she understood. With a wide smile on her face she turned to Matthew. "God will always accomplish his purpose," she said firmly. "Lincoln may not have at first had the desire to free the slaves. His sole interest may have been in the preservation of the Union. But I believe God has been planning freedom for the slaves from the very minute they first stepped foot on American soil—just like he planned freedom for the Israelites from Egypt." She chuckled, her heart light. "God has taken the circumstances and used them to turn Lincoln into the 'Great Deliverer' of the slaves." She laughed aloud now. "God will always accomplish his purpose one way or the other."

"Surely you don't think this war is God's will," Matthew said in astonishment.

Aunt Abby fixed him with a steely glare. "That is ridiculous and you know it! I believe God weeps for every soldier who is killed in this horrible war. But men weren't listening to God when they started this war, and I don't see many people listening to him now," she said firmly. "None of that changes the fact that God can take any circum-stances—however horrible—and perform his will." She walked over and put her hand on Matthew's arm. "I hate this war as much as anyone. But it gives me hope to see God at work in the midst of it."

Matthew covered her hand with his. "I'm sorry. I know you abhor this war, and I know you would never think it is God's will. No matter how hard I try to make sense of all of it, I just can't."

"Thank God," Aunt Abby said fervently. "If you could, I would really be concerned about you. War never makes sense."

Matthew opened his mouth to speak, then closed it.

"What is it?" Aunt Abby prodded.

"I'm not sure war never makes sense," Matthew said slowly. "If a foreign country were to come to America and attempt to conquer us, I think I would fight." His eyes clouded as he thought. "I think there may be times when war may not be the best answer, but sometimes it is not just an answer—it is a response to actions others have taken. There will always be bullies who want to enforce their will on others. Many times the only thing they understand is force."

Aunt Abby allowed his words to sink into her heart. She wasn't sure she agreed, but she certainly understood what he was saying. She would have to think about it for a while. "Can we at least agree *this* war doesn't make any sense?"

"Absolutely," Matthew said with a smile. "Now—all this talk has made me even hungrier than when I arrived. I believe you promised to reheat my meal. I'm going to hold you to it."

Aunt Abby laughed and headed toward the kitchen. "I'm a lady of honor," she said with a slight curtsy. "Dinner will be served in a few minutes. I discover I am famished as well."

Aunt Abby watched Matthew as he ate. "Why aren't you married?" she asked suddenly, then flushed. "I'm sorry! I don't know why I asked you that. It's absolutely none of my business." Aunt Abby was horrified with herself. Was she turning into one of those meddling old women?

Matthew finished chewing his last bite. "I'm surprised you haven't asked before now. Most people consider me an oddity."

"You are certainly not an oddity, Matthew. You are a wonderful young man." Aunt Abby chose her words carefully. "I worry about you. It must be lonely coming home to that empty boarding house room."

"It is," Matthew agreed quietly. "But I've watched my mother and father for years. My father once told me there was no other woman for him once he had laid eyes on my mother. They still love each other fiercely. I want that kind of love." A great sadness crossed his face.

"It will come some day," Aunt Abby said gently, reaching out to cover his hand.

Matthew shook his head and sighed. "I'm afraid it already has." He looked at Aunt Abby with an apologetic smile.

Aunt Abby was confused. "I don't understand."

Matthew sighed again. "I suppose I knew you would ask me eventually. I was looking forward to it, in a way."

Aunt Abby watched him closely. She had seen that troubled look on her husband's face many times. It was always when he had a burden he was tired of carrying alone. She waited quietly. Matthew would tell her when he was ready.

"I've met the woman I want to marry. I haven't been able to see anyone except her from the first day I met her."

"She won't have you?" Aunt Abby asked sympathetically.

"She has no idea how I feel. I can't tell her."

Understanding began to dawn in Aunt Abby's heart. "Oh, Matthew . . . "

Matthew nodded. "Carrie has eyes for no one but Robert," he said hopelessly. "I loved her the minute I laid eyes on her. The night you brought her to the dance here in the city. I saw her from across the room. The only thing important to me right then was to meet the beautiful girl who was exploding with life."

"And then you found out who she was."

Matthew nodded heavily. "I would never betray Robert. Not that she would ever see me that way," he added hastily.

Aunt Abby's heart went out to the young man. She could not bear the pain in his eyes. She struggled for the right thing to say.

"I'm rather relieved that you know," Matthew went on. "Just telling someone helps. And I'm sure you understand because you know how special Carrie is." He paused. "Promise me you'll never tell her how I feel."

"Of course," Aunt Abby said softly, reaching out and covering his hand warmly. "I promise."

Rose stopped to watch the men driving the wagons full of firewood. The mid-October day was still mild, but a few crisp nights had delivered the message that winter was on its way loud and clear. All the signs indicated it was going to be a severe one. She was sure that this far south it would not be as cruel as the winter she had experienced the year before in Philadelphia, but then she wasn't exactly living in a warm, well-insulated home.

"Annie won't be at school the next few days," Amos called as he drove the wagon by her. "She has a right high fever."

"I'll check on her today," Rose called back, watching as he waved and drove on. It had taken Amos almost two months to recover from the beating the Union soldiers had given him. With the exception of a slight limp, he was back to normal. At least his body was. There was a shadow in his eyes that never seemed to go away. Rose had been out to their house many times since the incident. Harriet rarely left the house anymore—fear kept her hostage in her own home. Every now and again, Rose could coax her outside if it was a particularly beautiful day, but she was never willing to go far from the porch. The children did all the gardening and outdoor chores while Harriet watched from inside.

Rose had talked with Amos about it. He had merely shrugged and said, "I don't know if she'll ever be the same. Those soldiers roughed her up pretty bad." He wouldn't say anything else. Rose had learned not to ask. It just made the shadows deeper.

Annie had shown up for school just a week after the attack. Fear had been stamped on her face when she appeared at the door, but she had a light of determination in her eyes as if the youngster had decided she wasn't going to let anything keep her down. School had been her salvation. After a few weeks the spontaneous crying had stopped and the shine had come back into her eyes. There were still times she clung to Rose, trembling, but they were fewer and further between.

"Supper is ready," June called from the porch.

Rose looked up, startled. She had been so deep in thought she wasn't even aware she was almost home. Home was now a small, weather-beaten frame house on the edge of the Great Contraband Camp. From her front porch she could see Slabtown. She could also see the burned remains of Hampton. It had been difficult to return to primitive conditions, but she didn't regret her move. She and June had grown very close, and she loved being more accessible to the people. They had worked hard to make their little home comfortable and welcoming. As promised, the superintendent had a new house built for Rose, but she and June had elected to give it to a newly arrived family of eight. The two women were quite happy where they were.

"One of your students brung a pie by today," June said, smiling. "I declare . . . "

"Brought," Rose corrected. "One of my students brought a pie by today."

"Brought a pie," June repeated, then frowned. "I don't think I'll ever learn how to talk like you."

"You're doing very well," Rose insisted, draping her light shawl on the hook by the door. She sniffed the air appreciatively. "Umm . . . Sweet potato. My favorite!"

"I sure do like living with a teacher," June laughed. "I hardly have to cook at all. Somebody is always bringing something." She paused. Just then little Simon squawked to get her attention. Turning quickly, she scooped him up in her arms. Little fists waved in the air as his cries turned to laughs of delight. "Here. Let your Aunt Rose take care of you for a minute. I got to get dinner on the table."

Rose reached for him eagerly. She never grew tired of playing with her tiny nephew. "Hello, sir. Were you good for your momma today?" She laughed as he kicked his feet and cooed, his eyes wide with delight. Suddenly her heart caught. What she would give to have a baby. Would things ever settle down so she could? Her mind drifted to Moses as it did dozens of time every day. Their one night together had been so wonderful, but in many ways it had increased her loneliness. Sometimes the ache of missing him was almost physical.

"You got a class tonight?" June asked sharply. "You're looking real tired."

Rose looked up. "It seems to be a constant condition," she said with a slight smile. "No, I don't have a class tonight. Marianne gave me the night off." It was the first in ten days. Students, hungry for knowledge, were crowding the school both day and night.

"Good!" June declared.

"I'm going out to Annie's house tonight. She's sick," Rose added. June snapped her lips shut and turned back toward the stove. Rose looked down at Simon. Yes, she was tired, but so was every other teacher. When they weren't teaching, they were trying to meet the other needs of their students. Most of her spare time was spent taking care of the sick, handing out clothing and shoes, or finding food for new arrivals. "You know I love my work," she said, more to herself than to June.

June spun around from where she was standing by the stove. "I know you do. If you didn't, so many folks wouldn't be loving you. But that don't mean it makes sense for you to drive yourself into the ground. You ain't a slave no more, Rose."

Rose almost laughed at the sparks flying from June's eyes, then she sobered. "I'm definitely not a slave," she said thoughtfully. "I would never work this hard for someone else. No, I'm working hard because this is what I'm supposed to be doing."

June looked unconvinced. "I may not be as smart as you, Rose, but I know the look of someone walking on the edge. You don't start taking care of yourself, you ain't gonna have nothing to give anyone." Having spoken her mind, she turned to the stove, her back rigid with disapproval.

Rose continued to play quietly with Simon, but her mind was pondering what June had said. Then suddenly, nausea gripped her. Taking a deep breath, she fought to control it.

"What's wrong?" June asked sharply.

"I . . . " Rose grabbed her stomach and bolted for the front porch. Several minutes later she turned back toward the door.

June reached out to help her back inside. "What'd I tell you?" she said sternly. "You been working too hard." Then she stared at Rose suspiciously. "What's that silly smile on your face for?"

Rose gazed at her quietly for a few minutes, hugging her secret to herself. Her stomach had been doing strange things for several days. She had ignored it, hoping she hadn't gotten some bad water. But now a knowing gripped her, just as it must have gripped millions of women before her.

Slowly, understanding dawned on June's face. "You mean . . . ?"

Rose nodded, her smile growing wider. "I'm going to be a momma," she whispered. Suddenly, more than anything in the world, she wanted her own momma to still be there. She could imagine the explosion of delight on Old Sarah's face. *"Rose girl, there ain't nothin' like bein' a momma. Ain't nothin' like knowin' God done trusted you with one of his little ones."*

June laughed with delight as she squeezed Rose's hands. "You're gonna be a momma!" she repeated.

Suddenly Rose was laughing out loud with her. After several minutes she sobered. "What's it like, June? Being a momma without your Simon around?"

June frowned. "It ain't the way I want it, but having little Simon makes it a lot easier to not have my husband. At least I have a part of him. Every time I look at my baby, I think about the fact that somewhere I have a man who loves me. Someday we'll be together again."

Rose drew strength from June's words. At the same time, her heart reached out—hoping that across the miles, Moses would somehow hear—and know—he was going to be a father. When would she see him again?

~Twenty-Two~

*C*onsciousness came slowly, unfurling like a fern before the spring sun. Images shot through Robert's mind in a dizzying spectacle. Exploding cannons mingled with the call of newborn calves romping in green pastures. Pictures of mutilated men overlaid the memory of his father's death. Soft breezes withdrew before furious storms. Raging pain subsided in dull numbness.

Robert . . . the whisper rolled through his mind again. *Robert* . . . The pictures quit spinning for just a moment. Looking deep into the fog, he could make out laughing green eyes. *Robert* . . . the voice became louder, more insistent. He fought to free himself from the blackness shrouding his mind, pressing down on his body. *Robert* . . . *!*

Robert opened his eyes. "Carrie . . ." he groaned. His words echoed back to him. He was alone. Disappointment collided with confusion. Struggling to focus his eyes, he looked around. Where was he? What was the heavy weight pressing down on him, making him feel so very tired? Gradually his mind cleared and his brain registered what he was seeing. Making no effort to move, Robert gazed around.

He was in a cabin. The fire flickering in the stone fireplace seemed to have been set recently. Place settings for four and a vase full of greenery rested on the crudely made table in the center of the room, with chairs scattered around. Plain muslin curtains hung at the windows. He was lying in the only bed. He looked at the quilt covering him, then continued his inspection. Stairs led up to what must have been a loft.

His brow creased in confusion. Where were his men? Where was the rest of his unit? Wherever he was, he had to get out of here.

General Lee was going to be calling for them any minute. His confusion increased as fatigue pressed down on him again. Sighing, Robert once more slipped into darkness.

Robert was aware of noises when he again gained consciousness. His mind was a little clearer this time. He lay quietly, gathering his strength before he opened his eyes and faced the world. His men had come back while he was sleeping. Now he would get some answers. Slowly he opened his eyes and turned his head. Instantly he snapped them shut again, his head swimming. Surely he had been mistaken. He hadn't really seen . . .

"Momma, I brung in the eggs from the chicken house. You'se got anything else for me to do right now?"

"No, Amber. You run on outside. There ain't gonna be many nice days left. I'll be callin' ya when supper be ready."

Robert's fists clenched under the cover. He hadn't been wrong. The little girl he saw when he had opened his eyes *was* colored! Where was he? Gradually, he forced himself to relax. They must be slaves. But how had he gotten back to the South? Why was he in this cabin? The questions once more pounded through his head, making the ever-present ache unbearable. Weariness pressed down on him again. He had to know where he was.

Robert heard the door swing open and he opened his eyes a mere slit. He wanted some answers before he let anyone know he was awake. He had to get back to his unit, but first he had to know what was happening.

"Momma, I sho be hungry."

"You always be hungry, Clint," the woman laughed. "Go get some more firewood. I reckon it's gonna be a chilly one tonight."

Now Robert was even more confused. He slumped back against his pillow, trying to make sense of everything. Just yesterday the weather had been hot and humid. How had it gotten cold in the middle of September? He lay still, pondering his situation. A sudden fear gripped him. What if they had captured him? What if these negroes were planning on hurting him when he woke up? He gritted his teeth together, waves of frustration washing over him. None of it made any sense. Surely he wouldn't be lying in their only bed if they meant him harm. The woman looked harmless enough, and the boy she had called Clint looked to be no more than fourteen. As for the little girl, she couldn't have been more than five or six.

Another blast of cool air entered the cabin. Robert didn't open his eyes again, but he knew someone else had come into the room. Was it the boy, or the girl?

"I got me a deer, Polly. A few more and I reckon we'll be set for the winter."

Robert managed to stifle his groan as the deep male voice boomed through the cabin. Holding his breath, he peered through narrowed eyes. Whoever this man was, he was formidable looking. His towering bulk made the woman he was standing beside look like a child.

"Anything from that fella over there?"

Robert snapped his eyes shut and tried to appear as if he was still asleep. The man had to be talking about him.

"No, Gabe. There ain't been no change. I'm beginnin' to doubt he ever gonna wake up. If it weren't for the fact he still be breathin' I'd think sho enough he be dead. It's been over a month now that he been lyin' there."

Robert felt his head explode with a new round of questions. Surely the woman was wrong! But why would she say it if it weren't true? A month? It took all his self-control to not spring from the bed and start shouting questions.

"I'm tellin' ya, Polly. I think we got to take that fella somewhere's else. Somebody gonna find him here. What are we gonna do when somebody finds a Rebel soldier lyin' in our cabin?"

"Shush, Gabe. That boy ain't goin' nowhere. You ain't thinkin' straight. First off, ain't nobody gon' drop by our house. And if they were, there ain't no way to know that boy there be a Rebel."

How did they know he was a Southerner? Robert's mind shouted. How did he get to this cabin? It was obvious from the conversation that he was still behind Northern lines. Vague images of a fierce battle floated through his mind, but they were too elusive to patch together.

"I told that fella who left him here that it weren't a good idea," Gabe growled.

"And I told him that boy was welcome. That we would do what we could to keep him from dyin'!"

"Yeah, well he ain't been awake for over a month!" Gabe retorted.

Polly's voice softened. "Look, Gabe. I know you be scared, but we can't just be throwin' the man out of our house. It's gonna be okay."

"Polly, that ain't just another man. That boy be *white*, for God's sake."

"Ain't no sin to be white," Polly said calmly.

"What if that fella is a slave owner?" Fear oozed from Gabe's voice.

"Then I reckon we'll cross that bridge when we get to it."

Robert detected the first hint of fear in Polly's voice as she answered him.

Who in the world had left him here? The questions were too much for his pounding head. He fought the cloud descending once again, but it was too dark—too heavy.

Only the flickering of the firelight filled the cabin when Robert woke again. The pounding in his head was not quite so bad, but thirst wracked his body. Should he let them know he was awake? He wasn't so sure about the man, but he was fairly certain Polly meant him no harm. His longing for a drink of water grew with each passing moment.

"Momma?"

Robert turned his head slightly. The room was too dark for anyone to notice that his eyes were open. Polly was seated by the fire, holding the little girl in her lap. The boy she had called Clint was in a chair next to her.

"Yes, son? Talk quiet—Amber is finally asleep."

"Momma, do you think Daddy is right? You think that fella is a slave owner?"

Robert frowned. Clint's voice was edged with anger.

"Not every white man owns slaves," Polly replied calmly. "You know that."

"Yeah," Clint admitted. "But I don't want no slave owner in our house. Not after everythin' you and Daddy went through. What if he tried to take you back?"

"I don't reckon that man is taking anyone anywhere," Polly said firmly. "You got to quit lettin' your fears get the best of you. If we quit carin' 'bout other people, then we gonna be just as bad as the slave owners."

Robert listened in astonishment, his own anger growing. How dare she . . . ?

"Don't you get tired of lovin', Momma?" Clint asked plaintively.

Polly's only response was a low laugh.

"I mean it, Momma. Don't you get angry sometimes? Don't you want to lash out at them folks that hurt you? Them folks that kept you and Daddy slaves most all your life?" Clint's voice was bitter now.

Robert watched Polly put out her hand and touch Clint's cheek.

" 'Course I get angry sometimes. I be just as human as anyone. But, son, there ain't nothin' wrong with gettin' angry. It's what you do with that anger that matters. You can blow up and hurt anyone who gets near you, or you can figure out somethin' else to do with it."

"What you do with yours, Momma?"

Polly chuckled. " 'I work off my anger, Clint. Some clothes get cleaner than others, some bread gets kneaded a little more than I reckon it should . . . " Her voice trailed off. "And when workin' it off ain't doing the job—I sing it off. Ain't no way you can be singin' and hatin' all at the same time."

"You sing an awful lot," Clint commented.

Polly laughed again. "I reckon I do, boy. I reckon I do."

Clint changed the subject. "Are you scared?"

"Scared?"

"Yeah. You know—scared that someone will find him here. Or what if he dies? Ain't you scared to have a white man die in your bed?"

Robert frowned. Polly and Gabe had given up their bed for him? Why?

"I guess I try not to think 'bout things to be scared of. I figure that man got brung to us for a reason. I reckon we'll know what it is if we wait long enough."

"Don't look like we got no choice but to wait. Don't seem that man is goin' anywhere."

Just then the door swung open.

"Gabe! I wondered where you be. It's gettin' right late."

Gabe strode in, his massive form blocking any light from the fire. Robert tried to push away his thirst. If he listened long enough he might find out more about where he was. He had been ready to let Polly know he was awake, but now that Gabe was here, he was suddenly afraid.

"Mr. Green down the road asked me to drive his wagon over past Sharpsburg for him," Gabe said, settling into a chair by the fire.

Robert heard a strange note of sadness in his voice.

"What happened? Sounds like there was trouble," Polly said.

Gabe shrugged. "Weren't no trouble." Then he hesitated.

"Come on, Daddy, you can talk," Clint pleaded. "I'm almost a grown man now. Amber is asleep. You ain't got to be afraid of me hearing."

"When you learn how to read minds, boy?"

"You always get quiet when you think me or Amber shouldn't not be hearin' what you gonna say."

Gabe chuckled. "I reckon you're right." Then his voice grew serious. "I had to drive past that battlefield over at Sharpsburg. The place this fella come from."

"It was bad," Polly stated quietly.

"I ain't never seen nothin' like it. I reckon the army done tried to bury all them men, but they didn't do such a good job. Looks like they just scooped dirt over what used to be a real purty cornfield." He stopped for several long moments.

Robert listened carefully. He still had no idea what had happened to him. Maybe he was about to get some answers.

"There were bodies sticking out all over. I reckon the rain done washed away a lot of the dirt. I ain't never seen. . . . " his voice broke, then he continued. "The smell is awful. Far as the eye can see there ain't nothin' but body parts. While I was watchin' a bunch of pigs come out to root around."

Robert felt sick, but wanted to scream and make someone tell him what had happened.

"Mr. Lincoln done called it a Northern victory. Doesn't look to me like nothin' but a bunch of slaughterin' went on. I reckon that fella who brought our man was right. Ain't nothin' good about war. Still—I'm gonna sign up when I get my chance."

"Sign up?" Polly asked, startled.

"Yeah. Old Johnny figures it won't be too much longer before they'll be lettin' coloreds enlist in the army. Not since Lincoln signed that sheet of paper. I don't be knowing anything about it, but I'll wait and see."

Robert could feel himself slipping away again. *No!* his mind screamed. What sheet of paper? How badly was the South defeated at Antietam? Just before the darkness claimed him again, Carrie's smiling face rose to comfort him. Sighing, he slipped back into the shadows.

Robert woke the next morning to the feel of a wet cloth on his face. He lay quietly for a moment, enjoying the warmth of it. Suddenly he remembered who was doing the washing. His eyes flew open.

"Dear Jesus!" Polly screamed, as the bowl she was holding spun through the air. Water sprayed in all directions as her hands flew to her mouth.

Robert stared at her. He had no idea what to say.

"You be alive, boy!"

Robert looked toward the door fearfully. If Gabe had heard his wife scream, he was liable to think something horrible had happened to her. Robert was quite sure the big man would act first and ask questions later. He opened his mouth to tell her he was sorry he had frightened her. Nothing but a croak came out.

The fear left Polly's face. Compassion rushed in to take its place. "You be needin' some of that water I just threw all over the cabin?" When Robert nodded, she rushed to the bucket beside the door and quickly filled a pitcher. Picking up a glass from the table, she hurried back. "Here you go, boy," she said gently, filling the glass and holding it to his lips.

Robert tried to struggle into a sitting position but he was too weak. He had only his eyes to communicate his frustration.

"It be okay," Polly said reassuringly. "You done been asleep a long time." Reaching underneath his shoulders, she lifted him.

Robert was astonished at the tiny woman's strength. Eagerly he sipped the water she held up to his lips. At first he felt like his mouth was full of sand and grit. Gradually he was able to take longer sips until finally he settled back. "Thank you," he whispered in a gravelly voice.

Polly sat back and examined him. "I reckon you got a lot of questions," she said simply. Then she shook her head. "I can't believe you really be awake. I wasn't sure you'd ever come to."

"How long?" Robert croaked.

" 'Bout a month—a little more. The first few days you had a raging fever. Did a lot of talking and thrashing around. After that— nothing. Your fever went away, but your body just seemed to give up. I dripped water into your mouth with a rag. I knew you had to have something in there."

"How bad?" Robert couldn't seem to make his tongue form more than two words at a time.

Polly frowned. "You been real sick. Auntie JoBelle didn't think you'd make it." She seemed to understand Robert's puzzled expression. "Auntie JoBelle be the healin' woman in these parts. She came over right when that fella brought you. Darndest thing," she mused. "She ain't never dropped by before. But there she was. Anyway," she continued, "she took four bullets out of ya. Had to carve one right out of your side. You almost caught one in your head. It just kinda left a groove 'long the right side. There sho was a lot of blood, but Auntie JoBelle said it shouldn't kill ya. She wasn't so sure 'bout the other ones." Polly paused. "She sho is gonna be surprised to know you done woke up. She stops by every now and again to check on ya."

"Who . . . ?" Robert ground his teeth in frustration that he couldn't communicate the way he wanted. He longed to jump out of bed, but his body seemed to weigh a thousand pounds.

"Who brought you here? I don't reckon we really be knowin'. He just appeared out of the dark. We'd seen him earlier that day—gave him some soup when he was passing through with the Union army . . . "

"Yankee?" Robert knew his face registered shock. Was it true that a Yankee had saved his life?

"Yep. It was a Yankee sho 'nuff," Polly said firmly.

Robert's mind raced. Had it been Matthew? Had his old friend somehow found him and saved him? "Red hair?" he whispered.

Polly's loud laughter rang through the tiny cabin. "I don't believe I done ever seen a colored man with red hair." She laughed louder as she thought about it.

"Colored?" Robert exclaimed weakly.

"Why, sho," Polly said. "It was a colored man who brung you here. Carried you in like you was a baby. Told us to do the best we could to save your life. Then he said he had to get back to his unit. Just turned and disappeared. You been here ever since."

Robert's mind was spinning again. Instead of getting answers, he was just getting more questions.

"That fella did say one more thing," Polly mused.

Robert turned to her eagerly.

"He told us to take care of you for Carrie."

"Carrie . . . " The very mention of her name made the longing rise in him like a spring flood.

"That your girl?"

Robert nodded, confusion inundating him. It was all too much. He could feel the fatigue settling in again. "So tired."

Polly resumed washing his face. "I reckon you are. You been asleep a long time but it weren't the kind of sleep that rests you. You're gonna need to be doin' a lot of that now." She finished washing his face. "You get some rest. I'll have some good hot soup ready for you when you wake up."

Robert closed his eyes as she spoke. Confusion still swirled in his mind, but mixed with the confusion was an odd sense of comfort. Polly would take care of him. He knew he would be safe here.

~Twenty-Three~

"Y ou say that man woke up today?" Gabe asked suspiciously.

Robert heard Gabe's voice as soon as he awoke. His eyes opened easily this time. He turned his head to listen to the conversation by the fire. The cabin was filled with the delicious aroma of chicken soup. His stomach sprang to life, reminding him it had been a very long time since he'd eaten. No wonder he felt as weak as a baby.

"Sho 'nuff!" Polly exclaimed. "He woke up! I talked to him for a while."

"Well, it's about time," Gabe said, pulling a chair over and sitting down in it. "I sure am ready for some of that soup."

"Where are the kids?"

"Clint will be in directly. He be finishin' up that load of wood we brung in yesterday. Amber was out gatherin' the rest of the persimmons off that big tree. I reckon she be here soon."

Polly nodded and dished up the steamy broth. "He has good eyes, Gabe."

"Who?" Gabe asked between big spoonfuls of soup.

"The sick man."

"What's his name?"

Polly looked confused. "Why, I don't know. I didn't even ask him."

Robert found himself feeling oddly guilty about eavesdropping. But these were just colored people, he told himself, and from the sound of things they were runaways, to boot. Why should he feel bad about listening to their conversation? He should lie quietly and learn as much as he could. He would be out of there in a few days as soon as his strength came back. But then he remembered the tender compassion on Polly's face as she had wiped his brow that morning. "Rob-bert," he croaked. His voice was just as gravelly as it had been earlier.

"What!" Gabe exclaimed, dropping his fork and spinning around.

"I told you!" Polly cried. She walked over closer. "What'd you say?"

"Robert," he said slowly, forcing the words over his thick tongue. "My name."

"Well, it's real nice to meet you, Robert. I'm Polly. This here be my husband, Gabe."

Robert nodded and managed a weak smile.

Polly turned and strode to the fire. "I got you some nice soup ready. Are you hungry?"

"Yes. . . . " Robert said weakly, his stomach growling loudly. He turned his head to look at Gabe. The big man was staring at him suspiciously. Robert tried to push down the fear that sprang up. Surely this man wouldn't do anything to him while he was sick. Hadn't he let Robert lie in his very bed for over a month? Slowly the fear abated. The man had every reason to be suspicious.

"Here you go, Robert," Polly said, hurrying over with a bowl of soup. "Gabe, get over here and help me lift him up against these pillows," she ordered.

Robert gritted his teeth with helpless frustration as Gabe sauntered over, lifted him as if he were no heavier than a feather, then settled him back after Polly had positioned a pillow behind his back. She held the spoon up to his lips. "I can do it," Robert gasped slowly. He tried to reach for the spoon, but the effort left him exhausted. He sank back against the pillow with a groan.

"You ain't had no food in your body for over a month," Polly chided. " 'Course you ain't got no strength. Just you let me get some of this good soup in ya. You'll be strong before you know it."

Robert nodded weakly, opening his mouth. Over Polly's shoulder, his eyes caught Gabe's. Robert flushed at the piteous look laced with anger, and looked away.

"Here you go, Robert."

The first spoonful of soup that touched Robert's mouth was the best thing he had ever tasted in his life. He swallowed slowly, relishing the feel of its warmth trickling down his throat, then opened his mouth again eagerly.

Polly laughed. "I ain't never met nobody didn't like my chicken soup," she said triumphantly. She had only given him half of the bowl when she laid it aside. She smiled when Robert shook his head. "Auntie JoBelle told me you had to eat just a little bit at a time if you done ever woke up. Said your stomach would give you a fit if we gave it too much. She said we was to give you a little bit every hour or so for the first day. I aim to do what she says," she stated firmly.

Robert longed to reach out and grab the bowl out of her hand but knew he was helpless to do so. Besides, maybe that old healing woman was right. She'd kept him alive, hadn't she?

Just then the door to the cabin swung open. Robert tensed, his eyes shooting to the entrance. Were the Yankees coming after him? Had Polly somehow managed to get a message to them? He sagged back against the pillow when Clint and Amber walked in, a gust of fresh air rushing in with them.

Clint's eyes immediately swung to his mother, then opened wide when he saw Robert sitting up. "He's alive!"

"He sho is," Polly agreed.

"Too bad," Clint muttered.

"Clint!" Polly cried.

Clint refused to back down. "I ain't glad he's alive! Why should I pretend to be? He ain't nothin' but a white man. A Rebel," he spat the last words out.

Robert could feel both anger and fear rising to choke him. This fourteen-year-old boy was big enough to kill him if he got the mind to—he had inherited his size from his father.

"He's a human being," Polly said firmly.

"I bet he owns slaves," Clint said bitterly. "I bet he's just like those evil people who hurt you and Daddy."

"I don't want any more talk like that," Polly said, rising and stepping over to her son. Even though he towered over her, she reached out and grabbed his arm. "We don't know nothin' 'bout this man. We ain't gonna judge somebody we don't know."

"Why don't you ask him?" Clint persisted. "Why don't we find out if we been keeping a slave owner in our house?"

Robert wished frantically that there was some way he could disappear into the floor. Was he going to lie to these people? Or tell them the truth? They would throw him out in a minute. As much as he wanted to be gone, he knew he didn't have the strength to make it on his own yet. He looked longingly toward the pot of chicken soup swaying over the fire, then back to the angry boy.

"Daddy, why's Clint being so mean?"

Robert swung his eyes toward the little girl. Something in his heart caught. He had seldom seen such beauty in a youngster. Her sweet face glowed as her bright eyes stared at him steadily. She had a high forehead and one long braid ran down her back.

Gabe walked over and swung her up into his arms. "Clint's goin' to stop bein' mean right now," he said firmly. "Ain't you, son? I don't much like this man bein' here either, but he's here. We gonna treat him right."

"Ain't you even gonna ask him?" Clint cried.

"Ain't no need to," Gabe growled. "I figure if he wasn't a slave owner, he'd have done said somethin' by now."

Robert groaned inwardly.

"And you gonna let him stay here?" Clint's voice was both furious and disbelieving.

Gabe walked over closer to Robert. "This man ain't in no condition to do nothin' to us. I can take care of my family."

Robert understood the look Gabe gave him. If he tried anything, Robert would have Gabe to answer to.

Polly had quietly watched the exchange. Now she walked over next to Robert. "You ain't got nothin' to be afraid of, Robert. I believe the Lord done brung you here. I ain't got no idea why, but sometimes you just got to wait 'fore you can understand the ways of the Lord." Then Polly turned to her family. "I don't want to hear another word 'bout this man not bein' welcome in our home. The Lord done brought him here. We gonna take care of him till he's better. Y'all got that?" she added sternly.

Clint nodded sullenly and stalked over to the fire. Gabe shrugged his massive shoulders, then turned back to his meal. Silence fell on the cabin.

Amber watched Robert for a minute, then edged her way over to the bed. "Hi," she said sweetly. "I'm Amber. I'm six."

Robert couldn't keep from smiling at the cute little girl.

"I be real glad you're here," Amber said seriously. "I always been wantin' to know a white person. I see's them sometimes, but I ain't never gotten to know one. I reckon you'll be a fine one to start with."

Clint snorted but didn't say anything.

Reaching out, Amber touched Robert's arm. "You get well real soon, white man." Then she turned and walked back to the fire.

Robert stared after her, bemused. Once again, silence fell on the cabin. His head was spinning with everything that was happening. Who was it that had pulled such a cruel trick and brought him to this family? Rage mingled with gratefulness. It was true that he might be dead if his rescuer hadn't found help for him, but surely there were white homes he could have taken him to. *He was colored.* Polly's voice echoed through his head, which was suddenly aching again. Whoever had saved him must have brought him to the only place he knew. He would be out of here soon enough. At least he was still alive.

"Momma, what do I got to read today?" Amber's clear voice rang through the cabin.

"You know what's you got to read," Polly said. "You ain't done with that book Miss Connors sent home with you last week. You go fetch it. I'll listen to you read."

Amber jumped up from the table, then noticed Robert watching her. She ran over to his bed. "I got me a real good book to read," she announced brightly. "It be about a dog named Bucko." She paused. "You know how to read?"

"Yes," Robert said, charmed in spite of himself.

Amber beamed. "That's good 'cause my Momma done told me I ain't never gonna be nobody 'less I learn how to read."

"It's white men who kept Momma and Daddy from learning how to read!" Clint snapped.

Amber's eyes opened wide. "Did you do that?" she asked Robert in a shocked voice.

Robert opened his mouth to answer, even though he had no idea what he was going to say. For some reason what this little girl thought of him was important.

"I told you Robert just needed to rest and get well," Polly said firmly. "This ain't the time for questions."

Robert closed his lips with relief. Amber gazed at him for a moment more then turned away. Seconds later she disappeared up the stairs to the loft, only to reappear with her prized book clutched under her arm. She fairly flew down the steps.

"I'd like to read to Clint today," she announced, running over to her brother. "May I?" she asked sweetly, staring up at him with liquid eyes.

Clint shot Robert a glance and shook his head. "No," he growled.

Amber climbed up into his lap anyway. "That white man ain't gonna care if I read to you," she said seriously. "Auntie JoBelle said if he was ever to wake up it was gonna take a while before he could leave. We gots to keep living, you know."

Clint glared down at her for a second, his gaze softening quickly. He smiled reluctantly and shifted her in his lap. "All right," he muttered. Amber smiled brightly and began to read.

Robert was fighting with the throbbing in his head when a sudden shot of pain jolted through it. He gasped as the pain reached out to claim him—consume him.

Polly was at his side in an instant. "You okay?" she asked anxiously.

"My head," Robert murmured, fighting to control the tears stinging his eyes.

"Gabe, get over here and lay Robert back down. He's done been up too long," Polly commanded.

Robert could barely feel Gabe's hands lift him. The pounding in his head blocked everything else out. He had just settled flat on the bed when the blackness claimed him.

The cabin was empty when Robert came to. He moved his head carefully, sighing with relief when he realized the pain was gone. Still, the same heaviness pervaded his body. He was glad to be alone. How awkward it was to be lying helpless in a room of people who didn't want him. Polly had been kind, but he was certain she would be glad to see him go, and Gabe and Clint were openly hostile. Little

Amber seemed happy to have him there, but once she found out he was a slave owner he was sure she would shun him as well.

Robert ground his teeth in frustration. He had never been so helpless in his life. He hated it! He had always been in control— always in charge. As his body tensed, he felt the pain in his head edge its way back. He took deep breaths, forcing himself to relax. He dreaded the darkness of his headaches. They must be the result of the bullet wound to his head. As his body loosened, he felt the headache sliding back.

Robert gazed longingly at the pot of soup still simmering on the fire. When would Polly be back? He was hungry again. *How does it feel to be helpless?* Robert shook his head and pushed the thought aside. He wasn't going to be helpless for long. He would be out of here in a few days. Then he would have to figure out how to get back across the lines into the South. The very thought of it made the pain edge back. "Don't think about it," he muttered through clenched teeth.

Suddenly Carrie sprang full-blown into his mind. He was back on Cromwell Plantation, watching her race down the road in front of him on Granite, her slender body swaying rhythmically, her long black hair streaming behind, her merry laugh floating to him on the breeze. He smiled. The pain subsided.

Robert was beginning to get the message his body was sending him. He dug back in his memory for more images. He watched as his mind replayed the day Carrie had shared her special, secret place with him. He could see her beautiful face raised to him, her glowing eyes speaking to him. He could feel her lips melting under his. "Carrie..." he whispered. "I'm coming, Carrie. I'm coming ... "

The door eased open. Robert turned his head quickly, Carrie fading in his mind as a large woman strode through the door, followed closely by Polly. Robert watched curiously. He felt no alarm.

Polly walked over. "I brung Auntie JoBelle to see you, Robert."

Robert studied the woman who had saved his life. Intelligent black eyes met his squarely, returning the examination. She was big but she wasn't fat. Short black hair, sprinkled with flecks of gray, softened a square face.

"Hello, Robert."

Robert was taken aback by the deep timbre of her voice. If he closed his eyes, he would think she was a man. "Hello," he managed. She continued to inspect him with her steady eyes. He was beginning to feel uncomfortable. What was she looking for? Suddenly he remembered this woman had saved his life. "Thank you."

Auntie JoBelle nodded her head briefly. "We'll find out how much there is to thank me for. I ain't never taken bullets out before. Hope I never gots to do it again." She turned to Polly. "Give the boy some more of that soup. Then we'll check things out."

Robert gulped the hot soup gratefully, then reached for the lone piece of cornbread Polly offered him. "Thank you."

"You be real welcome, Robert," Polly said with a gentle smile.

Robert gazed at her for a long moment. Why was this woman being so nice to him? She knew he owned slaves. How did she know he wouldn't try to take her back into slavery? He almost laughed bitterly at his own thoughts. If the South had really lost the battle at Antietam, these people probably weren't worried about it very much. A deep wave of longing to know what was going on with his unit washed over him. Had the North won the war? Was the South still fighting? The pain edged back into his head.

"You gots to relax, boy," Auntie JoBelle said suddenly. "Gettin' all tight ain't gonna do you no good."

Robert pushed the thoughts of the war out of his mind. He forced his mind to Carrie. It was the only thing that could keep the pain away.

"That's better," Auntie JoBelle said strongly. "You ready for me to check some things out?"

"I suppose so," Robert replied. What was this lady going to do?

"I know you still be weak as a baby," she commented. "But I wants to see if everythin' be working." She turned to Polly, ignoring Robert completely. "I been thinkin' 'bout this boy every night."

Robert grew anxious at the worried tone in her voice. "Am I going to be all right?" he asked.

Auntie JoBelle shrugged. "Reckon only time can tell us that." She came a step closer. "How 'bout movin' your arms for me?"

Robert nodded, then concentrated on trying to move. The two bowls of soup had restored some of his strength, but he still felt as though his limbs were rubber. Slowly, he lifted his right arm over the covers—then his left. His face flushed with his accomplishment.

Auntie JoBelle watched him closely. She grunted abruptly to indicate her approval. "Now your legs." Reaching down, she pulled back the covers.

Robert looked down and gasped, mortified to see he was covered with only a long nightshirt.

Auntie JoBelle laughed. "You ain't got nothing I ain't seen before, boy. You didn't think we were going to leave you in that filthy, ragged uniform, now, did you?"

Robert ground his teeth in frustration, determined to concentrate on moving so this overbearing woman would pull the covers back up.

"What's going on in here?" a deep voice demanded.

Polly spun around. "Auntie's just checkin' out Robert. He done moved his arms real good. Now he's gonna move his legs. Then," she laughed, "I think she's gonna quit torturing him and let him get some rest."

Robert was grateful that Polly understood what he was feeling, but he hated knowing Gabe was going to watch. Humiliation washed over him in waves as Gabe edged closer.

"Ain't no time like the present," Auntie JoBelle observed.

Anger flashed through Robert like a fire. He was *not* going to lay here like a helpless baby any longer. So he was weak—he'd fought battles when he was weak. He had been helpless long enough. Pushing himself up with his arms, he tried to swing his legs over the edge of the bed. Horrified, he stared down at them. Gritting his teeth, he tried again. They lay exactly where they had been moments before. Frantic now, he willed his legs to move.

"Jesus . . ." Polly said softly, then reached out to touch Robert's shoulder.

Robert shook her hand off and stared at his legs. Why couldn't he get them to obey his commands? *Move!* his mind screamed. Pain raced through his head, blurring his thoughts and vision until he collapsed on the bed with a groan of agony. He lay there, gasping, the silence in the room choking him.

Auntie JoBelle moved quickly, grabbing a wet rag to bathe his head. "Take it easy," she said soothingly. "Some things just take time."

The pain in Robert's head eased just enough for him to open his eyes. Gabe was staring at him with that mixture of pity and anger again. But this time there was something else. Robert struggled to identify it. Suddenly he knew. Gabe was looking at him with satisfaction.

Fury surged through Robert. Right before the darkness claimed him again, his mind acknowledged the truth. He was paralyzed.

Twenty-Four

"A re you ready, Carrie?" Janie called up the stairs.
Carrie sighed, signed her name to the letter she had
just finished, then stuffed it into an envelope. "I'm
coming," she called. She held the letter close for just a moment, laid
it on the stack of others on her desk, then scooped them all up. Mail
was very unreliable since the war started, but Carrie had to try every
avenue to find Robert. She had written letters to every known hospital between Maryland and Richmond. She had received responses
from only five of the fifty she had mailed letters to, but she knew it
would take time. At least she was doing something.

Thomas looked up from his chair in the parlor as Carrie walked
in. "I'll mail them this morning," he said, looking at the stack in her
hand. "And you know I'll check all the lists today." His eyes crinkled
with sympathy and understanding.

Carrie smiled, then leaned down to kiss him on the cheek.
"Thank you. Janie and I won't be home till late."

"I thought your days were getting shorter now that so many of
the soldiers from Antietam are leaving the hospital," Thomas
responded in surprise.

"They are," Carrie said uncomfortably. "Janie and I are going
shopping."

Thomas looked at her again, his eyebrows raised. "I see," he murmured.

Carrie gave him another quick hug, then turned and left before
he could ask any more questions. She and Janie exchanged a long
look as they reached the road. "It's getting harder now that winter is
coming," Carrie sighed. "With the days getting so much shorter, it's
going to be harder to come up with excuses for being late."

"I don't think your father totally believed you," Janie agreed wryly.

"I just don't think he needs to know about another one of his difficult daughter's activities," Carrie protested. "He would only worry if he knew we were going down to the colored hospital twice a week."

Janie shrugged. "You know what I think. I think you're doing your father a disservice. I think he deals quite well with his difficult daughter. It seems to me that he shows you nothing but respect, in spite of your differing beliefs."

Carrie frowned and searched her mind for a change of subject. Was Janie right? Should she tell her father the truth? An image of his lined, tense face rose up in front of her. She shook her head. "I'll tell him sometime," she said shortly, irritated more at the situation than at Janie. "How is Morgan?" she asked, knowing any mention of his name would take Janie's mind off of her. Morgan, a seventeen-year-old from Mississippi, had been brought in after Antietam.

Janie smiled instantly. "That boy is really something!" Then she frowned. "Not that the new doctor who arrived a few weeks ago should get any credit for the fact Morgan is still alive." Janie shook her head. "No one expected that boy to live. I surely didn't. When he came in, with that huge gaping hole in his abdomen, I was certain he would die just like the others in my ward who'd had similar injuries."

"He must have wanted to live very badly."

Janie nodded. "The human body is a wondrous thing. In spite of the horrors of such mutilation, it never ceases to amaze me how many of these men actually get well. I know we have to deal with a lot of death, but sometimes we forget how many more of them get well enough to go home, or back to the battlefield." She paused. "Morgan's wound is beginning to close all by itself. He's eating well and his spirits are high."

"You sound angry," Carrie observed.

Janie sighed. "I wish Dr. Wild was the physician in our ward. You are so lucky."

Carrie waited for her to explain.

"You've seen doctors use the moxa method."

Carrie shuddered, remembering the few times she had seen it performed. Some of the physicians at Chimborazo thought moxa a wonderful way of relieving pain. The moxa, a wad of cotton, was applied to the skin over an injury, then torched with the assistance of bellows. They believed that burning the painful wound relieved the pain. Carrie would never forget the reactions of the men she had watched. At first they had remained calm, watching in fascination as the flaming cotton glowed on their body. Then their eyes opened wide, until finally a scream ripped from their mouths as excruciating pain ripped through them. She had been told relief followed soon after, but she had seen nothing to indicate that.

"They didn't do that to him again, did they?" she asked, horrified.

"No, thank God. But as far as I'm concerned what they did was just as bad," Janie said grimly. "I told you he seemed to be coming down with pneumonia." Carrie nodded. "I learned a new treatment yesterday," she said bitterly. "They call it cupping."

Carrie groaned silently. She had read about cupping, but she let Janie talk.

"I couldn't believe it!" Janie exclaimed. "First the doctor ignited a small amount of alcohol in a cup. Then he inverted the cup on poor Morgan's chest. When the doctor picked it up, there was a huge blister there." Her voice caught. "Morgan was being so brave, but his eyes were so frightened." She gulped and continued, "The doctor lanced the blister, then put that flaming cup down on it again." Her eyes burned angrily. "I couldn't believe it!" she repeated. "When the doctor walked away, I went after him and demanded to know what he was doing." Now her eyes were flashing sparks. "He looked at me in that patronizing way and said, *'My dear. I realize a woman would have a difficult time with such a procedure. But I assure you it was for the young man's good. It is imperative to draw off blood to affect the cure of pneumonia.'*" Janie snorted. "He also said the procedure would make Morgan forget about his painful illness. I guess it would. How could he think about anything else but the pain after something so cruel!"

Carrie reached out her hand sympathetically. "I'm so sorry. Cupping is a ridiculous method. I've talked with Dr. Wild about it many times. He believes many methods in use today are simply a way of attempting to deal with things the doctors aren't able to understand. They think doing *something* is better than doing nothing at all."

"But they cause so much pain," Janie protested. "Have you told Dr. Wild how we treat the pneumonia patients in the colored hospital?"

"No . . . " Carrie said slowly.

"Afraid he'll throw you out for not practicing proper medicine?" Janie teased.

Carrie just looked at Janie, not wanting to admit how close her friend was to the truth. "Dr. Wild doesn't use those types of cruel methods," she said instead. "He utilizes a combination of drugs, good food, and lots of water. His patients seem to be doing well."

"What happens when the drugs run out?" Janie challenged. "You know as well as I do that opium and quinine are getting harder to obtain."

Carrie frowned. The blockade was making much-needed drugs scarcer by the day. Anger flared in her that the North would try to deprive men of medicine to relieve their suffering. "I don't know," she said finally, glad to see they had reached the hospital.

Carrie breathed a sigh of relief when she entered the hospital ward.

"Howdy, Miss Cromwell."

"You got a minute, Miss Cromwell?"

Carrie smiled and began moving from bed to bed in her daily ritual of giving and receiving the healing both soldier and nurse needed in their time of trouble.

"May I talk with you a minute, Miss Cromwell?"

Carrie looked up quickly when Dr. Wild's voice sounded over her shoulder. "Certainly, Doctor." She followed him out of the ward, grabbing her coat as she passed the rack. A brisk wind was blowing, making her grateful for its warmth as she hugged it close. November had roared in with colder temperatures than normal—it was going to be a bad winter.

Dr. Wild scowled as he pulled his own coat closer. "I'm afraid we're not going to have enough wood to make it through the winter. Dr. McCaw is doing everything possible to put in a sufficient supply, but wood is getting harder to come by."

Carrie's heart ached for the suffering that seemed to never end. She thought of the people in the colored section of town. They always suffered most when supplies ran short.

"Many people are going to struggle this winter," Dr. Wild predicted. He turned to look down at the river, whitecaps dotting its surface as the wind whipped at the water.

Carrie waited patiently. Dr. Wild seemed worried about something.

Finally he turned to her. "I hate to ask you this, but I need people I can trust. Dr. McCaw is afraid we are going to experience a severe shortage of drugs this winter. The blockade will be harder to run when it gets colder. He has asked me to inventory our remaining supply. Some of them seem to be disappearing without just cause."

"Someone is stealing them?" Carrie gasped disbelievingly.

"I'm afraid so," Dr. Wild said grimly. "Can you stay longer tonight and help inventory them?"

"I wish I could," Carrie said. "But I can't," she finished. "I'm so sorry."

"Plans with your father?" Dr. Wild asked. "I understand."

"No." Carrie didn't want him to think a social engagement was more important than his request. "It's . . . " She didn't know what to say.

"It's okay. I understand you have other plans. We'll be working on it for a while. Maybe you can help another time."

"I would be happy to." Carrie paused, something pushing her. She was learning to listen to her instincts. "Dr. Wild . . . "

"What is it?" Dr. Wild looked at her in concern. "Is something wrong?"

Carrie laughed. "No," she said quickly. "I just don't know how to tell you something." She and the doctor had become close friends in the past several months. She knew they shared a mutual respect for each other's abilities. Would he think less of her if he knew what she was doing? His opinion of her was important, but she realized it wasn't worth compromising her integrity for. If he thought less of her for doing what she believed was right, she would rather know.

"I can't help you because I promised the hospital down by the river I would be there tonight. I go there every Tuesday and Thursday."

Dr. Wild looked puzzled. "I don't remember a hospital down by the river. I thought I knew all of them."

"This isn't one you would be aware of," Carrie admitted. "It's a hospital for the coloreds down near the warehouses. They have a serious need for medical care."

"I see," Dr. Wild said slowly, with a curious look in his eyes. "How long have you been doing this?"

"About two-and-a-half months," Carrie replied. She was suddenly eager for him to understand. "The people down there can't get help from the other hospitals. A pastor—a friend of mine—started it."

"Who is the doctor?"

Carrie was instantly flustered. "I'm afraid you're looking at her," she said quietly. "They don't care about my credentials. They can't get anyone else to help."

"They're simply happy that you care enough to come down."

Carrie looked at Dr. Wild closely, but saw nothing in his eyes except interest. "Yes."

"What do you use for medicine? It must be very difficult to obtain."

"I'm afraid we can't get any at all," Carrie responded. "But we're doing fine." Now that she had decided to tell him, he might as well know the whole truth. "We're using other things. Herbs—and other plant remedies."

Dr. Wild continued to stare at her. "You amaze me, Carrie Cromwell," he said honestly. "Where did you learn so much about medicine that even us 'educated' doctors are ignorant of? It drives me mad that my patients are suffering for lack of drugs. The medical community is searching for substitutes in the absence of traditional medicines." He paused for a long moment. "May I come down to your hospital?"

Carrie took a sharp breath.

"I have no desire to usurp your authority there," Dr. Wild said quickly. "I would just like to come and see what you're doing. Perhaps I could learn something."

Carrie could hardly believe her ears. "I would like that very much. I have learned so much from you. It would be wonderful if I could give something back."

"Dr. Wild is coming down after he gets the people started on the inventory," Carrie told Jane excitedly. "Isn't that wonderful?"

"Why?" Janie asked bluntly. "Aren't you afraid he will make fun of our methods?"

Carrie had thought about that already. "I don't think he will," she said, shaking her head. "He's not like that. I truly think he wants to learn. He's deeply worried about running out of drugs this winter at the hospital."

When they reached the bottom of the hill, Spencer was waiting in his normal place. Carrie was grateful her father didn't question her use of his driver, and she was confident Spencer would never reveal where he took them. Now that the days were getting shorter, their trips down into the colored section of town were becoming more dangerous. Both she and Janie knew that—but it was a risk they had decided to take. Coming back through the crime-ridden streets of Richmond at night was not very wise, but the needs of the people made it imperative.

"How'do, Miss Carrie. Miss Jane. Same place?"

"Yes, Spencer," Carrie said with a quick smile. She and Janie climbed in and settled back. They were past Capitol Square, heading down the hill that would take them along the river, when Spencer pulled the carriage up short.

"Looks like trouble, Miss Carrie," he said softly.

Carrie craned to see over his shoulder, her blood turning to ice at the sight that met her eyes. Blocking the road was a group of scruffily dressed white men. Swallowing her fear, she stood up in the carriage and spoke firmly. "Please clear the road. We have business to tend to."

"Business like treating them niggers down by the river?" one man sneered, stepping closer.

The whole group formed a blockade and edged toward the carriage.

Carrie stared down at Janie for a quick moment, then raised her voice. "I don't see that what I do with my time is any business of yours," she snapped. "Now, please clear the road."

Another man laughed. "We heard you're real high spirited, Miss Cromwell. We figure you ought to just turn that carriage around and go on home." His words ended in a menacing growl.

Carrie could sense Spencer growing tense. She was sure he would protect her, but he would be no match for these men. He would be certainly hurt. Images of what could happen to her and Janie spun through her mind, but she pushed them aside. Now was no time to give in to fear. These men were like a pack of animals— they would smell fear in an instant. She would try to reason with them. At the very least it would buy her some time. "Why do you men care what I do with my time?" she demanded.

"We know all about you setting slaves free," one of the men stated, stepping forward boldly.

Carrie examined him. He appeared to be in his mid-forties, brawny from outdoor work, with tobacco-stained, gapped teeth. The bold look in his eyes made her nervous. He had obviously been drinking.

He continued his slurred sermon. "You know there's laws against anti-government activities. We figure you're helping them niggers go free when you're down there in the hospital. The boys and I figured we'd better do our patriotic duty and make sure that didn't happen any more."

"That's ridiculous!" Carrie snapped, her anger rising. "The people I treat are sick. They're not going anywhere. Besides, these people are already free."

"The people you *did* treat," another man remarked casually, stepping forward as he held up a large stick. "We ain't got no mind to hurt anyone so I reckon you just better turn around and go on back to your rich daddy. It don't sit too well with us to watch a white lady helping them heathens."

Carrie's blood was boiling as she cast about in her mind for a way to get through.

"What's going on here?" a sharp voice boomed from behind her.

Carrie spun around and looked at the well-dressed man standing on the sidewalk about ten feet back. "These men are blocking the road," she said crisply to hide her relief. "They refuse to move."

The stranger eyed the motley crowd of men for a few minutes, then slowly raised a pearled revolver. "I think the lady wants to get through, gentlemen," he drawled dangerously. "You best be moving on." His voice left no room for argument.

The men stationed in front of the carriage growled and began to move forward.

"I said move on!" the stranger barked, pulling back the hammer on his gun. "I'd hate to see some of you fellows shot. I happen to be sympathetic to what you're feeling, but this isn't the way to handle it." He paused for a long moment. "Now move!"

The group turned, scowling and muttering under their breath. The man who had threatened her whirled back around. "We'll be keeping an eye out for you, Miss Cromwell. Don't think this is over."

Carrie held her breath as they eased away. When they were several hundred feet from the carriage, she turned to the man who had rescued them. "Thank you," she said quietly, trying to calm the rapid beating of her heart.

"Don't bother," the man snapped. "Does your father know you are doing this, Miss Cromwell?"

Carrie could only stare at him, her heart sinking.

"I thought not. Thomas Cromwell would have enough sense not to let his daughter do what you're doing. I stopped that crowd this time, Miss Cromwell. I won't be around next time. Even if I were, I wouldn't step in again. If you want to take your life in your own hands by treating coloreds you will have to be responsible for your own foolishness. I rescued you this time because of the high regard I hold for your father. I find my high regard is somewhat mixed with pity now." He stopped and glared at her. "I've heard the rumors about your activities with your father's slaves. You are in the South, Miss Cromwell. Don't forget it." Having delivered his final word, he spun on his heel and stalked off.

Carrie slowly sank back into her seat, staring after him. "Well."

"You be wanting to go back to the house now?" Spencer asked in a shaky voice.

Carrie looked at Janie for a long moment, then turned back to Spencer, confident she and her friend were in agreement. "Certainly not," she said crisply. "We're going to the hospital."

Spencer whirled to look at her, his gaze a mixture of admiration and fear. "You heard what them men said?"

"Are you willing to let those people lie in that hospital without adequate medical attention?" Carrie asked steadily.

Spencer paused a long minute then slowly shook his head. "I reckon not, Miss Carrie." Picking up the reins, he urged the horse down the hill.

Carrie sat down across from Janie, exchanging a long look. Were they being foolish? Would those men be waiting for them farther down the hill? Carrie tried to push aside her fears, but the question remained. Was she being courageous to move forward in the face of her fears—or foolish? She sat ramrod straight, determined not to peer around as they continued to roll down the hill. If the men were watching, she would not give them the satisfaction of seeing her nervousness.

She did not breathe easily again until she and Janie were striding in the door of the hospital. Resolutely, she pushed away the image of what could happen when they left to return home that night.

"Thank God we made it," Janie said softly. It was the first words she had spoken since the encounter.

Carrie looked at her closely. Janie was trembling, her breathing uneven.

"Are you girls all right?" Pastor Anthony asked, striding forward. "You look shaken."

Carrie smiled weakly. "There are some people who don't approve of our work here." Trying to sound casual, she told him what had happened.

"They accosted two women in broad daylight? What cowards!" Pastor Anthony exclaimed angrily. Then he sobered. "I will see you home tonight myself."

Carrie didn't argue with him. The idea of having another man in the carriage was very appealing.

"Thank you," Janie said warmly. "I've been wondering how we were going to get home. Those men were just a little intimidating," she said, laughing shakily. Sudden tears sprang to her eyes but she brushed them away impatiently. "Just a delayed reaction," she insisted. "Let's get to work."

Carrie turned to Pastor Anthony. "I have a friend coming down tonight. His name is Dr. Wild."

"The doctor you work with at the hospital?" Pastor Anthony asked in surprise. "Is there something wrong?"

"Of course not," Carrie said reassuringly, then told him of Dr. Wild's interest in the herbs. "I'm glad he's coming. I would like him to look at a couple of wounds some of the men suffered working at the Iron Works. They aren't healing as well as I had hoped."

Pastor Anthony nodded. "I'll be happy to meet him." He paused. "I have someone coming I would like you to meet as well—my son."

It was Carrie's turn to be surprised. "I didn't know you had a son!"

"His name is Jeremy. He's twenty years old." Carrie tried to mask her curiosity, but Pastor Anthony saw through it. He smiled slightly. "His mother died when he was just three years old. I've raised him myself. He's a wonderful boy."

"I'm looking forward to meeting him," Carrie said warmly.

"And so am I," Janie added graciously. "If he's anything like his father, he is a wonderful man indeed."

"Jeremy is a businessman here in the city. He's in finance. His skills were in such demand that he was saved from having to go to war. I'm very grateful."

"You must be proud," Carrie added. Just then someone called her name from across the building. She moved away and began making her rounds, instantly caught up in the needs of her patients, the earlier confrontation fading from her mind.

There were only about thirty patients in the hospital that night. Only the most serious cases were kept here now that cold weather had set in. Pastor Anthony had managed to scrounge enough materials to partition off a smaller portion of the building, making it easier to heat. Some of the patients were still on the floor, but most had beds, pieced together from scraps of wood people from the church had brought in. The beds were quite crude, but they kept the patients off the floor.

Dr. Wild found Carrie in one of the back corners, talking to a lady suffering from pneumonia. "Quite a place you have here," he said cheerfully.

Carrie looked up quickly to see if there was any mockery in his eyes. He looked back at her steadily. "We've come a long way," she said, smiling. She had decided to act as if they were in any hospital in the city. She would make no apologies for the crudeness of the facilities. Patients were getting better—that's what counted. She turned to her patient. "Mrs. Banning. This is Dr. Wild. I work with him up at Chimborazo."

"You be real lucky then, Dr. Wild. Miss Carrie here be like an angel. I come in here knocking on death's door. I reckon, though, that the Lord gonna be calling me home another time. I'm feeling a heap better, thanks to her."

"I know exactly how lucky I am, Mrs. Banning," Dr. Wild said sincerely. "What has been keeping you here?"

"Why, I had me a rip-roaring case of pneumonia. Couldn't hardly breathe!" she exclaimed, bending double as a hacking cough seized her.

"That's enough talking, Mrs. Banning." Carrie reached into her deep apron pocket and pulled out a bottle. "I fixed you some more cough syrup. Some coughing is good for you—it will help clear the phlegm from your lungs—but too much will irritate your throat. I want you to take some of this every couple of hours. We'll see about you going home soon."

Dr. Wild watched her closely as she turned around. "What's in your cough syrup?"

"Hyssop," she said promptly. "I make it by mixing hyssop, aniseed, honey, and water. It is very effective. If the cough is extremely troubling, I mix pounded garlic in milk. My patients don't like the taste, but they can't argue with the results."

Dr. Wild nodded intently. "And what did you use to treat her pneumonia?"

"Two things," Carrie replied. "I gave her heavy doses of straight garlic, along with the garlic and milk mixture. I also used a warm infusion of white horehound sweetened with honey."

Dr. Wild stared at her in amazement. "Where did you learn all this?"

"Most of it I learned from one of my father's slaves. I became interested when my mother was quite ill. She died, but I'm convinced her last days were easier because of the herbs. Unfortunately I didn't begin the treatments in time."

"You believe she would have lived if you had?"

Carrie shrugged. "I don't know. She had been very sick for several days before she received any treatment at all. Modern medicine simply had nothing to offer her. There is a chance the herbs would have helped."

"Yet you use drugs," Dr. Wild commented thoughtfully.

"Of course," Carrie agreed instantly. "Many of them are very effective. But when they're not available, you can always find the herbs. Sometimes I think the herbs work better."

"And you learned all of this from a slave? Is she still alive?"

Carrie shook her head regretfully. "Sarah died last year. I miss her greatly. She was like a second mother to me." Instantly she looked to see if there was any scorn in Dr. Wild's eyes—she saw only sympathy.

"I'm sorry." Then he turned back to the herbs. "What if a patient has diarrhea? What would you use?"

"There are several effective herbs," Carrie responded. "I might use blackberry root or persimmon bark. I've also used rose geranium tea. If the case is very mild, I often treat it with meadowsweet plants or purple loosestrife."

"Fever?"

"Jimsonweed or dogwood bark."

"Gangrene?"

"Thankfully I've had no cases of gangrene here, but if I did, I would make a poultice out of charcoal, carrotseeds, and flaxseeds."

"Any tricks up your sleeve for maggots?" Dr. Wild teased.

"A salve made from the inner bark of common elder," Carrie said, smiling. She was rather enjoying their game.

"You're kidding! A slave woman taught you about maggots?"

Carrie laughed outright. "I said Sarah taught me *almost* everything I know. The use of herbs is not new. It's been around for centuries—long before there were drugs. I was so intrigued by what Sarah taught me, I have continued to read and study. There is an abundance of literature," she said teasingly.

Dr. Wild laughed. "All right, I guess I'm caught. My professors were so in love with the new drugs they never taught much about herbs. I wish now that they had. By the end of this war, most Southern doctors will have access to little else."

Carrie was relieved by his reaction. She was fully aware of the medicinal value of herbs. She knew, too, that many doctors turned their noses up at them.

Dr. Wild took a deep breath. "Will you teach me?"

Carrie thought quickly, then nodded. "Hands-on experience is the best teacher, you know."

Dr. Wild laughed loudly. "Meaning I would learn best if I were working with you here in the hospital?"

Carrie was amazed at her own daring. "Just one night a week," she bargained. "The rest I will teach you at Chimborazo."

"You have a deal."

"That's wonderful!" Carrie exclaimed. "We have a couple of cases here now that I would appreciate your opinion on."

"You know I'm going to want to put all of this in writing," Dr. Wild challenged.

"I thought you might," Carrie agreed. Reaching into her pocket, she pulled out a long sheet of paper and produced a pencil. "No time like the present to get started." She grinned, then motioned with her head. "I'd like you to take a look at Joseph. He has a very nasty break. I've set it, but I think it might need surgery. I'd like your opinion."

The next hour passed rapidly. Carrie gasped when she looked down at her watch. "Oh, my goodness. I have to be going. My father will be worried sick if I don't get home soon." She turned toward the door to look for Janie.

Just then Pastor Anthony appeared, a young man at his side. "Carrie, I know we only have a few minutes before we leave, but I wanted you to meet my son."

Carrie moved forward. "Hello, Jeremy," she said graciously. It was easy to see why Pastor Anthony was proud of him. Jeremy was almost six feet tall, with broad shoulders and a muscular build. His wavy blond hair was cut short, accentuating his high cheekbones and blue eyes. His dark tan revealed someone who loved the outdoors.

"Hello, Miss Cromwell. It's a pleasure to meet you." He turned to Dr. Wild. "And you must be the doctor my father was telling me about."

"Miss Cromwell is the doctor here," Pastor Anthony corrected.

"You're a doctor?" Jeremy asked Carrie in astonishment.

"Not technically," Carrie admitted easily. "But none of my patients have asked for my credentials so far. I also work at Chimborazo. I'm a lowly hospital assistant to this man who is a real doctor."

"One I couldn't do without!" Dr. Wild added. He stepped forward. "It's a pleasure to meet you, Jeremy. I've heard about you. I understand you're a whiz at finances."

Jeremy shrugged modestly. "I enjoy my work."

"We need to be going," Pastor Anthony said regretfully.

Carrie gathered her things, called good-bye to her patients, and climbed into the carriage with Janie and Pastor Anthony, Dr. Wild following closely in his own carriage. The ride home was uneventful, the streets unusually quiet.

"Are you going to tell me what you've been thinking about ever since we left the hospital?" Janie demanded, pulling the covers up to her chin.

Carrie looked at her for several moments. "It's odd," she finally said, then fell silent.

"There are a lot of odd things," Janie finally said in exasperation. "Would you be so kind as to fill me in on what odd thing you're referring to?"

Carrie smiled slightly. "Jeremy. I could swear I've seen him before." She paused. "Yet, I know I've never met him." Finally she shook her head and sighed. "I'm not going to figure it out tonight. He probably just looks like someone I've seen before."

Carrie reached up to turn off the lantern, then rolled over to stare into the darkness. She couldn't shake the feeling that she'd seen Jeremy before somewhere.

Twenty-Five

*C*arrie was up with the sun the next morning. She could hear her father moving around in his room as she knocked on his door. "Good morning," she called.

"What are you doing up so early?" Thomas asked in surprise when he opened the door.

"I wanted to talk to you before you left for the Capitol," Carrie replied, walking in and settling on the edge of the bed.

Thomas sat down in the chair next to his fireplace which sent off a cozy warmth into the chilly room. "What is it?" he asked quietly.

Now that Carrie was here, she didn't know what to say. She had rehearsed it in her mind a thousand times before she had drifted off to sleep the night before. It was then she had realized she'd made a mistake in not telling her father. "I need to talk to you about something I've been doing." She stopped, unsure of how to continue. When she looked up, her father was gazing at her steadily. There was something in his eyes . . . "You know already," she murmured, her heart sinking.

"If you are referring to your work in the colored hospital—yes, I know about it," Thomas agreed, then sighed. "Why couldn't you tell me?"

Carrie cringed at the hurt she saw in his eyes. "I'm so sorry," she cried. "I thought I was protecting you. I realized last night I was wrong not to have told you from the beginning. I didn't want to worry you."

"And you didn't want me to tell you you couldn't go," he said flatly.

Carrie didn't bother trying to deny her father's charge.

330

Thomas shook his head heavily. "I thought you knew me better than that."

Regret tore through Carrie's heart. Jumping up, she moved over and sank down on her knees to stare up into her father's face. "I'm so sorry." Suddenly she saw it clearly—she had fallen into the habit of lying to her father when she was helping his slaves escape the plantation. It had become almost second nature to her. Even now it was easier not to tell him what she was doing. But she also realized she was depriving him of the opportunity to face his own prejudices by hiding her actions. She was doing him a disservice by not trusting him. "Will you please forgive me?" she asked contritely.

Thomas nodded, then grew stern. "You have to promise me never to lie to me again. I'd rather be worried sick about you than think you don't trust me. I realize this war is crazy, but we're family—we have to be able to depend on each other."

"I promise," Carrie agreed instantly, searching her father's eyes. There was still a shadow of hurt lingering there, but she knew he would be okay. "How long have you known?"

"I've known you were hiding something from me for quite a long time. As far as what it was—about a week. One of my colleagues saw you going down there. I made some discreet inquiries and found out what you were doing."

Carrie sighed. She should have known someone would see her. "I'm afraid you may hear about it from someone else." Haltingly, she told him what had happened the night before. Her father's face whitened as she talked.

"Are you sure it's a good idea for you to be there?" was all he said when she finished.

"I have to, Father. I'm all those people have. It may not be much, but I'm making a difference."

Thomas studied her for a long while. Then he got up and walked to his bureau. "If you're going to be frequenting that part of town at night, I want you to take this with you." He reached into the bureau and pulled out a pistol.

Carrie was shaking her head before he finished speaking. "I couldn't take that," she cried. She had seen the results of gunshot wounds every day at the hospital. The very sight of the pistol made her feel sick.

Thomas walked over to where she had pulled herself up in his chair and pressed it into her hand. "If you're going to go into an area most men wouldn't think about going into, you're at least going to go armed," he said sternly, then paused. "I may have to acknowledge that my daughter is a grown woman with the freedom to make foolish decisions. That does not mean I have to sit idly by and do nothing while she gets herself killed. You're a good shot. I know you can handle a gun." His voice caught. "Do this for me, Carrie. Please."

Carrie gazed into his eyes and saw loving desperation there. Slowly she nodded and reached for the gun.

Carrie was laughing, running through tall grass dotted with wildflowers. Her dress flowed around her as she spun, her arms lifted in wild abandon. Suddenly, she turned. "Catch me if you can," she called gaily. Then she ran, moving faster and faster away from him. All Robert could do was watch her fade into the distance, her laughter taunting his inability to catch her. Then she disappeared. Only her laughter floated back on the breeze.

Robert jolted awake, sweat streaming down his face, even though the cabin was still gripped with an early morning chill. Burying his face in his pillow to stifle his groan, Robert tried to gain control of his trembling hands. The nightmares had become a constant reality, tormenting both his waking and sleeping hours. The situations varied, but they always mocked and taunted his helplessness.

"You all right, Robert?"

Robert's head shot up. He thought everyone was still asleep. Polly rose from her chair next to the fresh, crackling fire and moved over to put a cool hand on his forehead. "You be burning up!" she exclaimed. "You sick again, boy?"

Robert shook his head wordlessly.

Polly lit a lantern and carried it close to the bed, hanging it on a hook above his head. She gazed at him for several moments. "You been having them bad dreams again," she stated.

Robert stared at her. How had she known?

Polly read the question in his eyes. "I sit up at night lots of times. Be the only quiet time I have to myself. I got to have quiet to think. I see you thrashin' round in that bed. Don't you think I know you got lots of demons to fight after them battles and finding out you be paralyzed?"

Robert felt comforted by her understanding. "I'm awful thirsty."

"I reckon you are. You probably done sweated out everythin' you had last night." Polly made a clucking noise, then quickly filled a water pitcher.

Robert drank several glasses before his thirst was quenched. "Thank you."

Polly nodded complacently. "I figure we'll work on your legs again today."

"It's not doing any good, Polly." Robert scowled. "I know it puts a strain on your family. Why don't we just give it up? Just call the army and let them know you've got a Rebel soldier in your house. They'll take me off your hands," he said bitterly. He didn't know why they hadn't done it weeks before.

"What if I don't want you off my hands?" Polly asked serenely. "Nope. I reckon you're supposed to be here. That's what I keep hearing when I get quiet enough to listen."

"Listen to what?" Robert growled.

"Why, listen to the Lord, boy. Who else would be tellin' me such a hare-brained thing?" Polly laughed softly. Then her voice grew firm. "And I don't want to hear anything else about us not working with your legs. Ain't no reason to believe you ain't gonna walk again someday. Auntie JoBelle said she's seen it happen before. You just gots to keep believin' boy."

Robert had lost his ability to believe long ago. Any notion he had of a loving God had evaporated when he realized he was paralyzed. The only thing that kept him from laughing when he thought about God healing his legs was a respect for Polly. He didn't want to make fun of her beliefs. Why hurt the kind-hearted woman?

"Yep. We'll keep right on putting hot rags on your legs and making them move. One of these days I reckon they'll move on their own."

"What makes you believe in God?" Robert asked suddenly, then frowned. He hadn't meant to ask her that. He had no interest in even talking about God, but it was too late to retract the question.

Polly looked at him thoughtfully for several minutes, then reached over to pull up a chair. "I want to tell you a story, Robert." She stopped, gazing off into the distance as if she was looking at something, then turned back to him. "I was born on a rice plantation off the coast of South Carolina. My momma and daddy were fine people—loved me somethin' fierce. We was treated real good. Then our owner ran up onto some hard times. Had to sell all his slaves. We got put on the auction block one at a time. I was only five years old when I got bought by a fella in Virginia. Ain't never seen none of my family again." She paused, gathering her thoughts.

Robert watched her closely. Maybe it was because Polly had been so good to him that he could feel some of the hurt and pain radiating from her eyes. It was a new sensation for him. His mind darted to all the slave families he had sold on the auction block. For the first time he felt a twinge of discomfort.

"I was a mighty scared five-year-old when I got took to that plantation in Virginia. My owner was a hard man. He beat me. His kids beat me. Why, even his wife beat me if I didn't move fast enough for her. My heart got real hard—real quick. There was a powerful lot of hate in me." She shook her head as if she were trying to shake away the memories. "A lot of years went by. The hating in my heart grew stronger. Those kids who had beat me grew up. One of them had a baby." Her voice faltered. "I decided one day I was gonna kill that baby. Just as a way to let loose some of the hate."

Robert gaped at her. He couldn't believe Polly was telling such a story. He had seen daily evidence of her caring and gentleness.

"I had that baby to take care of all the time. One day I put a pillow over her face. I was plannin' on suffocating her. That baby was squawking and flailing something awful." Now her voice broke and her eyes filled with tears. "That's when the voice stopped me."

"The voice?" Robert was completely caught up in the story.

"Yep. There was a voice. Clear as my own. Told me to stop. Said I didn't want to do that." She paused, remembering. "I looked around to find out who be talkin' to me, but I was all alone."

"Did you stop?"

" 'Course I stopped. You ain't never heard a voice like that one. You didn't dare do what it told you not to. It was a strong voice—a stern one . . . " She paused. "And filled with the most love you could ever imagine . . . I took the pillow off that baby's head and cried and cried. Once I'd done crying, my hate was gone." Polly shook her head. "But what I'd done scared me somethin' awful. I decided right then and there I had to escape 'fore I did somethin' else."

Robert leaned forward so as not to miss a single word. "Go on," he urged.

Polly smiled. "It weren't too much longer before I just took off. All by myself. Didn't tell nobody where I was going. Didn't really know myself. I reckon I was about nineteen at the time. You lose track when the years spin by so fast." She paused. "My owner sent all kinds of slave hunters after me. Lots of times the dogs came so near I could hear them panting. They didn't never find me," she said in amazement. "Still—to this day—when I think about it, I know God was covering me up with some kind of magic blanket. He just wasn't figuring on me going back into slavery. I must have taken all the misery he was gonna allow."

Pictures of all the times he had gone after escaping slaves filled Robert's mind. Especially vivid in his mind was the picture of a little boy he had killed in retribution for other slaves who had escaped. He cringed, then stiffened as a surge of anger shot through him. They were his slaves. He could do with them what he wanted. *Couldn't he?* Anger mixed with confusion as he watched Polly's sweet expression.

"You done asked me what makes me believe in God. I believe in God every time I look at my husband and children. They be sure 'nuff miracles. I never thought I'd live long 'nuff to have any of that. I believe in God every time I remember where I came from. It be a miracle I'm still alive. And lately, I found me a new reason to believe in God."

She paused so long Robert felt compelled to ask, "What's that?"

The look she turned on him was direct, yet compassionate. "I believe in God every time I look at you because I don't hate you," she said flatly. "I should, you know. I know you done owned slaves back in the South. I don't know whether you treated them good or bad, but I know you owned them. That should be enough to make me hate you. But I don't. I reckon that's a pretty big miracle."

A stirring upstairs made Polly turn back toward the fire. "I got me some cooking to do, Robert. I'll just let you stew for a while."

Robert lay back against his pillow, pondering the things Polly had told him. Unbidden, words he had said to Carrie swam into his mind. *"Never again will I allow myself to be so caught up in the events of my world and my activities, that I lose contact with my own heart and mind. All of my achievements mean nothing if I lose myself in the process."* His own thoughts made him uncomfortable. Was he indeed losing himself? Had he already? Robert was relieved when Amber slipped down the ladder. He could put his thoughts aside for a while.

Just as she did every morning, Amber skipped to the side of his bed. "How you doin', Robert?" She gazed at him for a moment. "Your eyes look real funny. How come?"

"I don't know," Robert replied, forcing a chuckle. Could even a six-year-old girl see into his heart and know how troubled he was? "Are you going to help your momma finish your new dress today?"

A bright smile exploded onto Amber's face. "I sure am. Then we be goin' out into the woods and search for some of them red pokeberries. They make the purtiest red dye you ever saw. My Christmas dress is going to be the most beautiful one ever."

Robert smiled at Amber's joy, while his heart caught again with a familiar pain. How he wished he could be spending Christmas with Carrie. He had been so sure they would be married by now, sharing their first real Christmas together. Fiercely, he shoved the thoughts aside. What if he *was* home? There was no way he was going to let Carrie marry a paralyzed man. She was too vibrant, too full of life to be saddled with an invalid. He would never ask that of her. Amber's voice floated back into focus.

" . . . ever been out to get pokeberries?"

Robert shook his head, pulling his thoughts back from Carrie.

"Mr. Robert, will you let me read to you?" Amber asked, jumping quickly to a new subject.

Robert shot a glance at Polly, who merely shrugged and turned back to the fire.

"I'd like that," Robert said simply. Amber had completely captured his heart in the last month and a half. So far she had been warm and friendly, but still she had kept her distance.

"I'll get my book," she exclaimed, then turned and disappeared up the ladder to the loft. Seconds later she reappeared, her newest book clutched under her arm. As if it were the most natural thing in the world, she clambered up into bed beside him and settled down next to Robert's side. "I'll read now," she announced, then flipped through the pages until she found her place.

Bemused, Robert stared down at her tousled pigtails. A rush of warmth flooded through him. He glanced up to see Polly watching them, an inscrutable look on her face.

"You got to look at the pictures!" Amber commanded.

Robert obeyed instantly. He barely noticed when the rest of the family came down for dinner; he was too busy listening to Amber read.

Breakfast had been cleared from the table before Polly put the first pot of water on to heat. Robert's lips tightened as he watched.

Amber materialized beside her. "Can I help, Momma? I can do it, you know. I done been watching you put them 'presses on. It ain't so hard."

Polly smiled. "They be called compresses, Amber. And yes," she said thoughtfully. "I reckon you can help. If it's all right with Robert."

"Oh, Robert loves me. He'll like me helping," Amber said confidently. "Ain't that right, Robert?"

Robert smiled, the first genuine smile he had given since waking up. "That's right, Amber." The wonder of it exploded in his heart. How could he love a little colored girl when for so many years they had been nothing but animals—mere possessions—to him? He looked up to see Polly gazing at him with that unreadable expression again. Robert dropped his eyes to the patchwork quilt covering him. His feelings were too new for even him to understand.

Amber skipped over and pulled back the covers. "We gonna make you walk again, Robert," she said brightly. "Then I can show you my secret place down by the river." Her voice lowered to a whisper. "I ain't even took my brother there," she confided.

Robert smiled back as a rush of pain seared his heart. *My secret place down by the river.* Pictures of Carrie, and the day they had shared in her secret place, swarmed into his mind. He managed to stifle a groan as his fists clenched in frustration.

"I say somethin' wrong?" Amber asked anxiously, her eyes narrowing with confusion.

Robert shook his head quickly and scooped her up into the bed beside him. "Of course not! I have someone else who shared their special place with me once before—I just miss her, that's all."

Amber raised her hand to his cheek, her tiny face warm with innocent wisdom. "Ain't you glad you got somebody to miss?" she said simply. "I reckon love be a wonderful thing."

Robert lay back, stunned by her powerful words. He had not once thought about being glad he missed Carrie. Suddenly he saw the truth in what Amber was saying. At least he loved someone enough to miss her. At least there was someone in his life who was hard to be away from. His mind flew to the many soldiers he had watched die, merely shaking their heads when he'd asked if there was someone they wanted to have a message sent to. What an awful thing that must be.

"I bet she be missing you somethin' fierce, too. I reckon we ought to let her know where you be," Amber said, turning to her momma. "You gonna let her know?"

Polly shook her head, her kind eyes troubled. "Me and Gabe done talked about that." Her words were directed to Robert. "I've heard you call Carrie's name enough in your sleep to know how much you love her. There just ain't no way to get a message to her. Least not a way we know about."

"I know," Robert said slowly. Amber's words had opened his eyes for the first time to the pain and fear Carrie must be feeling. He couldn't bear to think of her worrying about him. Did she think he was dead? Had whoever rescued him managed to get word to her? He knew it was highly unlikely. A surge of determination shot through him. "We'd better work on my legs. I can't lie here for the rest of my life."

Polly grinned, approval lighting her face. "Now you're talkin', boy!"

Robert watched as Polly dipped a cloth into the steaming hot water, pulled it out with a stick, then carefully draped it over his legs. It took several minutes to cover his legs completely with warm clothes. When they were cool again, Amber pulled them off and handed them back to her momma, humming quietly the whole time. Robert strained to feel something in his legs, battling frustration as they lay numb and motionless.

Finally Polly stepped back. "I reckon they be warm enough." She picked up his right leg, bending it back and forth at the knee, then stretching it out full length, maintaining a constant up-and-down motion. "You gots to imagine you be movin' them by yourself," Polly commanded. "That's what Auntie JoBelle said."

Robert obeyed, a picture of Carrie's worried face pushing him on. For the first time since he'd woken up, he was more concerned about someone else than he was about himself. He still had serious doubts that this regimen would work, but he had nothing else to try.

Amber remained firmly planted by his side, smiling brightly. Every now and again she would reach out to squeeze his hand, all the while humming the same tune over and over.

"What are you humming?" Robert finally asked. Amber answered him by breaking into song, the catchy tune reverberating through the cabin.

No more auction block for me,
No more, no more!
No more auction block for me,
Many thousands gone.

No more peck of corn for me,
No more, no more!
No more peck of corn for me,
Many thousands gone.

No more driver's lash for me,
No more, no more!
No more driver's lash for me,
Many thousands gone.

Her sweet soprano faded away, then she grinned up at him again. "Some people who came through 'fore you got here taught it to me. Ain't it a nice song?"

Robert sensed Polly watching him closely. "It's a nice song," he agreed somewhat lamely. Then he looked at Polly.

"Yep. They were runaway slaves," she said firmly, answering the question in his eyes. "Our home done been part of the Underground Railroad for years. Nowadays folks just head north straight out, so it ain't in operation much, but we still open our home to folks who need a stoppin' off place. There's some stayed out in the barn a few weeks back." Polly gathered her rags, then picked up the pail of water. "Folks want to be free, Robert." She turned to Amber. "Why don't you run out and get some more water?"

"Yessum."

The door swung open and Gabe strode in. "Looks like we're gonna get some snow tonight," he announced. "I finished up my job over at the White farm early. Figured Clint and I ought to cut some more wood. We're gettin' snow awful early this year. It's gonna be a cold winter."

"That sounds like a mighty fine idea," Polly said a little too brightly.

Gabe walked over to warm his hands at the fire, watching her closely. "Everything all right in here?" he growled.

Polly nodded. "Me and Robert just be talkin' 'bout the Underground Railroad."

"What?" Gabe exclaimed. Then he swung around to stare at Robert. "We be real proud of what we've done to help folks. Ain't plannin' on stoppin' either." There was a hint of a threat in his voice.

Robert merely nodded. Amber's song had cut through to his heart. For the first time he was beginning to understand what Carrie had been trying to tell him. Colored people were just that—people. "How can you stand having me here?" Robert asked.

Gabe scowled, then shook his head and turned back to the fire. Polly ceased stirring her batch of cornbread and watched the two men. A long silence stretched through the cabin. Finally Gabe swung around. "I ask myself that question ever' day," Gabe said slowly. "I can't hardly believe I got me a slave owner lying in my bed. I get so angry sometimes . . . " his words trailed away. Then he straightened, his clear voice booming in the quiet. "I've had men treat me like I was nothing. I know what it's like to be hurt and have nobody to look after you. I was twenty-five when I done run away from my owner. It was mighty hard—and it's been mighty hard since—but ain't nobody ever gonna treat me like I'm nothing again." He paused for a long moment, then looked Robert squarely in the eyes. "I hated being treated like that. I wanted to be treated like I was a human being— not an animal. I reckon I should treat you the way I'd want to be treated." He shook his head. "Even though I know you wouldn't treat me the same way." His voice was bitter. "Some things you just got to do for yourself. Even if they don't make no sense."

Robert had never heard Gabe say so much at one time. "Thank you," he said, then stopped. He didn't know what else to say.

Gabe nodded abruptly and turned back to the fire, his back stiff.

Robert's thoughts were spinning. Slowly they began to settle. "You're right," he finally admitted.

Gabe swung around to stare at him.

"I wouldn't have treated you like a human being before." Robert struggled to sort through his thoughts. "Carrie—the woman I'm engaged to marry—helped her father's slaves escape through the Underground Railroad. I thought she was wrong."

"Yet you was gonna marry her?" Polly asked in surprise.

"Yes. Both of us realize love has to allow room for differences." Robert managed a smile. "But I know Carrie. She's been praying I would see things differently. The thing is," he said slowly, "I thought what I believed was the right thing. The church told me it was my duty to own slaves." Gabe snorted, but Polly raised her hand to keep him from speaking. "Carrie was right. I let hate take over my heart." He couldn't bring himself to tell Polly and Gabe about his father, about the little boy he had killed.

The only sound in the room was the crackle of the fire. Robert finally looked up. "I've been wrong. Being here—watching your family—knowing Amber . . . " his voice trailed away as he looked toward the little girl. "I've been very wrong," he whispered.

Twenty-Six

*M*atthew hugged his blanket close and peered out the door of his tent. His three colleagues were already snoring, but sleep was eluding him. Could it really be less than two weeks until Christmas? Peace on earth seemed to be nothing but a grim mockery. The sun would rise in just a few hours. When it did, Matthew was sure nothing would keep General Burnside from ordering an all-out assault on Lee's forces positioned on the heights above Fredericksburg.

Matthew scowled as he thought about the last two days. He had already written it down for the paper, but the details continued to swarm through his mind. Federal troops had been amassing outside of Fredericksburg since early December. General Lee had stationed his army there weeks before. Matthew knew the wily general would be well entrenched in the hills above the city. The Army of the Potomac had reeled under the dismissal of General McClellan as their commanding officer and were trying to adjust to their new commander. Matthew knew President Lincoln had made the best decision under the circumstances—it would be ludicrous to have continued with McClellan—but he wondered if the army was ready to give its all for a new general. He liked what he knew of Burnside but wasn't sure any man could take on Lee's army in its current position.

Two days ago, Burnside had sent his engineers out into the frigid predawn to begin building bridges over the Rappahannock. Lee's men had been well situated in the brick buildings along the river and had knocked holes in the walls facing the waterfront in preparation for the Federal assault. As soon as daylight appeared, they had begun firing, driving the Union engineers from the bridges time and time again. Burnside had finally ordered demolition of the buildings in the town. Over one hundred and forty guns had poured five thousand rounds of artillery into the city, already wisely abandoned by its inhabitants. By late afternoon a bridgehead had been established and Federal troops had poured into the city. Lee had ordered the withdrawal of his men to the protected heights, and now the Confederate general was merely waiting.

Yesterday a dense fog had blanketed the area, limiting visibility to just a few yards. Burnside had ordered an advance. Artillery had been sited and fields of fire laid for the infantry but by the time the fog lifted it was too late in the afternoon to order an assault. Matthew knew today would be a different story. Burnside was under pressure to perform. All of Washington was watching to see if he would continue McClellan's overly cautious campaign maneuvers. There had already been a long delay while Burnside waited for promised materials to construct the bridges necessary for his battle plan. Matthew was sure he would attack today.

The sound of a hoot owl floated to him on the breeze. Orange circles dotted the horizon for as far as he could see—glowing fires valiantly trying to push back the gripping cold. He shivered and pulled his blanket closer. Was Robert stationed with Lee's men in the hills? The thought of Robert caused his mind to shift to Carrie. He sighed, having long ago accepted the futility of trying to erase her from his mind. How could one erase such beauty and courage? He was sure it was some cruel twist of fate that had made him fall in love with the girl who loved one of his closest friends. He had accepted the impossibility of the situation, but he would never stop loving her. That he had also accepted.

"Think a hundred and twenty thousand men can take Lee's army?"

Matthew started as one of his colleagues inched up to stare out of the tent with him. Roddy was a war correspondent with a New York paper. "I don't know. I've heard Lee's men call him the King of Spades. My guess is that he's used his men to build some pretty impressive fortifications."

Roddy shook his head. "I hope it's not another Malvern Hill, with the Federals catching the bad end of it this time."

Matthew was silent. He had been thinking the same thing for the last few days—ever since he had arrived and taken a good look at Lee's position.

"Doesn't feel much like Christmas, does it?" Roddy mused.

"We should just cancel it this year," Matthew agreed with a faint smile.

"What was your favorite Christmas?" Roddy asked.

Matthew frowned. He wasn't sure reminiscing would be good for him. "I guess my favorite Christmas would be the one two years ago," he said, surprising even himself. "I spent it with a wonderful family on their plantation outside of Richmond."

"Rebels?" Roddy exclaimed. "You mean slave owners? I didn't think you were keen on slaves."

"I'm not," Matthew said quickly. "The Cromwells are a very unusual family. Thomas Cromwell is a fine man, even if he does own slaves. He believes there is absolutely nothing wrong with it. I disagree with him, but I can appreciate his dedication to his beliefs. He treats his people well. He is currently serving in the Virginia legislative body." He paused. "His daughter hates slavery as much as I do. She has helped many of his people go free." He smiled, remembering the things Carrie had told him at the prison when she came to visit. "She is quite an independent young lady."

"Evidently," Roddy commented wryly.

"They invited me to their home for Christmas. I had a wonderful time." Memories flooded his mind.

"How do you feel about West Virginia becoming a new state?"

Matthew pushed aside his thoughts to answer Roddy's question. "It's been coming a long time. Western Virginia has been far apart from the rest of the state on many issues for a long while. I'm sure my parents are happy. They have fought for this for years."

"Do you think our country will ever be whole again?" Roddy peered out of the tent again.

Matthew didn't answer. He knew Roddy was speaking more to himself than really asking him the question. Moving closer to the door, he stared out. He could see the glow of campfires on the hills towering over them. Tomorrow morning Americans would once again slaughter other Americans. There seemed to be no end in sight.

Could anyone dare sing of peace on earth when thousands of their fellow citizens were being butchered every day?

Carrie arranged a piece of Christmas greenery on the mantel. How she missed the plantation, especially now that Christmas was here. Visions of their elaborate celebrations rose up to taunt her. She sighed and pushed another sprig of magnolia into the arrangement.

"That's an awfully heavy sigh," Thomas commented, lowering his paper enough to stare over it. "Very pretty," he commented, his eyes sweeping the mantel.

Carrie dropped into a chair, still holding the rest of the greenery she had gathered from the yard. "Is it bad to wish for Christmases past? I know I have to live in the present but . . . "

"Bad to miss happy, peaceful times when our family was all together and our world was not being destroyed? I hardly think that's bad. I would be more inclined to doubt your sanity if you didn't long for them." Thomas put down his paper. "I appreciate all you're doing to make it special."

Tears blurred her eyes. "I have to do something . . . " She couldn't say any more. It had been almost three months since the battle of Antietam, and yet there had been no word of Robert. The hospitals that had responded to her letters had stated there was no record of him ever having been there. Hope died in her daily. If he was alive, surely she would have heard by now. Both North and South did a good job of keeping a list of prisoners of war. Robert's name hadn't shown up anywhere. It was as if he had simply disappeared. "I'm sorry," she whispered.

Thomas stood and walked to the fireplace to embrace her. "You can't give up hope, Carrie. We still don't know for sure."

Carrie nodded, then turned away, staring into the fire and taking deep breaths to regain control. Her father was right. Giving in to her fears would do no one any good. She squelched the sudden urge to fling the greenery into the flames. If she were out on the plantation she could jump on Granite and go tearing off across the fields. That always helped. *Granite* . . . another lump formed in her throat. She

had lost her beloved horse as well. Suddenly the allure of the plantation dimmed. There was too little to go back to—too many memories
it would be better not to dredge up.

"Have you heard anymore about President Davis' trip?" Carrie
asked. It would do no good to dwell in the past; she might as well
think about the present. President Davis had left Richmond several
days earlier, bound for Tennessee.

Thomas frowned. "It was very hard for the president to leave." He
shook his head. "But he knows that no matter what happens here in
Virginia, the Confederacy is probably doomed unless the tide in the
West can be reversed. I can assure you that is the only reason he
would leave during the current situation at Fredericksburg."

"Is it really that bad?" Carrie asked, more to keep the conversation flowing so she didn't have to think than because she was really
interested.

"I'm afraid so. There are thirty thousand Federals marching
down through Mississippi, headed for Vicksburg. The Union General
Grant is leading them. He is known for his aggressiveness. If
Vicksburg falls I'm afraid it's all over. All of our western states will be
broken off if the Mississippi Valley is held by the Federals. Then there
will be no good way to save what is left of Tennessee or any of the
Gulf States, for that matter. If we lose them, the rest of the country
can hardly hope to survive."

The morose sound in her father's voice caused Carrie to forget
about herself. She looked at him closely while he continued.

"President Davis has gone out to try to renew the patriotism in
those states. I'm afraid that area of the country has come under so
much attack the citizens are tiring of the war. There needs to be a
new surge of men into the army, but very few are coming forward."

Carrie bit her tongue to keep from saying she could hardly blame
them.

"The Southern generals are squabbling among themselves about
how to best take care of the situation. They know more men need to
be sent to Mississippi, but none of them want to go. According to
each general, if they were to lose any of their men, the positions we
presently hold would fall into jeopardy."

"Would they?"

Thomas shrugged and sighed. "It could be Davis' plan to strengthen Vicksburg while not losing our grip on the other areas is simply not possible. I'm afraid there isn't enough manpower in the country to pull it off." His voice sounded defeated. "Too many people are losing heart."

"Do you blame them?" Carrie couldn't keep from asking.

Thomas raised his head and looked at her. "They will lose heart if they lose all they hold dear. There are times when it is necessary to make great sacrifices if you are to achieve something great." His voice was bitter now. "I'm afraid there are too few people willing to pay the price for what they want."

"Maybe some of them never wanted it in the first place." Carrie picked her next words carefully. "Could it be that many men went into battle not fully understanding what it was all about—that the reality of it was more than they can handle?"

Thomas nodded heavily. "I know what you're saying, Carrie. But it's simply too late to go back and pretend the war never started. If we lose this war, our way of life is gone forever. Lincoln made that clear when he signed the Emancipation Proclamation." There was no anger in his voice, just a stark resignation. "We simply can't lose."

Carrie turned back to the fireplace and began to place greenery on the mantel again. There was no good answer to offer. All any of them could do was wait and see what happened.

Matthew woke with a start. Sometime during the long night he had drifted off to sleep. A distant call had rousted him awake. Taking a look around, he saw that his colleagues were still asleep. He stuck his head out of the tent; the area was once more shrouded with a thick fog. The fighting would not start early today. Within a few minutes, however, the whole camp began to stir. They would be ready for action as soon as the fog lifted.

Matthew put on his heavy coat and moved to the fire to make some coffee and cook his ration of bacon. Fog swirled around him, its dampness penetrating his heavy clothing with its chill. He had spent so many days studying the area that he knew it like the back of his hand. Behind him the Rappahannock River flowed north to south. West of the town there was a low ridge known as Marye's Height. Most of Lee's army was perched there. On the crest of the ridge was a pillared mansion surrounded by lawns and open areas, abandoned by the unlucky family who had found themselves sandwiched between the two armies. The ridge ended in a shallow stream known as Hazel Run. South of the stream was a chain of little wooded hills that stretched about three miles.

None of the elevated ground was really very high, but Lee's army occupied all of it. For purely defensive purposes, the position was extremely strong. Matthew was somehow certain Lee was not planning an offensive. He could not possibly have enough men after Antietam. Reinforcements had poured into McClellan's army after the vicious Maryland battle had decimated his ranks. Lee did not have the same advantage. Would the Federals just walk into Lee's snare? A burning in Matthew's gut told him the day was not going to go well.

At ten o'clock the thick fog lifted, floating away on the breeze as if it had no appetite for what was to come. Almost immediately, Burnside's artillery began to roar. There was silence from the Confederate heights, as if they were choosing to wait.

Burnside ordered his first assault at eleven-thirty. Matthew watched, sick at heart as the first wave of bluecoats surged up the hill. From his vantage point, he could hear the screams of men as they fell, mowed down by strong Confederate fire. The Federals continued to advance, leaping over the fallen men in front of them, their yells filling the air. Finally they were beaten back.

Another wave of blue flowed up the hill in a relentless assault. Equally relentless Confederate firepower drove them back again and again. Matthew stared in disbelief as the pile of dead continued to grow. He wasn't sure how the Federals could continue to advance with so many lifeless bodies blocking their way. At about three-thirty there was a lull. Matthew held his breath, hoping it was over—hoping Burnside would realize the futility of sending any more of his men to certain death.

He heard a distant yell and once again the Federals shot forward. Matthew groaned as nausea rose in his throat. This was not a battle; this was slaughter of the worst kind.

There was another lull at sunset. Surely it would be over now. Matthew stared in disbelief as yet another assault was ordered. The carnage finally ended around six o'clock, darkness cloaking the awful reality.

Matthew welcomed the numbness in his heart and mind as he moved out onto the battlefield. He had been at Antietam—nothing could possibly be worse than that. There was a stark difference on this battlefield. At Antietam the dead had been a mingling of blue and gray. Tonight there was nothing but blue—as far as the eye could see. If there were Confederate dead and wounded, they were on the hills. But on the open plains there was nothing but dead Federal soldiers.

Matthew stared up into the starry sky, wondering how the stars could dare shine on a night such as this. It better suited his mood to stare down into the white mist shrouding the river valley. The demolished town was swallowed in the fog. He felt as if he was groping along the shore of some nightmarish lake—a chillingly silent, nightmarish lake. Suddenly Matthew realized the night was not silent. As the rescue workers and correspondents emerged from the fog, they could hear the cries of the wounded. The noise rose on the still air, echoing all around them, wrapping them in its eerie sound. For a moment the echo died away, then was pierced by an agonizing scream quavering across the darkness, only to rise again as thousands of men joined in the desperate chorus.

Matthew shuddered and turned back. He had seen enough. He would document the terrible scene as best he could, but he knew there was no way for a reader to fully comprehend the horror. It was something that had to be experienced.

Early the next morning Matthew started back to the battlefield. He shuddered at the thought of returning to the scene of such grisly carnage, but he slowly trudged up the hill. As a journalist, he had learned to listen to his instincts.

Fredericksburg had been utterly destroyed. It would take the residents a long time to rebuild. They had been in the wrong place at the wrong time—one of the millions who could make that claim.

When Matthew reached the battlefield, he could only stop and stare. He understood instantly that the needy Confederates had plundered the field out of dire necessity, but nothing could have prepared him for the sight. Hundreds of naked corpses lay in front of the stone wall, stripped of every bit of clothing as well as their shoes. Frozen stiff, their stark bodies resembled little more than cleaned hogs. Matthew tried to push the horrible analogy out of his mind, but it remained. Even in death, the soldiers were no longer human beings—they were simply the bearers of new Confederate clothing. Matthew's loathing of the war took on a new dimension as he gagged then turned away.

Two days later Burnside ended the standoff, ordered his men back, took up his bridges, and admitted the whole assault had been a miserable failure. The Battle of Fredericksburg was over.

Christmas was just ten days away.

Twenty-Seven

Rose had moved beyond the initial sickness of her pregnancy. She was sure she had never felt better in her life. Aside from the ever-present ache of wishing Moses could share it with her, she was deliriously happy, smiling every time she felt her baby kick. She could hardly wait until May, not only because her baby would be born then—it would also mean the end of the brutal winter gripping the Southeast.

How thankful she was for the warm clothes Aunt Abby had sent her and June, but her heart hurt for the many people in the camps who were suffering from the cold. Barrels of warm clothing were arriving every day, but still there was not enough. Men were hauling in firewood from the surrounding forests, but houses were still cold, icy air whistling in through cracks. Sickness was rampant, with medical care insufficient and medicine scarce. Still, with all the troubles, the people Rose taught were glad to be here, glad to have a chance to learn and prepare themselves for the end of the war.

A smile exploded on Rose's face as she felt her baby give another fluttering kick. She held her hands lovingly to her stomach. "You sweet thing," she crooned. "You kick all you want. I can tell you have your daddy's spirit. You certainly have his strength."

June walked in just then, shutting the door behind her quickly to keep out the cold wind, then settling Simon on the bed to unwrap his thick clothing. "I declare, I feel guilty every time I walk out the door. My little Simon is wrapped up so warm, and I see so many children running around with hardly anything on."

Rose smiled sympathetically. "I understand. But our getting sick won't do anyone any good. Barrels of clothing are continuing to come in. Marianne is on another trip North. We will see the stream of supplies increase—she has a way of stirring compassion and giving in people."

"I hope they get here soon," June sighed. "Annabelle's two youngsters have taken sick. So have Julia's."

Rose frowned. "Is it serious?"

"Who knows anymore. Something can start out as a cold and end up something terrible. This is going to be a long winter," she said heavily. "I'm so afraid something is going to happen to Simon. You ought to be mighty glad your baby isn't going to be born right away!"

Rose searched for a brighter topic. "The plans for the Christmas party are going well. I talked to the superintendent. He actually convinced the fort commander to give us enough turkey and ham for everyone." Her words did the trick.

"No kidding?" June exclaimed, her face bright again. "I can't wait to see the looks on all the children's faces when they see the feast we're planning."

"I can't wait to see the look on the *adults'* faces," Rose laughed. "I know most of them give the best food to their children. It will be wonderful to have enough to go around. Even if it is just for one night," she said wistfully.

"Well, it's only three days away," June reminded her. "How is the decorating going?"

"The building is starting to look beautiful. Some of the soldiers even helped us move in hundreds of chairs. The children have been bringing in armloads of cedar, magnolia, and holly berries. Amos dragged in a huge tree. Annie picked it out herself. And guess who was with her?" Rose smiled excitedly.

June stared at her. "Harriet?" she asked in disbelief.

"Harriet!" Rose exclaimed. "This is the first time she's been willing to go more than a few yards from her house. She looked scared to death when some of the soldiers came in with a load of chairs, but they were very nice to her."

"I'm so glad," June said fervently. "She can't live her whole life being afraid. I know there are some Yankees who hate us and want to hurt us, but there are so many more who are wanting to help."

"We're making progress," Rose agreed. "Conditions are hard, but from everything Marianne has told me, they're much better than at this time last year. Our people are going to make it yet," she said firmly.

"Of course we are. If slavery didn't kill us off, then a hard winter ain't hardly gonna do the job," June said indignantly. "Especially now that Lincoln has made us free."

Rose shrugged and turned away to add another log to the fire.

June grabbed Rose by the shoulder and turned her around. "All right, now you're gonna tell me why you're not excited about what Mr. Lincoln done. That Emancipation Proclamation. I know you want us to be free. What's wrong? I been letting you get off with this half-hearted approval long enough. Tell me what you're thinking," she demanded.

Rose stared at her for a minute, then turned to hold her hands out to the fire. "I know it's a first step," she said quietly. "I'm grateful for that, but . . . "

"But what?"

"It doesn't really free anyone. It does nothing to free slaves in the North, and unless the North wins the war there is no way to enforce freedom for slaves in the South. A slave is still going to be a slave unless he runs away."

"But you heard what Miss Lockins said," June protested. "She said it was going to give the North a moral reason to fight. All of us are going to be free one day!"

Rose spun around. "I believe that, June. And I'm glad for what Lincoln did. I just can't help wishing it was more. I know there is no way to enforce freedom for the slaves in the South yet, but I had hoped he would completely abolish slavery in the North and set all the slaves free."

"It's coming," June said confidently.

Rose gazed at her. In the few short months June had been in the camps she had become a new woman. An intelligent young lady, she had learned rapidly, devouring every book she could get her hands on. She had even developed a nest egg by doing wash for the army. Her confidence had grown by leaps and bounds. "Why are you so sure?"

"I read about it in one of the newspapers. Lincoln is pushing the North as far as he can. He has to consider the political part of it, you know."

"The political part?" Rose asked, amused, yet impressed.

"People ain't gonna be pushed further than they want to be pushed. You push too hard and they're going to start fighting you. But if you just kind of lead them on, taking them a little step at the time, pretty soon they'll be right up there beside you. Then you can take them where you wanted to go in the first place."

Rose laughed out loud. "I can certainly tell you're Moses' sister."

June continued as if she hadn't heard her. "People are going to learn to hate slavery more and more. As the hatred grows, the demand to see it end is going to grow. Pretty soon Lincoln will be able to abolish it completely."

"I hope you're right," Rose said softly. "Oh, listen to me," she exclaimed. "I sound like a whiny baby. So many good things are happening. I just get impatient and I want to see it all happen at once. Of course I'm glad Lincoln made *any* kind of step toward all the slaves being freed. I hope it's coming soon."

"So what's really bothering you?" June asked astutely.

Rose turned back to the fire again. It was nice to have someone around who knew her well enough to discern when she was troubled. "I guess all this talk about Christmas has made me miss Moses." She shook her head. "I know you miss Simon, too. He doesn't even know he has a son."

"And the aching in my heart never goes away," June said simply. "One day we'll all be together again." Her voice broke. "If I didn't believe that I couldn't make it."

Rose tried to find comfort in June's words, but her earlier happiness had been snatched away by the cold winds of loneliness.

Carrie stepped into the hospital and stared in surprise.

Pastor Anthony strode up to her, a broad smile on his face. "I'm so glad you could come, Carrie. All the patients wanted you to celebrate Christmas Eve with them. I'm sorry Janie couldn't be here but I know she was needed at Chimborazo."

"I'm just glad most of our patients are home celebrating with their families," Carrie said, smiling. "Where did all these children come from?" There were at least ten girls, aged ten to fourteen, moving from bed to bed, laughing and talking with the patients.

Pastor Anthony looked at them fondly. "They are some of the girls from my church. They asked if they could come down and cheer up the patients. I helped them all get jobs at the munitions laboratory down on Brown's Island."

"They're just children!" Carrie protested.

"Yes, but the money they make is helping feed their families. I go down and spend time with them several times a week to make sure they're getting treated well. I've had no complaints so far."

"But after what happened to Opal's Aunt Fannie . . . "

"That was a horrible accident. But surely you realize occurrences like that are rare." Pastor Anthony reached out his hand and touched her shoulder. "We all must do things we'd rather not in times like these. The girls will be all right."

Carrie nodded reluctantly, watching the girls move from bed to bed. Smiles and laughter filled the hospital. Just then the youngest girl darted over and planted herself directly in front of Carrie.

"Hi," she said, suddenly shy. "I reckon you be Miss Cromwell—the doctor." She looked up admiringly, her chocolate eyes shining.

"Yes, I'm Miss Cromwell. But you can call me Miss Carrie." Carrie was immediately captivated by the little girl. She bent down to look into her face. "What's your name?"

"My name be Elvira. I'm ten!" She took a quick breath. "Merry Christmas!" Then as if embarrassed she had said so much, she darted off again.

Carrie laughed. "What a darling."

Pastor Anthony nodded. "Her mother was real sick until Elvira started making money to help feed them. Their father was conscripted to work on fortifications. Without him around, the family was going hungry."

Carrie nodded thoughtfully. The pastor was right. All of them were having to do things they would rather not. Still—her heart hurt when she thought of these beautiful young girls cooped up in the munitions factory for twelve to fourteen hours a day. She was glad Opal had taken Fannie's children out to the plantation. At least they were getting plenty of fresh air and food.

"We'd like to sing you a song, Miss Carrie. It be your Christmas present."

Carrie hadn't seen Elvira scamper back to stand in front of her. "I'd like that very much," she said, smiling.

Elvira turned and ran to join the other girls who were standing in the midst of the beds. All of Carrie's patients were propped up on pillows, even the sickest ones determined to take part. An elderly man pulled out a stick and began to beat time against the frame of his bed. Seconds later their pure voices, harmonizing perfectly, poured forth.

When I was a seeker,
I sought both night and day;
I asked the Lord to help me,
And He showed me the way.
Go, tell it on the mountain,
Over the hills and ev'rywhere;
Go, tell it on the mountain
That Jesus Christ is born!

Carrie clapped her hands in delight. "Thank you so much. That was a wonderful gift."

"That ain't all they got for you," Elvira cried. Evidently she had been made the spokesman for the group. Everyone else seemed quite content to let the precocious little girl do all the talking. She grinned and flew to peek under one of the beds. "There be a surprise for you here, Miss Carrie. For Miss Janie, too—only she ain't here."

Mystified, Carrie walked over and leaned down. Her face split into a smile as she pulled out a large basket full of sweet potatoes. She knew exactly how much of a sacrifice this was for her patients.

"People been bringing sweet taters all week!" Elvira sang out.

"She's right," Pastor Anthony smilingly confirmed. "Everyone who had some brought one over. It was the only way they knew to say thank you."

Carrie's heart caught in her throat. Blinking back tears, she smiled brightly. "I think it's the most wonderful Christmas gift I've ever received. Thank you." Suddenly the memories of past Christmases with their elaborate celebrations faded away. The basket in her hands represented a sacrificial act of love. "I'll never forget this," she whispered. "Thank you so much."

It didn't take Carrie long to do her rounds; most of the patients still there would soon be able to go home. A few new cases of pneumonia had been brought in but, taking everything into consideration, the negroes along the river were doing well. Carrie felt a deep sense of satisfaction as she called Merry Christmas to her patients and left.

Pastor Anthony walked her out to the carriage where Spencer was waiting. "You feel all right going home alone?"

"I'm not really alone," Carrie laughed, patting the pistol tucked into her waistband. She looked into the kindly pastor's eyes. "Besides, Spencer will be with me. I'm sorry you won't be joining us for Christmas dinner tomorrow, but I'm glad you're going to be spending time with your son."

"He's a good boy," Pastor Anthony responded. "We've shared a lot of Christmases together. Adopting him was the best thing my wife and I ever did."

"Jeremy is adopted?"

"Yes. My wife and I tried for years to have children, but we never could. Finally the Lord gave us Jeremy. He's been such a joy. I don't know that I would have survived Elizabeth's death without him."

"I'm glad you have him," Carrie said warmly. She wondered why the pastor had never remarried but then scolded herself—it was certainly none of her business. She turned to get into the carriage, then hesitated. "Your son reminds me so much of someone."

"Oh? Who is that?"

"I don't know," Carrie admitted with a wry laugh. "I just feel like I've seen him somewhere before." She shook her head. "I may figure it out one of these days."

A sudden shadow cloaked the pastor's eyes. He quickly recovered and pasted on a smile. It seemed odd to Carrie that her words could cause such a reaction, almost as if he was hiding something. But that was ridiculous. She pulled her thoughts aside as they said their farewells and she began her homeward trip.

Laughter and loud voices reverberated through the building. Rose watched the children dashing around excitedly. A wide smile split her face as adults joked and sang, their happiness a tonic to her own loneliness. The smell of pine pervaded the building, mixed with the aroma of turkeys and ham cooking just outside the door. Tables groaned under their weight of vegetables, biscuits, and sweet potato pies. Everyone had brought something. This was the first time in the months Rose had been in the camps that everyone was celebrating together. The building was bulging at the seams as people swarmed in and out, but no one seemed to mind. They were free. And it was Christmas Eve.

Tonight there was nothing but goodwill. The white teachers mingled easily with the inhabitants of the camp, leading games for the children and talking with the adults. Even some of the soldiers had asked if they could be a part. Rose smiled as she spied one soldier playing horse, laughing harder than the children as they piled all over him, then shrieking as he bucked them off.

"Miss Rose! Miss Rose!"

Rose turned quickly and caught Annie up in her arms. "What's wrong?" she asked in sudden alarm, then relaxed as she saw the excited gleam in the little girl's eyes. There was no hint of trouble.

"Ain't nothing wrong," she insisted as she squirmed out of Rose's arms. "I got a surprise for you!"

"What kind of surprise?" Rose asked, smiling again. Her students had plied her with gifts in the last week. Last night she had told June she might not have to cook again for a month.

"You gots to come outside for your surprise," Annie announced importantly.

Rose followed her willingly. She was ready for some fresh air after the closeness of the building. The sun had barely been up when she had arrived to help the other teachers finish the preparations. It had been a long day—but a good one. She took deep breaths, instantly revived by the cold, crisp air. "Okay. I'm out here. Where's my surprise?" she cried, entering the child's game.

Annie clapped her hands in delight. "Your surprise be right there!" she giggled, pointing into the shadows underneath a spreading oak tree.

Rose looked in the direction she was pointing but couldn't see anything. "Where?"

"You gots to walk over closer, Miss Rose. You'll see it!"

Rose was mystified, but did as ordered. She was almost to the tree when a towering form stepped out from the shadows.

"Merry Christmas, Rose."

"Moses!" Rose shrieked wildly. "Is it really you, Moses?" Dashing forward, she threw herself into his arms. "Moses!" It was all she could think of to say.

Moses held her close just for a moment then pulled back. "Rose . . . what . . . ?"

Rose took hold of his hand and laid it gently on her stomach. "I'd like you to meet your child," she said softly, tears gathering in her eyes at the stunned look on his face.

Moses stood motionless for a long moment, then a wide grin split his face. He cupped her stomach with both hands. Just then the baby gave a strong kick. His face lit up with wonder as he stared down. Finally he looked up, his expression one of awe. His hands left her stomach and moved up to caress her face. "I love you," he whispered. Then his lips came down to meet hers.

Rose pulled back to gaze up into his face again, when another voice split the darkness.

"I guess this means I'm going to be a great-aunt. I kind of like the sound of that."

Rose gasped and spun around. "Aunt Abby . . . ? Aunt Abby?" she asked incredulously. "How . . . ?"

"Oh, we'll have time for questions later," Aunt Abby chuckled. "Right now I'd settle for a hug if you can tear yourself away from your husband long enough."

Rose gave a glad cry and rushed to wrap her arms around the smiling woman. Tears were streaming down her face when she pulled away. "Right now I don't care a bit how either one of you got here. I'm just so happy you are!" Moses moved over and wrapped a protective arm around her shoulders. "How long can you stay?"

"Three days," Moses replied.

Rose looked toward the building when she heard a distant cry. "Moses!" June was racing down the stairs.

"I think June just saw you," she laughed. "Let's go in. I imagine you both are hungry. We'll have plenty of time to talk later, and I'd like you to meet everyone." From within the warmth of Moses' arm she reached out and encircled Aunt Abby. "There is so much I want to show you, Aunt Abby." She shook her head, still trying to believe they were actually there. "How . . . ?"

Aunt Abby shook her head. "I said there would be time for questions later. I have plenty of my own, you know. It's Christmas Eve. Let's go celebrate."

Moses gave June a big hug, then turned immediately back to Rose. His eyes traveled to her stomach. "What . . . ?"

Rose scolded him, saying, "You should at least introduce your sister to Aunt Abby." She laughed at the instant remorse on his face, then made the introductions, glad to see Aunt Abby immediately embrace June in a strong hug.

"Why don't we go inside and leave the lovebirds together for a little while," Aunt Abby said in a conspiratorial tone. "Will you introduce me to some of your friends?"

Rose watched them amble inside, then turned to Moses. He was still gawking at her stomach, his eyes wide with wonder.

"I'm really going to be a father?"

Rose reached up to touch his face tenderly. "This is going to be the luckiest baby in the whole world." She gave way to tears once more as she moved into the arms he held out. "I've missed you so much. I've wanted so much for you to know we were going to have a baby."

Moses frowned suddenly. "I should be here with you," he said fiercely.

Rose put a finger to his lips. "We'll be together in time. We're together right now. That's what is important. I will be fine here in the camps. You have a job to do."

A look of great sadness shadowed Moses' face. "The war . . . It's so terrible." He paused. "I have so much to tell you."

Rose ignored the sound of the party—her husband needed her. Drawing her coat tight, she led Moses back into the shadow of the tree, then pulled his head down to give him a long kiss. When they finally stepped back, Moses just looked at her. "What is it?" she asked softly, alarm beginning to ring in her heart. She had never seen him look so lost.

Haltingly, he began to tell her about finding Robert on the battlefield. "I took him to a colored family. When I think about it now, it seems like the most ridiculous thing in the world. At the time, it was all I could think to do."

Rose listened carefully, her heart going out to Moses as well as Robert and Carrie. "I wonder what Carrie must be thinking. Do you have any idea whether Robert is dead or alive?"

"None. I was hoping I would be able to get back there, but the army has been stationed around Fredericksburg. When I got leave I had to go through Philadelphia on army business and Aunt Abby asked if she could join me. I knew you would be thrilled."

Rose was still thinking about Carrie and Robert. "Poor Carrie." Tears sprang into her eyes as she envisioned the agony her friend must be feeling.

"Robert could be back home by now," Moses said unconvincingly. He pulled Rose back into his arms. "We'll keep on praying. That's all we can do."

Rose nodded, snuggling into the comfort of his arms. Moments later June appeared at the door.

"They're holding dinner for y'all," she shouted merrily. "You'd better quit kissing and come in."

Moses tilted Rose's chin up until her eyes met his. "It's Christmas Eve. God performed a mighty big miracle when he sent Jesus down here. I imagine he's still in the miracle business."

Rose drank in the strength radiating from him. Taking a deep breath, she forced a smile. The very act of smiling somehow restored some of the magic of the evening. "I love you," she whispered.

Carrie was up before dawn on Christmas morning. She still felt the glow from the night before. Quietly she eased to the window and looked out onto the cold, stark winter scene. A brisk wind rattled the frozen branches outside her room. Millions of stars twinkled and blinked in the clear sky, fading slowly as the sun began to pour forth its greeting.

Early morning had become Carrie's favorite time. It was here that she found the quiet she needed to make it through each day. She settled down on the windowseat, pulling her robe closer to ward out the frigid air. Her room wasn't much warmer than the outdoors. Fires were only built during the day in order to conserve wood. And those were only built in the main rooms of the house. Carrie didn't mind. Everyone had to make sacrifices. From now on, every time she felt the desire to complain she was going to think about the basket of sweet potatoes her patients had given her.

As she watched the sun rise, Carrie allowed herself to think about Robert. "Merry Christmas," she whispered. All logic said Robert was dead. But as long as he was alive in her heart, she was not going to give up hope. She pressed her face against the windowpane, not minding when her warm breath created a sheet of fog between her and the outdoors. She could still see the misty shape of the sun just peeping over the horizon.

Carrie's mind traveled back to the days, a couple of years ago, when she had been so eager to grow up; to test her wings of independence and soar into a new world. She had indeed soared into a new world, a world of war and fighting and men's angry passions—this world that was frightening and full of darkness. Why had she ever wanted to grow up? A sudden longing to be protected on the plantation surged up within her. Unbidden, Elvira's face floated into her thoughts. Following close on her heels was an image of her patients singing, then presenting her with the sweet potatoes. She could see Pastor Anthony's caring eyes as he bent down over a sick patient. She could see Dr. Wild studying a collection of wild herbs until he understood how they could be used to help his patients.

Carrie leaned back from the window and thoughtfully rubbed the steam away until once more the sun shone in brightly. She could no longer afford the luxury of looking at the world through immature, clouded eyes. Yes, there was darkness. There was also much light if she opened her eyes and allowed herself to see it. It was her choice.

Just then a tiny rock bounced off her window. Carrie smiled, tugged the window up, and leaned out, seeing Hobbs standing below. "We'll be right there," she called softly. When she turned around, Janie was sitting up, staring at her.

"Is it time?"

Carrie nodded. "Hobbs is waiting outside. I told him we'd be right out."

It took the two girls only a few minutes to dress, pull their hair back, and struggle into their heavy coats. The house was still quiet when they emerged into the frosty morning. Carrie had already made arrangements with May to have Christmas breakfast ready later that morning. She and Janie would be back in plenty of time to help.

"Merry Christmas," Hobbs said brightly, moving forward easily on his crutches.

"Merry Christmas," the girls echoed.

Carrie was amazed at how swiftly he had recovered from surgery. To be sure, his right leg was several inches shorter than his left, and it was still very weak from having been encased in plaster of paris for so long, but he was alive and he hadn't lost his leg. A wooden block was attached to the bottom of his shoe to make up for the length difference. He was using the crutches temporarily until the muscles in his bad leg got stronger. Hobbs would never be back on a battlefield, but he was still giving his all to his beloved South. He had become a permanent fixture at the hospital, helping Carrie and Dr. Wild any way he could.

"Do you think they suspect anything?" Carrie asked anxiously.

"Not a clue," Hobbs chuckled, his brown eyes dancing. Then he sobered. "There's a bunch of homesick boys needin' some cheering up in there. A bunch of them were writing letters home into the wee hours last night."

Carrie frowned. She could only imagine how they felt. She and Janie had found families for some of the stronger patients to share Christmas dinner with, but the vast majority of them were bound to their beds, far from loved ones and family. "Is the fiddle I found you all right?"

"It's more than all right!" Hobbs exclaimed. "I don't reckon I've ever held such a fine instrument."

Carrie sighed with relief. "I'm glad. Pastor Anthony told me it was a good one. He bought it for Jeremy when he was a kid but he lost interest quickly. It's been sitting in its case ever since. He said you could have it."

"Have it?" Hobbs echoed disbelievingly.

"Yes," Carrie said with a grin. She was glad to see something good happening to Hobbs. He had been through way too much for someone his age. "He said to tell you Merry Christmas. And to make sure you use it to make other people's Christmases merry—for a lot of years."

"I will," Hobbs promised solemnly. There was a glow on his face as he walked the rest of the way up the hill.

When they crested the hill, Carrie saw that almost everyone was there. The sun was well above the horizon now, but it had done little to take the bitter bite out of the north wind whipping across the knoll. She scowled at the dwindling pile of firewood stacked against the nearest trees. There simply was not enough to keep the men warm through the winter. What was going to happen if they couldn't get more?

"Quit scowling," Janie whispered. "You hardly resemble a bearer of Christmas cheer. We can worry about firewood later."

Carrie laughed. "Can you always read my mind?"

"No. But it's relatively easy to read your face. You show everything you're thinking and feeling," Janie teased. "It's Christmas, Carrie. Life will be waiting for us tomorrow. Let's enjoy today."

Carrie took a deep breath. "You're right. Life will be waiting for us tomorrow." She shook her head. "One of these days I'll learn that lesson well enough to hang on to it all the time."

"Let me know when you do," Janie laughed. "I'm not sure any of us have the ability to totally quit worrying—at least not until we get to heaven."

"I guess you're right," Carrie acknowledged. "I sure would like to be a little more consistent, though."

Hobbs approached on his crutches. "They're ready," he said excitedly.

Carrie and Janie moved up to join the rest of the group bunched outside the door to the first ward. Carrie could see similar groups all across the broad plateau. Her heart swelled with emotion. In spite of the fact they all worked long hours in the hospital already, these people had given up part of their Christmas to bring cheer to the patients. At Dr. Wild's signal, they formed a long line, two across, and streamed into the ward, singing loudly.

Joy to the world! The Lord is come;
Let earth receive her King;
Let every heart prepare him room,
And heav'n and nature sing,
And heav'n and nature sing,
And heav'n and heav'n and nature sing!

Tears formed in Carrie eyes at the looks of delight on the patients' faces.

Hobbs' fiddle exploded with life and joy as he played by the front door. He finished the first song, adjusted his chin, and swung immediately into the next carol.

Hark! the herald angels sing,
Glory to the new-born King!
Peace on earth, and mercy mild,
God and sinners reconciled.
Joyful all ye nations, rise,
Join the triumph of the skies;
With the angelic host proclaim,
"Christ is born in Bethlehem."
Hark! the herald angels sing,
Glory to the new-born King.

Carrie watched as all the patients joined in—men with missing legs, men with stubs for arms, men blinded from minie balls, men weak from infections ravaging their bodies. Hope and joy erased the pain and suffering from their faces. For these few minutes the reality of the war melted away. For just a little bit they could believe in peace on earth. It was Christmas.

Rose sighed contentedly and snuggled close to Moses' strong warmth. June and baby Simon were staying with Aunt Abby in the teachers' lodging. Several of the teachers had gone North for the holidays so it had been an easy matter to arrange a room for them. Christmas Day had passed in a haze of laughter, talking, and great joy. Even the wind whistling through the cracks in their house couldn't dim her contentment. There were plenty of blankets and Moses was beside her. She could ask for nothing more. "Moses," she said softly.

"I thought you were asleep," he chuckled, then rolled over onto his side and looked down at her.

"I've been thinking."

"Sounds serious," Moses teased.

"I want us to have a last name," she said. "I want our *baby* to have a last name."

"I've been thinking about that, too," Moses agreed, immediately serious. "I'd say it's time we made a decision. You have any ideas?"

"I've been thinking about it ever since I knew we were going to have a child." She hesitated. What if he didn't like her idea?

"And?" Moses prompted.

"I'd like our last name to be Samuels," Rose said firmly. "For your daddy—Samuel. You've told me how he longed for freedom—for himself and for his family. Now we're free. June is free. Our baby is going to be born free. What he dreamed for his family is coming true. Someday your momma and Sadie will be free . . . " Her voice trailed away. She held her breath, waiting.

"Samuels," Moses said slowly, letting the name roll off his tongue. Then he nodded, his handsome face outlined in the flickering flame of the fire. "I like it," he said with deep satisfaction. "You're right. My daddy wanted freedom more than anything in the world. He'd be pleased to know we were taking his name."

Rose released her breath.

"Samuels." This time Moses' voice was strong, their new last name bouncing off the cabin walls and floating above their heads. He grinned again. "Moses Samuels."

Suddenly Rose was laughing. "You should hear yourself. You sound like a little boy who just got a new toy!"

"And so what if I do?" Moses demanded, a gleam in his eye. "It's fun to be a little boy sometimes. They get away with all kinds of things!" He laughed loudly. "Like this!"

Rose shrieked with laughter as he quickly flipped her onto her back and began to tickle her. "Stop! Stop!" she cried. Her attempts to tickle him back were futile. Finally he gave in to her cries and stopped.

"I want you to know you deserved much more than that. I was merely having mercy on our child," Moses said smugly.

Rose stuck out her tongue impudently. "You're hardly more than a child yourself," she replied haughtily, quickly realizing her mistake as the gleam once more appeared in Moses' eyes and he began his torture anew. Her shrieks of laughter once more rang through the cabin.

~Twenty-Eight~

1863 blew onto the world with cold winds and frigid temperatures. Even the Deep South was gripped by the coldest weather they had experienced in years. If Mother Nature was trying to cool men's passions, it was a futile attempt. Fighting continued in the Mississippi Valley, while new battles erupted throughout Tennessee and Kentucky. Soldiers struggled to survive in frozen camps with inadequate food and shelter. Wives cried for their husbands while little children whimpered with hunger. Mothers patted their stomachs, remembering their soldier boys when they were little babies, still innocent and unharmed. Remembered—and longed for those times. Blood soaked deep into the soil on ravaged battlefields, then froze, staking its claim on land that would long remain fruitless.

Aunt Abby held Rose close until the impatient scream of the ship's whistle made her let go reluctantly. "I'm going to miss you," she said quietly.

"I'm going to miss you too, Aunt Abby," Rose replied, blinking back the tears in her eyes. She was so glad Aunt Abby had been able to stay on two more days after Moses had left to return to duty. They had talked for hours, and Aunt Abby had visited her school and met many of her friends.

"You'll think about coming to Philadelphia to have your baby?"

"I'll think about it," Rose promised again. The idea of being in Aunt Abby's house to have Moses' child was very appealing, but she couldn't imagine leaving the people in the camps.

Aunt Abby turned toward the ramp, then spun around for one final hug. "I'll make sure more supplies are coming your way soon. I thought I was sending a lot before. I realize now how pitifully inadequate it was. Once I've mobilized my forces at home, barrels will start pouring in." She waved her hand merrily, brushed away the tears in her eyes and darted up the ramp just before a shipsman started to pull it up.

Rose stayed where she was, ignoring the cold wind, waving until the boat was finally too far away to identify Aunt Abby. Only then did she turn and head back for the camps. The last five days had been joyous. She knew the loneliness would settle in as it always did, but the memories and love would carry her for a long time.

Robert stared down at his legs, willing them to move. Sighing, he reached for the limb suspended by a rope above his bed. Gabe had rigged the contraption for him. He'd said there was no reason for Robert's upper body to wither away just because his legs weren't working. When Robert had first attempted to pull himself up, he had been able to lift himself only a few inches before he had collapsed back onto the mattress. Gritting his teeth, he had reached for the bar again. Now he was doing twenty pull-ups at a time, his upper body once again hardening with muscle.

"Happy New Year!" Amber called, bouncing down the stairs and running over to climb up beside him. Leaning over, she gave him a resounding kiss on his cheek.

Robert smiled and hugged her close. "Happy New Year to you."

"I had a dream about you last night," Amber announced importantly.

"And what kind of dream did you have?"

"It was a wonderful dream!" Amber exclaimed. "At the end of it you climbed out of that bed and walked!" She reached down and patted his useless legs. "I just know them legs are gonna be walkin' someday. You just wait and see." She climbed down from the bed and scampered to the fireplace. "I sure am hungry, Momma."

"You always hungry, girl. I declare, I think you eat more than that big brother of yours!" Polly laughed, ladling out a big bowl of steaming grits and setting it on the table. Then she dipped another big bowl and carried it over to Robert. "Reckon we got to keep those muscles of yours growing," she said.

Robert nodded and reached for the bowl. He had grown to love this family. Somewhere along the way it had quit mattering to him that they were colored. They were simply the people who had saved his life. He had watched them laugh, talk, eat, sing, and learn together. Every night they would gather around the fire with a new book, Gabe struggling to read it aloud, Polly insisting that education was the way to a new life for them. Nothing would get in the way of it. Robert's respect and admiration for all of them had grown daily.

When Robert finished eating he turned to the window. Great banks of fluffy snow hugged the tiny cabin. A dull, gray sky, lowering to embrace the wintry landscape, promised more soon. Robert was glad to be safe inside the sturdy cottage. The little cabin might be rustic, but it was snug and cozy, even in this frigid weather.

The door swung open and Clint eased in, pulling off his boots so he wouldn't track snow. He shot a look at Robert but didn't speak. Instead, he turned to Polly. "Momma, wait until you see what I got!" There was no mistaking the excitement in his voice.

Robert had tried to befriend the boy, but Clint wasn't having anything to do with him. Robert couldn't blame him. The boy had heard stories all his life about what slave owners had done to his parents. Robert cringed. Thank God none of the family knew the things he had done. They would surely toss him out in the snow without a second thought. Robert was quite sure even gentle Polly would not let him stay.

" . . . President Lincoln signed it himself."

Clint's words pulled Robert back. He sat straight and watched Clint pull out a sheet of paper.

"The people who gave me this called it the Emancipation Proclamation. What does that mean, Momma?"

Robert sucked in his breath and leaned forward, wishing he could grab the sheet of paper out of Clint's hand. He wanted to read it for himself.

Polly shot him a look, then told Clint. "Why don't you go get your daddy. You can read this to the whole family." Excitement tinged her voice. "Hurry," she commanded. When Clint dashed from the house, she turned back to the fire, humming softly to herself.

Robert lay quietly, waiting. He was fairly certain he knew what was coming.

Gabe and Clint came pounding back into the cabin just as Amber crawled down the ladder. The whole family pulled up chairs around the fire. "You want to read it, Daddy?" Clint asked.

"You go ahead, son. You brung it home. You should get the honor of reading it."

"Do you already know what it is?" Clint asked.

"I've been hearing about it." His voice became stern. "This is a real historic moment, children. This be something your people have been fightin' for ever since we were brung to this country. You burn this moment into your brains and never forget it." He motioned with his hand. "Go ahead, son."

Clint cleared his throat importantly, held the paper up, and began to read.

"Whereas on the twenty-second day of September, in the year of our Lord, one thousand eight hundred and sixty-two, a proclamation was issued . . . containing among other things, the following . . .

"Now I, Abraham Lincoln, President of the United States, by virtue of the power in me vested as Commander-in-Chief of the Army and Navy of the United States in time of actual armed rebellion against the authority . . . "

Clint stopped reading and looked up. "Daddy, I know I be stumbling all over this. These here are some mighty big words. I can't figure most of them out."

"Those be some mighty big words, son," Gabe agreed, his brow wrinkled. "I ain't sure I can do much better than you."

There was a long pause, then Polly stood and reached for the paper. "Will you read this here paper for us, Robert? I reckon you won't have any trouble with the big words."

Robert wordlessly reached for the paper she held out to him. Polly turned up the light on the lantern above his bed, then moved back to her chair. When she looked at him and nodded, he began to read.

"... *as Commander-in-Chief of the Army and Navy of the United States in time of actual armed rebellion against the authority and government of the United States, and as a fit and necessary measure for suppressing said rebellion, do, on this first day of January, in the year of our Lord, one thousand eight hundred and sixty-three, designate as the States and parts of States ... in rebellion.*"

Robert quietly read the list of Confederate states, as well as the slave-holding border states. Then he continued.

"... *all persons held as slaves within said designated States, and parts of States, are, and henceforward shall be free ...* "

"Thank you, Jesus!" Polly cried. Then she said, "I'm sorry, Robert. You keep on reading, boy. Them words just be music to my ears."

Robert swallowed and kept going. " *. . . and that the Executive government of the United States, including the military and naval authorities thereof, will recognize and maintain the freedom of said persons.*

"*And I hereby enjoin upon the people so declared to be free to abstain from all violence, unless in necessary self-defense; and I recommend to them that, in all cases when allowed, they labor faithfully for reasonable wages.*

"*And I further declare and make known, that such persons of suitable condition, will be received into the armed service of the United States to garrison forts, positions, stations, and other places, and to man vessels of all sorts in said service.*"

"That fella who brought Robert said this was coming. I couldn't believe it then. But he was right!" Gabe crowed loudly. He laughed. "What else does it say?"

Robert tried to calm the pounding of his heart. His hands were shaking slightly as he held the paper closer to steady it.

"*And upon this act, sincerely believed to be an act of justice, warranted by the Constitution, upon military necessity, I invoke the considerate judgment of mankind and the gracious favor of Almighty God.*"

"Amen," Polly said fervently.

Robert lowered the paper.

"That be all of it?" Gabe asked.

"There's only the closing part left," Robert replied.

"Read it all, Robert. This here be an historic occasion. I want to hear it all."

Robert sighed, and continued, *"In witness whereof, I have hereunto set my hand and caused the seal of the United States to be affixed.*

"Done at the city of Washington, this first day of January, in the year of our Lord, one thousand eight hundred and sixty-three, and of the independence of the United States of America the eighty-seventh."

Robert lowered the paper as a deep silence filled the cabin. Amber was the first to speak. "Does this mean there can't be any more slaves, momma?"

"That's what it means, honey-child. Sure enough, that's what it means." Tears of joy glistened in her eyes.

"That there paper says colored people gonna be free from now on. Just the way God intended them to be." Gabe's deep voice rolled through the cabin. "Our people done waited a long time for this." Suddenly he swung toward Robert. "What you think about this Emancipation Proclamation?" he challenged.

Robert struggled to control his thoughts. He had known Gabe would ask him. But for the life of him he couldn't think of an answer. He didn't know what he was feeling. He was glad for this family he had learned to care for, and yet his overall feeling was a one of overpowering loss. During the reading of that document, he had seen all he had worked to build crumble before his eyes. A surge of anger shot through him.

The family waited expectantly for his response. Robert took a deep breath. He knew he had to say something. Should he say what they wanted to hear or should he be honest? He had grown to care for these people over the past weeks and he felt certain they felt the same way. They had known he owned slaves from the start and yet they hadn't abandoned him—he chose honesty. "It's just a piece of paper, Gabe. As long as the South is an independent country, the people will continue to own slaves. There will be no United States military to enforce this."

Gabe shrugged his massive shoulders carelessly. "That ain't nothing but a matter of time. There be thousands and thousands of colored men been waiting to help win this war. Now that President Lincoln got some sense in his head, I reckon the coloreds will be pouring into the army. You ain't seen fierce fighting till you seen people fighting for their freedom," he stated flatly. "It's just a matter of time till we win this war and head down to set our people free."

"The South isn't going to lose its independence." Robert's protest sounded weak even to his own ears. He knew the South was struggling for its survival. A strong influx of colored men into the Union army would be another kick in the teeth.

Polly walked over and sat down on the edge of the bed. "I can tell you be real upset, Robert. Why you so dead set against our people being free?"

Robert gazed back into the eyes holding his so steadily. He tried to explain. "It's not that I'm so set against your people being free," he said slowly. "I've changed a lot of my thinking in the time I've been here. I've learned I've been wrong about a lot of things."

"Then why you so afraid?"

Polly had hit what he was feeling square on. Robert made no attempt to deny it. "I've lived all my life on a wonderful plantation. My father owned it before me. It's called Oak Meadows. All I've dreamed of since this war started was going home and bringing it back to life. It's my whole life—all I've ever wanted. . . . " His voice faded away and he shook his head. "Without my slaves . . . " He laughed abruptly. "I know you must think I'm crazy."

"I think fear be a mighty powerful thing," Polly said slowly. "I think slavery be nothing but evil, but I can understand your fear. I done felt enough of it in my time." She paused, then looked him in the eye. "What I want to know is where the hate comes from."

"I don't hate you, Polly. I don't hate any of your family. I told you a lot of my thinking has changed," Robert protested. He was uncomfortably aware of the rest of the family listening to their conversation.

"Oh, I know you don't hate us," Polly said easily. "But you got a passel of hate in you, nonetheless. I hated for so long I sure 'nuff can recognize it. Hate eats at your heart, Robert. It marks you in a way folks who've been there learn to recognize."

Robert opened his mouth to deny what she was saying. Nothing came out. Instead, a vision of his father flooded his mind. With it came a surging wave of loathing. He slumped back against his pillow as it rushed through him. All he could do was stare at Polly.

"That hate gonna eat you till there ain't nothing left of the real Robert. Ain't never no good reason to hate 'cause it mostly just hurts you."

"I've got plenty of reason to hate," Robert cried wildly. His mind was screaming at him to seize control, but it was too late. "I watched a slave kill my father. He was a runaway. My father went after him . . ." Robert choked on his emotion. "I was only eleven years old when the slaves in the county revolted. My father was with the group of men who caught them. One of the slaves killed him—stabbed him to death." Blind rage blurred his vision. All he could see was his father lying in a pool of his own blood.

"Your father got what he deserved!" Clint yelled bitterly. "That man weren't trying to do nothing but be free."

Robert clinched his fists, a new wave of rage pouring over him as he realized afresh that he was paralyzed and helpless. "I got even!" he cried. "I got even!" He knew he should shut up, but now that the dam of feelings had been released he simply had no power to shut them off. "Last year another group of our slaves escaped. I went after them but somebody with the Underground Railroad had taken them off in a wagon," he said bitterly. "I went back into my slave quarters and taught the rest of my people what would happen if anyone else tried to run off." A high-pitched laugh erupted from his throat. He barely recognized it as himself. "The little boy I taught the lesson to didn't make it. Just like my daddy didn't make it," he said fiercely.

Shocked silence filled the room. For just a moment Robert felt a gloating satisfaction. Then a picture of the little boy he had killed, the horrified eyes gazing up at him as he had swung the whip down onto the tiny, bared back, rose before him. The bleeding, crumpled body laying lifeless on the dirt when he strode off, his anger still raging. The terror-stricken eyes seemed to float up from the body and bore into his heart, begging to know what such a little child had done to deserve such punishment.

Another picture rose up to block out the little boy's eyes. It was his mother, gently rocking in her chair when he had returned from the slave quarters. He could still hear her telling him he had become just like his father. *"You've got the same hardness and hatred in your heart."* The words echoed in his heart, bouncing off the walls of his mind till they spun and tumbled in wild confusion.

Then another vision reared up to taunt him. It was his father. Robert barely remembered anything about his father except seeing him lying in that pool of blood. Now he watched as pictures of his childhood unrolled before his eyes. His father yelling—treating him harshly—mistreating his mother. *"You're just like your father."* His mother's accusing words floated back into focus. *"You're just like your father. Just like your father!"*

Robert gasped as truth collided with the reality he had clung to all these years. "Oh, my God!" he cried in a broken voice. "I killed that little boy. I killed a defenseless, innocent little boy!" From somewhere deep in his gut, great sobs came wrenching forth, doubling his body as they tore through him. "I'm so sorry," he sobbed. "Oh, God! I'm so sorry . . . Please forgive me! Please forgive me!" Great waves of sorrow rolled through his heart, threatening to drown him, to suffocate him.

Suddenly he felt a presence move into his grief. A presence that picked up his shredded heart and handed it back to him gently. Even in the midst of his grief, Robert wondered if he was losing his mind. He could see the presence in his mind just as clearly as he had seen the little boy he had killed, yet the presence had no real form. It was simply there. Robert could feel great power, as well as an embracing love, reaching out to him. Wonderingly, Robert reached out for his heart. As the presence held it out he watched in awe as his shredded heart was miraculously transformed into a whole, healthy one.

Robert had no idea how long he had been sobbing before he began to gain control. Finally he gave a final gulp and was quiet. He dreaded looking into Polly's eyes. He knew he would see condemnation there, albeit justified.

"Feel better?" Polly asked quietly.

Robert raised his head slowly, not willing to believe what his ears were hearing. His eyes met hers. There was nothing but loving acceptance in her eyes. "You don't hate me?" he asked disbelievingly.

"I told you once I'd done all the hating I ever intend to do. I figure all the hating I did when I was young was enough for a lifetime. I sure 'nuff hate what you did to that little boy, but I don't hate you. I sure 'nuff hate what I almost did to that little baby I was taking care of, but God didn't hate me. I don't reckon I can hate you. You didn't do nothing I didn't want to do myself."

"I didn't know," Robert whispered. "I didn't understand." Finally he gained enough courage to look up at Gabe. "I'm sorry," he said weakly. "I know that doesn't change what I've done . . ." Robert sighed heavily. "I know you want me out of here. If you call the army, they'll come get me."

Amber didn't wait for her father to respond. Walking over to Robert's bed with a very serious look on her face, she stopped and stared into his face for a long minute.

Robert gazed back with no idea of what to say to the little girl. "Amber—"

"Hush, Robert," she said sweetly. "You done been crying too much to have to talk." Pushing aside his hand, she climbed into the bed next to him and looked up at him. "I love you. I don't care what you done. Anyway, I don't think you like that any more. My momma said she changed. I reckon you have too." Once she had made her announcement, she turned to stare at her father defiantly.

Gabe stayed where he was by the fire, his face hard and angry. Nothing was said while a log on the fire crackled and sputtered. As if the fire were melting it, the hardness on Gabe's face began to soften. After a long while, Gabe shook his head and settled back in his chair. "I don't reckon we'll need the army."

"I don't expect you to keep me here," Robert protested. "Not after what I've done."

Gabe held up his hand. "There's been enough hatin'. I hate what you did to that little boy, but I also know if I'd ever had half a chance I would have killed the man who owned me 'fore I ran away. I planned it in my mind a hundred times. No, I reckon the hatin' has to stop sometime." He paused for a long while. "Maybe this Emancipation Proclamation will help folks. Maybe it will make people stop to think long enough to realize folks are just folks—no matter what color they are. Maybe that'll stop some of the hatin'."

Robert exchanged a long look with Gabe, and for the first time understanding flowed between them.

Polly nodded. "Slavery done ripped the heart out of people. But it didn't just take it away from the colored folks—it done took it away from the whites, too. I figure that be the only way you can live with yourself."

Across the room Robert heard Clint give a disgusted snort. When he looked over toward the corner, Clint's glowering eyes locked with his. Robert understood. Clint was too young to sort through all the passions of his heart. Of course, age didn't really have anything to do with it. He had seen enough proof of that. He couldn't fight Clint's battles for him. Clint would have to fight them on his own.

Robert was exhausted, but he had never felt more peaceful. It was as if a spreading gangrenous sore had been ripped from him. His heart was sore but for the first time in his life he felt whole. He reached out to take Polly's hand. "Thank you," he said softly.

Polly looked satisfied. "Folks got to stick together, Robert. Colored and white. That's the only way any of us are going to make it. God might never have wanted us to be hauled to this country as slaves. But now that we're here I know for certain he wants the hatin' to stop. It's our job to make sure it happens—at least in our own hearts. I reckon those are the only ones we can really answer for."

Gabe threw another log onto the fire. The snow clinging to it hissed and sputtered until the licking flames melted it away into oblivion. "I reckon it's a lot like that dump I found the other day."

"What you talking about, Daddy?" Amber asked from the protective curve of Robert's arm.

"I found a pile of somebody's garbage down in one of the valleys not too long ago. Looks like somebody just drove a wagon down and pitched a bunch of stuff." He paused. "I remember looking at that garbage, then lookin' 'round at all the beauty surrounding it. It sure didn't fit with all that white snow heapin' up and layin' so nice on the branches." He smiled sheepishly. "Might seem crazy, but I figure that's what folks are like. Everybody's got some beauty in them— everybody's got some garbage. I reckon folks all got some stuff in them they'd rather just throw in the trash pile and pretend it ain't there. Lots of people hide it real good, but it's there just the same. Shouldn't come as no surprise. Seems that folks who try to hide it the most end up judging the most. Guess they figure if they judge other people's garbage, it makes their own not quite so dirty." He shook his head. "I know I've done it." He paused again, then spoke wistfully. "If people could accept that we all got trash in us, it sure would be a lot easier to accept each other. We got an awful lot in common—no matter what color we be."

Twenty-Nine

arrie moved gracefully around the dining room, putting finishing touches on the preparations for dinner. It seemed somehow too good to be true that all of her father's boarders had gone home for a few days or left town on government business. She was happy to have them in the house, but it was wonderful to have a few days with just Janie and her father.

"What time are Pastor Anthony and Dr. Wild supposed to arrive?" Janie asked, looking up from setting the table. "Matron Pember said she would be here around seven o'clock. Thankfully things aren't quite as busy at the hospital."

"They said they would arrive as close to seven as possible," Carrie answered. She stepped back to survey the room, then frowned. "It seems so odd to be having a dinner party when people all over Richmond are cold and hungry."

"I would hardly say three people constitute a dinner party," Janie responded. "It's not as if we're being elaborate. Soup, sweet potatoes, and biscuits are definitely not a feast."

Carrie nodded. "You're right." She knew she should just let herself enjoy the evening. The cold winter had indeed roared in as a brutal monster. There had already been several snowstorms. The accumulation wasn't substantial, but the accompanying frigid temperatures had made the shortage of wood and coal even more critical. Combined with the scarcity of food, the situation in the city was becoming increasingly bleak. She shivered and moved closer to the fire as another nordic blast rattled the windows. "I wonder where Father is? He said he would be home before now."

"Probably just taking care of some extra business at the Capitol," Janie said soothingly.

"Don't you get tired of constantly relieving my worries?" Carrie laughed.

"I don't think of you as a worrier," Janie protested. "You're one of the most optimistic people I know. Your problem—which I hardly think of as a problem at all—is that you care so deeply. You're always thinking about how something affects other people."

"I much prefer that viewpoint." Carrie smiled gratefully. Then her smile faded and she turned to stare out the window.

"Carrie?"

Carrie shook her head. "I'm fine," she murmured.

Janie walked up close behind her and laid a hand on her shoulder. "It's Robert." There was no question in her voice.

"Somehow," Carrie started slowly, "I thought a new year couldn't start with me still having no idea if he's dead or alive. I know 1863 arrived a few days ago. I'm afraid I'll be forever stuck in 1862."

"No, you won't," Janie said firmly.

"You sound very sure of yourself," Carrie commented dourly. Every time she thought she was getting used to living with the uncertainty, a fresh wave of grief and fear would sweep through her.

"Grieving is a very natural thing," Janie said gently. "But you are too full of life to remain under its weight forever. Time takes care of many things."

Carrie swung around to stare at her friend. "You think he's dead, don't you?" she said accusingly.

Janie returned her look for several long moments. "I think it's been almost four months since the battle." Her voice was blunt but kind.

Anger flared in Carrie then subsided just as quickly. She knew that reason deemed she accept the inevitable. Yet somehow she couldn't. She knew better than anyone that Robert was probably dead. How could she expect anyone to share her unfounded belief that he was out there somewhere, still alive?

"Carrie, I'm sorry," Janie cried contritely. "Until there is some final proof Robert is dead, I know you have to keep on hoping."

"Yes," Carrie agreed softly. The front door swung open and a blast of cold air announced her father's arrival. Carrie spun gratefully to meet him. Once all her guests were here, she would have no time to think of Robert.

"Sorry I'm late," Thomas called, shrugging out of his heavy coat and moving close to the fire. He held out his hands to the warmth, rubbing them together to restore the circulation. "Brutal out there," he muttered.

Carrie handed him a hot cup of coffee. "This should help." She gazed closely at her father. "You look angry."

Thomas scowled. "Lincoln has made a very grave error," he snapped.

Carrie contained a groan as she saw the lighthearted mood of her dinner party dissolving before it even started. She opened her mouth to inquire what Lincoln's current misdeed was, but was saved by the ringing of the bell. She hurried to answer the door.

"Matron Pember," she said warmly. "I'm so glad to see you. Please come in."

"Is it all right for my driver to wait inside?"

"Of course! It's too cold for anyone to be outside longer than is necessary. There is no need for him to come back for you." Carrie started to invite the driver in through the front door, then thought of her father. Stepping out onto the porch, she called, "Take your carriage around to the back. You can put your horse in the barn and go in through the back door. May will fix you something hot to drink."

"Thank you, ma'am," the driver said gratefully.

Thomas was helping Matron Pember off with her coat when Carrie stepped back inside. Moments later she heard a clatter of wheels as Pastor Anthony and Dr. Wild made their way to the house. Soon they too clustered around the fire warming themselves.

Pastor Anthony rubbed his hands briskly, then turned. "Happy New Year," he said, smiling.

Thomas spoke before anyone could say a word. "I do indeed wish it was a happy new year," he growled.

Dr. Wild was the first to respond. "Is something wrong, Mr. Cromwell?"

Thomas turned a look of disbelief on the doctor. "Surely you have heard about the Emancipation Proclamation! The whole city is in an uproar over it."

"Yes," Dr. Wild said carefully. "I've heard of it."

Carrie thought about trying to change the subject but she knew it would be futile. Until her father had vented his frustration, there would be no way to simply have a dinner party. She should have known it wasn't possible to pretend war wasn't affecting every area of their lives. She had read President Lincoln's document and she was thrilled such a huge step had been taken.

"Surely you know what the result of that heinous document is going to be!" Thomas fumed. "Why, there is going to be a slave insurrection such as we have never seen. The North has for all practical purposes invited millions of slaves to rise up while their masters are away. The South is soon to go through a reign of terror such as we've never imagined."

Carrie stared at her father, stunned by the fear in his voice. "Surely you don't think all the slaves are waiting for the time when they can kill the white people," she protested. "These people simply want to be free."

"You mark my words," Thomas responded sternly. "For years the South has feared uprisings such as the one Nat Turner led years ago. The same thing is going to happen again. All over the Confederacy."

An uncomfortable silence settled on the room. Carrie tried to think of some way to ease the tension.

Thomas turned to Pastor Anthony, "I'm sure you've heard plans being made by the coloreds you work with down by the river."

Pastor Anthony shook his head calmly. "I'm afraid most of the coloreds down by the river are simply interested in surviving the winter. They are thinking about food and staying warm. That seems to be all they can handle." He paused. "They're not alone. The whole city is under a terrible burden."

"Don't you understand what is going to happen soon?" Thomas demanded.

"It's not just that I don't understand it—I simply don't believe it. But I do think I understand why you're frightened."

"I'm not frightened," Thomas sputtered. "I'm furious that the North thinks they can try to destroy our country this way."

Carrie smiled to herself as Pastor Anthony merely nodded. Her respect and admiration for the pastor grew daily. She felt like strangling her father for being so blind. Pastor Anthony was giving him plenty of room to have his beliefs, while firmly disagreeing with him.

"I simply don't think most coloreds in the South have violent uprisings on their mind. I don't deny some have been driven to violence, but the vast majority of them simply want to lead their lives in freedom. They want to stay in their homes, remain in the South, but be able to dictate their own lives. My church down by the river is comprised mostly of free coloreds. They want the rest of their people to have what they have been able to claim for themselves. And they want for themselves, not only freedom, but equality." He paused. "Basically, all they want is what any of us would want if we were in their place."

The only sounds that could be heard in the room when Pastor Anthony finished were the crackling of the fire and the chiming of the clock.

"May I add something?" Dr. Wild asked.

"Please," Thomas responded.

"I can appreciate your views on slavery, Thomas, even though I don't personally agree with them. It seems to me, however, that Lincoln's proclamation is little more than a political move on his part. As long as the South remains in the hands of the Confederate military, there is little Lincoln can do to enforce his proclamation of freedom for slaves. There are millions of coloreds in the South who will be content to wait and see if the North wins the war. Only then will they begin to exercise the freedom Lincoln has granted them. If the South wins, I think life will pretty much go on as it has before."

"But so many of the slaves are running away!" Thomas stated angrily.

"Exactly," Dr. Wild said mildly. "Those slaves aren't looking to start an insurrection. They're trying to start a new life—in the North, where equality is a little easier to come by. The slaves who are determined to be free are going to run away—proclamation or not."

Thomas stared into the fire and barked a laugh. "To say I'm outnumbered here would be an understatement." His voice was not bitter, just resigned. He straightened. "Carrie, I'm sorry. I had no intention of spoiling your dinner party. I most certainly do not agree with your guests' feelings on slavery, but I have learned to accept yours. I can accept theirs as well." He paused. "I can also see what Dr. Wild is saying. Maybe my fear is not well founded. As long as the Confederate military continues to control the country, Lincoln has no way of enforcing this heresy."

Carrie was proud of her father. He was struggling with his beliefs and yet she also knew he was making a choice to be a gentleman in his home. "I think I hear May ringing the bell," she said with relief. "Why don't we all go in to dinner?"

Carrie stepped back to join Matron Pember. "I'm sorry things are a little tense," she said quietly.

"No need to apologize," Matron Pember replied. "I'm quite used to the passions sweeping our country. I see the results of it every day. I, too, experience some fear about what will happen if the coloreds truly become free, but I also realize it is inevitable. I'm afraid—by the very act of slavery—that we have put ourselves in a most unfortunate situation. I believe it will be the responsibility of the whites to ease the transition of the coloreds into our society, but I fear far too few of them will take up the challenge." She shook her head. "We are going to be in for a long period of storms, I'm afraid. The war is just the beginning."

Janie stepped forward to direct everyone to their seats.

"Let's pray," Thomas said. Everyone bowed their head as his voice rang through the room. "Our gracious Father, we need you to help make sense of the world we are living in. Thank you for your continual blessing and your supplying of our needs. May be find ourselves worthy of your love."

Carrie looked up as a quiet amen echoed through the room. "I want everyone to know the sweet potatoes were a gift from Janie's and my patients down by the river. It took great sacrifice on their part. I do hope you enjoy them."

There was silence for a few minutes as everyone began to eat. Carrie caught herself replaying her father's prayer over and over in her mind. She knew his faith was important to him. How could they both love God and still hold such opposing beliefs? *I love all my children* . . . The truth came as a gentle whisper in her heart. Love made room for opposing beliefs. Love was not confined to specific doctrines or church teachings. God may not like some of the things his children believed and did, but his love was big enough to encompass even that. And because he loved his children, he was never going to quit trying to show them truth. Carrie suddenly realized she was not big enough to understand God—how dare she judge the ones he had created? If he chose to love—could she do any less?

The truth smacked her hard in the face. She loved her father, but she had been judging him because he didn't share her beliefs. She had been feeling superior to him because her understanding was more advanced, more civilized than his. *I love all my children . . .* Carrie suddenly understood that God's love was not a love *in spite of*—it was a love that simply valued what he had created. Her arrogance left her humbled.

"Mr. Cromwell, may I ask you something?"

Thomas wiped his mouth with his napkin and smiled. "Certainly, Mrs. Pember. What is it?"

"I received a letter from my sister recently. You know she was banished to Ship Island, I suppose."

"Yes, Carrie told me Beast Butler was continuing his reign of terror in New Orleans," her father replied. "I was sorry to hear your sister has been adversely affected."

"Oh, she'll be all right," Matron Pember laughed. "I rather feel for the Union soldiers guarding her. I can assure you she has lost none of her spirit." She paused. "There was something in her letter I found rather curious, though. She has overheard some of the Federals talking. New Orleans is shipping out thousands of bales of cotton. From what she can tell they are not seized property. They seem to have been purchased from Louisiana planters. How is that possible? I understood no trade was allowed between the North and South."

Thomas sighed heavily. "I'm afraid that is a rather touchy issue. Even here in Richmond. I will make an attempt to explain what cannot really be explained." He paused for a long moment. "There is an age-old rule that one simply does not trade with the enemy in wartime. The issue becomes much more complicated in this present war. The North and the South are not foreign enemies, rather we are the estranged half of an economic whole. We have depended on each other for years. I'm afraid both sides are discovering that declaring war has not ended that interdependence."

"Which is why the South was so confident the North would not actually declare war on us?" Janie interjected.

"That's one of the reasons, Janie," Thomas agreed. "We believed the South depended on our cotton and tobacco too much to risk losing it."

"They don't appear to be losing it, if my sister's letter is right," Matron Pember observed.

"I'm afraid your sister's letter is correct," Thomas said heavily. "The necessity of exchange of goods between the North and South is an overwhelming economic force. Even though we're at war, we still have to have the other's goods." He grimaced. "The North needs our cotton, sugar, rice, and tobacco as desperately as we need their salt, clothing, and munitions."

"The North is selling arms to us?" Carrie gasped. "I find that difficult to believe."

"It's not that simple," Thomas replied. "They are providing us with many other goods. But no, with the exception of a few smuggled loads, the North is definitely not providing us with arms. At least not directly. Many of the planters, especially in New Orleans and Nashville, the two biggest occupied cities, are refusing to accept United States money for payment. They are accepting gold or nothing."

"I'm sure that makes some people hopping mad," Dr. Wild chuckled.

"You bet," Thomas agreed. "But most of the time they simply go along with it. The people operating the trading are so greedy for the huge profits they are reaping, they will give the planters whatever they demand. The planters, most very loyal to the Confederacy, are taking the gold and using it to buy arms. Boat loads are coming up from Nassau. I'm afraid without Yankee money our armies would be in much worse shape than they are now."

Carrie shook her head. "It just doesn't make any sense. The North is trying to destroy our armies in order to bring us back into the Union, yet they are providing us with the very things we need to keep fighting."

"War never makes sense," Pastor Anthony said thoughtfully. "But you're right. The whole situation seems ludicrous. Is President Davis aware of what is happening?"

Thomas laughed abruptly. "Oh, he's aware. He hates it as much as anyone, but there seems to be no way around it. I'm sure that somehow he hopes by keeping our armies strong we will eventually drive Yankee troops off our soil." He sighed. "The profits being made are phenomenal."

"By the extortionists?" Janie asked.

"Yes. Right now a sack of salt can be bought in New Orleans for a dollar and twenty-five cents. A trader can take it over to the other side of the lake still in Confederate territory and sell that same sack for sixty to one hundred dollars."

Pastor Anthony whistled. "That's a mark up of over six thousand percent!"

Thomas nodded grimly. "I don't believe a government has ever existed that could stop trade with a profit to be made like that. Especially when allowing it to continue yields certain benefits."

"How does the military feel about it?" Dr. Wild asked astutely.

"I'm sure the Confederate generals are a little confused. On one hand they are told to destroy all cotton they believe is being exported to the enemy. On the other hand, they are receiving memos advising discretion because it might be to their benefit to exchange produce for arms and ammunition." He snorted. "Secretary of War Randolph has stated that the Confederacy can violate its policy of keeping cotton out of Yankee hands, or it can risk the starvation of its armed forces."

"Is he right?" Matron Pember pressed.

"I'm afraid he is," Thomas said. "I'm afraid the reality is much the same here in Richmond. Our capital appears to be infested with Baltimore merchants who are importing huge quantities of goods from the North and selling them at incredible mark ups."

"Right here in Richmond?" Carrie gasped. "The people are suffering so much. How can the government allow that to happen? Most people cannot afford such prices!"

"It's not that simple," her father replied. "There seem to be only two choices. People can either pay exorbitant prices, or they can simply not have access to the goods. The blockade of the coast has affected Richmond severely. Combined with the influx of refugees, we simply cannot take care of the citizens without the Northern goods these men are bringing in."

"Is there any end to this madness in sight?" Janie asked, then held up her hand. "I don't expect anyone to be able to answer that question."

"It would seem to me that the South providing cotton to the North will ultimately lead to its own downfall, even if it is getting goods," Carrie said thoughtfully.

Thomas smiled slightly. "As usual, you are able to see things much more clearly than others. I'm afraid I agree with you. I believe that cotton, instead of contributing to our strength, may prove to be the greatest element of our weakness. I fear Yankee gold will accomplish what Yankee military strength might never—the subjugation of our people."

"People are only willing to suffer for so long," Pastor Anthony observed. "Especially when they don't really understand what they're suffering for anyway."

Thomas smiled halfheartedly, then picked up a piece of cornbread. "Do you think it might be possible to find a more pleasant topic of conversation?"

"Why don't we talk about the opening of the new theater?" Janie asked brightly. "I'm so glad they were able to rebuild after that disastrous fire. I understand the next show is going to be wonderful."

Carrie looked at her friend gratefully. She had so looked forward to the dinner party, but their conversation had left her deeply saddened. Now all she wanted was for her guests to leave so she could be alone. She vaguely registered the flow of conversation around her, but her insides were spinning and churning.

If only she could go back to Cromwell Plantation. Not to stay—just for a visit. She loved her work at the hospitals, but the crowded city was making her feel like a trapped animal. She was never alone—never had privacy. She longed for wide open spaces where she could breathe, where she could feel free.

Carrie smiled warmly at each of her guests as they prepared to leave. "Thank you so much for coming. Please be careful on the way home."

"What a nice evening," Janie said, closing the door.

"Yes." Carrie was thankful she had recovered from her dark mood enough to join in the chatter that had surrounded the table for the remainder of the evening.

Thomas walked up and wrapped his arm around her shoulders. "Carrie, I'm so sorry I started the evening out on such a sour note. I realize we are surrounded by trouble everywhere we turn. I should have been considerate enough to leave it out of the house for one night." He paused. "I like your friends very much. They seem like wonderful people."

"And I'm sure they feel the same way about you." Carrie smiled graciously, slipping her arm through his. "They've heard me brag about you often enough. I'm sure they realize you wouldn't have a daughter like me if you weren't a fair-minded man. Besides, I don't think they minded talking about it. It's just your daughter who sometimes wants to pretend the world isn't falling apart."

"I still feel badly," Thomas insisted. "I wish there were some way to make it up to you."

Carrie laughed and said, "Well . . . if you feel that way about it . . ." Was it really going to be so easy?

Thomas guffawed. "Why do I feel I just set myself up for something?" He moved over and sat down in a chair by the fire. "Okay, daughter. What is it you have up your sleeve?"

"I want you not to be upset when I tell you I want to go home for a few days. I want to go to the plantation. I need it," she added almost desperately. To her amazement, her father didn't look distressed. She knew how much he had worried about her before.

"I don't see any reason you shouldn't go," he said calmly. "I think it would be good for you. In fact, if I wasn't so busy at the Capitol I would go with you. This city is about to suffocate me."

"You understand?" Carrie cried.

"You are my daughter, aren't you? I watched you roam around that plantation free as a bird from the time you were a child."

"I need to feel free again."

"Yes. And you need your special place," Thomas said with a smile.

Carrie ran to him and threw her arms around him. "Thank you."

"You're welcome. Of course, I knew you'd be going anyway, whether I gave my permission or not. At least you don't have to carry the burden of thinking your father is worried sick about you." He paused. "I think you should take Janie with you. It will do her good to get out of the city, too. And I will feel much better if you have someone other than just Spencer along."

Carrie laughed again. "You were reading my mind," she accused playfully. Then she turned to Janie. "Will you go with me?"

Janie clapped her hands in delight. "I've been dying to see the plantation," she cried. "When do we leave?"

"We'll watch the weather. As long as there is not a lot of snow, the roads should be frozen enough to be passable."

"I can hardly wait," Janie proclaimed.

"I'm actually relieved you're going," Thomas said quietly. "I have heard plenty of horror stories about what the Union soldiers have done to the plantations. I would like to know what condition my home is in."

"You're going to freeze to death by that window if you don't come to bed," Janie chided from the protection of her own thick blankets. "You can't solve all the problems of the world tonight."

Carrie looked at her friend. "I know. It's just that I seldom see the city so quiet." More snow had started falling right after they had come up to bed. By the time they had chattered about their upcoming trip to the plantation, it was already several inches deep. She loved to watch the snow drift in lazy spirals, slowly dancing its way to the earth.

"What are you thinking about over there?"

"My father," Carrie said slowly. "I've been thinking about the Emancipation Proclamation. Dr. Wild was right. The only way for it to have any real impact is for the South to be defeated. I want the slaves to be free. If the South has to lose the war for it to happen— well—it just has to happen. But . . . "

"Your father is going to lose his way of life," Janie finished.

"Yes. Oh, I know he can rebuild the plantation and some of his people will choose to stay and work for wages. He can hire others as well. But his whole way of life is going to become extinct. He has worked so hard to preserve it. It's going to break his heart."

The dark clouds that had settled over America ceased their powerful advance. They hovered near the surface but the swirling and spinning stopped. What had been a chaotic dance was stilled into a careful watching. The first step had been taken that would cause their eventual retreat. In the broad scope of things the step was a tiny one—yet a step nonetheless. It was up to each person to let the spark ignited by Lincoln become a flame in their own heart. Only light would force the darkness away from the land.

～Thirty～

arrie was practically bouncing up and down on the seat when Spencer turned the carriage down the drive leading to the plantation. "We're here!" she crowed. Nothing seemed to have changed. The fields were snow covered. Their pristine beauty stretched as far as the eye could see, ending in a dark bank of trees on the horizon. Fluffy white clouds bounced through a vivid blue sky. A gentle breeze knocked tufts of snow off branches, their scattering flakes catching the sun in a dizzying dance of light. Carrie took deep breaths, feeling renewed.

"It's beautiful," Janie said, a touch of awe in her voice. "How could you ever stand to leave it?"

"You haven't seen anything yet!" Carrie leaned forward expectantly. "We should see the house in a minute." Her heart caught with a sudden fear. "I hope it's okay. What if it's gone? What if they've burned it? There may be none of my father's workers here." Her voice stuck in her throat. "I'm so looking forward to seeing Sam, Opal, and the kids. What if they're all gone?" Carrie had known she should be preparing for the worst, but her excitement the last two weeks had made it impossible.

"I'm just glad the weather finally cleared so you can get all your questions answered." Janie reached for Carrie's hand.

Carrie took it gratefully, squeezing it tightly. Her eyes were glued on the final curve. She would know in just a few minutes. Suddenly she was afraid to know. Turning her head away, she closed her eyes. Janie squeezed her hand tighter. Carrie still had her head turned away when her friend spoke.

"I wonder who owns that beautiful, three-story white home?" Janie asked in a teasing voice.

Carrie eyes flew open. "It's here. It's still here," she said softly. She was stunned by the surge of emotion that swept through her as she saw her home rise before her eyes. It stood, tall and elegant, banked by huge mounds of snow, the towering oaks surrounding it like frosted sentinels. "I'm home," she whispered. She made no attempt to wipe away the tears running down her face.

"Sure is a right nice place," Spencer said admiringly. "You reckon your daddy will need some help out here when we're all free and this war be over? I always thought working on a farm would be a mighty fine thing."

"I'm sure Father would find something for you, Spencer. He thinks very highly of you." Carrie had a hard time thinking past each day. Thinking ahead to when the war would be over was simply too much of a stretch for her. Right now all she wanted to do was enjoy being home again.

They were almost to the house when the big front door swung open and a tall figure stepped out onto the porch, shading his eyes against the bright sunshine.

Carrie leaped up, hanging onto the front seat of the carriage. "Sam!" she cried. "You're still here!"

Sam bent low to peer out at the carriage, then straightened with a shout. "Miss Carrie? That be you, Carrie girl?" He gave a yell of delight and turned to holler back into the house. "Miss Carrie be home!"

Carrie was out of the carriage before it had rolled to a complete stop. Seconds later she was wrapped in the old butler's arms. "Sam! It's so good to see you. I was afraid you were going to be gone."

"Don't figure I got nowhere to go better than here," Sam said, smiling. He held her out and looked her over. "I been wondering every day if you were able to get away from them Yankee soldiers. I reckon you did, sure nuff."

Carrie laughed and pulled away. "I have so much to tell you. But first . . . " Carrie beckoned to Janie and Spencer. "This is my dear friend Janie Winthrop. And this is Spencer. Please make sure he has a nice room."

"I reckon there be plenty of rooms, Miss Carrie. We don't seem to have a whole lot of company nowadays," Sam grinned. "You here to stay for good?"

"Just for a few days. I have to get back to the hospital." She saw the question in Sam's eyes. "I'll tell you everything. Just give me time."

All of them moved into the house, laughing and talking. Carrie had just reached to unbutton her coat when a shriek of delight sounded from the back of the house.

"Miss Carrie! I did hear Sam right. I thought I was imagining things. You're home. You're all right. Those soldiers didn't get you!" Opal dashed into the hallway and gave her a fierce hug.

Carrie hugged her hard, then stepped back. "I'm so glad to see you, Opal. I was afraid you would have taken the children and gone to the Contraband Camps."

Opal shook her head firmly. "The children and I are staying right here. We aren't leaving until this war ends and Eddie gets out of that prison. Besides, we're doing fine here. We're keeping the house nice and we got plenty to eat. From what I hear, we've got a lot more than those folks in the camps. I know we can go free anytime we want. Living here like this is like being free. It's fine for now. I've got the children to think about."

"The children are all right?"

"They're doing real fine. They still miss their momma and daddy, but they're growing like weeds with all this good food, and we're putting all your daddy's books to good use. Those are some mighty smart kids."

Carrie looked around. "Where are they?"

"I sent them out to tend to the pigs. Ain't too many, but the herd is growing again."

Carrie finally held up her hand. "I have a thousand questions, but I think we'd better bring our things in first."

"Spencer done went out to get them. You and Miss Winthrop just get yourselves warm," Sam said easily. "I know that had to be a mighty cold ride."

"Your home is so beautiful!" Janie exclaimed, walking over to caress the baby grand piano in the parlor. "Everything has been kept so nice."

Carrie turned to Sam. "You've done a wonderful job taking care of the place. Thank you." Her words were inadequate, but she knew Sam would be able to hear what her heart was really feeling. She gazed around. They had indeed done a splendid job. The house was just as she remembered it. Even the crystal chandelier was gleaming.

"Ain't nothing much to do around here," Sam said with a shrug. "Opal and the kids do a fine job keeping the place up."

"I was so afraid the Union soldiers would destroy it."

"They talked about it," Sam admitted. "They knew all about your daddy working with the government. That didn't sit too well with them. I heard 'em talking about what they were planning on doing to that Ruffin fella's place."

"They completely destroyed it. Even salted the fields," Carrie said sadly.

Sam grimaced. "Some of those soldiers were real mad when you got away from them. They came back in here snortin' and stompin'. Couldn't believe a girl had outwitted them!" he laughed. "A few of them were all for torching the place. I was plenty scared, I can tell you that."

"What stopped them?"

"Not what—it was who. That captain fellow. They called him Captain Jones. He said he ain't never seen nothing like you flying over that fence on Granite. That he was sure he saw blood on your shoulder, but still you just flew over that fence like a bird." He stopped for a moment. "They didn't shoot you, did they, Miss Carrie?"

"It was nothing," Carrie said casually. "Just a surface wound." She ignored Janie's look of disbelief. There was no reason to dwell on the past.

"That's good. Anyway," he continued, "that fella was so impressed he told his soldiers they couldn't touch one thing in the house. Said it was a tribute to your bravery. Those soldiers snorted and stomped some more, but all they did was take food. They didn't hurt one building on the place."

Carrie sagged in relief, suddenly realizing how tired she was from the long, cold ride.

"You go upstairs," Sam said. "I'll send one of the kids up with some hot water. I bet you and Miss Winthrop could use a warm bath."

"That would be wonderful," Janie sighed. "I think even my blood is frozen."

Carrie led the way up the stairs, collapsing on the bed as soon as she reached her room. "It feels so good to be home."

Janie gazed around the room curiously. "How *did* you get away from the Union soldiers? I've heard you tell the story a million times, but you never explained how you did it. There's no way out of this room." She walked to the window and looked out. "Surely you didn't climb out the window."

Carrie merely smiled mischievously. "It's a Cromwell secret," she said in a hushed whisper.

"You won't even tell *me*?" Janie said pleadingly. Then she laughed. "That's okay. Far be it from me to pry into family secrets. I'm simply glad you escaped unharmed."

Carrie knew she meant it. "I want to show you a special mirror," she said, jumping up from the bed. "My great-great-grandfather brought it over on the boat when he and my great-great-grandmother came to America. It stayed in its box until he had carved a home out of the wilderness. It's been in this exact spot ever since."

"How beautiful," Janie murmured. "It seems odd, though."

"What?"

"That a mirror like this should be in a bedroom. You would think something this beautiful and elaborate would be in a prominent place downstairs."

"That's what my mother thought, too," Carrie chuckled. "She tried to get my father to move it for years. He refused."

"Because of tradition?"

"Well, it was a little more than that," Carrie teased.

Janie looked confused. "I'm afraid I don't understand."

"I didn't either. Not for a long time. The mirror was simply a beautiful thing I confided my secrets to. I didn't realize it held a secret all of its own." Leaning over she ran her fingers lightly along the edge of the frame. Finally she found what she was looking for—a slender handle concealed by the frame—and tugged. Slowly the mirror swung out to reveal a gaping hole.

"Oh, my!" Janie gasped, her eyes wide. She moved forward slowly to peer into the dark hole. "*This* is how you got away from the soldiers."

Carrie grinned and told her the detailed version of her escape. "Moses saved my life. Or at least my honor," she added in a grim voice.

Janie was still staring at the hole, shaking her head in disbelief. "What an incredible place. It's like something you'd read about in a book—only it's real."

Carrie heard approaching footsteps and quickly closed the mirror door.

"Thank you for sharing your secret," Janie said quietly. "You can trust me to keep it."

"I know," Carrie said calmly as she moved toward the door, flinging it open. "Susie," she said warmly. "It's so good to see you again." Fannie's eldest daughter was becoming a beautiful young woman.

"Thank you, Miss Cromwell. It's nice to see you, too." Susie spoke with a quiet confidence. She nodded to Janie. "It's good to have you, Miss Winthrop." She turned back to Carrie. "I've brought you some hot water. There's more on the way." She paused. "It's good to have you back. This has been a wonderful home for us . . . until our daddy gets out of prison."

"The war has to end sometime," Carrie said encouragingly.

"Yes, ma'am. I just hope the North wins this war. If the South wins, my daddy could spend the rest of his life in prison." Nodding slightly, she turned away and retreated down the hall.

Carrie watched her go. The girl carried burdens much too heavy for her young shoulders. Of course, the whole country was carrying heavy burdens lately.

"She's a very beautiful girl," Janie said admiringly.

"Yes. She has been through so much. I'm glad to see no bitterness in her eyes. She just seems to have matured."

"Hard times can either make you or break you," Janie said thoughtfully. "I've seen some people come through hard times so much stronger and wiser—and more compassionate. I've seen other people become hardened and bitter."

"I pray every day that won't happen to me," Carrie whispered.

"Your heart is too tender to ever become hardened," Janie said firmly.

"I hope so," Carrie responded. Sometimes she wasn't so sure. There were so many times she yearned not to feel any more hurt. "I hope so," she repeated, wondering if she really meant it. Lately, she found herself trying to push pictures of Robert out of her mind. If she didn't think about him so much, surely she wouldn't hurt so badly. If she only made room for the present, perhaps the past would go away. Carrie felt herself clutching at the wall forming around her heart.

A knock came at the door, pulling Carrie from her thoughts. She hauled in the second bucket of hot water. Soon both she and Janie were luxuriating in the warm baths, allowing the hours of cold travel to be soothed away. A crackling fire sent fingers of warmth into the room, wrapping Carrie in a blanket of comfort. She laid her head back against the tub with a contented sigh and watched the glow of golden flames chase black shadows across the ceiling. The gentle breeze had turned into a stiff wind, making the windowpanes rattle in protest. Carrie sank deeper into the water and closed her eyes.

"Opal, you've prepared a feast!" Janie cried.

"She's right," Carrie said gratefully. "How did you pull this off so quickly?"

"It's not anything like you're used to eating around here," Opal protested, laughing.

"You don't know how fortunate you are to be on the farm," Carrie said seriously. "The food shortages in the city are becoming quite severe. Many people are going hungry and winter is hardly over."

"You going hungry, Miss Carrie?" Sam asked, frowning.

"No," she hastened to assure him. "Our diet is repetitive but we have enough. Thankfully my father still has money to pay the exorbitant prices. I just hurt for the other people."

"I wonder how Pastor Anthony is," Opal said. "I hate to think of that good man suffering."

"Pastor Anthony is doing extremely well," Carrie smiled at Opal's look of astonishment, then told about her and Janie's work in the hospital.

"I declare," Opal said wonderingly. "The Lord do know how to make all the pieces fit together, don't he?"

"That he does," Sam interjected. "The piece I'm interested in right now is getting this meal eaten while it's still hot."

Carrie laughed and slipped into her seat. "I won't argue with that bit of wisdom." She gazed hungrily at the ham and sweet potatoes. Mounds of corn bread were piled on a platter, with a pitcher of buttermilk resting beside it. A bowl of hot green beans was sending wafts of steam into the air. "I haven't eaten like this in months."

"If I'd known we'd be eating like this, I'd have made you bring me out here months ago," Janie laughed.

Carrie was working on her last piece of cornbread when she finally asked, "How are you doing this? I thought the Yankees took everything. The vegetables I can understand, but what about the ham and milk?"

Sam grinned. "Them soldiers done took everything, but they had a hard time controlling all them animals. Some of the pigs and cows they took just plumb didn't want to cooperate. I was out in the woods a couple of weeks after they came through and found a couple of pigs and a good-sized heifer roaming around. I didn't recognize 'em as being Cromwell stock, but I didn't reckon anybody else was gonna find 'em. Them pigs already gave us a good-sized litter, and that cow turned out to be a momma."

"He even found a bull roaming around out there," Opal laughed. "Now don't go gettin' the idea we're eating ham on a regular basis— but we put one aside for when you or your daddy come home." She paused. "He know about what you did yet?"

"With all the slaves? He knows." Carrie grew thoughtful. "I'm sorry I lied to him as long as I did, but I don't regret my actions. He's grateful to all of you who have chosen to stay and keep the place up, but he knows I've told everyone they can go."

"And he ain't real mad?" Sam asked incredulously.

"Well," Carrie smiled. "He wasn't real happy, but he realizes more and more slaves are simply walking off from plantations all over the South."

"Especially since the Emancipation Proclamation," Sam said proudly.

"You know about that?" Janie asked in astonishment.

"The grapevine works real well out here. It be the only way we had to communicate for a long time."

"And yet you chose to remain?" Janie asked.

"Yes, ma'am," Sam said firmly. "Now that my people be free, I reckon we can do whatever we want. I want to be a butler, and I like being here just fine. I reckon when this war be over Mr. Cromwell still gonna need a butler. I'll just be being paid for it—that's all."

"How are others in the area feeling about it?" Carrie asked.

"Oh, they's feeling different things. Some are just crazy with happiness—making all kinds of plans for what they gonna do. Others be plenty scared. They ain't never known nothing but somebody takin' care of them. They've gotten real used to it. The idea of being on their own is makin' them right nervous. And I guess some just ain't feelin' nothing. They figure they ain't free till this war be over—they ain't gonna get in a tizzy about it now."

"What are you going to do, Opal?"

"I'm going to be taking care of these children, Miss Carrie. Least till Eddie gets out of prison. Even then I figure he'll need some help with them. And I aim to start a restaurant," she said firmly.

Susie walked in with a hot sweet potato pie. "Opal is one of the best cooks I've ever seen. I think she'll do real well."

Opal reddened. "I'm hoping I'll do all right. I don't reckon there's anything else I want to do."

"Where would you open this restaurant?" Janie asked.

Opal shrugged. "I've always dreamed about going north, but the South is my home. I'm just not so sure I want to stay down here. That paper Lincoln signed may make all the slaves free, but that don't mean white people aren't going to see them as anything but niggers," she said contemptuously. Her voice grew thoughtful. "I reckon I want to live where I got the greatest chance of other folks seeing me as a person. Just a woman who wants to make her living cooking. I guess I'll figure it out when that time comes."

"How you think your daddy is going to take to not having a passel of slaves?" Sam asked.

Carrie shook her head. "I don't know, Sam. It's all he's ever known. I know owning slaves is wrong, but my father is not a bad man."

"I know that for sure," Sam said quickly.

Carrie smiled. "There's no telling what the South will be like when this war is over. So much has already changed. I don't think my father holds much hope that he'll be coming back to the way things were before the war started." She paused. "Sometimes people are so caught up in what is happening right now they simply have no time to worry about the future. And then sometimes the future looks so grim you convince yourself what you wish for could never really happen. The only way to know how you'll respond is to be in the middle of it with nothing to do *but* respond." She laughed shortly. "Am I making any sense at all?"

"Yes, ma'am," Sam answered. "The future be too dark for your daddy to see too clear, so he just ain't looking too hard right now."

Carrie laughed. "I wish I could see things as perceptively as you."

"It's always easier to see other folk's lives clear. What's hard is trying to figure out your own. That's when the seein' gets hard."

"Amen," Janie said softly. "It's easy to *think* you'd know how you would respond to a certain situation—being in the middle of it is a different story."

"I reckon it's like living in this house," Sam said slowly, almost reluctantly. "I always thought white people were evil for wanting to own slaves. Now, I don't own any slaves," he said quickly, "but I'm kinda the head slave around here. I get to live in this here house. I get to tell all the other slaves what to do. I'm always warm and dry and I eat whatever I want to. I don't got to answer to anybody when it's just me and the slaves here." He paused for a long moment.

Carrie gazed at him thoughtfully. It took a lot of courage for Sam to be so honest.

"I reckon if I was a white man," he continued, "I would be a slave owner. I hate to think that way, but I see how much I like being in control. I guess it's just a human thing to want to have power over other folks." He shook his head heavily. "I reckon what I'm trying to say is that it's real easy to judge folks when you ain't in their shoes. But all of a sudden, when you there, you realize you'd do the same thing." He sighed. "I ain't proud of it, but it be the truth. It makes me understand Marse Cromwell a whole lot better."

A long silence fell on the room. Opal was the first to break it. "I reckon I know what you mean. You remember Gilbert Hunt, that man who saved so many white folks during the theater fire so many years back?"

Carrie nodded. "Miles told me about him one day when we were in Richmond. He was a slave, but he finally was able to buy his freedom. Doesn't he own a blacksmith shop down in the black part of the city?"

"Yep. But that ain't all he owns. That man owns slaves."

"A colored man with slaves?" Janie gasped. "How can he do that?"

"I reckon it's like what Sam said. He had the chance to have power over someone and he took it. I've heard about several coloreds who own slaves. I couldn't believe it at first. Those people had come out of slavery themselves. They knew how bad it was. They worked hard to buy their own freedom—or their folks before them did." Opal paused. "I don't reckon owning slaves is a white thing. I reckon it's a power thing. People want someone else to make life easier for them—even if it means stealing someone's freedom." She shook her head. "Anyway, it's made it a lot easier for me not to hate white folks. I figure if coloreds had been the first ones to America, they might have brought white people over as their slaves."

Susie passed out slices of pie. Everyone was silent as they contemplated the complexities of humanity. The wintry wind battered the house, bringing with it a fresh, white blanket of snow.

Carrie was up early the next morning. The snow clouds had once more been driven north. She wrapped a thick bathrobe over her gown, added several fresh logs to the fire, and stepped over to the window. "Oh, my goodness!" she exclaimed, sucking her breath in sharply.

"Is something wrong?" Janie asked anxiously.

"Come look," Carrie invited. She wasn't sure she had ever seen such a gorgeous sunrise. Great purple and orange clouds, arranged in fluffy waves, spread across the entire sky. The blanket of snow caught the splendid colors and sent them shooting back. Great white banks covered everything, only the dark green tops of the boxwoods revealing the life that lay below. Great tufts of snow clung to the branches of the large cedars guarding the side of the house, causing the tender branches to bend almost all the way to the ground.

"It's beautiful," Janie whispered in an awestruck voice.

The two friends stood side by side until the magnificent colors had faded to a muted pink, and blue snatches began to gain dominion of the sky.

"You're shivering," Carrie said suddenly.

Janie laughed. "I guess so. I didn't put my bathrobe on." She turned and dove for her bed.

Carrie quickly laid more logs on the fire. Soon the room took on a pleasant warmth.

"What are you doing?" Janie asked a few minutes later, her covers pulled tight under her chin.

Carrie glanced over and laughed. "You look like a chipmunk peeking out of its burrow."

"I'm a warm chipmunk," Janie retorted. "Why are you pulling all those clothes out of your closet?"

"I want to be warm when I go riding."

Janie gasped. "You're going riding? Horseback riding? In this weather? Are you crazy?"

"I guess the answer is yes to all questions," Carrie said calmly. "I will hardly freeze to death." Suddenly she stopped pulling clothes out of the closet. "I'm going to make sure I don't freeze to death," she said firmly. "I'll be right back." Janie was still staring at her over the edge of her covers when she dashed out of the room. Soon she was back, her arms loaded with warm clothing.

"Those look like your father's clothes," Janie observed.

"They are." She undressed and began to pull on several layers.

"You're going to wear your father's clothes?"

At the long-suffering tone in Janie's voice, Carrie grinned. It was not a tone of disapproval, more one of resignation. "I learned the night I escaped the plantation that riding in men's clothing is much more comfortable than riding in women's. And it will be warmer."

Janie stuck one arm out of the covers. Once she was convinced the room had warmed up, she jumped out of bed and moved close to the fire. "As long as you're not planning on wearing them to the hospital."

Carrie laughed. "I'm not ready to create that much of a scene."

"Where are you going?"

Carrie was suddenly reluctant to share her secret. Janie was a dear friend—someday she wanted to take her to her special place. But today she needed to be alone. She didn't know how to answer the question. "I just need to get outside," she finally said, knowing from the look on Janie's face that her friend was aware that she was hiding something. Janie smiled, seeming to understand.

Impulsively, she gave Janie a big hug. "I love you."

"I love you, too," Janie responded. "Are you sure you're not going to get lost in all this snow?"

"I know this plantation like the back of my hand. I could never get lost." Carrie said reassuringly. "I'll be back before lunch."

Max twisted his head and looked at Carrie curiously when she heaved a saddle onto his big sturdy back. "I know, fella. You're not used to being ridden. But I promise it's a lot easier than pulling that carriage. I think you might actually have fun today." She laughed when the horse continued to stare at her. "Look, you're all I have. All my father's horses were taken by the Union army, and Granite is gone." Sudden tears blurred her vision as she thought of Granite. Quickly she brushed them away. Remembering wasn't going to do any good. Her horse was gone. Robert was gone. It was time to face it, time to let the past go.

That was the purpose of her trip to her special place. Only there—in the shelter of her secret haven—would she have the courage to do what she needed to do.

It took her only a few minutes to get Max ready. She smiled as she remembered the look on Spencer's face when she'd told him she was going for a ride. He obviously thought she was crazy but had bitten his tongue to keep from saying so. Sam had merely chuckled and told her to eat plenty before she left. He was used to her independence.

Carrie sighed in delight as she settled into the saddle. With the exception of the night of her escape, she had always ridden sidesaddle. That one experience had convinced her that those days were over—unladylike or not. Riding astride was so much more comfortable and enabled her to feel so much more in rhythm with her horse. Resolutely she pushed away the images of Granite that kept rising up to haunt her. Those days were over. She needed to harden her heart and press on to the future.

"Let's go, Max."

Max snorted and pranced forward, obviously delighted not to have a carriage behind him. He pawed at the snow, causing great sprays of white to float into the air, then snorted and shook his head.

"I know it's fun, but we'll get where we're going a lot faster if you'll quit playing," Carrie ordered with a laugh. She pushed him forward firmly. Max shook his head again, then settled into a ground-eating walk, the snow reaching just a few inches short of his knees. Soon the plantation house was out of sight, swallowed by the white snow.

Carrie gazed around, reveling in the fresh sense of freedom she felt. Suddenly she threw back her head and laughed loudly. Great wisps of steam shot from her mouth as her laugh echoed across the fields. A rabbit bounding through the snow stopped long enough to give her a curious look, then disappeared into its hole. Brilliant red cardinals and noble-looking bluejays lent the only flashes of color to the endless landscape of white and gray. A brilliant sun reflected diamonds of light off the snow, almost blinding her, while giving an incredible sense of clarity to the entire scene.

Carrie was glad—so glad she had come! She could feel the horrors of the hospital melting away, swallowed by the vastness of God's magnificent creation. She was impatient to get to her special place, but she wouldn't push Max. He had a long way to go through deep snow.

Over an hour later, Carrie found the break in the woods she was looking for. There was no trail. She didn't need one. Carefully she guided Max through the maze of trees, allowing him to go slowly so he wouldn't trip over a hidden log. Finally she broke out into the clearing. Thankful she'd worn her father's tall boots, she slipped out of the saddle, fed Max a couple carrots, looped his reins over a low-lying branch, then turned to stare out at the river. Great tears rose in her eyes and rolled down her cheeks.

"I'm here," she murmured. "I'm here." Carrie had wondered many times if she would ever be able to return to this special place. Slowly she walked toward the river, brushed a thick layer of snow off her boulder, and settled down. Warm tears continued their course down her cheeks.

Suddenly she caught herself and wiped her tears away. "Fine way to develop a hard heart," she said scornfully, taking a deep breath to regain control. Cupping her chin in her hand, she gazed out at the river. The unusually cold winter had formed great chunks of ice. Beyond the frozen shoreline she could see them bobbing, their creamy whiteness in stark contrast with the blue-gray of the water. Snow embraced the river, seeming to part just enough to allow the mighty waters to continue their journey to the bay. The whole world seemed to be a study in white and gray.

A commotion behind her caused her to turn quickly. Max had grown tired of standing still and was pawing, his giant hooves sending snow flying all around in a cloud of white. He had quite a satisfied expression on his face when he finished. Then he bent his head and snorted in pleasure.

"What did you find, boy?" Carrie's curiosity made her stand and move over to look.

Max didn't wait for her approval. Giving another snort of satisfaction, he reached down and tore off a thick mouthful of the green grass he had uncovered.

Carrie stared at the grass in amazement. To be sure, it wasn't the verdant green of summer, but it still held a definite tint of green. Somehow it had survived under its covering of snow, waiting for spring to uncover it and set it free once more.

Spring will come.

Carrie frowned. Of course spring would come. It did every year—no matter how hard the winter.

Spring will come.

The thought clung to her like a lifeline. Carrie watched thoughtfully as Max tore into the grass he had uncovered. When he had eaten all that was there, he started pawing again. Once he had unearthed more, he settled down to eating again.

Spring will come.

Suddenly Carrie understood. No matter how long or hard the winter, new life was waiting just below the surface. Her decision to harden her heart had pronounced winter on her soul—on her very life. There could be no growth, no new life, as long as she let the cold hardness of her heart block it out. Only by allowing God to melt it, to take away its protective covering, could she find the new life it was hiding.

There is always life beneath the snow.

Carrie saw it now. There would always be new life beyond the pain. But only if she allowed the new life to surface. Only if she let down the stone walls to let it in. The walls she was building to protect her heart were doing nothing but blocking out the new life God had to offer.

Carrie bent down slowly and picked a blade of grass Max had missed, then turned back to her boulder. Holding it tightly she lifted it to her lips. "Oh God . . . " The groaning in her soul was at once an expression of pain and a relinquishment of the walls she had built. Tears poured from her eyes as she grasped the slender blade of grass.

Memories of Robert—of all their special moments—roared through her mind. She felt the familiar ache, but this time there was something different. The memories brought a healing. It was as if the hurt was helping to cleanse her, burning away the chaff that had choked her growth—had choked the new life waiting just on the other side. The fire roared hotter as it swept over the walls, fed by the breeze of new life.

Finally the tears stopped. Carrie gave a final gulp, then blew her nose. Carefully she slipped the tiny blade of grass into her pocket. Whenever she was tempted to hide from life behind walls, she would pull it out as a reminder. Her heart was suddenly light. The questions still remained. The pain lurked on the horizon. But she would face them.

Spring would come.

Thirty-One

"Are you sure that's all you want to take?" Janie asked. "How in the world did you develop such a huge stock of herbs?"

Carrie's gaze swept the hundreds of bottles lining the shelves in the basement. "There wasn't much else to do the long winter I spent here before I came to Richmond. I spent hours down here every day. Something was driving me to do it."

"And yet you're only taking back that bag full?"

Carrie held up the large bag she had stuffed full and shrugged. "There's really not room for any more," she said regretfully. "I want to make sure I have some if someone in our house falls ill. Medicine is so hard to come by. I would take it all back if I could, but it just isn't possible this trip. Maybe I'll be able to come back this summer when we can bring a wagon out here."

She turned away from the shelves. "We'd better get going. I think Sam is right. There's another snowstorm on the way. Father will worry himself sick if we're not back by tonight."

The good-byes were brief but heartfelt. Sam, Opal, the kids, and the rest of the slaves still down in the quarters stood on the porch and waved until they were out of sight.

"What a wonderful place," Janie said fervently. "I will miss it. I know we're needed in Richmond, but I would love to stay here."

Carrie nodded thoughtfully. A few days ago she would have said the same thing. Now she was ready to face what Richmond held for her.

"What happened that day?" Janie asked suddenly.

Carrie smiled. She knew what day Janie was referring to. She groped for words to explain it. She knew Janie had been yearning to ask ever since she had returned from her special place.

"I'm not trying to pry," Janie said. "It's just that you seem so different."

"You're not prying. I'm not sure how to explain it." Carrie paused. "You said the night we got here that hard times can either make or break a person. I was very close to allowing them to break me." She stopped again. "I guess I'm just trying to grow up."

Janie nodded understandingly and reached for her hand underneath the thick layer of blankets Sam had tucked around them.

The snow was already several inches thick when Spencer finally drove the carriage into the barn. "I reckon I'll be headed home now," he said wearily. "Soon as I get Max here taken care of."

"Not until you've had some good, hot food," Carrie said firmly, trying to control her own shivering. "You take care of Max. I'll tell May to prepare you something to eat."

"Thank you, Miss Carrie," Spencer murmured, rubbing his hands together. "I'll be in shortly."

Micah was waiting just inside the back door when Carrie and Janie entered, stomping their feet to rid them of the clinging snow. Carrie took one look at him and frowned. "What's wrong?" she asked anxiously.

"There's been an outbreak of smallpox, Miss Carrie," he said soberly, then hesitated. "There's lots of people in the city who done got it."

Carrie's heart caught. "My father?"

"He's real sick," Micah admitted.

"How long?" Carrie asked sharply.

"Since the day after you left."

Carrie groaned. "What did the doctor say?"

Micah shrugged. "He wanted your father to go into the hospital, but of course he refused. Said if there was no treatment he would rather take his chances at home." He paused. "Is there really no treatment for smallpox?"

"I'm afraid not, Micah. At least not any commonly accepted treatment." She turned to May. "Please fix Spencer something hot to eat. He's freezing and exhausted." Then she turned to Micah. "I'm going up to check on my father. If you could fix some hot tea and bring it up, I would appreciate it."

"I'll bring it right up, Miss Carrie."

Carrie turned and ran up the stairs. Smallpox! She knew too well the dreaded effects of the disease. The patient first developed a high fever and horrible body aches. Two to four days later a rash resembling thousands of small pimples would appear on the face before spreading to other parts of the body. During the next week the pimples became larger and filled with pus until they finally scabbed over. Then the scabs would fall off in three to four weeks, leaving scars.

Her father was awake when she entered the room. "Hello, Father," she said gently, trying not to show any reaction to his flushed face, already covered with the rash.

"I'm glad you're home," Thomas said weakly. "I'm sorry this isn't much of a homecoming."

Carrie moved forward and laid her hand on his forehead. It was burning hot. Quickly she turned to Janie who had followed her up. "Please have Micah bring in buckets of snow. Then bring my bag of herbs to me."

She turned back to her father. "You can hardly run the government like this," she teased.

"Well, if you can give me a hard time, you must not be too afraid I'm going to die," Thomas replied hopefully.

"You're going to be miserable for several weeks, but you're going to be okay. Your fever is high but you still have a spark in your eye. I'm glad you chose not to go the hospital. There is nothing they can do for you there, and you would merely have been exposing yourself to even more infection. Home is the best place for you right now."

"I was afraid you would be angry," Thomas said sheepishly.

Micah stepped in with a huge tub of snow. Janie was right behind him with Carrie's bag. Carrie opened it quickly, heaving a sigh of relief as she pulled out several smaller bags bulging with cloves of garlic. "I'm just glad I've been to the plantation. I have everything I need to treat you right here. We'll have to let the disease run its course, but these will help with some of the symptoms at least." Digging deep she pulled out a bag labeled *Boneset*.

"What's that?" Janie asked curiously, watching over her shoulder.

"Aunt Sarah called it gravelroot. It's a combination of dried flowers and leaves. The roots are used for something else. Boneset is good for high fevers. I'll make a tincture out of it."

"How do you make that there tincture stuff?" Micah queried.

"It's not hard," Carrie smiled. "I'll steep the dried herbs in a mixture of vodka and water. The alcohol extracts the active ingredients, as well as acting as a preservative. I'll give Father five drops several times a day until the fever goes away."

"And the garlic?" Janie asked. "I thought it was good for coughs."

"Aunt Sarah called garlic the miracle herb. I think she was right. There is very little it's not good for. I'm going to mash the fresh cloves and rub them directly on the sores. It will keep them from getting too infected and may help with the scarring."

"I'm afraid no one will want to get near me," Thomas replied with a weak smile. "I should smell just lovely." Then he frowned. "Is my being home going to put all of you in danger?"

Carrie shrugged. "Smallpox is a very infectious disease, but Aunt Sarah taught me about a herb that helps you resist infection. Thankfully I brought some of it. It's called purple coneflower. I'll make a decoction of it by simmering the herbs in water for one hour. I would like everyone in the house to drink a half cup of the brew three times a day. It will have to be made fresh daily," she said firmly. "We'll just deal with new cases if they happen."

Quickly sne told Micah how to wet a towel in the snow and then hold it to her father's head. "I'll be back up in a few minutes. I've got to make the treatments."

Janie was silent until they reached downstairs. "I wonder if this winter is ever going to end. People are freezing and hungry already. Now they have to deal with an outbreak of smallpox."

Carrie nodded heavily. "Many people are going to die. They simply won't have the strength to deal with the disease. Father is one of the fortunate ones." She stepped to the window and stared out at the swirling snow. "Spring will come," she said softly.

Robert stared at his leg, willing it to move as Polly performed the exercises once again. Amber stirred the rags around in the hot water, waiting to cover his legs with them.

"You feel anything?" Amber asked excitedly.

Robert had grown used to Amber's continual question. At first it had irritated him because the answer was always no. Finally he had seen it as evidence of her undying hope and had been able to appropriate his own hope from it. He shook his head calmly. "Not yet, Amber."

"That's okay, Robert," she said brightly. "It's gonna be any day now."

It was a ritual that was as familiar as the sun rising. Robert took comfort from it. Polly and Amber were determined—he would be too.

After Polly finished the exercises, she pulled the covers up over his legs. "I reckon that'll take care of it for now. I'll fix us some lunch."

Robert nodded and gazed out the window. Dark clouds portended yet another snowstorm. He had never seen so much snow in one winter. Automatically he reached for the pole over his head. Still staring out at the snow, he lifted himself fifty times before finally relaxing back against his pillow. His upper body had grown quite strong. Now if his lower body would just cooperate.

Robert's thoughts drifted to Carrie. His love for her grew every day. Every time he looked at his legs he saw evidence he would never walk again, but the hope Amber instilled in him helped him deny that fact. If his heart could be so completely changed, surely he would walk some day. He smiled slightly, reveling in the lightness he felt. The miracle of it amazed him. Gone was the heavy burden of hate and bitterness. In its place was a peace that defied his understanding.

He yearned to share the newness of his heart with Carrie, to let her know he was alive. It had been five long months since the battle of Antietam. She must surely believe him dead. A dark thought taunted him. He tried to push it away, yet it persisted. What if Carrie had found someone else? He knew there were any number of men who would jump at the chance to be her husband. Had Carrie given up hope and turned to someone else? He shook his head firmly. Carrie wasn't like that. Even if she did believe he was dead, she would not give up her love for him so easily. That he was confident of.

"Will you read to me, Robert?"

Robert turned away from the window and smiled at Amber. "Sure, honey. What are we reading today?" This was another of their daily rituals.

Amber crawled up on the bed and handed him a book. "My daddy brought this home last night. He said it had a lot of big words in it."

"This is *The Last of the Mohicans*!" Robert said in astonishment.

"Is it good?"

"Sure it's good but . . . "

"But what?" Amber asked innocently.

"But it's an adult book. I'm afraid it might be over your head. I'm not sure how much of it you'll understand."

Amber leaned close and pulled his head down. "That's okay," she whispered in his ear. "I like it when you read anything to me, but this one is really for momma. She likes it when you read, too."

Robert smiled, opened the book and began to read. Amber snuggled in close to his side and closed her eyes to listen. Within a few minutes he could tell she was sound asleep. Robert glanced at Polly sitting by the fire and continued to read.

Robert woke the next morning to water dripping from the roof of the cabin.

Gabe came stomping in just moments later. "There's the nicest warm breeze you could ever imagine blowing out there. I reckon it's time for our false spring."

Robert knew what he meant. Every year, usually in February, winter took a deep breath and let spring creep into its territory. The air flow would turn southerly, bringing in soft, warm breezes. Snow would melt, birds would sing, and people would eagerly plan their spring gardens. When winter had teased the earth just long enough, it would let its breath back out, blasting the world with cold air and more snow. But the damage would have been done. The longing in people's hearts for the new life of spring would expand and grow stronger, till finally winter gave up and retreated until the next year.

Robert gazed out the window, wishing with all his heart he could feel the breeze. How he longed for fresh air and warm sunshine to touch his face. He had lived most of his life outdoors. All the months of confinement and inactivity had been unbearably hard.

Gabe swung the door open and propped it back with a chair. "Time for some fresh air," he said cheerfully. Then he laughed. "Think I can't read a man's face, Robert? I know how I'd feel if I'd been cooped up in that bed so long."

Robert's heart swelled with gratitude. "Thank you," he said softly. He lay back against the pillows, luxuriating in the fresh breeze bathing his face. He closed his eyes, enjoying the moment.

"Can I come up there with you, Robert?" Knowing he would give permission, Amber clambered up. "I'm gonna feel spring with you!" she chirped.

Robert smiled but didn't open his eyes. His mind had transported him back to the spring day he and Carrie had taken the packet boat *The John Marshall* up the river. A soft breeze had been blowing, warm sunshine had bathed the deck of the boat, and a band had played music while they danced. He could hear the music so clearly in his mind. As Carrie laughed and spun, he tapped his foot in time to the music.

"Robert!" Amber screamed.

Robert jolted forward. "What's wrong?" he asked sharply.

Gabe came dashing back into the cabin. Polly spun away from the fire, her eyes wide with fright.

"Your foot!" Amber screamed again. "I saw your foot move. Under the covers there!" She was so excited her words all ran together.

Polly approached them. "That so, Robert?"

Robert just stared at his feet. "I don't know," he said slowly. Polly reached down and pulled the covers back. Robert stared at his feet, willing them to move again. Nothing. With a sinking heart he realized Amber must have imagined it.

Amber read his mind. "I saw it move," she insisted. "I know I did." She paused. "You was smiling right before your foot moved."

"What were you thinking about?" Polly pressed.

"Dancing with Carrie," Robert admitted. His mind drifted back to the very real memory. "We were on a boat on the James River. We were dancing to band music."

"There!" Amber screamed again. "It moved! Did you see it move, momma?"

Robert shot a look at Polly. Her eyes were wide, and she was nodding her head. Robert stared at his feet again. He could feel nothing.

"Hum that tune, Robert," Polly commanded. "The one you and Carrie danced to."

Robert's heart was pounding so hard now he was having a hard time breathing. Taking a deep breath he began to hum softly.

"Louder!" Amber begged.

Robert complied. The sound of his humming filled the cabin and spilled out into the morning air. He saw it before he actually felt it. Then from somewhere deep inside, the sensation filtered into his brain. He stared at his right foot, hardly able to believe it as he watched it keep time with the music. He watched in wordless amazement as the withered muscles in his right leg moved and contracted.

"Thank you, Jesus!" Polly cried, grabbing Amber up into her arms and spinning around the room, great tears rolling down her cheeks.

Clint dashed into the cabin, obviously alarmed by all the commotion. "What's going on in here?" he cried.

"Robert done moved his foot," Polly exulted. "He done moved his foot. The Lord done give us a miracle!"

Robert stared at her, the reality of what was happening finally sinking in. A smile exploded on his face, even while tears blurred his vision. He had held on to hope for so long. Was it possible he would really walk again?

"Where'd Daddy go?" was all Clint said.

"He went after Auntie JoBelle," Polly said happily. "She just ain't gonna believe this!"

Robert brushed away his tears and stared hard at his foot. *Move*, his mind commanded. He laughed loudly when his foot obeyed.

"It's just his foot," Clint protested. "It ain't like he's walking!"

Robert sobered. Clint was right—he wasn't walking.

Polly whirled on her son. "You just hush up with that kind of talking. I'm ashamed of you. I didn't raise my son to be hateful and small. You best figure out where that be coming from and get rid of it!" she said firmly. "Now go out there and get that horse. I reckon Robert will ride it out of here one of these days after all."

Robert shook his head. "What are you talking about?"

Polly turned to him with a smile like sunshine. "We figured it would be better if you didn't know the fella who brung you here, brung you on a horse. Seein' such a beautiful animal and not being able to ride it . . ." She shrugged. "We just figured it would make things harder on you."

"I been feedin' that horse every morning and night," Amber piped in. "He sure do look a lot better than when he got here. Clint takes him out sometimes, but only when you be asleep. Ain't nobody ridden him, though."

Robert heard the door to the barn open. Holding his breath, he stared out the window, trying to guard his heart against a futile hope. It wasn't possible. It just wasn't possible that the horse was—

Robert recognized the ringing neigh even before the beautiful gray thoroughbred pranced out into the glistening snow. "Granite," he whispered, dashing away the tears blurring his vision.

"That be his name?" Amber asked.

Robert nodded, unable to take his eyes off the animal. "How? Who?"

Polly put her hand on his shoulder. "That fella who brung you just said the same thing about that horse. Said to take care of him for Carrie."

Robert pushed away the questions spinning through his mind. None of it made any difference right now. He gazed at Granite hungrily.

Granite let out another ringing neigh, then pawed the ground impatiently, staring at the house.

Polly laughed. "I reckon that big guy knows you're in here." Moving to the door, she called to Clint. "Bring him on over here."

Seconds later, Clint stepped into the cabin. Granite stopped short of the threshold but stuck his head into the cabin, his long neck reaching as far as he could.

"Hello, boy," Robert managed to say, tears choking his words.

Granite pricked his ears forward, then snorted softly, his velvety nostrils flaring.

Amber laughed and clapped her hands in delight. "He remembers you."

"Carrie has owned Granite since she was a child," Robert said quietly, his eyes never leaving the horse. "She gave him to me when I left for battle. Said she could trust Granite to bring me home." Once again hot tears rolled down his face. "I guess he might after all." He reached out for Polly's hand. "Thank you for taking care of him."

Polly just shook her head. "It weren't me. Clint's the one been taking care of that big animal. Amber's done the feeding but Clint has done everything else. I declare I think he's fallen in love with that animal."

Robert turned to Clint. The boy was looking back at him defiantly. "Thank you," Robert said. Clint just shrugged. Robert knew the boy hadn't done it for him. A thought came to him. "Do you know how to ride?"

Clint shook his head. "Ain't never had a chance."

"I'll teach you how when I can walk again," Robert stated firmly.

"On Granite?" Clint breathed, reaching out to pat the horse's glistening neck.

"On Granite," Robert promised, hoping it would create a bridge between them.

Auntie JoBelle came stomping into the house seconds later. "I hear we done got a miracle here. I can always be handlin' a miracle. There be plenty enough bad news to get a person down already." She walked over to Robert's bed. "Let's see that foot."

"Which one?" Robert smiled.

Auntie JoBelle turned to Gabe. "I thought he could just move one?"

"That was a few minutes ago," Robert said confidently. Seeing Granite, realizing that the possibility of going home could become a reality had bolstered his hope. Staring at his right foot, he willed it to move.

Auntie JoBelle gave a whoop when she saw it move. "Now let's see the other one," she demanded.

Robert stared at it hard. For several moments there was nothing. Then his big toe twitched.

Amber sat up and began to hum the tune Robert had been humming earlier. "Let your foot dance to the music," she urged.

Seconds later Robert's left foot began to move. Robert laughed as cheers broke forth in the cabin.

Auntie JoBelle sank down into the chair next to the bed. "I never," she said shaking her head.

"But I thought you said you'd seen stuff like this happen before," Polly exclaimed.

Auntie JoBelle smiled. "Weren't true. I done heard about it, but I ain't never seen it. Not till now. I just figured if Robert believed it could happen, it just might. Hope can be a mighty powerful thing. And besides, whether he walked again or not, he had to have hope to keep on surviving. It sure weren't gonna hurt him none."

The cabin erupted in laughter. Granite joined in, tossing his head and snorting loudly.

Thirty-Two

Robert leaned heavily on the crude cane Gabe had fashioned for him. His legs were still weak, but he was getting stronger every day. A month had passed since his feet had first moved. His progress was agonizingly slow, but he was improving every day.

His thoughts swung to Carrie almost hourly. How long before he would be well enough to try to cross the lines back into the South? And what would he do if he was captured by Union troops after all he had been through? He pushed the questions back firmly. He was learning to take one day at a time. Imagining trouble before it happened was silly. He would cross those bridges when he got to them. Right now he had a job to do.

Clint had just finished brushing Granite when Robert walked slowly into the barn. "He looks great," Robert commented. "Even with his winter coat on, he shines. You've taken excellent care of him."

Clint looked at Robert then turned back to Granite. "I've always wanted to work with horses," he said in a low voice. "Never figured I'd get the chance to."

Robert smiled. "You've definitely got the touch, but you'll go a lot further in the business if you know how to ride. I think today would be a fine day to start the process."

Clint gasped and spun around. "You mean it? You're actually gonna teach me how to ride Granite?"

"I told you I would," Robert said firmly.

Clint eyed him for a long moment, then nodded his head reluctantly. "I reckon you did," he muttered. Then his voice strengthened. "The saddle and bridle that were on him are clean. I oiled them up real good before the cold weather set in. I'll get them," he added eagerly.

Robert stroked Granite. Clint was just as excited as Robert had been when he learned how to ride. He had only been five years old when his father put him on a horse, but he could still remember the thrill. It had never dimmed for him. He could hardly wait until he could climb into Granite's saddle again himself. *Patience*, he told himself. *Patience.*

Clint reappeared, clutching the gleaming saddle and bridle.

Robert laughed. "I don't think it's been that clean since the day it was bought. Thank you for taking such good care of it." Clint mumbled something and looked at the ground. Robert understood. Clint was glad to have the opportunity to ride, but it didn't mean the boy was thrilled about him being the teacher. Robert knew Clint still didn't trust him. That was all right. Clint would have to work through things in his own time.

For almost an hour, Robert coached Clint in the basics of horsemanship. He firmly believed that most of riding was in the head. A confident rider gained a horse's trust much easier than a fearful rider. If Clint wanted to work with horses, he needed much more than the mechanics; he needed an understanding of the art of horsemanship. Clint listened to every word he said, drinking them in hungrily, his expression intense and concentrated.

Finally Robert was ready to put him in the saddle. Handing Clint the reins, he said, "Just walk him around over there in that pasture. I want you to get the feel of him."

Clint's eyes were wide but confident as he took the reins. Talking to Granite softly, he put his foot into the stirrup and swung up into the saddle.

Robert smiled with satisfaction as Clint's tall, muscular body settled lightly into the saddle. His form wasn't perfect, but he looked comfortable. "You know what to do," he stated quietly. "Go do it. When you're feeling completely at ease, ask him to trot."

Clint had made amazing progress by the end of the morning. His eyes were shining when Robert finally called him over. "What a horse!" he exclaimed, reaching down to rub Granite's neck.

"You did a fine job," Robert praised. "You have what it takes to make a fine horseman."

"Really?" Clint asked eagerly.

"I would let you work with my horses any day," Robert said.

The spark in Clint's eyes was replaced by a dark shadow. "I ain't ever gonna be one of your slaves," he muttered, swinging down from Granite and handing Robert the reins.

Robert took a deep breath. "I understand your bitterness, Clint, but I think you know I've changed. I'm not going to own slaves anymore. Your family has taught me so much." He paused, then decided to plunge ahead. "I think you're using me as an excuse to hang on to your anger and hatred. I know what it's like. You get used to feeling it; it becomes a big part of who you are. You're afraid you won't know yourself anymore if you let it go."

"What do you know?" Clint muttered angrily.

Robert took hope from the fact that Clint hadn't stalked away. "I was the exact same way," he replied. "I'd had hate living inside of me so long, I'd just gotten used to it being there. I held onto it as a protection against having to look at the truth. The truth was that I was judging a whole race of people by the actions of one man—actions I probably would have taken myself if I'd been in his position. It was easier to do that than look at the truth of who I had become." He paused. "It takes a lot of courage to look at yourself honestly and let God show you the truth. It took me a long time to become brave enough to do it. I don't know that I ever would have if I hadn't been paralyzed for months. I was so used to being in control. It took losing control before I could listen to anything else."

Clint stared hard at the ground for several minutes. "I reckon you ain't so bad, Robert." Then he took Granite's reins and strode into the barn.

With a glimmer of a smile, Robert watched him go. He knew that was Clint's way of saying he'd think about what Robert had said. He also knew it was the boy's way of saying Robert had been accepted. Whistling, Robert walked back into the cabin.

Carrie gazed around her sadly as Spencer drove the carriage down the road. It was almost the middle of March, and still the city was gripped by old man winter. Great piles of gray snow were pushed to the side of the roads lined with litter. Richmond had once been a proud, beautiful city. Two years of siege and overcrowding had exacted a heavy toll. Paint peeled from once immaculate storefronts. Shutters hung loose, swinging in the breeze. Wounded soldiers were everywhere, pushing through the snow on crutches. Prostitutes hung from windows, beckoning the men in for an afternoon of entertainment. Gambling halls sent music blaring into the streets. And everywhere were thin, pinched faces that spoke of hunger or illness.

"Your father doing better?" Spencer asked over his shoulder, driving carefully to avoid the deep potholes left from winter's freeze and thaw.

"Yes. He's been out of bed for several days. Almost all the scabs have fallen off and the scarring is very minimal. He's been doing work at home, but I think he'll be able to go back to the capital by the end of the week."

"That's good. Lots of people died from the smallpox so far."

"I know," Carrie said grimly. She was on her way to the colored hospital to check on her patients. As with any disease, it seemed the poor were always the hardest hit. It made her sick to realize the vaccine to prevent smallpox had been held from them by the Federal blockade. So much suffering could have been prevented. The colored hospital was full of people down with the dread disease. So far she and Janie had managed to avoid it. She could only pray their good fortune would continue.

It was not yet noon when she arrived. She had taken a full day off from Chimborazo to care for the patients down by the river. A winter of no fighting had lessened the load in the military hospitals greatly.

Pastor Anthony came rushing out the door. "I'm heading for the armory," he called. "I promised the girls I would come by and check on them this morning. I'll be back soon."

Carrie waved, then ducked into the building. She was soon absorbed in her work. Suddenly the sound of a prolonged roar bellowed from the direction of Brown's Island. Carrie was used to hearing explosions from the testing of ordnance at the Tredegar Iron Works, but something about the sound troubled her.

"Excuse me," she murmured to the elderly woman she was treating. Not understanding the sudden anxiety gripping her, she stepped to the door of the hospital.

A man appeared from nowhere, running down the street frantically. "It's the armory," he yelled. "One of the buildings blew up!"

Carrie raced inside, grabbed her coat and medical bag, and took off at a run. She knew she could make better time on foot than trying to fight traffic in a buggy. She blinked back tears as she raced down the road, heading for the collection of one-story frame buildings clustered on Brown's Island. She pushed herself to run harder when the image of several hundred employees—most of them young girls— rose in her mind.

She could see the smoke and flames long before she got to the island. A tide of people were flowing toward the bridge. She could hear the screams of frantic mothers searching for their children. Carrie wove her way through the crowd, breathing a sigh of relief when she finally broke through.

"You can't go over there!" a policeman barked, stepping in front of her.

"I'm a doctor," Carrie said crisply, holding her bag for him to see. A skeptical expression crossed his face, but he stepped aside. Carrie ran on, deciding it was no time for technicalities. Fear gripped her heart as she dashed across the bridge. Where was Pastor Anthony? Where were the little girls who had sang for her on Christmas Eve?

Carrie headed for the building. She groaned as she reached the site of the explosion. The armory had been reduced to a complete wreck. The roof was missing, the walls blown out, and flames were licking toward the other buildings. Men were pouring water on the fire as fast as they could. No one needed to be told what would happen if the flames spread to the surrounding buildings. Other people were picking their way into the ruins. Carrie watched grimly. She knew they were searching for survivors among the dead.

Suddenly a figure stumbled out of the smoke, clutching a tiny body tightly in his arms. They were within several yards of her before Carrie recognized who it was. "Pastor Anthony!" she cried, cringing at the burns on his face and arms.

"Carrie," he gasped. "It's Elvira. Please take care of her." Quickly he laid the injured little girl in her arms and dashed back to the ruins.

Carrie groaned as she looked down at the disfigured little body. Tears blinded her for a moment as she remembered the precocious child who had so delighted her on Christmas Eve. She knew before examining her closely that Elvira was too badly burned to be saved. She had only begun the process of removing the remnants of the little girl's clothes when Elvira gave a tiny moan and went slack. Carrie reached for the blanket one of the rescue workers was handing her and laid it tenderly over the tiny body. Gulping back sobs, she moved on to the next victim. There was nothing else she could do.

The next several hours passed in a thick haze. Carrie thought the horrors of battle could never be surpassed. But somehow this was worse. Over sixty children—too young to understand what war was all about, while working long hours to produce much of the ammunition that kept the Confederate army fighting—were laid out in long rows. Many were dead when they were pulled from the building. Others, still clinging to life, were blinded from their burns, their hair singed from their heads, their clothing hanging in tattered shreds. The wailing of children and parents became a steady chorus as medical personnel worked frantically to save whom they could.

Pastor Anthony appeared at Carrie's side again as she bent to help another little girl. "What can I do to help?"

"You can get someone to treat those burns," Carrie said crisply, choking back her tears at the tortured look on his face.

"Please . . . I need to help," he pleaded, tears rolling down his face. "I sent these little girls to work here." He shook his head heavily.

"Help me get her clothes off," Carrie ordered. "We're going to cover her body with flour and cotton, then saturate it all with oil. It's the best we can do until they can get her to the hospital." Reaching into her bag, she pulled out a bottle of chloroform she'd managed to find. She administered it to the moaning little girl, heaving a sigh of relief when she felt the body relax into unconsciousness. It was the only respite any of them had to offer.

"Elvira?" Pastor Anthony asked.

Carrie pressed her lips together and shook her head. "I'm sorry," she said softly.

Pastor Anthony groaned but didn't stop working on the unconscious child.

In some ways the girls who had died were the lucky ones, Carrie thought grimly. The survivors would know nothing but months of pain and agony—many would never recover.

Not until the last ambulance had trundled away did Pastor Anthony sink down to the ground wearily.

"Let me look at your burns," Carrie said gently. Her whole body ached with weariness and sorrow, but she was certain the pastor was suffering greatly.

Pastor Anthony shook his head. "They're not that bad," he said shortly. He dropped his head in his hands, his whole body trembling. "How could I have let those little girls work in such a place? Five of them are dead, five more are horribly burned. Only Marva and Florence escaped without serious injury." His voice broke. "And it's all my fault."

"Nonsense," Carrie said crisply. "Lift your head up so I can see your burns. Allowing your own wounds to become infected won't help any of those girls. You still have people who need you." Her heart ached for Pastor Anthony. She continued to talk as she treated his burns. "I know you're feeling responsible, but you simply can't blame yourself for what happened. It was an accident. The safety record here has been incredible since the war started. The girls were much safer here than they would have been on the streets. Without these jobs they might have died from starvation this winter." Dabbing at his burns with an ointment, she paused when Pastor Anthony flinched. "It was an accident," she insisted. "I heard some of the men talking."

"Yes," Pastor Anthony whispered. "It was an accident. One of the girls was trying to free a primer from a board. She had been warned against striking the boards before, but," he shrugged, "she did it anyway." He paused, taking a deep breath. "I had walked out of the building to get something for Elvira. When I came back in, I saw the girl strike the board against the table she was working at. There was a horrendous explosion. The girl was blown to the ceiling." He shuddered. "Right before she hit the ground, she was blown up again." He shook his head heavily. "Then everything started blowing up. When I came to again, all I could hear were screams of agony, and I could feel hot flames."

Tears poured down Carrie's face as she listened to the account. She wanted to plug her ears and scream that she could handle no more tragedy, but instead she reached out her hand and touched Pastor Anthony's unburned hand. "If it hadn't been for you, more of the girls would be dead."

Carrie was suddenly aware of the acrid fumes burning her nose, the clinging smoke clogging her lungs. She began to shiver as the cold seeped through her clothing. Now that the emergency was over, reaction was setting in. Gently she helped Pastor Anthony to his feet. She could see Spencer waiting with the carriage on the other side of the bridge. "I'm taking you home," she insisted. "I know you will want to visit the girls in the hospital later, but right now you need to get cleaned up. I have some chickweed ointment at the hospital. I want you to keep it in on all of your burns."

Pastor Anthony nodded his head, but said nothing all the way to his house.

Spencer helped him inside, then came back to the carriage. "The Pastor's gonna make it. He's a strong man."

Carrie felt her strength crumble now that there was nothing else to do. Tears blurred her vision. "Please take me home," she whispered. For the first time she noticed the burns on her own hands—caused by removing still-flaming clothes from the girls she had treated. "I just want to go home." She knew the pictures of those charred bodies would stay in her mind as long as she was alive.

One week later all the dead had finally been buried. Forty-five of the sixty-eight victims had died, their burns and wounds too serious to recover from. Once again funeral processions wound their way through the streets. The city seemed to be in shock. Losing young men to battle was one thing. But losing so many young, innocent children was another. Richmond continued to reel from one disaster after another. And just when they had every reason to hope for the arrival of spring to dull the agony of the long winter—the day before they heralded the advent of a new season—a foot of snow was dumped on the city.

Carrie trudged her way through the snow, heart-sore and exhausted. Several of her smallpox patients had died that day. Pastor Anthony's burns were healing well, but the haunted look in his eyes had not diminished. The whole city was gripped with a deep despair and darkness. As hard as she was battling to keep her own heart free from despair, she could feel its tendrils weaving their way through her defenses.

No one was home when she arrived at the house. She held her hands out to the fire, trying to chase the chill from her body— wishing there was a way to chase the chill from her heart. The clatter of boots on the front porch sent her hurrying to her room. She couldn't bear to face anyone after the day she'd endured. It might be cold, but at least she would have privacy in her room. As soon as she was safely inside, a force propelled her to the mantel standing guard over the cold fireplace. Smiling slightly, she reached out to grasp the treasure she had enthroned there. Once she had it in her hands, she moved to the window and stared through the frosted glass at the drifts of snow.

Carrie tore her eyes away from the cold scene and gazed down at the tiny blade of grass in her hands. It was dry and brittle now, but it still held a tinge of green. She allowed it to transport her back to her special place—back to the memories it caused to flood through her heart.

Finally Carrie looked back through the window. She could see people trudging up the street, their beaten faces speaking more loudly of their internal defeat than anything else ever could.

"Spring will come," she whispered. Her voice grew louder. "Spring will come." She spread her arms wide, new hope surging into her heart. "Spring will come. God promised."

Thirty-Three

Rose walked slowly to the waterfront to say good-bye to Carter and Teresa. The two teachers, exhausted from a long winter of aid to the Contrabands, were returning home for a month-long break.

"You sure you won't come with us?" Carter asked for the hundredth time. "I know how much your Aunt Abby wants you to come to Philadelphia to have your baby," she said anxiously.

Rose smiled, rubbing her stomach lightly. "Me and this little guy are staying right here. This is our home now. At least until the war is over. We'll be fine," she said firmly. The long winter had been cold and brutal, but the warm winds of April had brought a resurgence of new life. Her baby was kicking harder every day. She knew in her heart that it would not be long before he would insist on meeting his world. Part of her heart longed for Aunt Abby, but deep inside she knew she was where she was meant to be. More slaves would be pouring into the camps. If she left now, it would be several months before she could travel again.

Teresa gave her a fierce hug. "We'll be back to see that baby in a month or so. You take good care of yourself."

Rose hugged her tightly, blinking away the sudden tears in her eyes. She knew Teresa might not return. At the beginning she had worried about Carter, afraid her frail, gentle friend wouldn't be able to stand the rigors of camp life. But it had been Teresa, strong and confident, who had crumbled beneath the demands, the shadows in her eyes growing deeper with each passing day. When spring had finally come, she had grasped at it with a pathetic eagerness, but it had done little to dispel the shadows.

427

Rose reached for Teresa's hands, knowing she might never again have a chance to share with her friend what she was thinking. "My momma used to tell me something," she said softly. "She used to tell me that some people stagger under the burden of failure because they were never supposed to be doing what they were doing anyway. She said some people try to do things God never gifted them for in the first place. Then they feel like miserable failures because they don't succeed." Rose gazed deeply into Teresa's eyes. "My momma didn't believe anyone was a failure. She figured those folks just needed to find out what they're supposed to be doing. Once they find that out, they'll have all the abilities and gifts they need to perform it." She paused again. "Teresa, you're a very special person. If you decide not to come back, don't feel bad. It only means there is something else you're supposed to be doing."

Great tears ran down Teresa's cheeks as Rose finished. "Thank you," she gulped. "I thought I could help most by being a teacher."

"You can help most by doing exactly what you're gifted to do," Rose said firmly.

Teresa squeezed her hands again, then looked toward the boat when the whistle blew shrilly. "I guess we'd better be going."

The three friends exchanged fierce hugs again, then Rose stepped back and watched them board the towering ship. She waved until they were out of sight, then turned to move slowly back up the docks. Her baby gave a hard kick and Rose smiled joyously. "I sure am glad you waited till spring," she murmured, "but I must admit I'm rather anxious to meet you." She laughed when an even harder kick came in seeming response to her words.

Robert strode out of the house, taking deep breaths of the warm spring air. Tossing back his head, he welcomed the rays of the bright sun on his face. The snow was almost completely melted, daffodils and crocuses pushing through the earth. Trees were sporting a soft green hue as new leaves finally dared come out from their winter hiding. Birds trilled loudly. Just as Robert reached the barn, a doe and her fawn exploded from the woods, looked at him in alarm, then turned to dash back into cover, their white tails flashing as they loped away.

Robert laughed loudly. Granite heard him and answered with a ringing neigh. "Coming, boy," Robert called. Minutes later, he led Granite from the barn and swung into the saddle. It took much more effort than before his injuries, but he accomplished it fairly gracefully. His objective today was to ride for two hours. He had been practicing for three weeks now. The first time out his legs had only supported him for five minutes. But he had worked at it hard every day, and he could feel the strength pouring into his body.

"Bye, Robert!"

Robert turned to wave at Amber. "I'll be back soon." He stopped Granite when Amber suddenly raced from the cabin. Granite pranced impatiently until Amber was close. Then he calmed and lowered his massive head to allow Amber to stroke it.

"I got a surprise for you when you get back," Amber said with a grin.

"What kind of surprise?"

"It wouldn't be a surprise if I told you," she retorted, then turned and raced for the cabin.

Robert laughed and turned Granite toward the trail leading away from the cabin. Granite tossed his head joyfully and pranced down the trail. Robert's thoughts turned once again to Carrie. He was almost strong enough to try to make it home. With spring would come the preparation for more military maneuvers. He had no idea where the Army of the Potomac was now, but he was sure their eventual target would once more be Richmond. If he didn't leave soon, the risk would be even greater that Northern troops would block him from the city. Old fears of capture gripped him, but he resolutely thrust them aside. If he started thinking about everything that could happen, he would never do anything. There was only one way to get back to Carrie—he would ride Granite through the lines.

Amber was waiting for Robert when he rode back up to the barn. "You ready for your surprise, Robert?"

"Would it be all right if I got something to eat first?" he asked, smiling. "My ride made me very hungry."

Amber reached down behind a log and pulled up a wooden bucket. "Momma fixed us lunch. I helped her," she said proudly.

"In that case—lead the way. I will follow you wherever you want to go."

"I'm taking you to a very special place," Amber said mysteriously. "Ain't nobody knows about it except for me."

Robert's mind flashed back to the time she had promised to take him to her secret place when he was walking again. The little girl was keeping her promise. "I can hardly wait," he replied earnestly, hiding a smile when Amber's pretty face beamed up at him.

They were only a couple hundred yards from the barn when Amber seemed to sag beneath the weight of the lunch bucket. Robert reached down and took it from her hand. "I understand the one who is being taken to the special place is supposed to carry the meal," he said seriously.

Amber's expression was equally somber. "I didn't know that. Thank you for telling me." Then she put her finger to her lips. "We need to be quiet the rest of the way."

Robert's heart swelled with affection for the little girl as they glided down a trail, then pushed their way through thick overgrowth. She led the way confidently, a smile of secret importance plastered on her face.

"We're here," she finally whispered.

Robert gazed around him, charmed by the beauty of the small clearing they had come upon. A bubbling creek rushed over a myriad of shiny boulders, singing a melody of spring as it cavorted along. The soft green moss of the forest floor was dotted with vivid red, yellow, and blue wildflowers. A squirrel fussed at them from a nearby tree, then dashed to the highest branch to chatter its discontent.

Amber laughed merrily. "Mr. Squirrel must not like you being here. He'll get used to it, though. He never fusses at me when I'm alone anymore."

Robert sank down on the moss. "This is very beautiful," he said sincerely. "I understand why it is so special to you."

"It is right pretty," Amber agreed. "But that ain't why it's so special to me," she stated matter-of-factly.

Robert waited for her to explain.

"I found this place one day when I got lost in the woods. I was awful scared and lonely. I wasn't sure I would ever see home again. I was crying real hard. My momma said I was probably so scared I weren't thinking straight. Anyway, that little creek talked to me until I felt better. Then I just followed it until I came out to a place I knew." She paused. "I can think better when the creek talks to me. That's why I come here."

Robert was bemused. What on earth did a six-year-old have to think about that was so serious?

Amber seemed to read his mind. "I got me lots to think about. I thought about you a lot when you first came. I knew Clint didn't like you so much. He told me not to have anything to do with you. I came out here to think one day and the creek told me I should give you a chance. I guess the creek was right, 'cause I sure love you a lot."

Robert opened his mouth to speak, but she continued on.

"I think about some of the people who have stayed with us. One was a little girl my age. Her name was April. She was real scared the whole time she was here. She was sure them bad slave hunters were gonna catch her and her momma and daddy and beat them like they used to get beat on the plantation. They finally got away, but I've always wondered what happened to her."

"You care about people a lot," Robert said softly.

Amber seemed to ponder his words, then nodded. "Clint used to tell me people were bad. That they were out to hurt me. I used to believe him. Now I don't."

"Why not?" Robert was amazed at the innocent wisdom of the little girl.

"Well, he told me that about you, didn't he? And weren't he wrong?" she asked. "I reckon he could be wrong about a lot of people. I figure I need to get to know folks for myself. Then I can decide what they're really like. I don't reckon I need him to decide that for me." She paused, then stared up into Robert's eyes. "You know what I mean?"

Robert smiled down into her sparkling brown eyes. "I know exactly what you mean," he agreed. He was searching for something else to say when she spun around and reached for the bucket.

"I'm hungry! How about you?"

Robert licked his lips.

Amber laughed and reached down into the bucket. "Momma sent us a bunch of fried chicken and biscuits. I think she slipped some sweet potatoes from last year in here. She even sent us some cold milk," she said triumphantly, holding the jar high.

Robert heard his stomach growl in response. He leaned back against a rock and let the magic of the creek speak to him as he devoured every crumb of the food she put in front of him.

Clint was coming back from a ride on Granite when Robert and Amber arrived at the cabin. Clint's eyes were shining brightly, his face split with a huge grin. "Boy, is he fast!"

"Fastest horse I've ever been on," Robert agreed. "Have any trouble handling him?"

"He does everything I ask," Clint exclaimed. "I hope I can own a horse like him some day."

"You keep working. You have a natural touch with horses. No reason why you can't." Robert meant every word he said. The reality of that still amazed him sometimes. It no longer mattered that Clint was colored. He was talented and intelligent. That's what was important. He had helped Robert tremendously by getting Granite back in shape for the long ride south. Granite's muscles, grown soft by a long winter of inactivity, were once again strong and powerful.

"You're a rich man, ain't you, Robert?" Clint asked suddenly.

"Where in the world did that come from?" Robert asked, startled.

"I know I said I'd never want to work for you, but I'm kinda changing my mind. I know you're a whole heap different than you used to be," Clint responded. "I bet you got lots of good horses, don't you? Ain't you gonna need someone to work with them?" He paused. "And I figure Granite will be there since he belongs to your girl," he finished triumphantly.

"Got it all figured out, don't you?" Robert laughed. He sobered quickly as he studied the serious look on Clint's face. The boy had done a lot of thinking about this. "Clint, I would love for you to work with my horses. You have a natural touch. But I simply can't make you any promises. Except for one. If I have any horses left for you to work with, and if I have any money to pay you, I would be honored to have you work for me."

"But you're rich, ain't you?" Clint insisted.

Robert hesitated. "I suppose by many people's standards I was rich before this war started. I just don't know what it's going to be like when the war is finally over. For all I know, my home has already been destroyed. Because of inflation our money is practically worth nothing. If we lose the war it's going to hold no value whatsoever. I could already be a poor man."

Clint's face clouded with disappointment for several moments, then cleared. "You let me know where you are after the war, Robert. I figure I can help you rebuild. I just want to work with horses. I don't know nobody else to work with."

"You got a deal, Clint."

Polly appeared at the door of the cabin. "Dinner will be ready soon."

Dinner was over when Polly turned to Robert, asking, "What you got on your mind, boy? You been thinking hard enough to make me tired the whole time we been eatin'."

Robert hesitated, trying to figure out how to say what he needed to.

"You leavin', ain't you?" Polly asked bluntly.

"It's time for me to move on," Robert acknowledged quietly.

Clint and Amber stopped their game of checkers. Gabe looked up from the magazine he was reading. Not a word was said. They just stared at him. A long silence fell on the tiny cabin.

Amber was the first to break it. "You leavin' us, Robert?" Tears shone in her eyes.

Robert held out his arms, and she ran to climb into his lap. "I can't stay here forever," Robert said gently. "I have to go home."

"But I'm going to miss you!" Amber cried. "Why can't this be your home?"

"I'm going to miss you, too." Robert had known breaking the news was going to be hard. He hadn't been prepared, however, for the ache he was going to feel in his own heart. He had grown to genuinely love this family. If it hadn't been for Carrie, it would have been easy to stay here and let other men fight the battles he had learned to despise so much. Not only was he sick of the war—he could no longer find the heart to fight for the preservation of slavery. He knew the war was about more than that, but slavery had become the sticking point.

"You reckon you can make it?" Gabe asked, his deep voice revealing his skepticism.

"I'm much stronger," Robert replied. "If I don't go now, I'm afraid I won't be able to get through. Both armies will begin to move now that spring is here. It may already be impossible for me to get through the lines. But I have to try," he said firmly.

"Of course you do," Polly agreed.

"But, momma!" Amber cried.

"But, momma, nothing," Polly said sternly. "We knew when Robert got here that he weren't gonna stay after he got well. Now we know about his home. We know about Carrie. He done got a whole life down South." Her voice caught as tears glimmered in her eyes. "We gonna miss you, Robert, but I figure we'll see you again."

Robert nodded. "Soon as this war is over, I'm going to bring Carrie up to meet the people who saved my life."

Amber snuggled close to him but didn't say anything else.

"When are you leaving?" Clint asked gruffly.

Robert knew the longer he stayed, the more risk he would run of being caught by the Yankees. "I figured I would leave in the morning."

Clint stared at him for a long moment. "I reckon I'll go tell Granite good-bye," he said heavily. Heaving himself up from the floor, he disappeared outside.

Robert was stuffed with a hearty breakfast when Clint led Granite to the front of the cabin.

"I reckon it's that time," Polly said quietly.

Almost mechanically, Robert tied his blanket and several bags of food to the saddle. He was excited to be on his way home. But he felt as if his heart was breaking, to leave these people he had learned to love. Finally he turned to gaze at them.

Gabe's massive form was outlined in the door of the cabin. Polly was tucked under one of his strong arms, her eyes soft with sadness. Amber snuggled close to her momma, tears running down her face.

Robert struggled for words. "I—I just . . . " He shook his head. "I don't know how to say thank you. I simply can't think of the right words to tell you how much I appreciate what you've done for me. You not only saved my life—you gave me a new life." Tears blurred his vision. Wiping them away, he took a deep breath. "I will never forget what you've done for me."

"You've done just as much for us, Robert." Polly stepped forward to take his hand. "White folks ain't the only ones who need to learn to be color-blind. I reckon colored folks need to learn the same thing. You done taught us that." She chuckled. "I sure was mad at that fella who dumped you here and took off. Now I wish I could find him to thank him."

"Me, too," Robert echoed. "I wonder if I'll ever know who it was." He shook his head. It wasn't so important that he know now. Kneeling, he held his arms out to Amber. She darted into them, sobs wracking her tiny body.

"I love you, Robert. I love you!" she cried, wrapping her arms around him tightly.

"And I love you, Amber." Robert held her for several minutes, then gently pushed her away and wiped her tears. "It's not going to be forever," he reminded her. "I'll be back to visit just as soon as I can. And I'll bring Carrie with me."

"Promise?" Amber brushed at her tears, trying to sound brave.

"Promise," Robert said solemnly.

Polly pulled Amber back. "We got to let Robert get going. He's got a right long ride to Richmond."

Gabe stepped forward and held out his hand. Robert gripped it firmly, knowing no words were needed. Their hearts and minds understood each other—they were friends.

Finally Robert turned to Granite and took the reins from Clint. Clint held out his hand. Robert grasped it, then pulled the boy into a rough hug.

Clint hugged him briefly, then stepped away. "Like I said before—you ain't so bad for a white man," he said gruffly.

Robert grinned, swung into the saddle, and trotted away. He looked back for one final glimpse before the woods swallowed him and the tiny cabin was out of sight. Tears blurred his vision for several minutes before he straightened in the saddle and took a deep breath. Now that the good-byes had been said, his thoughts flew South.

He had a long way to go, but he was on his way home!

Moses leaned back against a tree, staring out over the Rappahannock River in the distance. He missed being a spy, but he had not been able deny Captain Jones' request. His captain had called him into his tent shortly after the new year and told him he had been given command of one of the many colored regiments being mustered into the army. Tens of thousands of negro men had promptly enlisted in the army when Lincoln released his Emancipation Proclamation. Captain Jones had asked Moses to come with him even though, as a colored man, he could not be given the commission of officer. Moses had pushed aside his horrors of battle and agreed. He owed the captain a great deal. He would do what was needed. If it meant he had to fight, he would fight.

The soft breezes blowing on his face turned his thoughts to Rose. Their baby would be born in another month or so. It ate at his soul not being able to be there, but it was impossible. Now that spring was here, the army was preparing to move. The long winter had passed with extensive reoutfitting and training of the demoralized Army of the Potomac. General Burnside had been replaced after his stunning defeat at Fredericksburg. General Joe Hooker had done an incredible job of revitalizing and motivating the tattered army. Now, over one hundred thousand strong, the mighty Army of the Potomac was perched on the banks of the Rappahannock River, waiting for the signal to once more advance on Richmond.

Thirty-Four

Carrie leaned against her windowsill, thankful for the warm breeze bathing her face. Spring had finally come to Richmond. The last major snowfall, a month before, had finally melted. Winter had bowed in submission to the warm southern sun. Trees were beginning to bud. Crocuses and daffodils were waving their heads gaily, rejoicing in the new life.

"Are you going downtown with your father?" Janie asked, turning away from the mirror after she had tucked the last strand of hair securely in place.

"Yes. He is determined to buy me a new dress now that winter is over." Carrie frowned. "It seems so frivolous. I have absolutely no need of a new dress, and they're so very expensive now."

"Your father wants to do something to show his appreciation for all the care you gave him while he was sick."

"I know," Carrie replied. She was so glad to see her father restored to his old self. The sickness almost seemed to have done him good. His enforced confinement had granted him more rest than he had gotten since before her mother died. He was now eager to get back into the fray. "I'll go. I'll find a dress. I'll even be properly appreciative. But," she added, "I still don't think I need one. I have absolutely nowhere to wear something fancy."

She jumped up when she heard her father's footsteps approaching, grabbed a light coat from her wardrobe, and opened the door before he had time to knock.

"Ready?"

Carrie tucked her arm in her father's. "Ready," she said brightly.

Thomas stuck his head in the bedroom. "Sure you won't join us?" he asked Janie.

"I have some letters I want to take care of," Janie assured him. "You two go have a good time. You need to be alone with your daughter."

"I won't argue with that," Thomas agreed. "Thank you."

Broad Street was crowded, but Spencer wove in and out of traffic without a problem. Even spring couldn't keep the city from looking bedraggled, but the spirit of complete despair seemed to have lifted. People were smiling as they strolled along in the warm sunshine.

Thomas clapped his hand to his head. "I forgot!" He turned to Carrie. "Do you mind if I slip by the Capitol? I promise it will take just a few minutes. I neglected to sign a document the governor needs this afternoon."

"Certainly," Carrie agreed easily. "I won't mind sitting in Capitol Square. The flowers should be beautiful by now."

The carriage rolled up to the Capitol and Thomas leaped out. "This should only take ten or fifteen minutes."

"Take your time. It's a beautiful day," Carrie assured him. "I'm going over to sit on one of the benches. Just call when you're ready."

Carrie had been sitting only a few minutes when a large group of people, mostly women, began to assemble quietly. She watched them curiously. As the group drew closer, one young lady broke away and sank down on the bench beside her.

"I just can't stand a moment longer," she said weakly.

Carrie gazed at her in sympathy. She was familiar with the thin, pinched cheeks that spoke of hunger. It would be a couple of months before gardens would produce food for the hungry. There was still a critical shortage. The girl resting next to her couldn't be much older than she was. She spun to glare at Carrie. "We aren't going to keep being hungry," she said angrily.

"What are you going to do?" Carrie didn't know what else to say. She didn't particularly want to get involved in a conversation with this stranger, but she could hardly ignore her.

"We're gonna get us some food," she snapped. She raised her arm to adjust her bonnet. When the sleeve of her threadbare dress fell away from her arm, she held it up almost as a trophy.

Carrie's heart sank. The girl's arm was nothing but skin and bones.

"Ain't much left of me," the woman said, noticing Carrie's staring eyes. "But that's going to change. This government has already taken all our men. My children and I have been hungry all winter. It's time for the government to take care of their own. Their soldiers aren't going to have anything to come back to at this rate."

"I'm so sorry," Carrie said sympathetically.

The stranger shrugged. "Maybe you are, and maybe you aren't. It doesn't really matter. We've decided to take things into our own hands. The bunch of us has talked about it. If we all stick together they'll have to listen. We're here to ask Governor Letcher for some food." She glanced up when someone across the courtyard called her name. "Well, looks like this is it." She stood abruptly.

"Good luck," Carrie said sincerely.

The woman glanced back over her shoulder. "Yeah. Thanks."

Just as Carrie turned to look toward the Capitol for her father, she saw a colored nanny walking with her little white charge down the square. The woman was looking down, talking while the little boy laughed excitedly. He broke away to run over and inspect a row of daffodils.

Suddenly he stopped. "Look, Judy. What are all those women doing?" he piped clearly.

The maid looked up and ground to a halt, her face registering disapproval. Quickly she grabbed his hand and turned around. "We got to get out of here," she said loudly. "You might catch something from them poor white people," she sniffed, then hurried away.

Carrie watched sadly as the group of women scowled and muttered. Her heart went out to them. She had seen so much suffering this winter. Without food there was no end in sight. She watched a group of the ladies, obviously the leaders, approach the Capitol. A few minutes later they turned away. The angry muttering in the crowd grew louder.

"I'm ready."

Carrie started. She had been watching the women so intently she had not even seen her father approach. "Did Governor Letcher help those women?"

Thomas shrugged. "He was at breakfast. He asked them to come back later when he was in his office. He said he would try to help."

Carrie gazed at the group thoughtfully. "I'm not sure that is going to make them feel any better. They seem pretty desperate."

"There are a lot of desperate people in the city right now," Thomas said grimly. "We're doing everything we can to help." He pulled her up from the bench. "And now I think we have a dress to buy."

The idea of buying a dress when hundreds were going hungry sickened her. Reluctantly she followed her father to the carriage.

Spencer urged the horse forward. "Them women are looking for trouble," he muttered. "We need to get out of here."

"Take us to Main Street, please, Spencer," Thomas ordered crisply.

Spencer turned down Eighth Street. Carrie watched as the women, yelling angrily to each other, surged down Ninth Street. There was going to be trouble.

Spencer had just turned onto Main Street, bound for the dress store, when the mob of women erupted onto the road in front of them. Spencer pulled back hard on the reins. The carriage shuddered to a halt.

Thomas frowned. "Turn the carriage around," he commanded.

"I can't, Mr. Cromwell. We be blocked in."

Carrie looked behind them quickly. Spencer was right. Crowds of bystanders, curious to know what was happening, had already surged out onto the streets, completely blocking the road.

Thomas cursed under his breath.

"They're just after food," Carrie assured her father.

"That might have been their original plan," Thomas scowled, "but when people decide to take things into their own hands, things can get out of control."

Just then the mob reached the Government Commissary. Carrie watched, fascinated, as the women pushed their way through the door. Minutes later she could see packages being handed out.

The alarm bell started ringing from the Capitol but no one turned away. The yelling and calling grew louder. Her father was right. Whoever had been in charge had lost control of the crowd. Women broke away and began pouring into the surrounding shops, grabbing bread, flour, hams, and shoes.

Bystanders began to move away. "Let's get out of here," one called. "Those women are dangerous."

"Shut the doors to the shop!" a man called, breaking through the crowd and yelling to a well-dressed man standing in the door of a nearby store. The man rushed forward, pushed the other man inside, and slammed the door shut.

Seconds later, the mob was at his door. They pushed at it angrily. "These rich people can't make us starve any longer," a woman screamed. Pulling out a hatchet from the bag she carried at her waist, she hurled it through the storefront window. The crowd roared triumphantly as the glass shattered and fell away. "Get what you want, ladies!"

"Father!" Carrie gasped, suddenly frightened.

Thomas was already stepping from the carriage. "We're getting out of here," he said grimly. "You come with us, Spencer."

"But what about the carriage?" Spencer asked anxiously.

"This mob is taking carriages up and down the street. Until someone takes control there is no way to stop them. So far they're not harming anyone, but that could change any minute."

The mob continued their rampage, smashing windows and taking whatever they could reach—silks, bonnets, jewelry, tools. They were no longer just searching for food—it seemed they were taking everything in sight. What had begun as an orderly demand for food had turned into a full-scale riot. The people of Richmond, frustrated and angered by a war they didn't understand and a long winter of suffering, were out of control.

A fire truck appeared at the end of the road. Firemen jumped from the truck. Seconds later great streams of water poured into the crowd. Yet it did nothing to dissuade the mob. The yelling grew louder as the crowd grew angrier. Moments later a contingent of city guardsmen, well armed, burst around the corner. Holding their guns to the sky, they fired a few warning shots.

The crowd stopped looting, but the yelling and muttering did not diminish. The guardsmen formed a line at the end of the road. The crowd swung to meet them.

"Surely they won't shoot the city's own people!" Carrie cried.

Thomas shook his head grimly, then grabbed her arm. "Here comes the President!"

Carrie craned her neck to see.

President Davis stepped up onto a wagon. She could hear little of what he said, but it was obvious he was making an appeal to the crowd. She saw him pull out his watch. Obviously, he had delivered an ultimatum.

"We ain't leaving!" one woman near Carrie screamed.

This time President Davis' response was loud enough for Carrie to hear.

"You must go home. I have no wish to use guns against our fine citizens. They are here to turn away our invaders. Disorder such as this will only result in famine because the farmers will refuse to deliver food to the city. I will share my last loaf with you," he called. "It is imperative that we bear our trials with courage and stand united against the enemy. I do not wish to injure anyone, but this lawlessness must stop. I will give you five minutes to disperse, otherwise you will be fired upon," he called firmly.

Carrie held her breath, praying the crowd would not incite more violence. Seconds ticked away, the guardsmen raising their rifles to a ready position. President Davis stood tall, holding his watch in front of him. Finally the crowd began to drift away, their angry mutterings still floating on the breeze around them.

Carrie sagged against her father in relief.

Thomas scowled, then reached into his pocket and pulled out some bills. He pressed them into her hand. "Please go find a nice dress for yourself. Spencer can drive you. I'm sorry I can't go with you, but I'm sure things are in an uproar at the Capitol because of this. I won't be able to join you."

Carrie handed the money back to her father. "I don't need a new dress," she said firmly. "I was merely buying one for you. I can't do it after watching all those suffering people."

"Most of those *suffering* people were common looters wanting to steal whatever they could get their hands on," Thomas snapped.

Carrie shook her head. "I saw those women when they were assembling in the square. They were just after food. I know things got out of control, but the people in this city are stretched to their limits."

"Everyone is stretched to their limits."

"You're right," Carrie said calmly. "But I think it is probably harder to be stretched to your limits by something you had no control over in the first place. I can't imagine telling my children they are starving for the honor of the glorious South."

Thomas sighed. "I suppose you're right." He hesitated, then shoved the money back into her hand. "Here. Take it and use it to buy something for the colored hospital. I imagine you can think of something they need."

"Now that I can get excited about," Carrie grinned. "Thank you. There are many needed things I can buy with this."

She watched her father stride down the street toward the Capitol, then she turned to Spencer. "We have some errands to do."

The morning passed quickly. She bought the supplies needed at the colored hospital, returned home, and dressed for her afternoon shift at Chimborazo. Sinking down on the windowsill, she stared out. She needed some time to think before she went to the hospital. She shuddered as she remembered the looks of desperation on the women's faces downtown. Spring had indeed come, but what would it take to heal the ravages of the past winter?

The residents of Richmond had endured bitter cold, deep snows, starvation, a smallpox epidemic, the explosion at the armory, and increased lawlessness. Spring was certain to bring renewed efforts by the Union to take the city. The last Carrie had heard, the Union army was still camped across the Rappahannock. When would they begin to move?

Memories of Robert rushed into her mind. She could see him so clearly—smiling down at her, asking her to marry him, promising to come back soon. Carrie took a deep breath and brushed away her tears. The hurt had not diminished over the months, but at least she had learned to quit running from it. "I still love you, Robert," she whispered to the wind.

Carrie finished her shift at the hospital and stepped outside. Now that it was warmer, the windows were left open, but still she longed to be in the fresh air. The battles would start again soon. Before long the buildings would be crammed with wounded and dying men. For today, she just wanted to enjoy the wonder of spring.

Carrie walked over to the edge of one of the clearings and sank down on a rock. Cupping her chin in her hand, she stared down at the river. It was once again running free. The thick ice that had imprisoned it all winter had melted before the warm winds. Carrie smiled as the water exploded around the boulders, the rapids of the James River shooting spray into the air that caught the sun, then falling in a shower of colors. A soft breeze loosened her hair from its bun, ringlets framing her face. Carrie turned her face to the sun, soaking in the glorious rays. One could almost believe there was no trouble in the world on such a beautiful day.

The clatter of hoofbeats grabbed her attention. She turned just in time to see a horse cantering up the road to the hospital. The shadows under the trees made it too dark to see anything. Carrie shrugged and turned back to her view. She wasn't going to let anything disturb her peace today. There were plenty of people in the hospital who could take care of any emergency that might arise.

Carrie wasn't sure what made her turn around several minutes later. Her heart was whispering something she couldn't decipher. Several yards away a tall figure stood quietly, watching her. The day seemed to fade into slow motion.

Carrie gasped, her hand flying to her mouth. Her heart skipped a beat, then raced back into motion. "Robert?" she whispered disbelievingly. Her heart and mind refused to accept what her eyes were telling her.

Robert took several quick strides and was standing in front of her. "You were so beautiful sitting in the sun. Exactly as I remembered you. I just wanted to watch." His deep voice tremored with emotion.

"Robert?" Carrie reached out her hand tentatively to touch his cheek. "Is it really you?" Her head spun. This had to be a dream.

Robert suddenly threw back his head and laughed. "It's me," he called loudly to the birds flying overhead. "I'm home!"

Carrie's disbelief suddenly changed to exploding joy. "Robert! It's you! It's really you! You're alive!" she cried. Tears rolled down her cheeks as her laughter rang out to match his. "You're home!"

Robert grabbed her in his arms and began to dance around the clearing. Picking her up, he spun her in great circles. Finally he set her down, then folded her into his arms. "I'm home," he whispered, just before he lowered his head to claim her lips.

Spring had come.

About the Author

Virginia Gaffney is the author of four books, including *Under the Southern Moon* and *Carry Me Home*. Her lifelong fascination with the Civil War in the South provides a rich background for her writing. She lives and works in Richmond, Virginia, where she is an avid outdoorswoman.

Coming in Book 4 of
The Richmond Chronicles ...

As Union forces renew their efforts to take
Richmond, newlyweds Carrie and Robert face separation once more. Carrie, on a desperate search
for medication needed in the hospital, faces a decision that could cost her everything. Meanwhile,
Robert fights at Gettysburg, only to be captured
and face the horror of a Northern prison. A moving
story of honor and love.

Available Winter 1998

Harvest House Publishers

For the Best in Inspirational Fiction

Virginia Gaffney

THE RICHMOND CHRONICLES

Under the Southern Moon
Carry Me Home
The Tender Rebel

Lori Wick

A PLACE CALLED HOME

A Place Called Home
A Song for Silas
The Long Road Home
A Gathering of Memories

THE CALIFORNIANS

Whatever Tomorrow Brings
As Time Goes By
Sean Donovan
Donovan's Daughter

KENSINGTON CHRONICLES

The Hawk and the Jewel
Wings of the Morning
Who Brings Forth the Wind
The Knight and the Dove

ROCKY MOUNTAIN MEMORIES

Where the Wild Rose Blooms
Whispers of Moonlight
To Know Her by Name
Promise Me Tomorrow

CONTEMPORARY FICTION

Sophie's Heart

Dear Reader,

We would appreciate hearing from you regarding this Harvest House fiction book. It will enable us to continue to give you the best in Christian publishing.

1. What most influenced you to purchase *The Tender Rebel?*
   - ❑ Author
   - ❑ Subject matter
   - ❑ Backcover copy
   - ❑ Recommendations
   - ❑ Cover/Title
   - ❑ Other_____

2. Where did you purchase this book?
   - ❑ Christian bookstore
   - ❑ General bookstore
   - ❑ Department store
   - ❑ Grocery store
   - ❑ Other_____

3. Your overall rating of this book?
   - ❑ Excellent ❑ Very good ❑ Good ❑ Fair ❑ Poor

4. How likely would you be to purchase other books by this author?
   - ❑ Very likely ❑ Not very likely ❑ Somewhat likely ❑ Not at all

5. What types of books most interest you? (Check all that apply.)
   - ❑ Women's Books
   - ❑ Marriage Books
   - ❑ Current Issues
   - ❑ Christian Living
   - ❑ Bible Studies
   - ❑ Fiction
   - ❑ Biographies
   - ❑ Children's Books
   - ❑ Youth Books
   - ❑ Other_____

6. Please check the box next to your age group.
   - ❑ Under 18 ❑ 18-24 ❑ 25-34 ❑ 35-44 ❑ 45-54 ❑ 55 and over

Mail to: Editorial Director
Harvest House Publishers
1075 Arrowsmith
Eugene, OR 97402

Name _____

Address _____

State _____ Zip _____

Thank you for helping us to help you in future publications!